Marriage

Readers' Choice Award winner

MURIEL JENSEN

delivers three heartwarming, humorous tales:

THE UNEXPECTED GROOM

"I do, I do…I did?"

MAKE-BELIEVE MOM

Last she heard, having a baby took nine months!

MIDDLE OF THE RAINBOW

He said "I do" when he didn't…

Dear Reader,

When my husband proposed a week after we'd met, I was a tender twenty-three with big plans to live in Italy and write the great American novel. But Ron was thirty-five and a seasoned newspaperman ready to settle down.

I offered a long string of arguments on why I didn't want to get married.

He listened, then countered with, "Fine. Can we talk about them after the wedding?"

And that was when I saw the love in his eyes that would recognize no obstacle because he couldn't imagine life without me.

So, I became a "Bride by Surprise," and discovered the wonders of saying yes to love that seems to come at the wrong time—just as Charlotte, Barbara and Regina did— and soon learned that there is no wrong time to give love and that giving it only generates more getting it.

It's also the reason my life's pursuit is no longer the great American novel, but the romance novel. Because I believe in it.

Warm regards,

Muriel Jensen

MURIEL JENSEN

Bride by Surprise

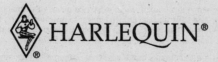

HARLEQUIN®

TORONTO • NEW YORK • LONDON
AMSTERDAM • PARIS • SYDNEY • HAMBURG
STOCKHOLM • ATHENS • TOKYO • MILAN • MADRID
PRAGUE • WARSAW • BUDAPEST • AUCKLAND

HARLEQUIN BOOKS

by Request—BRIDE BY SURPRISE

Copyright © 2000 by Harlequin Books S.A.

ISBN 0-373-20180-X

The publisher acknowledges the copyright holder of the individual works as follows:
THE UNEXPECTED GROOM
Copyright © 1993 by Muriel Jensen
MAKE-BELIEVE MOM
Copyright © 1994 by Muriel Jensen
MIDDLE OF THE RAINBOW
Copyright © 1992 by Muriel Jensen

This edition published by arrangement with Harlequin Books S.A.

Visit us at www.eHarlequin.com

Printed in U.S.A.

CONTENTS

The Unexpected Groom

Chapter One

"My life sounds like the plot line of a soap opera." Charlotte Morreaux, alone in her classic white Duesenberg, reviewed her current situation as she drove through the wooded canyon northeast of Los Angeles.

"Wealthy heiress falls in love with up-and-coming corporate executive in her father's company. Executive leaves heiress standing at the altar. While heiress begins life anew by leaving father's employ to open specialty wedding shop, executive falls in love with daughter of heiress's father's partner. No problem. Heiress number one holds no grudges. However, heiress number two's mother does. She dislikes heiress number one and is always finding innovative ways to embarrass her."

"Charlotte, you *have* to help me!" Kendra Farnsworth had pleaded the day before on the telephone. "My wedding dress is a horrid monstrosity! Please bring a selection of dresses from Borrowed Magic to the shower Sunday afternoon. I'd much rather have one of your vintage dresses than this…this thing!"

Charlotte heard the rustle of taffeta in the background and guessed that the offending dress had been shoved aside.

But I wasn't coming to the shower, Charlotte said to

herself. There isn't enough money or power or amaretto truffles in the whole world to make me....

"Bitsy Tate's coming," Kendra added in all apparent innocence. In reality, the announcement had the same effect as holding a French cannon to Charlotte's temple. "I told her I was calling on you to save my wedding."

Bitsy, who wrote Bitsy's Tidbits for the *Times,* had made her gossip column's reputation on Charlotte's embarrassing abandonment at the church the year before. As a reporter, Bitsy was brutally honest and thorough. Nothing escaped her attention—or her column. As a woman, she leaned toward viciousness—and she was a friend of Elizabeth Farnsworth, Kendra's mother.

"She thinks it's all very poetic," Kendra went on in her breathless ingenue voice.

Charlotte smiled to herself. It *was* poetic. Like something from the pen of Ogden Nash.

"Of course I'll come," she'd replied with forced enthusiasm. "I have a few things you might like."

She was already imagining an 1890s gown with a pinaforelike front that would enhance Kendra's blond fragility. Charlotte Morreaux might look poetic and tragic in front of Bitsy Tate, but Borrowed Magic would be brilliant.

With a sigh of resignation, Charlotte turned onto the back road to her father's estate. It would help, she told herself bracingly, that the shower was being held on her home turf. Kendra's father and Charlotte's father had been partners in the ever-booming field of high technology since their daughters had been children. Both men appeared completely ignorant of the antagonism that existed among the Morreaux and Farnsworth women.

Charlotte liked Kendra. Though Charlotte was oldest by three years, and though the girls were very different in interests and attitude, they'd managed to get along when their fathers' alliance forced them together throughout their childhood and teen years.

Their mothers hadn't fared as well. Elizabeth's standard for selecting friends was a complicated equation of ancestry, social status and bank balance. While Edward Morreaux held the latter with a vengeance, he was the son of a North Dakota farmer and chose his friends for their intelligence and their ability to sit still while he explained his current project in great detail.

Caroline, Charlotte's stepmother, traced her roots to one of the signers of the Declaration of Independence, but she had no pretensions whatsoever. And she didn't mind prodding those who did.

What resulted between her and Elizabeth was a kind of creative one-upmanship that had carried through the years.

Charlotte was smiling over thoughts of her father and Caroline when she saw the other car. It came at her from the side road, a low-flying blur of red.

Startled sharply to awareness, she turned out of its way as two sets of brakes screamed. She was flung forward and then back as metal crunched and glass shattered. The Duesenberg shuddered and then settled, her scream and the reverberations of the crash pulsing around her like a bad aura. Then all was silent.

She blinked, wondering what had happened, when her door was yanked open.

"Charlie? Charlie!" A concerned voice shouted in her ear as hands grasped her shoulders, then ranged clinically down her arms and over her ribs. A grazing touch over the tip of her breast penetrated her shocked disorientation.

She turned vaguely to the source of the noise and focused on a very familiar face.

"Oh, no," she groaned. "Not you. Not today."

Bourbon-brown eyes glanced up from a hands-on examination of her legs. Then Derek Cabot fixed a devastating smile on her. "I'm afraid so, Charlie. How've you been?"

His fingertips dipped under her knees and swung her legs around as he nudged the car door aside with his shoulder. "Stand up. Let's see if you're okay."

She tried to shake his hands off. "I'm fine."

"I'd like to see for myself."

Charlotte gave him the Duchess of Winter look. Though it had been a year since she'd left the company, Derek thought of her often, and he always thought of her in her persona of titled gentry.

He took hold of her wrist and pulled her to her feet. "Your patrician glare doesn't frighten me, remember?" he said, frowning at her, then putting a diagnostic hand to her forehead. "You look a little disoriented. Do you feel dizzy?"

"Yes," she admitted, batting his hand away. "Seeing you always upsets me. What are you doing here?"

"I was invited to the shower."

That seemed to annoy her. "Why?"

He put his hands in the pockets of his brown slacks and leaned his weight on one leg. "There are people who like having me around. I'm sorry if that upsets you."

She rotated a stiff shoulder muscle. "My dismay at seeing you is purely chemistry. I don't like you. Aaagh!" She had turned as she spoke and noticed for the first time the accordion-pleated front fender of her classic car now permanently affixed to the trunk of a fragrant eucalyptus.

She went to it, like a mother to an injured child. "Look what you did to my Duesie!"

"What *I* did?" he replied defensively, coming up behind her. "When you're driving something older than you are, you should slow down at intersections."

She rounded on him, her long, straight blond hair flying out like a banner, her pale iris-colored eyes giving him that look calculated to make him feel like a peasant.

"It is *not* an intersection—it is a lazy country driveway crossed by a rural road! Who does sixty down a curving rural road?"

"I do," he replied. "I have places to go. Unlike some people who are content to dawdle along as though time will stop for them."

She huffed impatiently. "Oh, God. Let's not have that argument again. This is a wedding shower, not a power meeting."

Derek reached into the dash of his Porsche for his cellular phone. He'd forgotten, he thought, waiting for someone at the garage to pick up, how much he enjoyed being shouted at by her. He always had, which was a good thing, because that was the way they'd exchanged most information when they'd worked together—at the tops of their voices. Opposite work styles had made dealing with each other almost impossible. Still, he was enough of a scrapper to feel that the relationship would have possibilities in another setting.

"Canyon Car Care."

"Les, it's Derek." He winked at Charlotte as she approached him, frowning. Apparently she didn't like him taking over resolution of the accident. Too bad. "I just hit a classic Duesenberg. A '31?" he asked her.

"Thirty-two," she corrected. "La Grande Phaeton."

He repeated the information to Les. "Right side's a mess. Front fender's crunched against the tire. Can you pick it up on a flatbed? I don't want it towed."

"Right away."

"Good." He gave him the location. "The owner and I are already late for a party, but I'll be by the shop this afternoon."

"How's the Porsche?" Les asked.

"Perfect," he answered. "She hit a tree, not me."

"Lucky break."

As Derek leaned into the car to replace the receiver, Charlotte folded her arms—another gesture of the Duchess of Winter. She looked as though she were considering the disposition of an unruly serf.

"I might have wanted my car taken to my own garage," she said.

He straightened away from the car and acknowledged that possibility with a nod. "But Canyon Car Care is the best. He works on a Daimler and a Bentley that I've seen there from time to time. And my insurance company's used to dealing with them."

She raised a wheat-colored eyebrow. "Then you do admit responsibility for the collision?"

He couldn't deny it. He'd been going too fast, spotted the Duesenberg, knew who had to be driving and, for one critical split second, let his mind wander from the road to the woman.

"Yes," he said. "I do. Come on. I'll drive you up the lane. We'll send one of your father's men back to stay with your car until Les picks it up."

She studied him dispassionately for a moment, then turned and went to the left rear door of her car.

He watched her move with interest. For a woman who

carried herself like untouchable royalty, she had the most seductive tush he'd ever had the pleasure to observe—it was just a little too round, with the most enticing sway in the snug skirt of the teal forties-era suit. He'd often thought of it as stamped with a royal crest.

"No hat today, Duchess?" he asked, forcing himself to think about something else.

She pulled three deep, wide boxes out of the back and placed them in his arms. The Borrowed Magic gold-on-white logo glinted in the early-afternoon sunlight of the southern California fall.

Then she reached in again and emerged with a picture hat the same color as her suit. She placed it on her head at an elegant angle.

She followed him to the convertible, rearranged the boxes when he placed them in the back, then allowed him to seat her and close her door.

But she looked a little disconsolate when he slid in behind the wheel. He thought he knew why. He'd taken Caroline to the Children's Hospital Ball the night before when Edward had been waylaid by a long-distance call at the last moment.

"I understand one of the dresses you've brought is going to save the wedding of the decade," he said.

She glanced his way in surprise. "How did you know?"

"Caroline told me. It's generous of you to come through for Kendra," Derek said. "Considering the circumstances."

Charlotte drew in several deep breaths, trying to relax. "Actually, I'm not that big. I'm thinking of it as business. Borrowed Magic is obliging a client, not I."

"No good," he said. "You *are* Borrowed Magic."

"Please." Her voice was a little high. "I'm having

enough trouble bracing myself to face everyone as it is. Why don't you just pull up in back and we'll go in through the kit—"

But he was already driving around the colonnaded front of the plantation-style house. A stately row of liquidambar trees just showing tips of red lined the circular drive.

A white-coated young man came to open Charlotte's door while another opened Derek's and took the keys from him.

"Is this the weekend I get to take the Porsche to the beach, Mr. Cabot?" the boy joked.

"Funny, Naldo. I need a favor." Derek explained about the accident. "Will you go keep an eye on it for Miss Morreaux?"

Naldo grinned at Charlotte. "Anything for Miss Morreaux. I'll take care of it."

"A duchess doesn't go in through the kitchen," Derek said, taking Charlotte's elbow and asking the second attendant to bring in the boxes. "And, anyway, you once lived here. You belong here."

"Every man and woman in there," she said quietly as they crossed the broad veranda, "knows that Trey Prentiss literally left me at the altar."

He looked down at her as though her dilemma confused him. "Then it seems to me *he* should be the one embarrassed, not you."

She closed her eyes to summon patience. "Yeah, well, it doesn't work that way. All anyone knows is that Trey is handsome and brilliant and that I must have done something pretty awful to have scared him away like that at the last minute. Particularly since he's obviously willing to head for the altar again with someone else."

"That's because marrying Kendra doesn't take any

guts. Marrying you would.'' He pushed a spot between her shoulder blades that made her stiffen her spine. ''Come on. Let's have the wintry royal smile. When you do that, you always look as though nothing touches you and nothing matters to you. People admire someone who can remain above the struggle.''

She wasn't sure she liked that assessment of herself, but the door opened at that moment, and Plowright, the Morreauxs' butler, gave them a broad smile and swept them inside.

Caroline was upon them immediately, plump and fragrant and exuding the warm generosity that had made her and Charlotte fast friends. Though Charlotte had been prepared to resent her when her father had brought her home, Caroline had filled the dark, lonely void with a wonderful sweetness coupled with an innocent and often hilarious propensity for causing trouble. She'd been the best friend Charlotte had ever had.

Charlotte was taken in a silky embrace, then held at arm's length and studied with a concerned green gaze.

''Are you all right?'' she asked softly.

''I'm fine,'' Charlotte assured her with more bravado than she felt. ''Unfortunately my car isn't. Derek just made a Japanese fan of it.''

Derek smiled as Caroline embraced him. ''She exaggerates. Two months with a good body-and-fender man and a small fortune, and the Duesenberg will be good as new.''

''Meanwhile,'' Charlotte said, ''I'll be getting around Los Angeles on roller blades.''

''Char—lie!'' The throaty cry came from beyond the foyer and halfway across the gray-and-rose living room where the shower guests were congregated.

Every one of the hundred or so heads turned in Charlotte's direction. She would have given her entire seven-figure inheritance to be somewhere on a mountaintop in Tennessee.

Kendra, slender and doll-like in red wool, remained standing in the middle of the living room, arms extended toward Charlotte so that Charlotte was forced to walk the gamut of guests and go to her, or appear the vengeful woman scorned, the sore loser. She went.

"Kendra," she said graciously, injecting her voice with warmth. "I'm happy for you." She saw a flare of light as a camera flash lit the scene. Over Kendra's shoulder, she saw Bitsy Tate taking notes, and Darby Grant, the photographer who worked with her, sighting through his lens for another shot.

Charlotte pulled away and added quietly, "The dresses are in the foyer."

"*Won*derful." Kendra reached a hand out for Trey, who stood just beyond them. "I can try them on here after the shower and you can tell me what you think. You won't *believe* the mess Jean Michel designed for me."

Jean Michel was one of the West Coast's most sought-after designers. Charlotte couldn't imagine that he'd created a monstrosity. Kendra had always had a flair for drama.

"Darling." Kendra drew Trey closer. It was the first time Charlotte had seen him since her own wedding rehearsal. She squared her shoulders and smiled.

"Please," Kendra said to Trey. "Thank Charlotte for saving the day for us."

Charlotte had always thought Trey Prentiss resembled Mark Harmon with his boyish yet jaded smile. He seemed even more handsome at that moment, taller, blonder, more charming.

He gave Charlotte a sheepish, self-deprecating grin as he extended a hand toward her. "Hi, Charlie," he said. "It was good of you to do this for us, considering…well, I mean after I…"

She'd have found it very satisfying to simply stand there until he finished the sentence—"…after I made a fool of you and myself." But she knew every ear in the room was listening and she simply couldn't be that cruel.

She put her hand in his. "Happy to do it," she said, her voice firm and convincing. "Borrowed Magic promises you a beautiful bride."

"Well, there you are!" Edward Morreaux's voice boomed in Charlotte's ear and she turned gratefully for her father's bear hug. "Hear you and Derek 'bumped into each other' on the lane." He laughed at his clichéd joke. "Bound to happen. *He's* always in a hurry, and *you* never know where you're going." He shook his head, smiling, as though he considered that an amusing situation.

He took two glasses of champagne from the tray of a passing waiter, handed her one and put the other in Derek's hand as he approached.

Kendra and Trey wandered away and conversation began to buzz again.

Edward beamed at his daughter. "Damned if you aren't turning out to be an entrepreneur in your own right. Everywhere I turn, someone's telling me about someone they know who bought or rented a dress from your shop, or had you design their wedding. I guess you were wasted all those years as head of public relations for Morreaux–Farnsworth."

Charlotte cast a glance at Derek. "Funny that we didn't notice it until Derek came along." She smiled at the man in question, her expression carefully neutral. "If you hadn't put him in charge of my department, we might still think I was doing a good job.''

"Your work was always late,'' Derek pointed out quietly.

"I was trying to do it well.''

"The requirements of PR are often very immediate. You were too much of a dreamer.''

"Now that's all water under the bridge,'' Edward said placatingly. "It all worked out for the best. You left to do your own thing, Charlie, and you're happy, and our news releases are getting out on time. *I'm* happy.''

"Charlotte, darling!'' Elizabeth Farnsworth, tall and elegant in a silky café-au-lait designer suit, took Charlotte in her famous touchless embrace where lips never met cheek. "You're looking well,'' she pronounced with what must appear to everyone else to be auntlike affection. Only Charlotte saw the dislike in her eyes. "What's new with you?''

Politely, Charlotte began a brief résumé of the past few months, the shop next door into which she'd expanded, the accessories she'd added.

"No,'' Elizabeth said softly, maliciously. "I mean, what's new in your love life?'' Then she added with a deepening of that suspect smile. "A few more years, darling, and you'll be thirty. It's time to make plans.''

Charlotte was torn. She could shock everyone by telling Elizabeth it was none of her business. She could make up a wild tale about a Turkish prince, or she could admit that she hadn't been on a date in a year, that she hadn't wished herself home in front of the television after the first hour. But she had an image to maintain for her business.

She opened her mouth, prepared with a tactful reply,

when Caroline appeared at her shoulder and said loudly, cheerfully, "Go ahead and tell them, Charlie."

The simple sentence with its suggestion of mystery reverberated through the room. People who had wandered into the parlor or out into the foyer wandered back. Edward looked up from a discussion with several of his golf buddies. Trey and Kendra, nuzzling in a corner, turned in her direction.

Charlotte had a well-developed sense of self-preservation. And it had grown even stronger over the past year. The obvious question was, "Tell them what?" but a significant look in her stepmother's eyes prevented her from asking it.

Elizabeth, however, did it for her. "Tell them what?"

Charlotte felt gooseflesh rise on her arms when her stepmother smiled and giggled. That was always a prelude to trouble. It meant she had a plan. And every plan she'd ever had meant disaster for someone.

"Well…" Caroline put a hand to the back of Charlotte's waist and smiled at her guests who were pressing closer. "I'm afraid Kendra and Trey have to share the festivities this afternoon. Charlotte has come home not only to see that Kendra has the perfect wedding dress…" She sent a benevolent smile in Kendra's direction. Then she turned it on Charlotte. "But to announce her marriage."

Charlotte heard the communal gasp and felt as though it had escaped from her own body. Marriage! Oh, God. Soap opera plot line number two! Out of the corner of her eye she could see Bitsy writing. A flash lit the side of her face. Elizabeth appeared to be suffering a spasm at the prospect of the spotlight being stolen from her daughter.

"Impending…marriage?" Elizabeth asked.

"Accomplished," Caroline corrected with obvious satisfaction.

There were more gasps, more exclamations.

"To whom?" Elizabeth asked in a demanding tone.

Even Charlotte waited for the answer. Caroline had been so convincing thus far, she felt sure her stepmother must have a reply.

She obviously didn't. Thus was the nature of Caroline's disasters. An ingenuous innocence carried her so far, then abandoned her. In defense of her stepdaughter, she'd tried to put Elizabeth Farnsworth in her place by showing her that, despite the past, Charlotte was as capable of finding a husband as Kendra was. She simply hadn't thought the scenario through. She hadn't cast the part of the groom.

Prepared to die of humiliation in front of these people yet again, Charlotte was shocked when a strong male voice behind her said with convincing firmness, "To me."

An arm came around her and pulled her close. Warm, dry lips pressed a kiss to her temple. "Ladies and gentlemen," the voice said. "May I present Mrs. Derek Cabot?"

Chapter Two

Cameras flashed again as the crowd moved in with squeals of delight and congratulations.

"What," Charlotte demanded of Derek under her breath while smiling at friends and neighbors, "are you doing?"

"I've no idea," he replied, an arm still around her while he reached the other out to shake Caleb Farnsworth's hand. "Caroline looked like she needed help."

Edward caught his daughter's eye from across the room. His expression was apologetic but resigned. He glanced at his wife fielding questions from the excited guests and shook his head with the same loving tolerance he'd shown for the past eleven years. He gave Charlotte an almost imperceptible shrug that reminded her that he never knew what to do about Caroline, either. She'd get no help from that quarter.

"Well, isn't this rather sudden?" Elizabeth asked, her eyes filled with calculating suspicion. "I mean, word was Charlotte quit the company when Edward brought Derek back from the New York office because they couldn't get along."

Caroline, radiant with Derek's rescue, shrugged grandly and laughed. "Well, you know how it is with sparks. Sometimes you get a fire, and sometimes you just get beautiful fireworks.'' She glanced at Charlotte and Derek and winked.

"When did you get married?'' Elizabeth insisted.

"While I was on a business trip.'' Derek replied with the smallest hesitation that might have been mistaken for a moment taken to enjoy the memory. He squeezed Charlotte and gave her an intimate look that suggested they shared the memory. "I asked her to join me and we decided it would be nice to travel together forever.''

"How romantic!'' someone gushed.

Charlotte was afraid to breathe. Deception was not her strong suit, and getting involved in an intrigue with Caroline held terrifying prospects. An intrigue that involved Caroline *and* Derek was too awful to contemplate.

"I think we should…'' she began, planning to make a clean breast of everything.

"Toast the newlyweds,'' Caroline interrupted with a sweep of her elegantly braceleted arm. "Excellent idea. Plowright, more champagne, please.''

"Caroline, you can't…'' Charlotte began, prepared to confront her, in front of everyone if necessary, to stop this silly charade.

Caroline turned to her with the same smile that had once proven to the teenage Charlotte that, though her stepmother was her friend, she was no pushover. It had preceded a month's grounding and loss of car privileges.

"Don't tell me I can't, darling,'' she said under her breath. "That always makes me crazy. You know that. Just follow Derek's lead. He's doing beautifully.''

"He's lying!'' Charlotte whispered harshly. *"You're lying.''*

Caroline rolled her eyes. "Don't be tedious, Charlie.

We have Liz Farnsworth on the run and I'm not giving up the chase for anything.''

"Relax," Derek said in her ear. "Here comes the champagne."

She turned to look up into his dark brown eyes, now alive with amusement, and said urgently, "Derek, everyone will tell everyone else. Tomorrow it'll be in Bitsy's column."

He did not seem concerned. "In a few days interest will wane and the whole thing will die a natural death. The important thing right now is not to embarrass your parents."

"*You're* going to be pretty embarrassed when everyone discovers you lied."

Plowright served the champagne himself. Derek accepted a glass from him and a second for Charlotte. "Nothing embarrasses me," he said. "That's the up side of not giving a damn what people think of you. Now get it together. You're supposed to look like a radiant bride."

When everyone was holding a champagne glass, Caroline smiled up at her husband, who had come across the room to join her.

"I think this is a job for the father of the bride," she said. Her eyes were filled with unrepentant deviltry.

Charlotte saw him return the look with a promise of retribution. But when he looked out at his friends, his smile appeared genuine, his manner one of the delighted, indulgent parent.

"To surprises," he said, a little edge of irony in his voice that made Charlotte and Caroline exchange a look. "To the little everyday charms that make love develop where you would least expect to find it…" He turned to Charlotte with a look that told her something she couldn't quite grasp. "To the magic that makes it all work, that takes two very different human beings and makes them one loving unit." His eyes went from Charlotte to Derek. "To Mr. and Mrs. Cabot."

Charlotte stared at her father while everyone else drank. Where had that come from? For an impromptu toast delivered on the heels of a phony announcement, his words had been touching and, by all appearances, heartfelt.

"Drink," Derek urged softly. "Elizabeth's watching."

Charlotte downed her champagne, not out of obedience, but out of a desperate need to feel the alcohol warm her stomach. It was threatening to revolt.

She was grateful when attention finally turned back to Kendra and Trey. Everyone found chairs or made themselves comfortable on the floor while the couple opened presents.

Charlotte tried to lose herself in a corner, but Bitsy made a point of relinquishing her chair in the middle of the room.

"Oh, please don't..." Charlotte tried to protest, but Bitsy was adamant—and expectant.

"I need to be moving around," she insisted. She looked from one to the other and asked with veiled suspicion, "Is this one of those business-decision marriages? A merger of stocks rather than hearts?"

For an instant Charlotte didn't know what to say. The temerity of the press often astounded her. Then she knew what it would take to get Bitsy off their backs, at least for the duration of the afternoon.

She looked up at Derek, barely made eye contact while wondering how to get her thought across to him, when he showed her that he understood completely.

With one hand, he swept her hat off, with the other he circled her waist, pulled her to him and made everyone around them, including Bitsy, gasp when he looked down into Charlotte's eyes. Even a *Forbes* magazine reporter could not have mistaken the look for business.

Then he lowered his head and opened his mouth over hers.

It's an act, Charlotte told herself. That made it easier to play her part. It also made her realize that if what she felt was make-believe, she had the potential to play Hamlet.

She was instantly, completely seduced. His tongue invaded her mouth—to demonstrate their passion for each other to their audience, she was sure—but it did its work with a tender finesse that astonished and excited her.

His hand in her hair held her still as he went a little deeper, probed a little farther, then flattened his other hand against her back until her breasts, through the gabardine suit and the leaf-lace bra beneath it, were spread against the wool-blend houndstooth of his jacket.

Her eyes closed, her brain turned to oatmeal by the surprise, she experienced the embrace with all the sensual detail she'd have known had they been naked.

A little frisson of sensation rippled up the center of her being and made her tremble in his arms.

When he raised his head, it was a moment before she could open her eyes. When she did, she was aware first of the conflicting emotions in his. She saw triumph, a trace of shock and the unmistakable arrogance of a man who knows he's made a woman respond to him.

Then she became aware of the silence and remembered where she was. Color flooded her face.

Derek straightened her with a hand between her shoulder blades and grinned at Bitsy.

"Yes," he replied. "Definitely a business-decision marriage." He sat in the chair and pulled Charlotte down into his lap and patted her hip. "I've always loved her bottom line."

Everyone laughed except Bitsy, who looked him in the eye and told him without words that he might be a business genius, but she was also extremely gifted—at ferreting out the truth. That he may have fooled everyone else, but she suspected there was more to this marriage than met the eye.

Then she raised her glass, offered her congratulations, then left them as Kendra and Trey began to open their opulent packages.

"Oh, God," Charlotte exclaimed under her breath. "She doesn't believe us."

"She doesn't want to believe us," he corrected quietly, resting his forearm familiarly across her knees. "But I think that's because, deep inside, we convinced her."

"That doesn't make sense. Why would she *not* want to believe us?"

"If your livelihood depended upon scandal," he pointed out reasonably, "would you want to believe we were really happily married? She'd have much better copy if she could convince everyone you were broken-hearted over Trey, or that your stepmother had perpetrated a sham marriage to show up the Farnsworths."

"That's what she did."

"I know, but do you want all of greater Los Angeles to know it?"

"Oh, God." Charlotte thought that over and decided the best thing she could do for all of them was disappear.

She tried to stand, but Derek held her in place. "Where you going?" he whispered.

"Moscow," she replied, pushing against him. "It's free now. I'll change my name, make a new start..."

He looped his arms around her waist and laced his fingers to keep her there. "We've got this under control. Just relax and trust me. You're the romantic, remember? Doesn't this feel just a little like you're caught in a fairy tale?"

She hooked an arm around his neck and smiled because she noticed Bitsy's photographer poised for a shot in their direction. "It feels a little like I'm in a bad nightmare. And it's all your fault!"

"You seem to be forgetting Caroline's involvement."

"Caroline would have been forced to admit she was lying if you hadn't stepped nobly forward and declared yourself my husband."

He frowned at her seriously. "You'd have preferred that? Caroline humiliated and you still a spinster?"

"I *am* still a spinster. Although I prefer using 'career woman.' It's just the poor people we've deceived who think of me as a bride." Then she sighed as she came to terms with the other half of his question. "Of course I don't want Caroline humiliated, but she can't just create her own reality like that."

"She did it for you."

"I know that," she said impatiently, "but look at the mess she's made. Tomorrow someone, probably me, is going to have to tell the press it was all a joke."

"Why?"

"Because it isn't true!"

He frowned at her again, careful to do it with a loverlike indulgence for the sake of all the glances that continued to wander their way. "For a woman who wrote press releases that sounded like novels, and embroidered the facts until they were barely recognizable, you've taken a very pedantic turn. Can't you just relax and play the game?''

"Marriage is not a game," she said stiffly, practically.

"How do you know?" he countered. "You ever been married?"

"No," she replied patiently, "but if I were, I wouldn't think of it as a game."

"Maybe that's why most marriages don't last," he suggested as the crowd oohed and aahed over a pasta maker. "They forget to play."

"The point," she said, "is that we've deceived people."

"Oh, I don't know." He became suddenly grave. "I always thought we could have had a relationship under different circumstances. That kiss made me sure of it."

There had been something there. Something she'd never experienced before, even with the man she'd been about to marry.

She averted her eyes and pretended to study the crowd. "We were acting. That wasn't real."

"We were acting," he said, "like a man and a woman with something important to say to each other."

She had felt that. But she didn't want to. She turned a lavender-gray gaze on him. "We said all we had to say to each other the day I quit."

"That was business," he said. "I'm talking about life. Love. Sex."

"I don't want those with you," she said brutally.

But it was like striking armor with a whiffle ball. He didn't seem to notice.

"That's not what your lips told me."

"If you don't stop talking about this," she said in a stern undertone, "I'm going to scream, slap your face and march indignantly out of here and let everyone in the room think whatever they like."

"And you would give Bitsy material for days."

That was true, but Charlotte chose not to think about it. She concentrated her attention on Kendra and Trey, ignoring Derek as much as was possible considering she was sitting in his lap.

It wasn't long before the procession around the room of towels and cappuccino makers and health spa certificates began to blur. She snapped her eyes open several times, thinking that she shouldn't have drunk the second glass of champagne when she'd had only three hours' sleep the night before worrying about this afternoon.

Then a firm, warm hand began to rub wide, relaxing circles up her spine and the blur slipped away into darkness, taking her with it.

DEREK HAD ALWAYS wondered what it would be like to hold Charlotte. Of course, he'd always imagined her awake when he considered it, but accepted that having her asleep at the moment was probably better. Awake, she'd have never stayed.

But now the crowd had thinned. Edward, Caleb, Trey and a few others were playing poker in the den, and Caroline, Elizabeth and Kendra were upstairs with the dresses Charlotte had brought.

The room where he sat had been darkened and the furniture left strewn around in deference to the sleeping duchess in his arms. Caroline had whispered that it could all be put to rights in the morning, then had winked at him conspiratorially when she left the room.

She considered him part of her deception because he'd

come to her rescue. Ordinarily that might have made him nervous. He's seen her in action before.

But this was not an ordinary situation. He had Charlotte Morreaux in his arms. It was difficult for him to think about anything else.

As he studied Charlotte's eyelashes, the thinly mascaraed silky fans fluttered open.

Her head came off his shoulder abruptly and she looked around at the darkened room empty of people.

"What happened? What time is it?" she asked, her body tense with confusion. His hands were loosely clasped around her and he freed one to steady her back.

"We were caught in a time warp," he replied, "this is our living room on the planet Uranus, and the year is 2457."

She turned to him with a perplexed look. Then, because she was still sleepy and probably because they were alone and her guard had slipped, she smiled at him.

"Why do we have so many chairs?"

"Because on Uranus," he answered, straight-faced, "women are fertile twenty-two days of the month and gestation is only four months long. We have—" he did a quick perusal of the room "—thirty-seven children."

She giggled and settled back against him.

That was a nice surprise, he thought. She awoke with a sense of humor. He valued that in a woman.

"Where are they all?"

"Ah…on the road. We have a basketball team, a rock group, a construction company and an all-female marching band. They're supporting us in our old age."

She giggled again, and after a moment of silence he felt her deep sigh. He enjoyed the moment. Soon enough she would remember what had happened, remember that she disliked him intensely.

"I've always wanted four boys," she said, her tone dreamily conversational. "And a place on a stream where they could build a raft and pretend to be pirates."

It was easy to take the fantasy on another turn. "Sort of a Tom Sawyer–Peter Pan fusion. I don't know. That encourages play. How would they support us with a little raft?"

"Oh…" Her eyelashes fluttered against his jaw as she considered. A strange weakness invaded his body. "They could carry freight," she said, "transmit regular weather reports and set out lobster pots."

"That could work. But I don't think we have lobsters on Uranus."

"We're back in L.A."

"We don't have lobsters in L.A., Charlie."

She was quiet a moment, then she sat up slowly. "Well, that's always been the trouble with dreams. In reality, you can never fit them into your life." She gave him a curiously bittersweet smile and tried to stand.

"Hey." He held her down with a gentle hand on her arm. "I haven't found that to be true. I've always dreamed of holding you and…here we are."

She leaned an elbow on his shoulder and looked into his eyes, her expression still soft with sleep and the left-over raft scenario. Strands of her blond hair fell on his jacket. "This isn't a dream, Cabot," she said softly. "It's a lie."

"There's not that much difference between the two," he said, reaching up to tuck the hair back behind her ear, needing an excuse to touch it. "A dream is something that exists only in your mind. In most cases, a lie is just a creative interpretation of what is. In either case, it would probably just require a little work on the subject's part to make the dream a reality and the lie a truth.''

She stared at him a moment, succumbed to a smile, then just as quickly frowned. ''You have a scary brain, Cabot.''

''Charlie!'' Caroline exclaimed, flipping on the living room light. The shadowy little haven dissolved. ''I'm glad you're awake. Elizabeth has the most wonderful idea.''

Caroline's faintly concerned tone didn't support the words. Elizabeth smiled down at Charlotte and Derek.

Charlotte settled back against her pseudo groom, partly for the sake of the sham she didn't seem able to elude, and partly because Elizabeth's cold smile suggested the tangle was about to draw even more tightly around her, and the solidity of Derek's chest was very comforting.

''Really?'' she asked. ''What is that?''

''Kendra's in love with all the dresses you've brought,'' Elizabeth said, ''but I think she'll be deciding on the Victorian with the choker neckline and the wide frills on the shoulder.''

Charlotte nodded. The pinafore dress. She had known it would be perfect.

''Trouble is,'' Elizabeth went on, ''the mood of everything else is out of sync—the bridesmaids' dresses, the flowers, the centerpieces for the reception.''

Since she didn't look particularly displeased about the fact, Charlotte waited.

''Kendra and Caleb and I have talked it over and decided the best solution would be to hire you to make the changes, to have you as a guest at our home next week to help us do what's necessary to get everything done at the last minute. Money's no object, of course.''

A week with Elizabeth? Desperation took hold of her. "But you'll be entertaining the wedding party," she said calmly. "You'll have your family from out of town…"

Elizabeth shrugged. "But we have so much room." She sank gracefully into the chair opposite them and smiled with pretended empathy. "Since you're such newlyweds, I wouldn't dream of separating you. I thought you could stay in the smaller of the two guest houses so you can have some time together. The press will be staying in the bigger one."

Charlotte tried not to show terror. She knew the Farnsworth estate well. The two little guest houses behind the big house sat on opposite sides of the rose garden, but shared a common lane to and from the house. And the house the press would share had a picture window; it would be impossible for anyone in the other house to make a move without being seen. She suspected Bitsy would be watching her and Derek every moment.

To her relief, Derek demurred before she had to. "I'm sorry," he said sincerely, "but I'm in the middle of Farnsworth–Morreaux's plans to acquire Windsor Tech. I wouldn't have the time…"

"Nonsense!" Caleb Farnsworth came into the room, followed by Charlotte's father. "Elizabeth has so many plans for me next week, I won't be able to come into the office, but if you were on hand to meet with me when I had a moment, and if Edward were to join us, we could go over Windsor Tech's notes and work the points into our contract."

"Excellent idea." Edward was quick to agree. "We could get some serious work done free of the everyday office crises." He clapped Caleb on the back and grinned at Derek. "It'll be almost as good as a hunting trip."

Elizabeth blinked; Caroline looked up at Edward with

a pitying look. Charlotte thought he might not be that far wrong—she was beginning to feel like an exhausted prey about to be run to ground.

Charlotte turned pleading eyes on Derek, lost for a believable excuse. He simply raised both eyebrows with an innocence that belied the pull at his bottom lip.

"Well, we never did have time for a honeymoon," he said. "What do you think?"

Artful, she thought. He'd put it back on her. She couldn't refuse the invitation without looking unwilling to help and probably bitter over Trey. And she also couldn't refuse for Derek's sake when the partners who employed him obviously thought the situation ideal.

Before Charlotte could answer, Kendra's head peered around the corner of the hallway. On it was a coronet of crystal-beaded flowers and leaves. Yards of netting hung from it to the floor.

"Is Trey gone?" she whispered.

"Yes," Elizabeth replied. "But he made me promise to have you call him after dinner."

"Oh, good." Kendra, flushed and radiant, emerged from the corridor. The slim-fitting white satin bodice was beautifully accented by a wide flounce of lace that trimmed the shoulders and crossed her breasts to meet at the waist and make it appear even narrower than it already was. A diaphanous skirt contributed to the fragile look of the bride.

Kendra did a turn in the middle of the room, obviously waiting for praise.

"You're breathtaking, Kennie," Caleb said.

"It is beautiful," Caroline agreed softly.

Elizabeth reminded, as though she couldn't help herself, "It is borrowed, darling. Are you sure?"

"I'm sure," Kendra said firmly. Then she went to

kneel in a riffle of white near Derek and Charlotte's chair. "But now we have to fix everything else. You will come and help me, won't you? There'll be so much to do! We have to do something about my attendants' dresses, and I was just going to have calla lillies, but now that will never do. Please, Charlotte. You *have* to help me."

Charlotte wanted desperately not to do this, but she was able to relate to Kendra's dilemma on a curiously unselfish level. This was Kendra's wedding day, and just because her own had been botched, she wasn't unsympathetic to Kendra's wish that hers be perfect. It should be every woman's right. And it was Borrowed Magic's job.

"Of course I will," she said, and for a moment Derek almost had both women in his lap.

As Kendra scurried off, Bitsy Tate wandered out of the kitchen, stirring coffee in a china cup.

Charlotte started, unaware that the reporter had remained behind when everyone else had left.

As though reading her mind, Bitsy glanced her way as she sipped, then put the cup in its saucer and smiled slowly. "Well, I had to see how it all turned out, didn't I? This is a lovely little drama. Guaranteed to be front page of the section. So you will be staying with the Farnsworths even though you haven't even had time for a honeymoon yet?"

Charlotte accepted that she was in an indefensible position. Surrender was her only option. But she wouldn't forget who had helped put her there, and she vowed to see that it would be as difficult for him as it would be for her.

She gave Derek a seductive smile and traced her index finger tauntingly over his bottom lip, deciding that paybacks could start now. "Every moment we're together is like being on a sunny tropical beach. Isn't it, darling?"

He nipped the tip of her finger and made her yelp and withdraw it. Then he smiled wickedly into her eyes. "Paradise," he concurred. "When do we move in?"

Elizabeth studied them a moment, then smiled stiffly and replied, "Tomorrow morning. Then you'll be on hand to meet everyone at lunch."

"There's no reason Edward and I have to be there," Caroline tried to withdraw gracefully. "We're just a few miles away. If you need us, we can be there..."

"Now, now," Elizabeth insisted. "Our home is half again as big as this." She gave a quick look around that seemed to suggest the Morreauxs' four thousand square feet simply wasn't adequate. "There's plenty of room. And you can help me with my mother. She wants to spend all her time in the kitchen and I can't spare the pounds." Another eloquent glance suggested that Caroline's weight was a lost cause already. "Well, Caleb. Let's round up our daughter and be on our way."

Everyone gathered at the door as the Farnsworths took their leave. Derek hooked a familiar arm around Charlotte's shoulder, ignoring her warning glare.

Elizabeth dispensed her touchless hugs and thanked Caroline and Edward for hosting the shower. "It was so thoughtful of you. Kendra's into quaint little things these days and it was all so appropriate."

Caleb and Edward seemed to notice no undercurrent in the politely spoken thank-you. Caroline ignored it, a veteran of many years of Elizabeth's social tyranny.

Charlotte barely resisted administering a good shove into the potted geraniums.

The moment the door closed on the Farnsworths, Charlotte turned on Caroline.

"Caroline, what in the name of heaven have you done?" she demanded, confronting her under the gleaming chandelier.

Caroline returned glare for glare. "Well, good heavens, girl. Someone had to step in for you! Elizabeth asks you what's new, obviously to put you on the spot, and you launch into a business report!"

"At least that was honest!" Charlotte retorted. "Caro, you lied to a house full of people and members of the press! Tomorrow it'll be in the *Times* that Derek and I are married!"

"Charlie, don't shout at her," Edward said, putting a protective arm around his wife's shoulders. "I'm sure Caroline meant well."

"Dad…" Charlotte made a conscious effort to lower her voice. "Tomorrow Derek and I have to move into their guest house and live there together for a week until the wedding. In case you've forgotten, we are not married. We don't even like each other."

Edward failed to look properly horrified. Instead he smiled at Derek. "Good save, son. I did think Caro was dead in the water there for a minute."

"Good save?" Charlotte repeated incredulously. "Good save! He made it worse! He confirmed the lie!"

Edward rolled his eyes and patted her shoulder, like one would a child having a tantrum. "Charlie, you get so upset about the strangest things. Think of what this whole thing will do for your business. When everyone sees Kendra in that dress, they'll all come flocking to you for vintage dresses. Everyone will want a wedding like hers."

"And when Bitsy Tate puts her hand to this," Derek added, "she'll have you so smothered in wistful romance, sheer stardust will bring all the dreamy young girls to you. The jilted bride who nobly saved her ex-fiancé's wedding.''

Caroline smiled slowly. ''They'll say you were able to do it because you've found love at last with a handsome devil who came up the hard way and won your heart.''

Charlotte put a hand to her stomach. ''I'm going to be sick.''

''You're going to be famous,'' Caroline corrected.

Chapter Three

"I'll take the side by the door," Derek said, following Charlotte into the guest-house bedroom.

Charlotte took one look at the pink-and-white flow-ered wallpaper, the eyelet bedspread and the half-dozen lace-trimmed pillows stacked against the wicker head-board and quickly turned around. She collided soundly with the chest of Derek's tweedy jacket.

"You can have both sides," she said, pushing past him and back into the small oystershell-and-green living room. She dropped her makeup case, her suitcase and her suit bag in the middle of the floor and went into the small, corridor kitchen.

"And where are you going to sleep?" Derek leaned a shoulder in the kitchen doorway and watched her fill a kettle shaped and painted like a fish. "The bathtub's stylish but very uncomfortable looking."

"I'll sleep on the sofa." The kettle on, she opened cupboards looking for a cup. She found a complete set of blue pedestal pottery mugs.

"It doesn't open," he said.

"Not a problem." She instituted another search for tea bags, instant coffee, anything. "I don't move in my sleep."

"I sleepwalk," he said. "You won't be any safer in the living room than you'd be beside me."

She cast him a glower that told him what she thought of his attempt to lighten the mood. It couldn't be done. She'd awakened without a sense of humor this morning. He'd driven her home the night before, after stopping by the garage to assure her that her beloved Duesenberg was being well cared for. When they'd parted company, she'd been resigned if not happy with the prospect of the week ahead.

This morning, living a week in this little house with the press on one side and the Farnsworths on the other seemed impossible. She couldn't do it.

Derek took several steps into the narrow room. "What's happened since last night?" he asked quietly.

She pried at the top of a square tin of tea. When she couldn't budge it, she said impatiently, "Seems like nothing around here opens."

He reached a long arm out, took the tin from her and opened it effortlessly.

"You haven't answered my question," he reminded her as he handed the tin back.

"Want a cup?" she asked. "It's—" she studied the product name so she wouldn't have to look at him or answer him "—a delicate blend of oolong and orange pekoe."

"I would love a cup," he said, reaching into the cupboard where she'd gotten a mug and pulling down another. "I'd also like an answer."

Cornered, she unwrapped two tea bags and pretended to think. "Well, let's see. I packed a few things, took a shower, brushed my teeth, had my nightly cocoa and pretzels and went to bed with the latest Regency novel."

"Most amusing," he said, opening the door on the

small refrigerator and peering inside. "That unwilling-ness to be open is the same quality that made you so difficult to work with."

She spun toward him, hands on her hips. "*I* was not difficult to work with. *You* were difficult to work with. You wanted to boss everything about me, not just my job."

"That isn't true. You're just so spoiled and stubborn you take every suggestion as a criticism."

"You tried to tell me who...whom...to date!"

He interrupted his perusal of the contents of the re-frigerator to throw her a grin. "And I was right, wasn't I? Prentiss turned out to be a jerk."

"He isn't a jerk," Charlotte corrected righteously, "he's a coward. There's a difference."

"Not in my book."

"At Farnsworth–Morreaux, I may have had to work by your book. In my life, I did not."

"So you ran away."

"I quit."

"Same thing."

"Not in *my* book."

He pulled out a clear square box of blueberry muffins and placed it on the counter. "Your book was written so long ago, no one's heard of it. Your book was prob-ably originally taken down on papyrus. Your book is just like *you*—beautiful and romantic but entirely impracti-cal."

"I believe in facts carefully researched, skillfully as-sembled and tastefully distributed. Until you came to F and M, that was not considered a crime."

He opened the cupboard again and pulled down plates.

"I don't want a muffin," she said.

He replaced a plate and opened the refrigerator in search of butter.

"Why do you think your father put me in charge of your department?" he asked. "Because it was weeks behind and Prince Prentiss wasn't doing anything about it. He was apparently afraid of you at work as well as in bed."

Charlotte swatted him with a handy towel. "How dare you say a thing like that! How dare you express an opinion on a subject you know nothing about!"

He gave her a glance she couldn't read, then neatly pulled the head off a muffin and buttered it. "You haven't been well loved," he said. "I can see it in your eyes. And if he'd really taken you over the top, it'd show in his. And it doesn't."

"Oh, right. Like sexual experience is a visible thing."

"It is. It's subtle, but it's there."

The kettle whistled. Charlotte snapped off the burner and lifted the three clear glass bubbles at the fish's mouth to pour. Derek held first one tea bag while she poured, then the other.

"Trey wasn't afraid of me," Charlotte insisted, consciously controlling her tone, wondering why a few minutes in Derek Cabot's company always had her shouting. "He just believed in letting me do my own work in my own way."

"Which resulted in it not getting accomplished."

"Why can't you admit," she said, lifting her cup and placing her other hand protectively under it, "that you just never liked me?" And she marched out of the kitchen to the living room.

Derek popped the last bite of muffin into his mouth and followed her, wondering how a smart woman could be so dense.

"My personal feelings had nothing to do with it," he said. And the moment the words were out of his mouth, he knew they'd been a mistake. They echoed in the small, stylish little room like the lie they were—only not for the reason she thought.

"You didn't want me there," she said, putting her cup on the glass-topped coffee table and sitting in the middle of the green polished cotton sofa, "because you decided even before you knew me that I was the spoiled, stubborn daughter of the boss who'd gotten her job on relationship and not on merit, and you couldn't stand that because no one's ever given you anything. You've had to fight for it. So you had to fight me."

He put his cup beside hers and pulled off his jacket, thinking that she was absolutely right. He'd felt precisely that way—and he'd been right. She'd taken the job because her father wanted her near him, and she'd done adequately when the company had been smaller.

But recently, acquisitions and diversity of product had happened with a swiftness that required a PR department that could act as quickly. It had taken him only days to see that Charlotte's relaxed, carefully attentive style couldn't cope.

She was already dressing like a woman from another time, and her locker and her desk drawers were filled with fashion accessories that looked like artifacts to him. She talked continually about one day opening her own shop.

The morning they locked horns over the production delay of a sales brochure, because her promotional copy hadn't been ready, had given her that opportunity.

What she'd never understood was that their mutual antagonism was based on more than their different work styles. Her closeness made him edgy. When he was near, she became defensive. He thought it was time he found out what it was all about.

"Actually, I liked having you around," he admitted easily as he tossed his jacket on the rocker at a right angle to the sofa. "I just knew you should be doing something else. Anyway…" He sat in a corner of the sofa and squared one leg on the other. "We shouldn't be talking about the office. We're supposed to be on our honeymoon." He grinned wickedly. "We're supposed to turn this into that sunny, tropical paradise you told the Farnsworths about."

She edged over one cushion, noting unhappily that the sofa was squishy. One night on it and she'd probably have to wear a back brace for the next month.

"I was just playing the role."

"And very well. All you have to do is keep it up for a week and we're home free."

She sipped tea, then thought she should explain her position in no uncertain terms. "I'm only doing this because I wouldn't hurt my parents for the world…"

"I understand."

"And Borrowed Magic is just beginning to take off. I can't afford any bad press right now."

"Of course not."

She sighed dramatically at his amenable acquiescence. "You needn't patronize me."

He turned to face her, setting his cup on the table and frowning. "Do you have to take issue with everything? I was simply agreeing with you. I also don't want to see Ed or Caroline get hurt, and bad press is a bad thing. Ease up, will you? If you keep up this attitude, everyone will wonder what I saw in you."

"No, they won't. It's considered very strategic to marry the boss's daughter." Still, she knew he was anything but an opportunist—at least in that respect. He'd never once done anything anyone might have construed as an attempt to reach her father through her. In fact, he'd found it more expedient to get her out of the way. She had to ask. "Why are *you* doing this?"

He reached to the table for his cup and took a sip before answering.

"Your father reminds me of mine," he said, thoughtfully resting his cup on his bent knee. "Only mine died too young to see all his big ideas grow."

That surprised her. She'd never thought of him in relation to a family. He seemed so solitary. "What did your father do?"

"He sold and repaired small appliances," Derek replied, a fond smile on his lips as he absently turned his cup. "He had a shop in Salem, Oregon, and another in Corvallis. He was always going to move into a mall, open a big furniture store and put his repair shop in the back, but he was always too busy to stop and put a deal together." The smile faded suddenly and he took another sip of tea. "He had a fatal heart attack when I was a sophomore in high school."

Charlotte was a little shaken by that information— Derek Cabot loved his father and missed him.

"And," he went on, the past gone from his eyes, the future alight in them, "I couldn't resist the temptation to satisfy my curiosity about you."

She blinked at him. "Curiosity about what?"

"About whether or not you would remain the Duchess of Winter in my arms and in my bed."

"The Duch...who?"

"The Duchess of Winter," he replied, putting his cup down again. "You know, that imperious woman you always become when you want to put someone off." He mimicked her raised eyebrow, her cold glance, then, comically, the dismissing toss of her head.

"Of course that doesn't work as well if you don't have this long veil of blond hair, but you know what I mean."

"I do not!" she denied, a giggle just below the surface of her indignation. His interpretation of her behavior had more humor in it than criticism. "I don't do that."

"Please," he said. "You do one of the three all the time. You have a few other signature moves I could never duplicate, so I didn't try. Are you afraid if you find a man who makes your heart pound your dignity might slip?"

"Of course not." She replied with the same glance she'd just denied using. "Nothing could make my dignity slip."

"Oh..." he said slowly, studying her with serious intent. "That's almost too much of a challenge to walk around. Do you want to test that?"

Trepidation filled her. And a subtle excitement. But she was off men at the moment and she'd never been one to flirt with danger or tempt the fates.

"Thanks, but it was tested a year ago when I walked up the aisle and there was no one there to meet me." She made herself look directly into his eyes. "I was bloody, but unbowed. And so I shall remain."

"Bruised and stiff. That about describes you." He reached a hand along the back of the sofa and ran a fingertip across her cheekbone. "That's got to be uncomfortable. I'll bet I could buckle your knees."

He saw her eyes widen. She thought so, too? Well. Wasn't life full of the damnedest surprises.

"That would make me fall," she pointed out primly.

"I would be there to catch you," he explained. "That's the whole point."

"You know," she said, at a loss to answer him and needing a way out of the conversation, "you worry a subject to death. Forget it. I am quite happy the way I am, thank you." She glanced at her watch and stood. "We should be changing for lunch."

"Changing what?"

"Clothes." She looked down at her fashionable silk sweats. "I'm going to put on a dress."

He unfolded slowly to his feet. "Do people still do that? I thought changing for meals was something people did only in the movies about high society."

"Yeah, well, this is the Farnsworth estate," she said, throwing her dress bag over the back of a chair and rummaging through it. "Elizabeth sleeps with the social register under her pillow. And we seem to be living the *Philadelphia Story*. I keep thinking the director will come through any moment and shout, 'That's a wrap. Take ten, people.'"

"Drama's good for the soul." Derek picked up his bag and headed for the bathroom. "You can have the bedroom," he said over his shoulder. "Change in there. I'll sleep on the sofa, but I should probably leave my bag in the bedroom so we don't raise the suspicions of anyone dropping by."

"I will be happy to sleep on the sofa," Charlotte insisted nobly.

"Well, I *would* enjoy your company." Derek smirked from the bathroom doorway.

She straightened, a Victorian floral print clutched against her, to frown at him in exasperation. "I meant, while you were in the bed."

He pretended surprise. "Oh. Here I thought I was go-

ing to get to buckle your knees, after all. Take the bed,''
he said, pushing the door closed to end the discussion.

EVERY NERVE ENDING in her body was dancing. Charlotte tilted her head sideways to brush her hair, then
swung her head to settle it against her back. She tied it
at the nape of her neck with a thin black ribbon.

The little tremor raced along under her skin, a curious
sensation she didn't recall experiencing before. Nerves?
she wondered. No. She was no stranger to deadlines and
stress. She'd supervised enough weddings in the year
she'd been in business to learn how to cope.

This was different. This was personal.

Big surprise, she told herself, smoothing the lace collar that sat neatly on the romantic rose print of her cinch-
waisted dress. You're living a lie with a man who seems
determined to unsettle you. This is nerves with a vengeance.

But she knew it wasn't. The moment she opened the
door and spotted Derek standing in the middle of the
small living room, a fresh blue shirt under the tweedy
jacket, she knew it was...awareness. Sexual awareness.

Good, she told herself ironically. You're required to
give the performance of a lifetime over the next six days
or humiliate your parents and kiss your business goodbye, and you're experiencing runaway estrogen.

Derek extended an arm toward her as she approached.
She was just about to slap it away and tell him to keep
his theatrical attentions for the benefit of their audience
when she realized they did indeed have one.

Bitsy Tate sat in the rocker, a white high-heeled san-
dal on the oystershell-colored carpeting propelling her
gently back and forth.

"Bitsy thought we might as well walk to the big house together," he said.

Charlotte slipped smoothly into his arm, a sweet smile in place. "Are we in danger of being unable to find it ourselves?" she asked.

"I just thought when you're looking into each other's eyes all the time," Bitsy said, standing and shouldering her bag, "you often miss the obvious. But I could give you a head start, if you'd prefer."

"We'd be delighted to have you join us," Derek said, offering his free arm. "Mornings, we love company. Nights, we like to be left alone."

At the door, he stepped out from between the women to open it and usher them through. As Charlotte passed him, following Bitsy, he asked loudly enough for the reporter to hear, "Did you find my keys?"

Charlotte understood the question was intended to assure Bitsy they were sharing the room. She decided the best part about acting was the opportunity to improvise.

"They were under the dresser," she said. "Must have happened when you cartwheeled off the bed. Ow!"

His pinch of retribution was swift and stinging. Bitsy, fortunately, seemed to take it as newlywed play.

KENDRA'S TWO ATTENDANTS had also arrived that morning, one a little redhead from Houston, and the other a Harvard-accented Bostonian with yards of curly dark hair. Kendra explained that they'd been college friends and met in Gstaad every winter and Cozumel every summer. Charlotte had been surprised when she'd first learned Kendra would have only two attendants. She'd imagined she'd want half a dozen beautiful young women streaming up the aisle.

"Of course, that'll stop now." A bright little woman

in a boldly patterned muumuu and sneakers with white socks wandered into the palatial, vaulted-ceiling living room where Kendra was making introductions. She put a floury hand around Kendra's waist, oblivious to the expensive crepe fabric of her dress. "Now you'll have to stay home with your man and raise babies."

"Mother," Elizabeth said with strained patience, pulling the woman's arms from around her daughter, "we just got that dress at Susanna's. I thought you were helping in the kitchen."

"I was," the woman replied cheerfully, "but I thought it was only polite to come out and greet my granddaughter's friends."

Elizabeth tried to turn her back toward the kitchen. "Well, we're just about to…"

"Chow down. I know, I'm fixing it." Elizabeth's mother pulled deftly away from her and turned to study the new arrivals with interest. "Hope you like this stuff. It's quiche. Looks a little insipid to me. I thought a good hearty stew would have been nice, but you know Lizzie. Gotta watch her gut."

She backhanded Elizabeth's midsection with a hearty laugh. Elizabeth doubled over and Caleb steadied her with a distinctive twitch to his lip.

Charlotte had to take action or burst into laughter. She extended her hand for a floury handshake.

"I'm so pleased to meet you," she said. "I'm Charlotte Mo—" She stopped herself just in time, giving an apologetic smile around the room. "Cabot. Charlotte Cabot," she said. "I'm a newlywed. I keep forgetting I'm not a Morreaux anymore."

"I'm Babs McGuffy." Elizabeth's mother shook Charlotte's hand, then looked up at Derek with interest. "You the groom?"

"Yes, ma'am," he replied, offering his hand. "Derek Cabot."

"You're a looker, Derek," she said, then stood on tiptoe and beckoned him to lean down. He complied and she added in a loud whisper, "But you got to work at this a little harder if she's forgetting that she wears your name."

A ripple of laughter passed among the women, except for Elizabeth who was still trying to recover from Babs's backhand. Edward and Caleb grinned at each other. Charlotte felt the color rise to her hairline.

Derek took the advice with a respectful nod. "You're absolutely right. I'll apply myself."

"Course, I understand Elizabeth and Kendra here stole you right out from your honeymoon to help save this shindig. No wonder the little lady's not sure of herself." She turned her full attention on Charlotte. "You're the one responsible for that dress Kendra's going to wear?"

The question had a suggestion of condemnation. Charlotte angled her chin because the dress was perfect for Kendra. "Yes, I am," she replied.

Babs nodded, treating her to the same backhand she'd given Elizabeth, except that this one landed on her elbow—and broke it, Charlotte was sure.

"Beautiful dress. Gives some class to this show. Only real thing here—except for my cake. Come on, I'll show you."

Babs locked Charlotte's wrist in one hand and Derek's in the other and headed off at a quick pace toward the back of the house.

Charlotte shrugged helplessly at the Farnsworths and their guests. "Excuse us," she said as she was tugged along.

Derek caught her eye over the much smaller woman's head and she could see that he was enjoying this. She had to admit she was, too. Babs was a delightful surprise in this stronghold of social correctness.

Derek was surprising also. Gone was the demanding, exacting man she'd so despised at the Farnsworth–Morreaux office. In his place was a casual, taunting, sexually aggressive man who was determined to find a chink in her armor before this week was over.

The laughter in his eyes drew her and charmed her. But she had to resist. She was here on business, though everyone else thought she was honeymooning in her spare time. And she wasn't about to let Derek Cabot seduce her just to prove to himself that he could.

The functional white kitchen was almost as big as a restaurant's and boasted every sophisticated aid and appliance that might be found in one. Charlotte had seen it before. The Farnsworth dinners were legendary.

A plump older woman in a serviceable apron looked up from arranging orange slices on salads. She smiled fondly at Babs, then recognized Charlotte.

"Congratulations on your wedding, Miss Morreaux," she said, turning an interested gaze on Derek. "Good morning, sir."

"Pauline, this is my husband, Derek Cabot," Charlotte said, horrified at how easily the words tripped off her tongue. "Derek, this is one of the finest cooks in all of southern California, Pauline Miller."

Unable to free himself from Babs's grip, Derek waved his free hand at her. "Nice to meet you, Pauline. I've enjoyed many of your dinners, though we've never met. I'm looking forward to lunch."

Pauline studied him a moment, then nodded at Charlotte. "Good work, Mrs. Cabot."

Babs freed her captives, then whipped the towel aside that covered a large pottery bowl of some deep vanilla-colored doughlike substance filled with nuts, raisins and other dried fruit.

"Smell that," she ordered the pair.

Simultaneously Charlotte and Derek obeyed, dipping faces several respectful inches from the substance.

Charlotte caught the tang of sourdough.

"Making it from my own starter," Babs said.

Though Charlotte wasn't much of a cook, she knew that a cup of starter was used to create new recipes, while flour and sugar and milk were added to the starter on a regular basis to keep it alive and growing.

It was a staple that had come west on wagon trains, moved to new homes with married daughters, was shared with neighbors and traveled along generations with a steadiness that was comforting to think about.

Derek leaned down to take a whiff and smelled the sweet, yeasty aroma of a living thing. Wrapped in the aroma was a floral fragrance that was Charlotte.

Charlotte felt his chin touch her hair, smelled the open-air fragrance of his after-shave and the light touch of his hand at her back as he leaned over her.

Everything inside her seemed to move just a little faster—heartbeat, breath, blood. She straightened abruptly.

Derek dodged her quick move and returned her suspicious look with one of innocence.

"I wanted to make Kennie's wedding cake with this," Babs said, lovingly replacing the cloth. "Brought the starter with me all the way from the Bitterroot Valley in Montana. But Lizzie says her guests won't understand if they don't have some mile-high thing from the spiffy bakery on Rodeo Drive." She rolled her eyes. "Going to have crystal birds on it." Then she sighed, smoothing the cloth with a gesture that was both thoughtful and sad. "So we're going to have this with dinner. Funny, isn't it, that all the homey old things don't fit in the world today. It's gotten so narrow and…and plain." She whispered, "That's why I never come here 'less I have to."

Charlotte put an arm around her and squeezed comfortingly. "I can't wait to taste it. Of course, I'm into old things, too, so I think it would be appropriate anywhere."

Babs smiled up at her, the sadness gone. It was apparent she'd long ago accepted that she and her daughter had little more than a blood connection.

"It's too bad I wasn't around to make a cake for *your* wedding."

Charlotte decided then and there to call her if the event ever came to be. "Well, it was kind of a quick thing. We didn't even have a cake."

Babs suddenly looked pleased about that. "Well, I'm going to make one, just for the two of you to share. You know, all the nuts and fruit in here promise fertility." She winked and waggled an arthritic index finger at Charlotte. "And with you forgetting your married name, it's bound to help."

Derek met her helpless glance and laughed softly.

"Thank you, Babs. I appreciate having you on my side."

"Mother? Mother!" Elizabeth's sharp voice sounded from the doorway. "I'd like Pauline to serve lunch now. Will you bring *the Cabots* out, please." There was a subtle emphasis on "the Cabots" that underlined her lack of conviction that that was indeed what they were.

"All right, all right." Babs pushed Charlotte and Derek before her with a roll of her eyes in Pauline's direction. "Let's go before Princess Grace has a hissy fit. I'll be back to help you serve, Pauline."

"Mrs. McGuffy, you're supposed to be a guest here," Pauline said, shooing her away. "I'll take care of things."

Babs dismissed her protests with a wave of her hand and led Charlotte and Derek toward the dining room. "Only society folk would decide cooking was too much work and hire someone to do it for them, then force that person to do it all by herself. Does that make sense to you?"

BABS BUSTLED in and out of the dining room, helping Pauline serve and clear away. Everyone accepted her sharp observations in stride, except Elizabeth who seemed torn between wanting to kill her mother and wanting to die herself.

Charlotte couldn't help enjoying her discomfort because it was all of her own making. Babs offended no one but Elizabeth and her inflated opinion of herself.

After lunch, Charlotte went upstairs to Kendra's room to look over the bridesmaids' dresses while the men closed themselves in Caleb's study. Elizabeth followed her mother into the kitchen, presumably to set down a few rules.

Charlotte had to admit that the dress from which she'd rescued Kendra was a beaded monstrosity. A high neck with padded shoulders was covered with sequins and bugle beads across the shoulders and tapered to a V at the waistline. Beading came up from the waist in a high, scalloped pattern.

It might have suited a taller, broader-shouldered woman—like Elizabeth—but it made Kendra look as though she'd donned a very expensive dress destined for the football field.

Sitting on the edge of Kendra's bed, Charlotte winced as Kendra did a turn in front of her.

"I can't believe that *this* is what came of mother's design! It cost her a fortune, and it's so ugly! She and Jean Michel are squabbling over whose fault it is."

Charlotte doubted there was any question. Elizabeth had probably had her mind set on what *she* wanted, forced the idea down Kendra's throat, then steamrolled Jean Michel into doing it.

Kendra pushed it over her head with little regard for the expensive beading and tossed it on the bed behind Charlotte. Then she slipped the beautiful Victorian dress over her head. It settled into place like a cloud, making Kendra beautiful despite her tumbled hair.

Briane, the redhead from Houston, came out of the bathroom with the broad-shouldered, full-skirted plum-colored dress Elizabeth had probably thought would carry on the theme of her creation.

Kendra and Briane looked at each other, frowning at the now discordant note of the soft, Victorian bridal dress, and the beautiful but blatantly contemporary bridesmaid gown.

Denise, the brunette, emerged from the next room in the same creation in purple. It looked even worse.

"What'll we do?" Kendra demanded plaintively.

Charlotte's love of the challenge fabrics and fashion took over and any resentment she might have felt for Kendra faded away. She could fix this little nightmare. What was more, she wanted to.

"Okay." She stood and studied the dresses with a critical eye. The dresses had a basic simple line that would be easy to turn into their purposes.

"Scissors," she said to Kendra.

"Scissors?" Kendra repeated worriedly.

"To remove the shoulder pads."

"Right." Kendra delved into a little desk across the room and returned with a pair of ornate embroidery scissors.

Charlotte reached into the shoulder of Briane's dress and began to snip.

"Watch it in there," Briane joked, careful not to move. "That's only a triple A, but it's precious to me."

Charlotte appreciated the woman's sense of humor. "Maybe we should stuff the shoulder pad down the bodice," she suggested.

Denise laughed. "With her luck, they'll slip and she'll walk down the aisle with a flat chest and well-developed kneecaps."

Everyone laughed at the absurd mental image.

"Okay." The pads removed, Charlotte smoothed the now pliant fabric over Briane's shoulder, stepped back and saw instant improvement.

"That's better, but it's so plain," Kendra said, grumbling.

"I was thinking..." Charlotte did a turn around the girls, who stood dutifully in place like a pair of mannequins. "I'll tailor the dropped shoulder, find tulle to match..." As she spoke she lifted the first layer of silky overskirt to bring it around Briane's shoulder. "And we'll make a small cape that we'll catch here with a little silk flower." She gathered the fabric at Briane's bosom, then looked up at Kendra for approval. "It'll be quick and easy to do, and it'll make the difference. What do you think?"

Kendra tilted her head right, then left, and smiled in

disbelief. "I think it's perfect. But what about the head-pieces?"

She took one of the little whimsies of netting lined up on the dresser and put the plum-colored one on Briane's head. It looked too contemporary for the dress's new look.

"It doesn't fit anymore, does it?"

"Picture hats would be nice," Denise said.

"But there isn't time to find them in the right colors," Kendra said worriedly. "Is there?"

Charlotte shook her head. "I don't think so. But we could make coronets of silk flowers or fresh flowers. That would be very Victorian."

"Fresh flowers would mean you'd have to do them at the last minute," Kendra said thoughtfully. "And what if something went wrong?"

Charlotte was beginning to think there was hope for Kendra. Elizabeth would never have considered that. She'd have thought fresh flowers the right choice and wouldn't have cared that someone would have to create them under great pressure at the last moment.

"I know where to go for silk flowers," Charlotte said. "And at the shop I have some dried flowers I could use and some pearls and beads that would add interest and make them unique."

The women nodded unanimously.

Kendra rummaged in a desk drawer and produced a small white envelope she handed to Charlotte. "Here are the swatches we used to have our shoes dyed, and I'll write you a check."

"Oh, don't," Charlotte said, following her when she went back to the desk. "I'll just get what we need and we'll settle up when we're sure everything…works."

Charlotte's attention was caught by a beautiful paint-

ing over Kendra's desk of a brass pot of flowers. The
light in the brass gleamed warmth, and the softness of
the flowers was almost touchable. She noticed the
scripted *K* with which Kendra signed her sketches as a
child.

"Kendra," she said in amazement. "I didn't know
you were painting."

"I'm not, really." Kendra stepped back to give her
painting a critical study. "I've taken a few classes when
Mother hasn't had me completely tied up in one of her
guilds or leagues or clubs."

"This should be hanging downstairs."

"Don't be silly." Kendra's tone was wry. "It didn't
cost enough." Then, realizing she'd been critical of her
mother's scale for success, she tossed her head and
laughed lightly. "My style isn't unique enough to be
noticed."

"Wouldn't devoting some time to it help you find
your special…something?"

Kendra shrugged. "Maybe. But I have other plans
now. I'm getting married."

"Kendra…" A thousand arguments rose to Charlotte's lips, but Briane came to lean a companionable
elbow on Kendra's shoulder. "Are you lucky to have a
friend who's a wedding expert!"

"Really." Denise hooked a thumb in the direction of
the pile of beads on the bed. "You should have consulted her before you ordered this horrid dress."

Kendra looked at Charlotte, and for a moment there
was more in her eyes than the spoiled young woman
with whom she'd grown up. Though publicly she still
seemed to be a clone of Elizabeth, something within her
had changed.

A new connection was made between them. It had

more to do with respect than affection, but it was there all the same.

"Thank you," Kendra said. "I appreciate your disrupting your honeymoon to do this for me."

Charlotte shrugged and slipped into her role. "You know how the men of Farnsworth–Morreaux are. Time away from the office is unheard of. Derek would rather be here than on some sunny beach."

"I'm not going to let Trey be like that," Kendra said with quiet firmness.

Charlotte nodded. "More power to you. If you'll excuse me, I'll go hunt down what we need and let you know how it's going at dinner."

"Good. See you then."

Charlotte raced down the mahogany stairway, anxious to get as far away as possible from this movie set of a home and into the crowded, smog-shrouded, gas-choked reality of downtown Los Angeles.

She was all the way to the garages before she remembered that she didn't have a car. Then she turned in the direction of Derek's Porsche and wondered whether or not he had the keys on him.

The chauffeur, white sleeves rolled up, appeared from out of the shadows of the garage, a chamois in his hand. She knew him well. He'd driven her and Kendra many times when they'd been girls.

"Can I help you, Miss Morreaux? I mean, Mrs. Cabot?"

"Do you have Mr. Cabot's keys, Henry?" she asked.

"Yes, I do."

"May I have them, please?"

"Certainly." He disappeared into the shadows and returned again with a small brass ring of four or five keys. He held it out to her and she was about to slip her index finger into the ring and take it from him when another male voice said with quiet command, "Don't even think about it."

Charlotte turned in guilty surprise to find Derek standing behind her.

"Oh..." she said with exaggerated brightness, then added for Henry's sake, "Darling. I thought you were in a meeting."

"I was." He replied, taking the keys from her hand. "I'm out. Going somewhere?"

"I, ah, have to pick up a few things for the bridesmaids' dresses. Since my car is still in the shop, I was sure you wouldn't mind my taking yours." She smiled at Henry to remind Derek that he was there, and that he probably wouldn't understand any references to theft.

Derek gave Henry an even look. "Ever let your wife drive your cherry Mustang, Henry?"

Henry replied gravely. "Never, Mr. Cabot."

"Sound policy. I don't let Mrs. Cabot drive this." He grinned. "Remember that next time she asks you for my keys."

Henry nodded. "Right, sir."

Charlotte rolled her eyes. "I have never had an accident," she pointed out, looking at one man, then the other. "Can either of you say that?"

"I had an accident once," Henry admitted, "trying to get out of the way of a woman making a U-turn on a freeway on ramp."

Derek added, "And I was once rear ended by a woman trying to parallel park."

Charlotte put a hand over her eyes. "Well, I'd love to stand and listen to you two praise each other, but I have to get to Flowers and Fabrics in downtown Los Angeles. Would either of you two care to drive me?"

"My pleasure, ma'am," Henry said. "That's what Mrs. Farnsworth pays me for."

"Thanks, Henry," Derek said, giving his keys a toss. "I'll do it. You stay and protect the stable from other marauding women."

Henry laughed heartily. "If I'm approached by marauding women, they can have everything I've got."

Derek opened the passenger side door for Charlotte and grinned over her head at the chauffeur. "You're a man after my own heart, Henry Phillips."

"You know," Charlotte said as they backed out of the garage and turned in a tight circle to head down the driveway, "I am so grateful you're not my husband, I can't tell you."

He gave her a lazy smile. "I know you are. But before this is over, you'll wish I were. *You* might even propose to *me*."

"In your dreams, Cabot."

"You are, Charlie," he said, shifting and sending the little car down the lane like a rocket. "You are."

Chapter Four

It was alarming, Charlotte thought, to be moving at top speed in the midst of six lanes of freeway traffic and look out the window into the face of a tire named General. Most cars looked enormous beside the small Porsche. Pickups looked huge, and semis freighting goods to and from the shipping capital of western America looked like Goliaths. One wrong move on Derek's part and they'd have been nothing more than a speck in the tread of some triple trailer.

"Nervous?" he asked, glancing her way as the traffic slowed at a popular off ramp.

"A little," she admitted, embarrassed to find she had sunken down in her already low seat.

"Is it me or the traffic?"

"You sit up a lot higher in the Duesenberg," she said, trying not to wince as the traffic moved on and he battled a van for a spot in the next lane and won. "I'm not used to watching the traffic from the viewpoint of the muffler. Haven't you ever thought about getting something bigger? Something higher?"

"This is more maneuverable. And I have good reflexes. You're safe, I promise you. This our exit?"

"Ah, yes. Then take a left. The shop's about three blocks down on the right side."

"Got it."

They were there in five minutes, and pulled effortlessly into an on-street spot that would have taken her ten minutes of inching forward and back with the Duesenberg. There might be advantages to this little car, she thought, but they were apparent only when one left the freeway.

Derek tossed his jacket in the back seat, then came around to help her out. The curb was higher than the floor of the car.

She bounced up beside him, ruffled and conscious of controlling her short, silky skirt.

"Geez!" she exclaimed, tugging everything back into place. "Climbing out of that thing is like rising out of a basement. Do I look like I've been working on a furnace or something?"

He grinned, reaching out intrepidly to refasten the pearly button that had come undone at her scooped neckline. "No, but my temperature's up," he said with a direct look into her eyes.

She looked back, determined not to blush. "There's no one watching now, Cabot. You can be yourself."

"This is it," he said.

"Derek…"

"One more thing."

"What?"

He took the angled-cut end of the black ribbon that secured her hair and tugged until the straight, blond mass fell free. He tossed the ribbon into the car and closed the door. "There." He studied her a moment, then reached a hand into the thick mass and combed his fingers downward through it. Something happened in his eyes—an emotion, a feeling, appeared there she couldn't analyze.

"It feels," he said seriously, "like the music from a cello."

She stared up at him, snared by the velvet darkness of his eyes. And by the thought. Her mind played back a melody she'd once heard in a cello solo; she didn't remember where or when. It had been smooth and honeyed and heartbreaking.

He put an arm around her and led her into the shop.

RELAX, DEREK TOLD himself as he trailed after Charlotte while she wandered from aisle to aisle. The store was acres of fabric in every shade of every color and every texture the mind could conceive. You know yourself. You do chancy things all the time. It's a large part of your success.

But this is a woman, he argued with himself, not a business deal. A fearless, aggressive approach was more likely to frighten than stun or impress. What's called for here is a little style, man. Rein in the horses. And keep your hands in your pockets.

She stopped so abruptly he collided with her. She gave him a quick, apologetic smile over her shoulder, obviously only vaguely aware of him. The moment they walked into the store, she seemed to have turned into someone else.

She pulled a bolt of purple stuff off a table and tried to put it in his hands. "Would you hold this, please?"

He made a reluctant sound, looking around, afraid he might be recognized. "Do I have to?"

She looked first surprised, then exasperated. "Yes, you have to. I've been humiliated on more than one occasion, thanks to your quick thinking to save my step-mother. You can do this little thing for me.''

He resisted when she tried to hand it to him again.

''You'll have to make it worth my while,'' he warned.

She studied him a full ten seconds before she asked in dry tones, ''And what would that entail?''

''Something wifely,'' he replied. ''A back rub. A kiss for no reason.''

She turned to place the bolt atop the other bolts to unroll it and check the shade, but the surface was already a jumble of bolts that hadn't been replaced. She turned back to him, exasperated. His hands would provide the only flat surface around.

''You have the duration of our stay at the guest house in which to do this,'' he encouraged.

She pushed the bolt at him, sure she would find a way to evade him.

The bolt bounced in his arms as she unrolled it, then he found himself looking at her through a haze of pale purple gossamer.

''Perfect,'' she said, rolling the fabric back up and plunking it back in his arms. She pulled out a bolt of a deeper, redder purple. Pleased with herself, she smiled at him and turned him toward a row of carts.

''Let's get something to put these in,'' she said, ''before I have to bargain away my virtue.''

''Two bolts,'' he said, holding them to him posses-sively when she tried to take them from him and drop them into a cart. ''That means I get the rub *and* the kiss.''

Charlotte shook her head at him, holding back a smile through sheer cussedness. ''No wonder Daddy has you negotiate all contracts. Come on. I want to look at the silk flowers.''

"Oh, God."

A second room at the back of the store held the silk representation of every species and subspecies of flower known to man, in their genuine colors and in some creative applications.

"A brown rose?" Derek plucked one from a trellis that attempted to make them appear real. "I've never seen a brown rose."

She replaced the rose, then tucked her hand in his elbow and pulled him from the display of full-blown roses to the smaller tea variety, and pushed him gently around the back of the floor-to-ceiling cascade. "I'm looking for a lavender rose—a delicate shade that'll coordinate with both of these." She held out the fabric swatches of plum and purple. "You try the back."

"Lavender roses?" he asked doubtfully, doing as she asked. "I've never seen that, either."

"Well, you obviously haven't sent many roses," she said, reaching for one that looked promising, then deciding it was too cool a color. "The Sterling Silver, a beautiful lavender rose, was developed years ago. And I think there've been others since then."

"When I send roses," he said, his voice sounding vaguely distracted as she lost sight of him around the wide display. "They're red."

"That's so conventional."

"It says something personal," he replied. "It doesn't say, 'I looked all over to find you an exclusive hybrid created in some laboratory because God didn't want it that color.' It says…"

She came face-to-face with him suddenly around the side of the display. She straightened with a start as he pinned her against the silky bank of roses, his eyes dark and challenging. "'These red roses express my passion for you, the color of my heart, my blood, my fire.'"

She looked back at him, her pulse tripping, her lips parted in surprise and the subtle beginnings of excitement. It occurred to her that excitement was a strange thing to find in a shop filled with fabric and silk flowers, but he seemed to create his own atmosphere, his own reality.

"I would never send you a lavender rose," he said, taking a step back and allowing her finally to draw an even breath.

He drew a dusky-rose flower from behind his back and held it out to her. "This it?"

"Ah, yes, I think so." She held the swatches to it and found that the strong but misty shade suited both. "Exactly right." She smiled up at him, hoping that confronting the attraction she felt would free the mystery inherent in it and make it disappear.

"You might be wasted in the corporate world, too," she said, following him around the display to the right shade. "Want to come to work for me?"

The roses were higher than she could reach, and she waited while he plucked down several dozen.

"Tempting as that is in some ways," he said, "I need the excitement of world-class deals and dangerous chances."

She studied him consideringly as he dropped the last rose in the cart. "Those don't sound like the preferences of a man who'd send red roses." She was gaining a new perspective on him. "I think you're more complex than you appear. Possibly even than you yourself realize."

He was beginning to suspect that himself. "What now?"

"Umm..." She looked around, her hand on the front

of the cart. "Baby's breath, and those little five-petal purple things. And maybe some tiny beads."

"Lead on."

He watched her rummage through a deep bin of tiny flowers. With a silky rose in one hand, she brought flower after flower up to hold against it until she found the right shade.

"You know, speaking of complexity," he said, pulling up a flower and touching it to hers to check the shade, "you're an interesting case. What made a young woman who was left at the altar go into the wedding business? Isn't that a little masochistic?"

"No." She lifted a handful of flowers and uncovered a vein of little five-petal things in the right shade. Derek dutifully tossed them into the cart. "These other weddings have nothing to do with me," she said, replacing the top layer of flowers and smoothing them into place. "My business is to lend romance to the weddings with my dresses and my finishing touches. It's business. I'm removed from any personal involvement."

"Charlie," he scolded softly. "That's a crock."

In the middle of the aisle, with silk flowers of every color cascading all around them, she turned to him in mild annoyance. "And how do you know that?"

"I worked with you for a year. You become personally involved in everything you do. And I remember how you lit up when Prentiss walked into the room. You certainly can't claim to have no emotional involvement in this particular wedding."

She rolled her eyes and took control of the cart. "That doesn't mean that Borrowed Magic can't do its job."

"As I've pointed out before," he said, following her to a display of beads and beaded garlands at the far end of the shop. "You are Borrowed Magic. Maybe it would be healthier to admit that it's just a little painful."

"It isn't," she said, fingering the garlands festooning another trellis. She reached for one with beads no larger than the head of a pin. "I don't care anymore."

"About Trey or about getting married?"

"Both."

"Is that why you find it so difficult to pretend to be married to me?"

She unhooked the fine-beaded garland and looked for a moment as though she would like to strangle him with it.

"I find it difficult," she said, enunciating slowly, "because it's a deception that is going to trip us up and embarrass everyone."

"It won't," he said, "if you just relax and go with it." He studied her eyes for a moment, then asked with sudden insight, "Or is it too difficult to pretend that you really married someone?"

Charlotte closed her eyes and drew a deep breath. When she opened them again, he saw wariness in them, a little residual anger and a confusion she did not appear to want to deal with.

"You have two choices," she said, tightening her grip on the pearl garland. "Being garroted by a string of beads, or being quiet."

It was only when the words were out of her mouth and she was looking into his intrepid grin that she remembered his claim to love the challenge of world-class deals and dangerous chances.

She dropped her threatening pose. "You're not afraid of me," she said. "Is that what you're trying to tell me?"

He laughed, thinking how genuine she was under the Duchess of Winter cloak.

"Actually," he said, growing serious suddenly and cupping the back of her head in his hand, "on a level I don't really understand—I think I am."

She was stunned by his admission. So stunned, that when he lowered his head to kiss her, she couldn't step back.

His mouth was warm, gentle, coaxing. It held none of the bold assumption of control that had been intended to confuse Bitsy at the shower the previous afternoon.

This was a communication between them, tender and warm, an experience of touch, a probing of sensations, physical and emotional. It seemed to chip at a resistance that was already peeling away.

Derek had dreamed for months of holding her unresisting body in his arms. And now he had it—in the middle of a fabric store. Fate had the damnedest sense of humor.

When he felt her lean against him, he forgot where they were and thought only of who they were—man and woman. He felt the potential ripen between them as she responded with a closemouthed but heartfelt kiss.

He fought against the need to part her lips, and simply paid her back in kind. It wasn't nobility that drove him. It was the knowledge he'd learned while working with her that, once pushed, she tuned out and turned off. And that was precisely the reverse of what he wanted.

Charlotte needed more, but was afraid to initiate it. Pretending to be husband and wife, they were in a precarious position and she didn't want him to misunderstand. She didn't want him to think—she didn't want him to *know*—she was just beginning to understand the tension that had always existed between them.

If she opened her mouth under his, he would think she wanted to explore it and she didn't. She was smarter than that.

She pulled away and looked up at him, a little surprised he hadn't insisted on more. And just a little disappointed.

"We have to be back in time for dinner," she said faintly. "Babs talked Pauline into making stew."

He nodded, catching the corner of his bottom lip in strong white teeth as though the touch of hers might linger there. The notion pleased her.

"We'll have time to pursue this later."

She tried to pull herself out of the warm languor his embrace and his kiss had caused. She smoothed her dress and tossed her hair back. "I don't think that would be a good idea," she said briskly.

He dissolved her briskness first with that deadly smile, then with a quick but thorough kiss.

"With all due respect," he said, pausing to wink at a pair of high-school girls whose cart contained all kinds of things in purple and gold, "who listens to you?"

As the girls moved on, still staring at him over their shoulders with dreamy expressions, Charlotte reached up to the trellis for two more strings of tiny beads and seriously considered winding them around her own throat.

He *did* have a thing for danger, but he wasn't dragging her into it. He wasn't. She pushed the cart toward the checkout stand, leaving him to follow, and admitted to herself that her denial sounded very, very thin.

THOUGH THE GUESTS had been in residence only a day, Charlotte noticed that the happiness and charm inherent in a wedding were taking over the formal correctness Elizabeth always applied to everything.

Seated together at one corner of the table, Kendra, Briane and Denise laughed uproariously and continuously. Charlotte watched in fascination. This was a side of Kendra she'd never seen, a side that had apparently developed in Gstaad and Cozumel with her friends and become a part of her makeup—a part Elizabeth couldn't affect. Judging by Elizabeth's frowning concern, she had tried and failed.

Edward, Caleb and Derek were engrossed in business talk at the other end of the table, while Caroline bubbled over to a distracted Elizabeth about the beautiful array of gifts arriving daily that had been set out in the parlor.

Trey and Charlotte, seated across from each other, were forced to find something to talk about.

"Isn't this stew wonderful?" she asked, thinking as she heard her own words that as a conversational gambit it was pathetic. Still, it was *some*thing and she wouldn't let it go. She tapped the side of the small round of bread that had been hollowed out to accommodate the stew.

"Imagine serving it in a bread," she said. "I've never seen that before. I wonder why it doesn't leak out?"

Trey looked at her for a moment as though considering whether or not the question was important enough to answer. Then he said politely, "I imagine because the stew is thick, the bread inside soaks up the liquid, and the crusty outside seals it all in."

Very well thought out, very logical. She had once admired that he could be so intelligent as well as romantic. Had that been just a year ago? It seemed like an age.

"What are you doing in the company these days?" she asked. "I haven't kept up very well since I opened Borrowed Magic."

"Windsor Tech's administrative offices are in London," he replied, looking modestly pleased with himself.

"When our deal goes through, Edward and Caleb are sending me there to restructure. I've always kind of felt like London was my city."

"Paris is mine," Charlotte said dreamily, forgetting the awkwardness between them. "I spent the most wonderful summer of my life in Paris when I was about twenty. Montparnasse, Notre Dame and the Place du Parvis, soup at Bistro Allard." She sighed. "I think it was Paris that made me fall in love with the old and the romantic."

Something subtle flickered in his eyes. She saw it and felt a vague sense of alarm, though she didn't know why.

"So you haven't changed?"

She looked around the table and noted that everyone was still engrossed in their conversations. She wasn't sure why she should feel uncomfortable answering that question, but she did.

"No," she replied. Then couldn't resist asking, "Have you?"

"Yes, I think so," he replied, glancing Kendra's way. She and Briane were leaning on each other in laughter. "I have a better understanding of what I need."

She smiled. "I'm happy for you." Then added to herself, *I wish I knew what I needed. I used to think I knew until you botched it up for me. Ah, well. Lucky escape.*

"And I'm happy for you," he said, indicating Derek with a jut of his chin. The look in his eye held a grudging respect coupled with an obvious dislike. "You got the man who never has to think twice about anything."

Charlotte turned to Derek, who had pushed his plate aside and listened while her father and Caleb talked about Windsor's London office. Though impeccably groomed in a pin-striped suit, dark hair combed slickly back, except for a loose wave at his precise side part, he did not look like social-register material.

He looked like what he said he was—a man with angles and edges made to deflect the danger he loved to challenge. Yet overlaying that was a veneer of charm that might deceive one into thinking otherwise, that worked in his favor when he made those world-class deals. She'd seen him in action. He seduced with that charm, then moved in for the kill with a wit and intelligence that had startled even the young woman who'd grown up in Edward Morreaux's household.

She put a hand on his arm, partly to prove possession to Trey, and partly because she felt a need to.

He turned at her touch, an eyebrow raised in question. Then he glanced at Trey and drew his own conclusion. He placed his other hand over hers and leaned forward to kiss her cheek.

"You'll have my undivided attention later," he said in a low voice rich with sexual suggestion, "I promise." Then he turned back to Edward and Caleb.

Had they been truly married, she'd have been annoyed at playing second fiddle to a business discussion. But as it was, the little ploy was effective in convincing Trey that Derek wanted her—a satisfaction she found it difficult to deny herself.

Charlotte turned back to the table to find that Elizabeth and Caroline had been watching also. Caroline looked delighted. Elizabeth's suspicions looked just a little shaken.

After dinner Trey and Kendra took Briane and Denise to a Karaoke bar.

"Oh, come with us," Briane coaxed Charlotte and Derek. "If Denise even *looks* as though she's going to get up and sing 'Memories,' I'll sedate her, I promise."

Charlotte refused with a smiling shake of her head.

Derek hooked an arm around Charlotte's neck and said, "Thanks, anyway. Neither of us can carry a tune in a bucket. And I think Charlie wanted to work on your dresses tonight."

"You found everything?" Kendra asked. "My goodness, I'd left it to you so completely, I forgot to worry about it."

Charlotte nodded. "If you don't mind, I'll take the dresses to the guest house where there's a little less distraction and work on them there. I should have one of the capes for someone to try on tomorrow morning. If it's all right, the other will be easy."

Denise looked at Charlotte with admiration. "When and if I get married, I'm sending for you to come to Boston." Then she added impishly, "You're sure you don't want to come and listen to me sing 'Memories'?"

Briane and Kendra turned on her simultaneously.

"I was kidding!" she insisted as the other two dragged her off toward the door. Trey followed in their wake, gathering his jacket and Kendra's, looking as though he could think of preferable ways to spend the evening than in a Karaoke bar with three rowdy women.

"You two get to bed early," Caroline encouraged with a straight face as Elizabeth handed Charlotte Briane's dress stored in a zippered plastic sleeve. "Don't let her work all night, Derek."

He smiled quietly back. "Never fear," he said with a quality in his tone that made Caroline beam and Edward look at his daughter and his right-hand man in sudden interest.

Charlotte hurried off down the walk.

"I *wish*," she growled at him when he caught up with her, "that you wouldn't do that." She waggled a fist under his nose. "One day you're going to say something in that suave, seductive voice and I'm going to let you have it!"

"Your fist?" he asked. "Or the seduction?"

She made a small sound of pain and continued to march toward the guest house. "The only thing that saved you," she grumbled, "is that Bitsy Tate wasn't there to write everything down."

"Where was she, anyway?"

"At the Karaoke bar, presumably setting up to record the happy couple humiliating themselves for posterity."

She stepped aside at the door of the guest house to let him unlock it. He frowned at her as he inserted the key. "You're serious?"

"Yes. It's the wedding of the decade. Nosy people want to know every lurid little detail. The Karaoke bar will make a great side story for the tabloids."

"She wouldn't do that as a guest in their home," Derek said. Then at Charlotte's look that proclaimed him a naive innocent, he added with a grin, "No kidding? Then we'd better watch our step. I'm not wild about ending up on the cover of the *Enquirer*."

Charlotte raised a haughty eyebrow as he ushered her inside. "You're the one in danger," she said. "I've been humiliated to cinders once already. I'd hardly notice a second time." She mimicked a tough-girl voice. "So don't push me or I'll spill my guts to the press."

He caught her arm as she would have walked past him to the bedroom. He took the dress from her and tossed it onto the sofa, then looked down into her eyes. His own were darkened by the early-evening shadows. His hands were a painless but firm pressure on her upper arms.

"I want to warn you," he said quietly, "that it's dangerous to threaten me."

She believed him without question. But it was important that he believe she would do as she promised.

"And you should know," she countered, "that I'm still Edward Morreaux's little girl, and if he thought you'd done anything to hurt me, or frighten me, your career on this continent—on this planet—would be over in a heartbeat."

His grip on her tightened. "That was another threat."

"It was a warning," she said, trying not to wince, "that you're not the only one with power."

"At least I'm using my own."

That annoyed her because it was true. "No, you're not," she said angrily. "You're using the power you acquired by putting me in this combustible position. If we weren't caught in this stupid farce, I'd simply slap your face and go home."

"You know," he said, dropping his hands from her to fold his arms, "it's interesting that you think of me in such violent terms. At the office you were always threatening to knock my block off, or sock me in the kisser. Do you read Sam Spade before you go to bed, or are your feelings for me so strong and so suppressed that they erupt in images of hot physical action?"

"Oh, please. I wouldn't…!"

Charlotte's angry denial was quickly arrested when he caught a handful of her hair and brought her to him.

Fear and excitement rose simultaneously within her. "If you try to kiss me now," she warned, her head tilted back because of his grip on her hair, "you'll need a lip transplant. Trust me on this."

"Bitsy and her photographer are coming up the walk," Derek said sotto voce, leaning over her like Rhett over a helpless Scarlett. "And the door is open. Unless you were absolutely sincere about not noticing a second humiliation, you'd better follow my lead."

They stared at each other for an instant, two strong wills challenged, two cherished careers in danger of falling victim to Bitsy's Tidbits.

Resigned to her fate, Charlotte was aware of his large hand completely cupping her head, of the scent of roses that wafted in from the garden, of Bitsy's gasp as she and Darby walked along the path—and stopped.

Derek lowered his head and, caught between fury and fire, Charlotte parted her lips.

Chapter Five

Derek congratulated himself on maximum use of a slim advantage. Edward always said it was his best strength.

Personally he didn't give a damn what Bitsy Tate thought or wrote, but it was becoming a good tool with which to assure himself of Charlotte's cooperation.

And her cooperation delighted him. He felt her slim arms come around his neck, then a hand wandered over his ear and into his hair.

Sensation raced over his scalp and down his spine. When she touched the inside of his mouth with the tip of her tongue, he forgot who was watching and why.

His tongue parried and teased, turned her hesitant foray into his mouth into a battle for supremacy.

Her heart racing, her body flushed, she returned kiss for kiss, nibble for nibble, drinking from his mouth as he drank from hers. She finally lost the battle when she had to draw away to gulp in air. It was a loud sound in the quiet, darkening evening.

Then it was followed by a little cry of surprise when Derek lifted her off her feet, kissed her long and reverently and turned to the bedroom.

Over his shoulder, her eyelids heavy with passion,

Charlotte saw Bitsy staring openmouthed, Darby looking wistful.

The bedroom was cool, the corners filled with shadows as Derek kicked the door closed, then leaned against it. He expelled a long groan of a sigh, then walked forward several paces to drop Charlotte in the middle of the bed.

For one instant of ambivalence, she wondered if he might join her. But he went to the small walnut chair at the foot of the bed and sank into it like a man who couldn't stand up another moment.

"Either you've had a private craving for my body from the moment we met," he said, stretching his legs out and letting his arms fall over the sides of the chair. "Or you're the next Meryl Streep."

Charlotte remained supine on the cool bedspread, unwilling to sit up and look into his eyes.

"Well..." she said softly, "there's a lot at stake."

"I thought you said you wouldn't mind being humiliated a second time."

It was easier to admit she'd lied about that than that she *had* always wondered what he'd be like as a lover, and that the need for an answer grew more demanding every time he touched her.

"So I exaggerated. I'd rather Bitsy thinks I'm this saintly woman who'll come to the rescue of her ex-fiancé's current fiancée. It's worth more to me to walk away from this with my dignity and my good business name intact than to expose you for the villain that you are."

"Expose me," he repeated thoughtfully. "Interesting choice of words. You have been repressing, haven't you?"

"Don't you have something to do," she asked lightly, "that would involve leaving the room?"

"No," he replied lazily. Then he straightened and pushed himself to his feet. "But I guess I should if you're going to get to work on that dress."

He went to the light switch to flip it on.

"Don't do that!" Charlotte said urgently.

He stopped, his hand suspended. "Why not?"

"If Bitsy's watching the house, which I wouldn't put past her, she'll wonder why we put a light on when you carried me in here obviously intent on…you know."

Derek flipped the switch, filling the room with intrusive, artificial light. Charlotte sat up indignantly.

"Relax," he said, coming to the bed and smoothing the tumbled hair from her face with a warm, gentle hand. "She'll think I put the light on so that I can look at you."

She stared up at him, unable to form one coherent word.

"And she'd be right," he added softly, giving her chin a playful pinch. Then he turned to the door. "I'll bring you the dress and put on the coffee."

"How does it look?"

Derek, stretched out on the sofa with the latest escapade of Spenser, Robert B. Parker's fictional private detective, looked up to focus on Charlotte. It was after midnight.

She had fashioned a narrow, gauzy cape for the plum-colored dress, and had fastened it at the little dip just above the delicate swell of her breasts with a little bunch of the five-petaled purple flowers. Under it, she wore the dress Briane would wear the day of the wedding.

She had twisted her blond hair up and out of the way,

and he felt himself go weak at the perfect line of her long, slender neck and softly sloped shoulder. The need to put his lips there was like a primal force. He had to give himself a minute to find his voice.

"The cape looks lovely," he replied gravely. "You look indescribably beautiful."

She fluffed out the skirt a little nervously. "It is a beautiful dress. I was trying to give it a demure Victorian look. Does it work?"

He cleared his throat. "Well, I might not be the best one to ask. I find it more alluring than demure, but then I'm the type who always looks under and around things to see what's there."

She had to laugh. "I imagine that's gotten you into trouble on more than one occasion."

"It has," he admitted candidly, "but the satisfaction of knowing was always worth it. Turn around."

She complied, this time showing him the beautiful shape of her well-formed back, and the intriguing column of her neck against which wisps of hair lay in tempting disarray.

He had to think about something else.

"What are you going to do with all the flowers we bought this afternoon? And the beads?"

"Garlands for their hair," she replied, her eyes sparking with enthusiasm. "I'll be working on those as soon as I have the capes finished."

He smiled, sharing her obvious delight. "You really do love this stuff, don't you?"

She shrugged a beautiful, gauze-covered shoulder. "It's me. The slow, laid-back romantic you so despised in the office."

He put the book aside and stood. "For the last time," he said, "I didn't despise you. Anyway, you should be grateful to me. If it wasn't for the fact that *you* despised *me,* you'd still be at Farnsworth–Morreaux instead of doing what you love to do.''

She looked at him for a long moment, long enough that he raised an eyebrow in question. She opened her mouth to say something, then changed her mind and turned to the bedroom.

''What?'' he asked, hoping for a translation of that curious expression.

She turned at the bedroom door, studied him a moment, then relaxed against the molding as though reaching a decision that removed some burden from her.

''I didn't despise you, either,'' she admitted. ''In fact, when you weren't shouting at me, I thought you were pretty interesting.''

That was hard to let pass. He took several steady steps forward, but knew when to stop. He asked from several feet away from her, ''You want to know just how interesting?''

She met his eyes and he saw the answer. His heart thumped against his ribs.

''I do,'' she replied finally, softly, ''but I want to know a few other things first.''

What? he wanted to say. Ask me anything. But she had smiled enigmatically and closed the door.

He went into the kitchen to make a fresh pot of coffee. It wouldn't prevent him from sleeping—Charlotte had already accomplished that.

CHARLOTTE SMELLED Derek's toothpaste and after-shave before she even opened her eyes. Anger rose hotly in her at the realization that he lay beside her. On the heels of their mellow mood of the night before, his assumption of sexual privileges made her furious. But she was determined not to give him the satisfaction of a display of temper.

"What are you doing in the bed?" she asked coolly without opening her eyes.

"Bitsy," he replied calmly, "is in the garden behind us with binoculars."

She opened her eyes at that and rolled her head on the pillow to look into his eyes. "You're kidding!" she whispered.

He lay beside her, his hips covered in a towel, his hands crossed over his stomach. "I'm not. I brought you a cup of coffee to help you wake up and saw her through the window. Do you leave your drapes open at home when you go to bed?" The question held disapproval.

"No," she replied. "But I don't have roses outside my bedroom window, either. So what do we do now?"

He smiled at the ceiling. "I could take off my towel."

"Choice number two, please," she said.

"Ah, Charlie," he said plaintively, "what is romance without imagination? Choice number two is that you kiss me good-morning, I pass you your cup of coffee, and we snuggle up to discuss the day."

"Derek," she said, "you're taking shameless advantage of the situation."

He stared at her a moment, apparently confused that she should be surprised. "Of course."

He was leaning over her, his bright dark eyes a threat to her sense of self-preservation. But the aroma of freshly brewed coffee wafted past his shoulder and under her nose.

"The coffee does smell wonderful," she said, waffling.

He gave her a knowing smile. "You can tell yourself

it's really the coffee you want if that makes you feel better."

She raised an imperious eyebrow. "It is the coffee I want."

"Sure. Then give me what I want."

To confound Bitsy, and to wipe that self-satisfied look off Derek's face, Charlotte applied herself to the work of deception.

She put a small, but strong hand to Derek's bare shoulder and pushed him back against the pillow. She tried not to dwell on the warm, suedelike texture of the flesh under her fingertips, of the muscled chest she felt against the thin fabric of her nightgown as she leaned over him.

She saw surprise register in his eyes, then lazy pleasure as he lay back, apparently willing to let her assume control.

She gave the kiss everything she had—and she was a little alarmed to find that she had so much. Desire burst from her the moment she covered his mouth with hers. Memories of the other kisses they'd shared rose up in her memory to make her eager to share this one. That, combined with the need to show him she could wield a little power, too, made her aggressive but artful.

Derek was sure he was in heaven. When she knelt astride him and covered his face with kisses, he thought he might be hallucinating. When the kisses trailed down between his pecs and over the jut of his ribs, he knew he'd died and gone to heaven. When the kisses stopped at the barrier of his towel, he thought he'd caught a glimpse of what hell could be like.

"Don't stop," he said, his voice hoarse, "she might still be watching."

Charlotte sat back on her heels, a Duchess of Winter tilt to her chin and the downward cast of her eyes.

"She just walked away."

It surprised him a little that he hadn't seen that move coming on her part. After all, it was a page out of his own book. Take a small advantage and make the best of it. It did surprise him to find that he wasn't annoyed. He was now more intrigued than ever, and more determined to uncover—hopefully literally one day—the woman under the duchess.

He laced his hands behind his head and grinned up at her. "You must have really wanted that coffee."

She reached across him for the cup and saucer. He resisted the impulse to sample the thinly covered delicacies that moved forward, then back, within an inch of his lips.

"Deception is the key, isn't it?" she asked, backing carefully on her knees off the bed.

"It is," he called after her as she headed for the bathroom, his eye on the tempting sway of creamy flesh under the flimsy little gown, "as long as you don't deceive yourself!"

"YOU'RE A GENIUS," Kendra said in amazement, looking over Briane's shoulder into the cheval mirror.

The cape fell delicately from Briane's shoulders, the precise shade of the dress, the very touch the garment needed to take it from the modern gown it had been, to the more old-fashioned but demure dress it had become.

Denise looked over Kendra's shoulder with a smile of amazement. "How can that little bit of fabric make so much difference? I can't believe how right it looks."

Briane lifted one side of the flimsy little cape and

smiled at her reflection. "I deserve to look wonderful, since I *didn't* get to sing 'Memories,' after all."

"Oh!" Her friends turned on her instantly, playfully swatting and teasing. Charlotte took the other dress and returned to the guest house to work on the cape.

Derek, Trey, Edward and Caleb were closeted in Caleb's den, and she planned to enjoy the quiet that had been such a part of her life before she'd answered Kendra's call for help and attended the shower.

Sunshine poured through the window of the little bedroom where she'd set up her portable sewing machine on an end table and pulled up the bedroom chair. Through the open window, she heard the birds singing happily, and inhaled the fragrance of the rose garden.

With such aesthetic accompaniments, the work should have been easy. Unfortunately the open window and the roses reminded her of that morning and made it difficult to roll a straight hem on Denise's plum-colored cape.

The worst part was that the memories were not unpleasant. They were delicious. They reminded her of how much she'd missed since she'd decided to bow out of man-woman relationships. More than that—they made her realize how much she had yet to experience. Derek had made her feel things, want things, she used to think were fantasies. Maybe they were, but now they were hers.

She worked through lunch and was just beginning to feel as though she were making headway when a rap on the door brought her head up.

"Yes?" she called.

There was an instant's silence, then a male voice called back quietly, "It's Trey."

For an instant, Charlotte stared at the door. Something told her letting him in would not be a wise move, but she put it down to unnecessary discomfort over the situation and thought it important that he not know she felt any.

She opened the door wide and gave him her warmest smile. "Hi," she said cheerfully. "Kendra isn't here. I think the girls said something about going to Rodeo Drive for a few last-minute things she needed for her trousseau."

He nodded, his hands in the pockets of raw-linen pants. A soft yellow sweater covered his long, lean torso. His rangy, athletic form once used to make her heart beat faster. She stood still for an instant, waiting for it to happen. Nothing.

"I know," he said. He gave her a charmingly embarrassed under-the-eyebrows look. "I wasn't looking for Kendra—I was looking for you."

"Really?" She tried to sound only mildly interested.

"I need to talk to you," he said, glancing over his shoulder as though concerned about being discovered. "Preferably while Bitsy is going over the reception menu with Elizabeth."

Dodging Bitsy seemed to be becoming a major part of everyone's life.

"What did you want to talk about?"

"Can we talk inside?"

"Trey..." she began, prepared to refuse him entry.

"Charlie, please," he said quietly, "there are some things I need to get off my chest."

An apology was the last thing she wanted to hear, but she didn't think she could in all conscience deny him the basic right to explain himself.

She stepped aside and gestured him into the small living room. He took the chair that faced the sofa, and she went into the kitchen for the coffeepot and two cups.

After pouring, she settled in the corner of the sofa farthest away from him.

Trey left his cup on the table and leaned forward in his chair, bracing his elbows on his knees. His gray eyes were apologetic.

"First, I want to thank you for helping Kendra when it must be awkward for you. She told me at lunch how you've fixed the bridesmaids' dresses to coordinate with the dress you brought for her."

A sweep of her hand dismissed it as a problem. "Her father and mine have been friends for a long time."

"But you're still honeymooning," he said. "I don't suppose that occurred to her. She is spoiled."

His disloyalty to Kendra annoyed her. "So I've been told about myself on more than one occasion."

"No," he said. "You've been indulged, but you haven't been spoiled. There's a difference. In fact, I think it's a little shameful of Kendra and her mother to have called for your help on this, considering that you and I were once involved. They had to know it would be hard for you."

She shook her head serenely and lied through her teeth. "It hasn't been. Briane and Denise are fun to work with, and I've really enjoyed meeting Babs."

He straightened and sighed. "So you really don't care at all anymore?"

Thin ice, she warned herself, but found there were a few things she had to get off her own chest.

"Trey, you left me standing at the church in front of four hundred people. That tends to change a woman's feelings for a man."

He seemed almost pleased by that flash of temper. Then he hung his head. "I know, I know. I was a rat, a clod, an idiot, a louse…"

He looked up at her, and she said calmly, "You may continue."

He leaned against the back of the chair and raised his eyes to the ceiling. "What can I say? There isn't a word bad enough to describe what I did to you, and none strong enough to tell you how often and how much I've regretted it."

"Thank you," she said. "I appreciate knowing it gave you a few bad moments, too. But now it's over and the best thing you can do for all of us is not give it another thought."

"How can I do that?"

"By concentrating on your fiancée."

He sighed again. "My fiancée is concentrating on her friends. I've hardly been alone with her since they arrived."

"Then think about your promotion and your office in London," she said a little airily. "A woman tends to be a little distracted by the details of her wedding, particularly when her mother is determined to make it the cover story for *Bride* magazine. And it's been a while since she's seen her friends. They're such a relief from the company she and her mother usually keep. Give her a break."

He caught her gaze across the width of the coffee table. "You, on the other hand, were always doing thoughtful little things for me. You never forgot I was around. I didn't realize then how precious a commodity is a woman's complete attention."

Twit, she thought. Aloud, she said generously, "That's life. Live and learn. We often don't realize what we have until we've lost it."

He stood and paced across the room. "In defense of myself," he said in quiet but what seemed genuine dismay, "I can explain my behavior only by saying that I realized you were more than I could handle."

"What you *didn't* realize," she said, "was that you wouldn't have *had* to handle me. I'm able to handle myself. You'd have had only to love me."

"I know that now," he said with a regretful glance down at her that touched her as nothing he'd said previously had. "At the time, I felt threatened and overwhelmed."

She felt his sadness and her own, but under it all was the knowledge that it was over, and that she'd moved beyond the woman she'd been when she'd loved Trey. She tried not to bemoan the fact that he had someone and she didn't.

"I think you and Kendra will be very happy," she said, getting to her feet and ushering him to the door. "Things have a way of working out."

She pulled the door open. He walked reluctantly through and said with that sadness still in his eyes, "But she isn't you. Ooof!"

Trey had turned to make a dramatic exit and collided with Derek coming up the steps.

"Sorry," Trey said with a quick, guilty look at him. Then he moved around him and hurried down the walk back to the big house.

Derek stepped inside and pushed the door closed behind him. The flicker of jealousy he'd felt when he'd been coming up the walk and saw Trey standing in the open doorway ignited inside him like a tree struck by lightning.

He tossed his briefcase on the chair and confronted Charlotte, hands on his hips.

"Why don't you just invite Bitsy in for tea and tell her this is all a scripted performance?"

Surprised by his vehemence, Charlotte folded her arms and faced him down. She knew she looked guilty. She *felt* guilty, but she she also knew guilt was simply the by-product of the circumstances.

"We were just talking," she said calmly, "and Bitsy is in the kitchen with Elizabeth and Pauline, going over the menu for the reception."

"Bitsy," he said significantly, "was right behind me when I left the house."

She refused to betray concern. "So? She's a reporter. Hopefully she'll be less likely to jump to conclusions than you are."

He gave her the same pitying look she'd once given him when he'd suggested the same to her. "Please," he said dryly. "What did he want?"

"To talk to me."

"About what?"

That did it. He continued to stand there, feet planted like an inquisitor, fully expecting her to relate in detail the few moments she'd spent with Trey.

"This is a charade, remember!" she shouted at him. She wasn't certain what made her so suddenly volatile, either, unless it was hearing her former fiancé admit that he now regretted treating her like unclaimed freight. Or maybe it was having Derek, who was partially responsible for this entire fiasco in the first place, treat her as though *she* were guilty. "My private life is none of your business. And if it were…how dare you suggest I'd make time with another woman's fiancé—even though he once was mine!"

It would be smart to back off, he told himself. He'd had no right to call her on what had probably been a very innocent visit. But he was used to operating on instinct, and at the moment it told him Trey was having second thoughts about the woman that got away. Unfortunately neither Trey nor the woman knew she now belonged to Derek Cabot.

"Whoa," he said quietly, trying to placate her. "I'm concerned about how it looked to someone else. We're being watched on all sides, you know. Elizabeth is probably hanging out an upstairs window even as we speak."

"I don't believe you for a minute!" she shouted, obviously unimpressed with his reasonable approach. "I think you've taken on this job of pretending to be my husband like just another Farnsworth–Morreaux project. You want to bully me into operating your way, just like you did before. Well, I don't work for you anymore!"

Charlotte yanked the door open, anxious to escape from him and the confining little house. "I've been my own woman for a year," she said angrily, her hand on the doorknob, prepared to slam the door behind her, "and nothing's going to change that!"

She turned, her chin in the air—and spotted not only Bitsy and Darby, but several other members of the press whom Kendra had said would be coming and going all week.

She began to feel as though she were trapped in a Regency novel—except that instead of a parlor farce, this was a front porch farce. People came onstage, upset everything going on, then exited to make room for the next onstage disaster.

She stopped still, aware that her mouth hung open.

She vaguely registered footsteps behind her, then a strong, gentle hand moved up into her hair. Derek turned her toward him while the interested audience watched.

"I didn't mean that I don't want you to keep your shop," he crooned in a lover's voice. "I meant that I want us to have more time to spend together. Does that really deserve all this shouting?''

His eyes were inches from hers, his lips even closer than that. For an instant, she forgot what the problem was and lost herself in the tender magnetism that seduced her closer. She groped for reason. ''I...you...''

''I know, I know,'' he said with disarming self-deprecation. ''I'm very hardheaded and maybe sometimes you have to shout to be heard.''

''You...accused me...''

''Of being a workaholic. I know. I'm sorry. It's just that I've been there, and now that we're married I don't want us to miss one precious moment together because one or the other of us is putting in overtime. Just give up working weekends, that's all I ask.''

''Most weddings...'' she said distractedly, resuming her role, ''are on weekends.''

''Then we'll have to coordinate days off during the week.'' He kissed her chastely, apologetically. ''Come back inside and let's...'' He paused to kiss her less chastely this time. Then he pretended to notice the press on the walk for the first time. His grin of embarrassment was frighteningly skillful.

''Ah, sorry,'' he said. ''We...had a difference of opinion and now we're going to make up. Excuse us.''

He pushed Charlotte through the doorway and closed the door behind them.

She slipped out of his spell with a thunk.

''And you call me a good actress,'' she said with the famous duchess's sarcasm. ''If De Niro had seen that performance, he'd be worrying about the rest of his career. I begin to wonder just how often you've pretended to be some hapless woman's husband.''

''This is the first time,'' he said, taking hold of her

arm, "and I'm so good at it because the role of your lover seems to fit me very well. As well as it fits you to be mine."

"I would not be your lover if…!" Whatever the dire circumstances were that would never allow such an event were never spoken.

She was pulled into his arms and kissed into silence.

She drew back, shaken and confused. "Don't think that all you have to do is…"

He kissed her again, and this time she didn't even fight it, because at least he was right about that. The role of lovers did fit them well. They had yet to carry a kiss that far, but they'd certainly learned to make an art of the kiss itself.

As Charlotte clung to his neck, she felt something new in his arms. This was more than the physical dynamite usually generated whenever they touched, this kiss had a message.

He could have left her on the little porch to explain away her anger to the press collected on the walk. If she had been exposed for the liar he and Caroline had made her, the scandal would have attached itself to her, not to him, because of her history with Trey. She was sure Derek knew that. He had far less at stake here than she did, yet he'd come to her rescue.

Then she remembered that he'd always come to her rescue. When press releases had been late, he'd always been the one who stayed half the night in the office with her to get it together and get it right. He'd always grumbled about it, and reminded her that she'd have to move faster, but he'd seen her through it.

Because he cared? That possibility so stunned her that she pulled out of his arms and stared up at him. Then she saw it in his eyes. He did care. This was real.

"Oh, no," she whispered, as though someone had just handed her a cobra.

He knew precisely what had alarmed her. It had alarmed him, too, when he stopped to think about it. The trick was simply to feel and not analyze.

"I'm afraid so, Charlie," he confirmed with a grin. "You're in love with me."

She remained incredulous. "And you're in love with me."

"Yes."

"Well…" She uttered a little gasp of dismay and spread her arms, turning in exasperation. "Great." When she faced him again, she said irritably, "You know, this is all your fault. You entrap me in this big lie, you come on all charming and possessive and lure me into relaxing with you, then you spring *this* on me."

"*I* spring this?" he demanded, knowing it was critical that he didn't laugh. "I didn't do this by myself, you know. You're the one with eyes like the dawn and a backside that drives me wild. You're the one who melts every time I touch you, and who looks at me as though I'm the one thing in your life that's forbidden but that you want above all else."

She stared at him, startled, because that was precisely how she felt.

"You expect a man to not respond to that?"

She didn't have an answer. But she had to tell him where they stood. "Well, I, for one, am not doing this."

He raised an eyebrow. "You think you have a choice?"

"We all have choices. People fall in love and think they *have* to be drawn in by it, they have to lose their minds and their plans—provided they do get as far as the altar—and provided the other one doesn't leave them there.'' She studied him one more exasperated moment and marched off to the bedroom.

He followed her, noting in concern the defiant look in her eyes. When she pulled her suitcase out from under the bed, he knew he had to take control.

He sat on the edge of the bed and watched her prop the case open on it and turn to the chest of drawers.

''I'm out of here,'' she said. ''I'm tired of Kendra's wedding controlling *my* life.''

''You promised a lot of people you'd see this through,'' he reminded quietly.

''Big woo,'' she said flatly, tossing silky underthings at the suitcase. ''Other people break promises and seem to get on just fine. People who know them don't even seem particularly disappointed in them. The sky does not fall.''

''That's because...'' A pair of black lace panties fell over the side of the suitcase. He picked them up and studied them. ''There are some people you expect things from, and some people you know won't come through for you. When you learn to tell the difference, you don't get hurt.''

She snatched the lacy scrap from him and slapped it into the case. ''The same rules don't apply to everyone, is that what you're telling me? Do I see the male tendency to a double standard rearing its ugly head?''

''No. I'm trying to tell you as gently as I can that, for all your denials, you haven't recovered from what happened to you last year. And recovery is taking too long.''

Fury and indignation warred for supremacy. She indulged them both by slamming the lid of the suitcase down and shoving it across the bed. ''Like you know all about it!'' she shouted at him.

''I know something about it,'' he returned mildly,

"because I know you very well. You thought you'd found a kind and gentle man who was your ideal of the laid-back romantic. What you didn't realize was that he's laid-back because he's indecisive, and he seems romantic because the seductive gesture is easier than standing toe-to-toe with a woman and telling her what you can give and what you expect in return."

She walked away from him because he was absolutely right. She couldn't have put it into words, but she could see that was precisely what had happened.

"The trouble here is," he said, coming up behind her and placing his hands on her shoulders. She wasn't going to like this, but he was used to getting the broadside of her anger, and it had to be said, "That I think you truly are over Trey, but you haven't recovered from the fact that the Duchess of Winter made an error in judgment."

She spun around under his hands to look up at him, anger and pain bright in her eyes. He rubbed gently over the points of her shoulders in comfort if not apology.

"And it's become easier to pretend that it's a matter of trust, rather than a matter of self-doubt. You pretend that men in general—me in particular—aren't worthy of your trust, instead of admitting that you can't bear the thought of being wrong a second time."

She brought her arms up to break his hold and went to the window. She inhaled deeply of the scent of roses.

"My point is," he said, picking up a cosmetic bag that had fallen over the side of the bed, "that in my estimation Trey is a jerk and you don't owe him anything, and Elizabeth is like something out of Tennessee Williams who is interesting to watch but who the hell really cares what happens to her? But they're not the only ones who'd get hurt here if you storm out four days before the wedding and speculation and scandal take over.''

She groaned and dropped her forehead on her arms folded on the sill. He pressed his advantage subtly, carefully.

"There are your parents, Caleb, Babs, Kendra. Am I wrong, or is she showing signs of being a real person?"

She didn't answer, but took another deep draft of air.

"Then you should consider all the things that would be said about you if you walk out now. They'll think you can't stand the sight of Trey and Kendra together, that you and I have quarreled and that you can't keep your relationships together. Bitsy might try to talk to Caroline to find out what happened, and God knows how that would turn out."

"All right, all right!" Charlotte spun away from the window. She walked past him to the suitcase, dumped its contents into the middle of the bed, then slammed the case shut, locked it and tossed it under the bed.

She scooped up the undies and dropped them into the still-open drawer, then closed it with a bang. She turned to face him, temper and hurt feelings in her eyes.

"You're absolutely right about me," she said. "I hate being stupid. And I'm not going to do it again."

He grinned and leaned back against the dresser, bracing his hands on the surface on either side of him. "You'd have to be dead to assure yourself of that. You're only human, Duchess. Emotion overrode intelligence. It happens to the best of us."

"Has it happened to you?" she challenged.

He nodded, his gaze snaring hers. "It's happening to me right now. I've been just a little in love with you since the night we stayed up to get the videophone press release out on time." He sighed with resignation. "It became terminal when you almost hit me behind your father's house in your classic tank. I know it isn't smart, but I'm not running away from it.''

''Of course not. You love to rise to the challenge, test your endurance, push the limits of mind and body. I just want to help other people have nice weddings.''

''To make up for not having one yourself.''

Charlotte expelled a frustrated breath and went to the closet where she'd stored the plum-colored bridesmaid's dress.

''We're talking in circles,'' she said, pulling out the plastic bag looped over the hanger of the last dress to be altered. It contained the half-finished cape. ''And I have work to do.''

''Fine.'' Derek straightened away from the dresser, shaking off the urge to throw her onto the bed and make her listen to him, then make love to her. Generally he was short on patience, but he could be long on finesse when he forced himself. ''I'll put on the coffee.''

''No,'' she said, sitting down at the sewing machine, squinting at the bright evening sunlight shining directly on her from the window. ''Don't do anything thoughtful or sweet. Just let me be.''

He went to draw the drape in direct defiance of her directive. He paused as he passed her chair to pinch her chin between his thumb and forefinger and raise her face to him.

''I'll do as I please, Duchess,'' he said. ''And the only thing I will let you be is mine. Get used to it.'' And he walked away.

Chapter Six

Charlotte awoke with a vicious headache. The second cape had not gone well and she'd finally had to cut a new piece of tulle and start over. She'd worked until two in the morning, propped up by the coffeepot Derek had placed at her elbow before going to bed at midnight.

She slipped out of bed and into the mint-green cover that matched her flimsy peignoir and peeked into the living room. Derek was still asleep on the sofa. She wasn't surprised. She'd heard him tossing and turning until long after she'd finally turned out her light.

A desperate need for a cup of tea made her pad quietly into the kitchen and fill the kettle. Then she tiptoed across the carpet to peer out the window over the sofa. It was raining! In September in southern California that was unusual enough to make her stop and stare.

She went to the door and pulled it open, letting the slightly cooler air flow in. The mellow light filtering through the cloudy sky made her feel curiously melancholy.

This was the kind of day that defined romance—a moody sky, a couple huddled under an umbrella, stopping for lunch at a cozy café or running home to share it in a cozy nook.

I, she thought, *will get to share it with a lap full of silk flowers while I make headpieces for the bridesmaids.*

She was about to turn back to the kitchen when she noticed Bitsy and Elizabeth coming down the walk.

No. Please. Not this morning. Not with Derek still asleep on the sofa where he'd obviously spent the night rather than in her bed.

She wasn't sure what told her they wouldn't be taking the turn to the guest house where the press was staying, but she knew they were coming here.

She raced to the sofa, grabbed Derek's shoulder in both hands and shook him.

DEREK CAME AWAKE with the sincere conviction that he was caught in a clothes dryer. A very strong force buffeted him back and forth, and when he tried to sit up to evaluate his situation, the blanket was ripped from under him, rolling him onto his back.

"God!" he groaned, falling back against his pillow only to thunk his head against the arm of the sofa. His pillow had also been confiscated by the throttling force.

Confused and woozy, but determined not to be taken without a fight, he swung his legs over the side of the sofa. A fast-moving something in green silk landed in his lap, forcing him back down. Arms circled his neck, lips found his mouth and kissed him to complete wakefulness.

For a moment Derek thought he'd been caught in a time warp. This resembled in close detail a dream he'd entertained on a nightly basis when he'd been about fourteen.

Then he realized that he was caught in a web of straight blond hair and flower-garden perfume. He didn't know how to explain Charlotte's behavior, but made a swift decision on the spot and quickly capitulated on the previous one.

He didn't *care* what had prompted her change of heart, and he would gladly be taken however the hell she wanted to take him.

"Charlotte? Derek? Kids, yoo-hoo!"

The delicious little fantasy crashed around his ears. He recognized the voice at the door as Bitsy's and understood exactly what had happened.

He wasn't sure why the truth annoyed him so completely. They'd been playing games for the benefit of the Farnsworths and the press since the moment Caroline had made her fateful announcement. He supposed it was because he'd been half-asleep and vulnerable and easily convinced that Charlotte's sudden ardor had been real.

Understanding how he felt didn't lessen the annoyance, however. And he felt the need to deliver a payback.

Charlotte tried to slip off his knees to answer the screen door through which both women peered.

But instead of letting her go, he stood, tossed her over his shoulder and went to the door himself.

"Derek!" Charlotte whispered angrily, pounding one fist on his back.

He ignored her.

"Good morning," he said to the two stunned faces in the doorway. He gently swatted the hip on his shoulder. "Sorry. She gets difficult sometimes and the only way to deal with her is to take away her choices." Then he leaned down and let Charlotte slide until her feet hit the carpeting. "Look, Charlie," he said with good humor. "Guests. Come in, ladies."

He opened the door as Charlotte stood aside, impotent with surprise at his audacity, affected, despite her fluster, by the bare-chested sight of him in cotton pajama bottoms.

"Sounds like the kettle's boiling," he said. "Good timing."

"I'm sorry," Bitsy said in a tone that sounded anything but. Charlotte could see her eyes dancing with the prospect of the first few paragraphs of her next column. Cabots Prefer Rough Stuff Behind Closed Doors. Read On For Details. "But I hadn't realized you were making alterations to the bridesmaids' dresses. I promised the fashion page I'd reshoot for them. Elizabeth said you have the dresses here."

Charlotte's professional self came to the fore, a circumstance she thought fortunate since her personal self was flustered and unable to cope.

Graciously she brought the dress out while explaining about the addition of the cape.

"The headpieces are floral garlands, but I haven't put those together yet."

Elizabeth frowned. "When do you think you'll have one for Bitsy to photograph?"

"I'll have to be certain Kendra and the wedding party approve first," Charlotte replied. "But I should have one ready by dinner tonight."

"Fine. Shoes and bouquets will remain the same?"

Charlotte shook her head. "Shoes will, but the girls had intended to carry a single calla lily—elegant but stark. Now they'll carry old-fashioned nosegays in the deep colors of the headpieces."

Bitsy hastily made notes. Then she looked up as Derek came back into the room with a tray of cups and a steaming teapot. He'd also bowed to propriety and put on his pajama top. Bitsy looked disappointed.

Derek presided charmingly over tea, pulling Charlotte

into his arm when she sat beside him on the sofa. Even Elizabeth seemed to relax. Slowly but surely, Charlotte realized, he was convincing them that the loving, sparring, playful couple he and she pretended to be was real.

But when their guests left, Elizabeth carrying the dress over her arm, Derek's charm evaporated into a curious, moody quiet. He helped her clear away cups, then excused himself to shower and change for a mid-morning meeting in Caleb's study. The uncharacteristic mood so surprised her that she swallowed her complaint about being thrown over his shoulder like an old bolt of fabric.

A quarter of an hour later he came out of the bedroom in light pants and a soft gray pullover. In his quiet mood, he looked like a stormy study of man in monochrome. His angles seemed sharper, his features darker, his height and breadth dramatically exaggerated.

He made her feel curiously out of tune, out of place. She didn't like it.

"Something wrong?" she asked as he went to the end table where he'd left his watch.

He gave her a quick, cool glance as he slipped on the expansion band. "Strange question," he replied. "I thought in your estimation everything was wrong."

She considered whether or not to pursue this. But this was a side of him she'd never seen, and there was a challenge inherent in being kept at arm's length—particularly when she remembered what it was like to be *in* his arms.

"I meant with you, not with the situation," she replied quietly, fiddling with one of the silk flowers strewn around her on the sofa. "It's unlike you to be so... remote."

He raised a mocking eyebrow. "You asked me last night to let you be. This is what it's like."

She didn't like it. It occurred to her that this didn't make sense when she had indeed asked for it, but it didn't seem to matter.

"You told me you would do what you pleased."

"Maybe it pleases me," he said, "to let you be. God knows it has to be easier than trying to figure you out."

"I wasn't aware," she said a little stiffly, "that I was that complicated."

He snatched up a ring of keys near where the watch had been and gave them a thoughtful toss. "Maybe I'm the one who's grown complicated. Maybe I don't like to wake up with a woman in my arms and discover she's there as part of the script."

He dropped the keys in his pocket and reached for the doorknob.

That brought her to her feet. "Wait a minute!" She approached him, hands on her hips. He rolled his eyes and waited.

"Do you mean to tell me," she said slowly, "that you're angry with me because I tried to save the charade this morning just as you've done half a dozen times since this all started? Would you have preferred that I let the ladies find you asleep on the sofa and give them proof that we aren't sleeping together? That we aren't married? That we can hardly exchange a civil word?"

She was right, of course, and that somehow made it worse. He had no idea what was happening. He never acted on emotion. Even when his feelings were involved, he made decisions based on logic—in business and with women.

But this woman had scrambled his brain. He wanted her desperately, even knowing he'd probably never have a moment's peace with her. And here he was, acting like an outraged boy because he'd misread a move she'd had little choice in making. He couldn't explain it.

He pulled the door open. "I'll see you at dinner in the big house," he said, and closed the door behind him.

CHARLOTTE'S HEADACHE had reached colossal proportions by early afternoon. She tried another cup of tea, a small bowl of soup, several aspirin, but nothing worked.

Paradoxically, the headpiece was coming together beautifully. The roses combined gracefully with the five-petaled little flower and the baby's breath to create a fanciful, romantic wreath. The tiny pearls, looped delicately in scallops around the circle, gave the flowers a touch of elegance.

Charlotte placed the wreath on her pounding head and peered into the mirror. She frowned when she saw that the silk stood up stiffly, without the naturally relaxed inclination of real flower petals.

She pondered the problem. Steaming would do it, she thought. The small appliance used to loosen wrinkles from fabric would be ideal. But her steamer was at the shop and the thought of driving on the freeway with her headache seemed too enormous a task. All she wanted was to take a hot bath and a nap.

Then it occurred to her. The steam from a hot bath would be just as effective as a steamer to assure her that it would do what she hoped.

Filling the tub with hot water, Charlotte pulled off the robe she'd never changed out of, placed the coronet of silk flowers on her head, and climbed into the bathtub.

She muttered a little cry as she displaced the steamy water, then rested her head back against the inflatable pillow. The ends of her hair dragged in the water, but she didn't care. Tying it back would have compounded her headache.

As the hot water began to soothe her tense muscles, Charlotte rested her arms on the side of the tub, and crossed her feet on the waterspout. She closed her eyes and tried to analyze Derek's behavior that morning.

Nothing computed. She'd tried over and over again throughout the day to find a reason for his sudden distance and couldn't. She went over everything that had happened, and everything they'd said to each other.

Then, in the quiet of her little self-created steam room something came together in her mind. "Maybe I don't like to wake up with a woman in my arms," he'd said, "and discover she's there as part of the script."

Her mind played over her frantic reaction when she'd spotted Elizabeth and Bitsy on the path, the way she'd torn the blankets from him and leaped on him when she saw the women try to peer through the screen door.

He was angry because he'd awakened thinking she meant the kiss and the embrace, then discovered she'd done it as part of their loving couple act.

She groaned in the steamy, afternoon light. If you only knew, she thought, how easy it is to touch you, to kiss you, to let you hold me. If you only knew how much it makes me wish this wasn't an act, that we did have the right to be together.

"Oh, Derek." She groaned again with the knowledge that they were as different temperamentally as their cars, she reaching back into the past for happiness, he moving ahead, always forward, ever faster, in search of a new challenge, a new chancy endeavor.

DEREK WALKED INTO the guest house, aware instantly of the unusual silence. Then he heard the quiet splash of water, and a soft little groan. He followed the sounds in concern to the open bathroom door and stopped on the threshold, momentarily paralyzed by the sight that greeted him.

He knew he wasn't dreaming, because he could feel the wood of the doorway molding under his right hand, the warm mist of the steamy air against his face. He heard the gentle splash of the water in the bathtub, and the soft little sound from the woman in it. This had the texture of reality.

But he couldn't believe what he *saw*. Charlotte lay naked in the water from which steam rose and swirled. It was no surprise, of course, to find her naked in her bath, but he had difficulty determining the significance of the coronet of flowers in her hair. Then he decided it didn't need significance. It gave her the look of some exotic nymph performing her ablutions in a natural spring.

She was every bit as perfect as he had imagined. Water lapped against small, round breasts, pink and bead-tipped from the hot water. The narrow waist and the slight flare of hips were indistinct, but she raised languid arms beaded with moisture and he couldn't dispel the notion that she'd cast a spell.

Still unaware of him, she raised one leg out of the water, gracefully pointed her toe to stretch it, rotated her foot at the ankle, then dropped her leg back into the water with a splash and a sigh.

Then she struck him to the core of his being with a softly spoken, woebegone, "Oh, Derek."

He heard the need in it, and felt his own need respond. He moved into the room and she sat up, startled. When she realized it was him, the fear slowly left her eyes and a sweet resignation took its place.

"Hi," she said softly.

He sat on the edge of the tub, reaching across her to brace his hand on the other side of it. Steam rose up to coil them in its misty arms.

His eyes went over the fine structure of her chin and jaw, the bright pink of her cheeks, the glow in her eyes and the fine mist of steamy dew that covered her. He raised his gaze to the wreath of flowers in her hair and smiled.

"Is that how a duchess bathes?" he asked, his voice quiet and deep in the tiny room.

"It's the prototype for the wedding," she replied just above a whisper. "The flowers were stiff and I thought steaming them would help, but I didn't have my steamer with me. And I needed to soak. So..."

Of course. That was how she did things. If there was a relaxed, romantic way to accomplish something, she found it. The need to touch her became unbearable. He ran his index finger lightly across a flushed cheekbone. "I heard you say my name a moment ago," he said.

She nodded, the gesture fascinating him as the flowers tilted gracefully in her hair. "I'm sorry about this morning." Her eyes grew wide and dark and he felt himself drawn into their beckoning depths. "The kiss was real, even though I did it because Elizabeth and Bitsy were at the door." She shrugged a delicate, fine-boned shoulder. "In some weird way, I feel as though it's all real."

It was. He had to show her.

Derek stood, reached down to take her hands and pulled her to her feet. He took a thick gray towel from the rack, wrapped it around her and lifted her out of the tub.

Charlotte felt as though her heartbeat might strangle her. For a moment he continued to hold her. Her arms looped around his neck, she looked into his hot, dark eyes and felt her own desire erupt like a fountain.

She closed the half inch that separated their lips and opened her mouth over his. He kissed her hungrily, taunted her with his tongue, nipped at her bottom lip, dipped his head to plant a kiss on the bare flesh above her towel.

"Derek!" she breathed into the wiry crispness of his hair.

He heard the passion in her whisper and felt it fuel his own. He swung her to her feet, unwrapped the towel from around her and, holding it in both hands, secured her in one arm and buffed her back and hips dry with the other end of it.

Then he wrapped it around her from behind, pulled her back against him and rubbed slowly, gently, over her breasts and her stomach. He leaned over to pass the towel over her thighs and she turned in his arms to catch him in her warm and fragrant embrace.

She nipped his ear, kissed his cheek, then raised his face and looked into his eyes. Hers held a love that was easy to read, and a thousand mysteries he didn't understand.

His held a fathomless passion and possession so strong she knew she'd feel it even without his arms around her.

"This will change everything," she warned softly.

He ran his thumb over her bottom lip, concentrating on it a moment before he looked up again into her eyes. "No, it won't," he insisted. "It'll just reaffirm the truth. We belong to each other."

Then he tossed the towel aside, lifted her into his arms and walked into the bedroom.

Chapter Seven

Derek placed Charlotte in the middle of the bed, then went to the open window through which they could hear the sounds of laughter at the pool, the drone of bees in the rose garden and, from somewhere distant, the sound of a lawn mower.

He pulled the window closed and smiled at her as he came back to the bed.

"I've had enough of snoops. It's one thing when we're onstage…" He sat beside her and leaned over her, a serious frown replacing the smile as he framed her face in his hands. "But quite another—" he leaned down to kiss her tenderly "—when we finally have the opportunity to write the scene ourselves."

Then he fixed her with a smile that was both gentle and devilish.

She expected him to make some witty remark, some astute, sophisticated observation—but instead he just looked at her, a hand braced on either side of her on the mattress.

She ran both hands up the front of his sweater. "What are you thinking?" she asked.

He caught one hand and planted a kiss in its palm. "That you don't look like the haughty duchess at the moment.'' He ran a fingertip down the middle of her from her clavicle to her navel. ''You look like some wicked little druid.''

He took the coronet from her hair and reached up to put it carefully on the bedside table.

Charlotte felt that light strum of his finger awaken every nerve ending in her body. It was important, she thought, that he know who she really was.

''It's just me,'' she said, tracing the line of his jaw with her fingertips. ''The woman who so frustrated you for a whole year because she had a tendency to look backward rather than forward, and because she tended to operate with a slowness that annoyed you.'' Her fingers moved over the sturdy square of his jaw. ''You're sure you want to do this?''

Derek slipped a hand under her, splayed it against her back and brought her up with it to within an inch of his own body. Her wide eyes questioned him.

''I've watched you work,'' he said, kissing her forehead. ''I understand your fascination with the past a little better.'' Then he tilted her sideways into his arm and cradled her there, running a hand gently down the smooth flesh of her side and over her hip. ''And some things,'' he said, lowering his voice intimately, ''are done best when they're done slowly.''

And then it began, the languidly deliberate exploration of every little inch of her body, every plane of it and every secret shadow.

Charlotte, aroused by his possessive touch and his reverent fascination, felt desire ignite as his hands moved over her, learning every little detail, she was sure, and even a few secrets her heart held.

He charted her breasts with a slowness that reduced her to absolute stillness.

When he put his mouth to the pearled tips of her, she felt it draw up the dignity she'd tried to reserve, the control she'd unconsciously tried to maintain.

''Derek!'' she whispered as she struggled to retain at least one protective mechanism.

But he was drawing a line of kisses down the middle of her body, over her stomach, to the juncture of her thighs.

Flame licked at her with the tip of his tongue and caution shredded and fled in the fingers with which she gripped her pillow.

She was aware first of a sense of surprise that it made her feel free rather than vulnerable.

Then she realized what freedom did for one. Her body trembled on the very edge of infinity, then flung her out without fetters of any kind.

She'd never experienced that before. She'd always remained partially connected, at least some thread of reality caught in her grasp and anchoring her.

But this time she was soaring free, as though the vastness of what she felt needed the eternal space of forever. But then she became aware of being there alone.

''Derek.''

She said his name softly, but he heard the edge of wonder in it. She groped for him, as though not sure where she was.

''Here,'' he said, lying down beside her and enfolding her in his arms. ''Right here.''

He expected her to need to lie still for a moment, to ground herself. But he'd apparently mistaken her purpose when she reached for him. She hadn't needed him to reassure her; she'd wanted to take him with her.

She knelt beside him and slipped her fingers up under

his sweater, traced the hem of his undershirt to the barrier of his slacks and tugged to release it.

He let her work over him without trying to help, enjoying the seriousness of her concentration, the feverish flush on her cheeks.

The undershirt free, she knelt astride him, slipped both hands under him and tried to lift him to a sitting position as he'd done to her. Without his help, she found it impossible.

She gave him a sweet, scolding look. "Are you going to help me?"

He lay passive, thinking nothing had felt this delicious in recent memory. Even past memory.

"I want to see your next move," he said shamelessly.

Still astride him, she sat back, almost ruining the slim chance he had of remaining in control of his body long enough to see what direction her resourceful mind would take.

She raised an eyebrow and he caught a glimpse of the duchess. He felt a trepidation that called to that part of him that loved to flirt with danger.

Without a word, she unbuckled his belt, unzipped his slacks, and scooting backward over him, tugged on them.

The sensation that raged through him as she slid over him made him arch involuntarily, giving her just the advantage she needed to slide his slacks and briefs over his hips and off.

She came back to him, kneeling over him braced on her hands, and smiled with blatant self-satisfaction into his eyes. She had every right to it.

"That's the difference between us," she taunted softly, pausing to blow a warm breath across his chest. "You think every little detail done exactly to your specifications is so critical to the outcome of a project. But I prefer to explore the alternatives. There are other ways to get things done than by the charge-ahead means you always choose.''

That gentle scolding administered, she tried to scoot backward again, intent on showing him just how inventive she could be.

But he had plans of his own. And a desperation he'd never known before.

He sat up to yank off the sweater and shirt, tossed them over the edge of the bed, then lifted her at the waist and lay back, placing her precisely where he wanted her.

He slipped into her and her body welcomed him with the ease of two people made for each other. He plunged deeply and she leaned to accommodate him, bracing on the hands they laced together between them.

He watched the little pleat form between her eyes that accompanied a little gasp of pleasure. Then she smiled at him with a helpless little inclination of her head that said what he already knew—there wasn't a word for how this felt, for how perfect, how all-pervading it was. It went deeper even than his body probed inside hers. It touched everywhere, everything.

Then urgency made him unable to concentrate on anything but the demands of their connection. He began to move under her and she leaned in counterpoint. Swaying together, following the paths of two separate but concentric circles, they turned on the pivotal point of a shared desire—and a shared love.

The knowledge, now irrefutable, broke over both of them the same moment fulfillment did, releasing them from everything that held love back or down, freeing them from all but each other.

CHARLOTTE STRETCHED languidly the length of Derek's warm body, then let her head fall back against his chest with a contented sigh.

"We really should stop this," she said, planting a kiss in the mat of hair under her cheek, "and get dressed for dinner."

Derek felt too replete to move. "Man does not live by bread alone," he philosophized drowsily.

Charlotte laughed against him. "Whoever said that hadn't seen Babs's sourdough starter." She sighed again. "If only someone would deliver dinner here so that we could eat it in bed."

"That's almost too hedonistic to contemplate."

"Or we could pack it into a basket with a bottle of chardonnay, put the basket in my Duesenberg and drive to Monterey."

"Your Duesenberg is in three pieces at the moment," he reminded.

She groaned. "That's right. And a picnic basket wouldn't fit into your Porsche. So I guess we have to go to dinner."

He shifted, holding her closer. "Let's not. I'll bet they won't even miss us."

She nuzzled closer. "I promised to have one of the coronets ready to show Kendra tonight. Bitsy's anxious to photograph them."

The mention of the coronets reminded him of the almost mythical way this entire afternoon had begun. And that reminded him that he would never get enough of her. Already the feeling of satiation was being replaced by a gnawing, growing need.

"If you insist," he said, rolling to turn her onto her back. "But I'll need a memory of this afternoon to see me through the wedding party's giggles, Elizabeth's endless discussion of details and Trey's longing looks at you.''

"I believe," she said, halfheartedly pushing him away, "that you've collected three memories already. Or was that four? I think I fainted on you the last time."

"I'd like to believe that, but I think you just fell asleep."

"Well, I hadn't had much to eat...."

He cupped a hand under her hip and the other under her back to break her ineffectual resistance. "We're back to that again, are we? Well, the sooner you cooperate, the sooner we'll go to dinner."

She gave him a dramatic, long-suffering sigh. "Oh, all right. If you have to have it your way...."

His way, she decided an instant later, was rather wonderful.

ELIZABETH DID NOT censure them when they arrived twenty minutes late for dinner. She didn't have to. She simply turned to the butler, who appeared at her elbow, and said with a regal flick of her hand, "You may finally serve dinner, Chadwick."

"Yes, ma'am."

Everyone gathered in the living room studied Charlotte and Derek speculatively. Charlotte was sure that to anyone who knew her well, the events of the afternoon showed on her face.

She'd seen the difference in the mirror as she applied her makeup, though she couldn't have described it. Something subtle about her had changed.

Despite the carefully applied eye shadow, her eyes looked wide and mystified, and her carefully outlined and painted lips, the same berry as her short, full-skirted dress, had a tendency to smile without reason.

Derek, looking into the mirror over her shoulder to knot his tie, smiled at her puzzled expression.

"I look," she said with a confused little shrug, "like my own country cousin."

He had dipped his head to study her, a very masculine smile curving his lips. Then he placed a light kiss on the side of her neck. "The duchess," he said, "is gone."

Charlotte was saved from the varied but merciless inspections when Kendra approached her, pointing to the paper bag she held in her hands.

"Is that the headpiece?" she asked anxiously.

"Oh! Yes. Briane?" Charlotte, Kendra, Briane and Denise converged on the mirror over a Queen Anne table. Charlotte placed the coronet on Briane's hair and stepped back to let Kendra examine it.

As they decided unanimously that it was perfect, Denise took it from Briane and tried it on.

"It has every subtle shade," Kendra marveled. "And the pearls are a nice, romantic touch." She put a hand to Charlotte's arm and squeezed gently. "You've come through again. I'm going to have the most devastatingly gorgeous attendants any bride every had."

It wasn't until they were seated at the table that Charlotte realized Trey was absent.

"Isn't Trey joining us for dinner?" Caleb asked, noting the empty chair.

"He wasn't feeling well this afternoon," Kendra explained, grinning at her friends. "He hasn't quite recovered from all the stingers he had at the Karaoke bar. He's napping."

Caleb looked at Edward as though to suggest that the current generation hadn't their stamina or their capacity to party.

Caroline's knowing gaze swung from Charlotte to

Derek, then settled on Charlotte again with a dazzling smile.

Charlotte looked away, afraid to think it could all be so easy. Any moment the glow would wear off and she'd probably ask herself why she'd been so impulsive and so impractical.

Then Derek, seated across from her, smiled at her with their new intimacy in his eyes, and she truly wondered if it could ever be a valid question.

Babs helped Pauline serve again. As Charlotte bit into the succulent shrimp cocktail, she looked up to catch Derek's eye. He gave her that look again that she was sure created a bright aura around her and made hot color flood her face.

Dessert was Babs's cake served with a whipped-cream frosting. Everyone raved, including Kendra.

"This *is* delicious, Grandma," she said, studying the morsel on her fork. "And it's very pretty." She turned to Elizabeth. "Mother, couldn't we have this instead of the bakery cake? It would be even better tasting, and in keeping with the Victorian theme."

"The cake is ordered," Elizabeth said. "Bitsy has photographed the bakery's model topped with your crystal lovebirds."

"But couldn't we… "

Elizabeth sighed. "Kendra, you've already caused everyone enough trouble, first rejecting Jean Michel's dress, then forcing me to move heaven and earth to find another dress and change everything else to coincide."

Charlotte saw Caroline's eyebrows go up as her glance turned in Charlotte's direction.

Charlotte bit back a wry grin. It was interesting that Elizabeth considered herself the one inconvenienced.

The gathering dispersed after dinner—Kendra and her

attendants upstairs where Briane could try on the head-piece with her dress, and Babs to the kitchen with Pauline where she felt most comfortable. Elizabeth went off to her bedroom office to tie up some detail of the reception, and Caleb, Caroline, Derek, Charlotte and Edward relaxed in the living room to sip brandy and talk about the tickets Caleb had bought the soon-to-be newlyweds for their honeymoon in Tahiti.

Then he drew out another folder and passed it to Derek, who sat on the arm of Charlotte's chair.

Derek put his glass down and frowned. "What is this?"

Caleb cleared his throat and blustered. "Nothing much. Just something to make up for having your honeymoon interrupted because of my daughter's wedding."

A blush of guilt flooding her face, Charlotte watched Derek's long fingers open the folder. He pulled out a pair of airline tickets and shot Charlotte a warning glance before saying with pleased surprised, "Tickets to Paris. Caleb, this isn't necessary."

Caleb looked embarrassed. "Didn't want to send you to Tahiti," he said with a dry twist of his lips. "Didn't think you'd want to bump into Kendra and Trey when you finally got to get away. Caroline assured me Paris is one of Charlotte's favorite places."

Charlotte knew she looked stricken. Derek leaned down to hug her as though sharing her surprise and whispered quietly, "Stop it. Do you want to hurt his feelings? It's going to be all right."

Charlotte made herself smile and thank him with a stunned courtesy Caleb seemed to find completely convincing.

"I brought some brochures home," Caleb said, patting his pockets. "What did I do with them? Oh, yes. I left them in the study." He groaned at the prospect of pushing his portly girth out of the deep chair. "I keep thinking I should get one of those chairs that throws you to your feet, but I can't help but wonder what happens if you miss."

Everyone laughed. Charlotte stood, desperately needing a moment alone. "Let me get them for you, Caleb," she said. "I was just going to see if there was any coffee left, anyway."

Derek gave her a look that was part concern, part warning. She patted his cheek.

"Be right back."

"On my desk," Caleb called after her.

Charlotte went directly to the study across the hall, the story about the coffee was nothing but a gambit to explain her eagerness to get away. She closed the big oak doors behind her and leaned against them in the dark.

She put a hand to her chest where her heart fluttered. Tickets to Paris. An expensive gift invested in gratitude for the disruption of a honeymoon that had never existed in the first place.

She was torn between thinking things had gone too far, and thinking they'd finally gotten to the point where they should be. After all the role-playing, she and Derek were truly in love, but that seemed to make it more difficult rather than easier to carry on the charade.

Confused by that thought, she groped along the wall for the light switch, but encountered nothing but the feel of genuine wood paneling. She turned to the other side of the door—and was stopped dead by a furtive sound behind her. A hand to the wall to retain her bearings, she stood still and listened.

She heard more movement, the rustle of clothing, what sounded like a stifled breath. Before alarm could take hold of her, she told herself reasonably that she was in a house filled with people that was located within a locked gate. This could not be an intruder. But who was it?

"Hello?" she said cautiously.

There was another long, pulsing silence, then more quiet movements.

Now a little worried, she inched toward the door. "Who's there?" she demanded in a firm voice.

There was another instant's silence, then a low, seductive voice came out of the dark. "It's me, Charlie."

"Trey!" she said with relief. For an instant, the quality of his voice hadn't registered, only the familiar sound of it. "What on earth are you doing here?"

Then she remembered Kendra saying he was napping to get over a headache. When he didn't answer her question, she remembered also how his voice had sounded— predatory and vaguely reckless.

"Oh, Charlie," he said, his voice even deeper, thicker than before. A hand caught hers in the dark and drew her farther into the room.

"Trey," she said, finally understanding what was happening, trying to draw her hand away. "Trey, stop it. What's the matter with you?"

"You know what the matter is." Suddenly his voice was in her ear and his arms were around her, taut with emotion barely held in check. She felt moist lips against her cheek and knew he'd missed her lips because she was tossing her head, pushing against him.

"Stop this right now!" she whispered harshly. "Your fiancée is just upstairs and her father is just across the hall!" She added belatedly, "Along with my husband!"

"Charlie, this is all wrong and you know it," he whispered urgently against her cheekbone, having missed her mouth again.

"You're damn right, it's wrong!" She tried to kick him and missed, pushed against him with all her might, but he was unusually strong in his ardor.

"I don't mean *this,*" he said, finally zeroing in on her mouth and kissing her. She kept her mouth closed stubbornly as she continued to push at him. Revulsion and fury washed over her. "I mean the way it's ending up, you with Cabot, me with Kendra. She's more beautiful than you are, and she's more amenable, but she isn't you."

"Trey, you're supposed to marry her in two days!"

"I can't."

And that was what finally gave her the strength to shove him away. There was a gasp of alarm from him as he fell backward, then a scream from her as he caught at her skirt and took her with him.

She felt pain as her thigh collided with something hard and angular, then her shoulder knocked against the same object as she fell against it. There was the sound of furniture falling and glass breaking. She landed on something that expelled a loud, "Ooof!"

Darkness and surprise disoriented her. As she tried to recover, there was another crash. The study door burst open and someone flipped on the light. It glared harshly over the condemning little tableau on the floor.

A globe on a floor stand lay on its side, the meridian still rocking, the globe within it still spinning on its poles pins. The falling globe had collided with a glass-topped coffee table and knocked it over. The glass had cracked, and a fluted crystal dish lay overturned, little foil wrapped candies spewed all over the tweedy brown carpet.

Charlotte and Trey lay in a tangle among the legs of the coffee table. Trey was on the bottom, his head against the uppermost leg, his own legs trapped between the two legs on the other end of the table. Charlotte was draped across him, her dress hiked up to her thighs.

She pushed against the side of the coffee table to squint up at the door and found almost everyone in the household there.

Derek and her father made up the front row, both staring at her in confusion and concern. Behind them were Caleb and Caroline, also staring. Caroline had a hand to her mouth. Kendra and her attendants were behind them, Kendra coming around the little crowd to peer in openmouthed dismay at the compromising scene. Elizabeth arrived with a gasp of dismay.

Charlotte put a hand to her spinning head and groaned. Trey exacerbated the situation by reaching up to put a hand to her face. "You okay, Charlie?" he asked solicitously.

Then everyone was galvanized into action. Derek came forward to pull Charlotte to her feet, Edward and Caleb helping Trey.

Charlotte, still trembling a little, looked into the controlled temper in Derek's dark eyes and explained inanely, "I was looking for the light."

"Light switches are usually found against the wall," Elizabeth said, studying the disorder on the floor.

Even to Charlotte's own ear, the claim sounded like a lie. And when she blushed, she was sure it looked like a lie.

She turned to Trey, daring him to extricate them from this embarrassing scene. Whatever notion she might have had that he'd assume all blame to save her dissolved when he cleared his throat.

"I was asleep on the sofa," he said, grinning at Kendra who was looking at him with open suspicion. "She just fell over me." He turned to Charlotte in all apparent innocence and asked, "What were you doing in here, anyway?"

Charlotte wondered how often she herself had fallen for that charmingly embarrassed smile. Who could be angry with anyone who looked so vulnerable and innocent?

It occurred to her to tell the truth. But her mind asked with a hint of gallows humor, *Why start now?* And if anyone should reveal the truth, it should be Trey.

"I'm sorry about the table, Elizabeth," Charlotte said wearily. She wanted desperately to extricate herself from this wedding and go home. She longed for the quiet, simple life she'd lived in her old North Hollywood home before this had all begun. "I'll have the glass replaced."

"Don't be silly," Caleb said when his wife righted her wounded table in obvious displeasure. "Are you all right?"

Caroline came to put an arm around her. "You should sit down, Charlie. You don't look well."

"I'm fine," she said. "But I'd like to go back to the guest house, if you'll all excuse me."

"I'll make you a cup of tea," Caroline offered.

Edward frowned into her eyes. "You don't look fine. Did you hit your head?"

"No." Charlotte shook it and immediately regretted it. The headache with which she'd begun the day was back with a vengeance. The intervening time, she thought, had certainly been eventful.

"I'm sure it would help her to get off her feet," Derek

said, sweeping her up into his arms to do precisely that. "I'll take care of her, Caroline."

Charlotte was happy to lean her face against his shoulder and close her eyes as he negotiated the gauntlet of the suspicious audience and left the big house.

He said nothing as he carried her through the fragrant darkness and up the well-lit path to the guest house. At the door, he braced a knee against the wall and rested her on it while he retrieved his key.

Then they were inside, and he was putting her down in the middle of the bed. It reminded her of how he'd done that very thing only hours ago, and the lovemaking that had resulted and changed something vital within her.

"Stay still," he said, slipping off her shoes. "I'll put the kettle on."

He left the room in darkness, but put on the hallway light. She heard him at work in the kitchen, then his footsteps as he returned to the bedroom. He tossed his jacket at the chair and came to sit on the edge of the bed beside her.

"Are you really all right?" he asked, pulling the other side of the bedspread over her.

"Yes," she replied, "except for a few bruises where I landed against the coffee table."

"Then what the hell happened?" he asked. "I thought it was over between you, yet I keep finding you together."

She tossed the spread off and sat up. "It *is* over between us," she said angrily, her temper and her composure in shreds. She snatched the pillow from beside her and held it threateningly, "And if you dare suggest that what happened in the study was the result of some...some rendezvous...I'll..."

He took the pillow from her, tossed it behind her and

pushed her gently back against it. "Then what happened?" he insisted.

She yanked the spread back over her, angry, disappointed and depressed.

"He kissed me," she said simply.

Derek reached over to turn on the bedside lamp. It cast a small puddle of light over the two of them.

"What?" he asked ominously.

"He was sleeping off the headache Kendra mentioned at dinner. Only she didn't mention he was doing it in the study. I blundered in in the dark, he woke up and heard me, and...and I guess he was probably..." She groped for a kind explanation. "You know, feeling last-minute panic, and maybe some leftover guilt from leaving me at the altar and..."

"You're telling me," Derek suggested dryly, "that he kissed you to make up for abandoning you in a church filled with people?"

Her look scolded him for deliberately misunderstanding. "No, I mean that when he gets panicky, he doesn't think straight."

"When he gets panicky," Derek amended, "he does whatever it takes to save himself."

She leaned into the pillow with a sigh. "Yes, I know. I shoved him away, he fell over the coffee table and grabbed for me as he went down. That's how we ended up...all entangled."

"No one believed his lame story for a minute. 'I was asleep and she fell over me.' He may as well have said, 'We fell off the sofa in the throes of passion.' Why didn't you say something?"

She winced as her head throbbed. "Because Kendra was standing right behind you."

"You don't think she has the right to know her fiancé was kissing his old flame?"

"I don't know." She rubbed between her eyebrows. "Maybe he really does love her, but he's just being a jerk. I fell in love with him because he was sensitive and sweet in a world filled with ruthless, hard-driving men." She cast him a glance that lumped him in their number. "Then the morning of our wedding, the only thing that arrived at the church was a messenger with a note from him that said he couldn't go through with it because he knew he'd fail me one day. He was probably right, because I'd have expected something from him. I'm not sure Kendra does. He's handsome and smart and her family likes him—that's the standard by which she's been brought up. She doesn't need anything for her personal self. They could probably make each other happy."

The kettle whistled and Derek answered its call with a profane, insightful observation.

He was back in a moment with two steaming mugs. He handed her one, then resumed his place on the edge of the bed. She scooted sideways and patted the place beside her.

"Want to sit with me?"

He did and he didn't. He was still full of angry, jealous questions, observations he'd like to make about the handsome, perennial fiancé. But Charlotte looked pale and tired, and there was evidence in her eyes that the episode with Prentiss had upset her. He put his cup down on the table and slipped into the small space she'd left him.

She leaned her head against his shoulder and sighed. "At least with a man who's straightforward, you know what to expect. You know the limits of the relationship.''

He wasn't sure he liked the way that sounded. ''You've found limits in our relationship already?''

She raised her head to sip her tea, then rested it against him again. ''Well, you know. You're very open about thinking my involvement with the past is silly and a little weird. I like to wander around while you bulldoze ahead, and I'm always looking for the sweet little things you don't even notice. There'll be a lot we won't be able to share. But at least I know that. You haven't pretended to be one thing and turned out to be another.''

He frowned into the shadows beyond their little pool of light. ''It's a rule that opposites attract,'' he reasoned. ''What results from two people who are very different is a healthy balance.''

She was silent for a moment. Then she put her cup aside and lifted his arm to place it around her. She found a comfortable spot on his chest and closed her eyes.

''Right,'' she said, too belatedly to convince him that she meant it.

Chapter Eight

"What's on your agenda for today?" Derek asked as he peered around the bathroom door, pulling a simple white sweater over his head.

Charlotte, stretched out in warm bathwater to soak away her bruises from the night before, smiled lazily as she watched his head emerge from the round neck.

She loved the serious, sturdy look of him that hid a sparkling sense of humor and a deep, hot passion. It occurred to her that the woman she was today would probably not even look twice at Trey Prentiss.

"I have to finish the other headpiece," she said, "and I had promised to pick up a pair of patterned stockings from my shop for Kendra to wear. Presuming she's still speaking to me."

Derek ran a hand through his hair to smooth it and moved into the humid little room.

"If you take any flack because of what happened last night," he warned, "*I'm* telling everyone the truth."

"Hopefully," Charlotte said calmly, "they'll all just think it wasn't half as bad as it looked. They might even believe I just fell over him."

"Looking for the light switch that was a good fifteen feet away?"

"You're not helping." She sat up and winced as the movement forced pressure against the bruise on the back of her shoulder.

"What's the matter?" he asked, coming to lean over her.

"Nothing serious. Just a few bruises from falling over the coffee table."

Derek looked at the angry red-and-purple blotch the size of a saucer on the slope of her shoulder and swore.

"God! Is that the only one you've got?"

Without warning or ceremony, he hauled her out of the water and checked her over. Ignoring her protests that she was fine, he found a purple welt on her thigh and one on her backside.

"That's it," he said. "It's time Prentiss and I had a man-to—"

She wrapped her arms around him, the touch of her warm, soaking body penetrating his clothing. "They're just bruises that'll fade in a day or two." Her wide eyes mesmerized him as they pleaded prettily. "And though they are his fault, we fell because I pushed him. Please don't spoil Kendra's wedding."

"Charlie, he..."

Her eyes fell to his lips and prevented them from moving coherently.

"I don't care about him," she whispered, running the tip of her tongue along his bottom lip. "I just want to think about us." Then her tongue parted his lips and he was lost.

He made love to her swiftly, responsively, wrestling her for control of the encounter, then gladly relinquishing it when she insisted with artful boldness. Then he rolled her over and made love to her again, retaining the initiative this time just to show her the scope of pleasure he wanted to offer.

He was twenty minutes late for the meeting in Caleb's office. With Charlotte in his bed, he thought, he was going to spend his life twenty minutes late for everything.

"YOU'RE SURE YOU don't mind taking the contracts to the office safe?" Edward asked Derek.

Caleb had already left the study in response to the butler's urgent message from Elizabeth, and Edward and Derek sat over cups of coffee that rested on the cracked glass top of the coffee table.

"Not at all," Derek assured him.

"You didn't have other plans for today?"

The question was innocent enough, but Derek had worked with Edward in one capacity or another for twelve years. It was his job to read between the lines of every contract and every conversation and evaluate the unspecified and the unspoken.

He grinned at his boss as he leaned over to pick up his cup. "I apologized for being late."

"The two of you have been late for everything."

"Your daughter doesn't respond to being rushed."

"My daughter is determined and strong-willed, but very gentle deep down, maybe even fragile." Edward smiled honestly. "I know you to be honest and fair, but hardheaded and ruthless. And I know she's fallen in love with you."

Derek remembered her strong resistance to his overtures and, last night, her practical assessment of their situation—an assessment he didn't particularly agree with, but found excessively reasonable all the same.

"She's tougher than you realize, Edward," he said.

He took a sip of the strong, hot coffee, then put it down, thinking how much he'd come to enjoy sharing tea with Charlotte. "But you know I've never injured or broken a delicate deal. And I always see that everyone wins."

Edward sighed, his expression growing thoughtful. "But you're very young. I wonder if you realize how different women are from business."

Derek nodded. "There was a time when I used the same approach on both. But I learned the difference when Charlie worked for me. Don't worry. I'm far more reliable than Prentiss."

Edward made a scornful sound. "Tell me something I don't know. He ducked out of this morning's meeting on the pretext that the jeweler needed to see him. I think he just didn't want to face you. What the hell happened last night?"

Derek knew Charlotte wouldn't be pleased that he told her father, but there were some things on which she wasn't the final authority.

"He made a move on her while she was groping around in the dark. She shoved him, he grabbed for her and they fell over the coffee table."

Edward's response was pithy and obscene.

"Precisely," Derek said. "But I'll have a talk with him when he comes back from the jeweler. Warn him what'll happen to his own family jewels if he isn't careful."

Edward laughed wickedly. "All right. See you at dinner."

IN A PAIR OF pink sweats appliquéd with roses, Charlotte went to answer the authoritative rap on the guest-house door.

Caroline pushed her way in, a paper bag of something

aromatic in her hands. "Point me to the kitchen," she said.

Charlotte complied, following her to lean in the narrow doorway while her stepmother found the still-half-full kettle, the tin of tea and a pair of mugs.

"I'll tell you up front," she said as she worked, "that your father sent me here to...to sort of...feel out the situation, so to speak." She looked up to wince apologetically. "Poor choice of words. To assess the situation, to see if you're...happy. Plates?"

Charlotte walked into the kitchen to pull down two.

"What's in the bag?"

Caroline opened it and removed two fat, fragrant croissants.

"Yum!" Charlotte said.

"And not only that, they're filled with raspberry. Should we skip the butter, or be truly decadent?"

As Charlotte considered, Caroline warned, "I'm going to be asking some tough questions."

Charlotte retrieved the butter from the refrigerator and led the way to the sofa.

Croissants halved and buttered and filling the small room with their aroma, Caroline tore off a bite of hers and sat back in her corner of the sofa.

"Okay. Spill your guts. Tell me everything. And give me details—your father will ask."

"You mean last night?"

"I mean Derek, and then last night."

Charlotte didn't want to answer questions, but she had to admire her stepmother's style. It was precisely this no-nonsense candor that had endeared her to Charlotte.

"Derek," Charlotte said, after chewing and swallowing her first bite, "is pretending to be my husband, remember? You wrote the play."

"Don't try to put me off with that," Caroline said, propping a designer loafer on the wicker tabletop. "Judging by the glow on the two of you, no one is pretending anything anymore. You've been intimate, haven't you?"

"Caro!"

She waved a bite of croissant helplessly. "Don't kill the messenger. Your father will ask."

Charlotte gave her a disbelieving glance as she reached for her tea. "I believe you're the one who's interested. Dad's always let me have my privacy."

"And so did I when you were in high school and relationships were a vast emotional experience. But those days are long gone now, Charlie."

Charlotte rolled her eyes over the rim of her cup.

"Oh, you know what I mean. You're still a youngster, but you should be old enough to forget all your old traumas and know a good thing when you see it." Caroline put her croissant aside in order to study Charlotte carefully. "Do you?"

"I think so."

"So...are you?"

"What?"

"In love!" Caroline shouted impatiently. "Have you gotten over Trey? Are you out of your shell? Are you willing to try again with a man who makes Trey look like an adolescent?"

"Yes. Yes. Yes." Charlotte counted over all the questions, then added tardily, "Yes."

"Hallelujah!" Caroline leaned sideways to give her stepdaughter a hearty hug. "Thank God! I thought the way you were behaving in the beginning, you might blow the whole opportunity. He's perfect for you."

Charlotte shook her head as she put cup and croissant aside. "Actually, we agree on so little."

Caroline heaved a theatrical sigh. "Then you're meant for each other, my sweet, because that's married life in a nutshell."

Charlotte had to laugh. "Come on. Dad does absolutely everything you ask of him."

She agreed with a nod. "But only after he's said no, been forced to listen to my arguments, then been swayed by my brilliant oratory."

"I think that's called nagging."

"An ugly word for such inventive tactics. Has he mentioned marriage?"

"No, he hasn't mentioned marriage. We were only thrown together four or five days ago. We just…" She stopped, finding it difficult to make the admission in the face of Caroline's eagerness to hear it. "We're just getting to know each other."

Caroline shook her head at her as though she were simple. "He's been in love with you since your father brought him back from New York. And I think you were in love with him, but you were engaged to Trey. I believe that's what was behind the fireworks between you two—he thinks all things business, personal and financial should be handled the same, and when he couldn't deal with you that way, it made him angry.

"And you were drawn to him, intrigued by him, probably even felt something for him—but you were engaged to someone you thought was ideal, so it confused you. You took it out on yourself and everyone else in the vicinity."

Charlotte listened to the detailed analysis of that awful year just before she quit her father's company, and concluded that Caroline was probably right.

"That's all over now," she said, propping an elbow on the back of the sofa and frowning. "But the issue of Trey remains. Did Elizabeth or Kendra say anything to you about what happened last night?"

"No. I haven't seen Kendra all morning, and Elizabeth has been very much business as usual. What *did* happen?"

Briefly, undramatically, she related her encounter with Trey.

"You aren't serious!" Caroline exclaimed in shocked fascination. "Do you believe that young man? What did you do?"

"I shoved him. That's how we ended up entangled with the coffee table."

"Well." Serene again, Caroline took another sip of tea. "I'm sure Derek will take care of him, just as he's taken care of the table."

Charlotte lowered her hand. "What do you mean?"

"It was replaced by a new one this morning, just as I was coming over here."

"That isn't his responsibility."

"Of course it is. At least everyone will think it is. A responsible man makes good on his wife's charges and breakages." Caroline lowered her cup and said with a knowing glance, "And I imagine he's taking care of Trey Prentiss at this very moment."

DEREK HAD LITTLE TROUBLE finding Trey. Charlotte's ex-fiancé returned just as the furniture truck left with the damaged table. From the study window, he saw Trey slip around the back of the house and disappear into the garden and the tents being set up for the reception.

He found him sitting on the canvas bottom of the tent at the farthest end of the lawn. He leaned back on his hands, looking pensive and uncertain, his head thrown back as he stared at the ceiling of the tent. Derek supposed he might have looked poetic and tragic to someone who had patience with indecision and a lack of loyalty.

Derek walked into the shadowy interior. Trey sprang to his feet, taking a cautious step backward before he could stop himself. Then he seemed to force himself to relax and pretend he hadn't been avoiding him since breakfast.

"Good morning," Trey said with exaggerated cheer. "I was just going to check on Charlie. How is she this morning?"

"That's what I want to talk about," Derek said, wandering in his direction, hands in his pockets.

"Oh? She's all right, isn't she?"

"She's bruised," Derek said, stopping a few feet from him. He knew he didn't have to tell him whom he considered responsible.

"I didn't..." Trey began to protest.

"She told me what happened," Derek interrupted, slowly taking his hands out of his pockets. "She's bruised because she tried to get away from you and you brought her down when you fell."

"She shoved me."

Derek would have taken great satisfaction in hitting him just for that. He had no patience with people who couldn't relate cause and effect.

"Because you kissed her when she's married to me, and you're engaged to be married to someone else tomorrow."

Anger flared in Trey's eyes and Derek watched with interest, wondering if Trey was going to allow temper to overcome good sense. He hoped so.

"Charlotte and I had some good times. We share a history you can never be a part of, and you can't just blot it out by..."

Derek closed the small space left between them in two strides and resisted the impulse to grab him by his shirt collar and choke him.

"You listen to me," he said quietly, his arms loose and ready on the chance that he changed his mind about being reasonable. "You flatter yourself to think she remembers anything about you except the fact that you changed your mind about marrying her at the last minute and didn't even have the guts to show up in person and tell her."

He had to draw a breath, because the memory of that morning in the church infuriated him still.

Trey seemed unable to breathe even though he wasn't choking him.

"Even if she did consider she had a 'history' with you," Derek repeated the word scornfully, "I wouldn't give a damn about it. All I care about is her future, and that takes place with me. If you so much as come near the guest house before we leave, if you even speak to Charlotte in a crowd, much less try to see her alone, I'll grind you to powder, Prentiss.

"Now." He smiled pleasantly. "My advice would be that you don't do anything to scotch your relationship with Kendra, because that's the only thing that's saving your job at Farsnworth–Morreaux. Have a nice day."

Derek turned to leave and Trey took a step after him. Derek stopped and turned, halting him in his tracks.

Humiliated and angry, Trey said, "You're a bastard, Cabot!"

Derek nodded, his expression grim. "You'd do well to remember that."

"HE CHANGED HIS MIND, Henry," Charlotte was saying to Henry as Derek walked around the garages. "He's decided that was narrow-minded and chauvinistic and that I can drive the Porsche, after all. So please get me the keys."

Henry frowned, obviously torn between an unwillingness to deny a favorite guest anything, and a possessive, protective attitude toward the Porsche left in his care. Not to mention the promise he'd made to another favorite guest.

"He didn't tell me that, Mrs. Cabot," he said stoutly, his tall body blocking the open door at the end of the long bank of garages.

Charlotte, looking like a charming version of the duchess in a flowered dress and a broad-brimmed hat, said with the confidence of a beautiful woman to whom little is denied, "It was a recent decision. Reached just this morning, in fact. The keys, Henry."

"He didn't tell me," Henry repeated doggedly. "Why don't I drive you in the limo?"

"He went straight to a meeting in Mr. Farnsworth's study," she replied courteously. "Now I have to go to my shop to pick up a few important things for the wedding. I have a dozen stops to make and I wouldn't want to keep you out that long. You wouldn't want to be responsible for doing anything to make the wedding less than perfect?"

Taking pity on the poor man's dilemma, Derek made his presence known. Henry looked as though he'd been granted a death-row reprieve. Charlotte looked charmingly embarrassed, but only for a moment. She immediately turned her interesting technique on him.

"How would you like lunch at Dominick's?" she asked, knowing it was one of his favorite places.

"Followed by taking you shopping?" He handed Henry his briefcase. "Would you get the car, please, Henry?"

"Yes, sir."

As the chauffeur disappeared into the garage, Charlotte looked at Derek with disapproval. "You were eavesdropping."

Derek folded his arms, trying to hide the desire that rose swiftly in him at the sight of her, the terminal weakness he felt when she smiled at him, the memories of this morning brought back so sharply.

"I like to think of it," he said, "as studying tactics. Yours are truly amazing. One lie after another without so much as a blush or a flicker of an eyelash."

As the Porsche's motor growled to life, Charlotte moved out of its path to stand beside Derek. She smiled up into his eyes.

"*You* taught me to be an actress," she said.

He curled an arm around her waist and leaned over her upturned face. Greedily he watched the welcome in her eyes. "But you're not acting anymore, are you?"

She stood on tiptoe to close the gap and kiss him. "No," she said as Henry, in the Porsche, roared out of the garage in reverse. "I'm not. Are you?"

As Henry pretended not to watch, but polished the driver's side-view mirror with a rag from his pocket, Derek kissed her again to remind her what they'd shared and what still lay ahead of them after the demands of the day.

"Did that feel like acting?"

"No." She devoured him with her eyes one more moment, then smiled innocently. "Then you're not upset about the car?"

He turned her around and sent her toward it with a

gentle swat. "Yes, I am. And just for that, you can drive."

"But...you'll be watching me. I'll be nervous."

"Just pretend I'm not here, and that Henry let you have the keys."

Henry looked in concern at Derek as he closed Charlotte into the driver's side.

"I came close to giving in, Mr. Cabot," he confessed. "You might consider giving Mrs. Cabot her own keys, or parking the Porsche at the Gables across the road." He pointed to the neighboring estate. "My conscience can't take being torn like this day after day."

Derek clapped his shoulder, then walked around the low-slung hood and leaped into the passenger seat without opening the door. "It's okay, Henry. This afternoon ought to settle the issue. Either she'll wreck it, or prove to me she's capable of driving it."

Henry looked doubtful of the outcome. "I'll see Chadwick has a brandy ready for you, just in case."

Chapter Nine

Charlotte had never expected to be seduced by power. It was against everything she stood for, everything she'd tried to sweep out of her life. But she was discovering that the power of a brilliantly designed, quickly responsive and maneuverable sports car was something else entirely.

Derek decided that letting Charlotte drive the Porsche was good for his character. Bad for his nerves, but good for his character.

Used to the steady solidity of her Duesenberg, Charlotte was quickly growing more confident with the Porsche's nimble responses. She drove faster than he did, changed lanes with abandon, found herself caught between one truck trying to pass another and floored the accelerator so that they shot out of the confining and potentially dangerous space like toothpaste from a tube.

"Remember," he said, trying to keep his voice calm, "that it isn't a motorcycle. And there's a cop somewhere in Beverly Hills who wasn't even impressed by Zsa Zsa."

She laughed and reached out to pat his knee. "Relax, husband," she said, heading for the fast lane. "This car is something else!"

He let his mind be distracted for an instant from the danger confronting the car he'd bought with his first substantial bonus, which symbolized his hard work and success, and with which he'd been through a lot, and concentrated on Charlotte's profile.

She had tossed her hat into the back and her platinum hair, which had been wound into a knot when they'd hit the freeway, was now streaming out behind her like a vapor trail.

"Do I detect the polluting encroachment of speed in my old-fashioned girl?" he asked.

She maneuvered around a slow compact. "Yes, I think so," she replied with no obvious regret. "It's fascinating isn't it, to be going fast and still feel in complete control?"

"I think that's a profoundly philosophical observation." He resisted covering his eyes when she slipped back into traffic just as it slowed to accommodate a truck changing lanes up ahead. She did it smoothly, easily, and he thought with surprise that he didn't know all there was to know about Charlotte Morreaux. "That's kind of what life's all about. Going as fast as you can while remaining in control."

"Now there's where we differ," she said. "I think life can only be enjoyed when you slow down to figure out what it's all about. Speed and power are a high, I'll admit it, but only for a little while. They make the scenery a blur. You can't say you've lived when you don't remember what life looked like. Uh-oh. That's my exit coming up."

Derek looked over his shoulder. "There's a pickup in the next lane that thinks it's a Ferrari. Please don't try to intimidate him into letting you in."

Charlotte gave him a scolding grin. "For someone

who espouses the 'live hard, die young' philosophy, you certainly are jittery.''

"That's because you've got it wrong.'' He put a hand to the dash as she did just what he'd hoped she wouldn't do. With a wave and a kiss blown to the driver of the pickup, she slipped past him to take the next turn. "The live hard part is right, but I intended to be doing wheelies in my walker. Charlie—damn it!''

There was the sound of brakes, and gears shifting down. Derek turned again to see just how close to death they were and was surprised when the driver shook his head tolerantly and blew the kiss back to Charlotte.

"See?'' she said, traffic roaring on as they turned onto the relative quiet of Camden Drive. "If you're nice to people, they're nice to you. Want to have lunch before we shop? You look a little peaked.''

CHARLOTTE SAT on the edge of Mrs. Harmon's desk while Derek locked the finished contracts away.

Mrs. Harmon, Derek's secretary, who looked like Mayberry's Aunt Bea, operated like a high-powered brain trust, and had the sense of humor of a stand-up comic.

"Hmm,'' she observed with interest as Derek left them. "You two have finally seen the light?''

Charlotte pretended to misunderstand. "What light? I had to come to town and so did he.''

"Really.'' The single word had a flat, disbelieving sound. "And that's why you're pretending to be husband and wife in a tiny little guest house?''

Charlotte gasped and looked around, returning a wave sent her way from far across the office. "How did you know about that?''

"Ginny in accounts payable told me.''

Another gasp. ''How did *she* know?''

''She had lunch with your mother the other day.''

Charlotte groaned and put a hand to her eyes. ''No. It's supposed to be a closely held secret. It just happened because...''

''I know, I know.'' Mrs. Harmon cut her off. ''The shower. Caroline publicly announcing you'd been married and neglecting to secure a groom—and all this in front of Bitsy Tate. Fortunately Mr. Cabot saved her—and you.''

Charlotte leaned toward her from her superior position, trying to look fierce. ''You will not say a word to anyone, is that clear?''

Mrs. Harmon smiled beatifically. ''Too late. KTLA called me. I'm going to be on the evening news.''

For an instant, Charlotte wasn't sure whether or not to believe her. That was precisely the last chapter she'd envisioned to their dangerous scenario. Exposed publicly for lying like a rug.

Then Mrs. Harmon smiled. ''Just kidding. Now what about you and the boss?''

''We're going shopping,'' she said. ''That's all.''

''For rings? Baby things? I understand you're going to Paris for a couple of weeks.''

''Talk about an efficient grapevine,'' Derek said, coming up behind Mrs. Harmon.

She tilted her head back to watch him walk around her. ''You're surprised? We sell communication stuff to NASA, remember?''

Derek frowned at his secretary with mock ferocity. ''Encourage these rumors,'' he said, ''and you'll find yourself on the next shuttle—with a one-way ticket. Anything I should know about that won't keep until Monday?''

She shook her head. "Never fear. I'm in charge."

Derek smiled at her with genuine affection. "Thank you, General Haig. See you next week."

"Aren't you going to Paris next week?" she asked sweetly as Derek and Charlotte walked away.

Derek cast her a scolding glance over his shoulder.

"ACTUALLY, IT'S NOT a bad idea when you give it some thought." Derek leaned against the glass door as Charlotte unlocked her shop. Without an assistant to help her, she'd closed the shop for the few days she was a guest of the Farnsworths.

"I am not going to Paris," Charlotte said firmly as she pushed open the door. "And that's final."

"That's narrow-minded," he corrected, following her into the cool, quiet shop. "You threw away our first honeymoon to run to Kendra's aid, and now you're throwing away our second?"

Charlotte closed and locked the door behind him and studied him in concern. "You're allowing the role to invade your reality, Derek."

He caught her arm and pulled her closer. "*You* have invaded my reality, Charlie. I'm not sure I know up from down anymore."

She looped an arm in his and led him companionably across a thick, rose-colored carpet. "This way is up," she said, pointing to an ornate oak stairway that wound upward in a graceful turn into an open gallery.

To the right of the stairs was a large open room in opulent Victorian design with an elegant settee in the middle and lace sheers and velvet drapes on the windows. At one end of the room was an out-of-character but practical three-way mirror.

On the other side of the stairs was an identical room. Behind the stairs were large double doors.

"What's back there?" he asked.

"A veritable warehouse," she replied, "of classic wedding dresses, bridesmaids' gowns and suits for the men in the wedding party. I seat my clients comfortably in one of the rooms, and bring clothes out for them to make their selections."

He smiled with new respect. "And you refer to this as a 'shop'?"

She shrugged a slender shoulder. "The word signifies elegance or chic, rather than size. Like 'boutique,' only less pretentious." She smiled, too. "Why? Did you imagine me slaving away in an old storefront with five dresses that I rotated over and over?"

He wasn't sure what he'd thought. But this beautiful, well-planned atmosphere wasn't it.

"No, of course not. I guess I just didn't realize the demand there must be for this sort of thing."

"Many brides are really into outdoing each other, looking unique. Others are sincerely searching for the dress and the atmosphere that expresses the romance they feel inside. And in this day of—" she slanted him a grin as she led him up the rose-carpeted stairs "—speed and power, it's easier to borrow romance from another time."

He stopped her halfway up the stairs, his eyes darkening to jet as he looked down at her.

Her eyes lightened to silver as they caught the early-afternoon glow from the leaded-glass window on the landing.

"You find yourself lacking romance?" he asked softly.

She considered a moment as he steadied her on their

precarious perch with a hand at her waist. "Yes," she replied finally.

His eyebrow rose in surprise. "After last night and this morning?"

She smiled gently, wondering if a man like him could be expected to understand the difference. "That was passion. It's strong and deep and I doubt that anyone could be considered truly alive without knowing that aspect of life. But I'm talking about romance."

"Isn't there romance in passion?" he asked in obvious confusion.

"Yes, but it also exists in and of itself, and that's its purest form. It's all tenderness and sweetness...and magic." She sighed indulgently when she saw in his eyes that he was skeptical.

She looped her arms around his neck and inclined her body against his.

"Remember this morning?" she asked.

"No," he said wryly. "My temperature goes to three hundred and six all the time. Why should I remember?"

"My point precisely." She cupped his head in her hands and brought it down to her. "I'm going to kiss you," she said, her lips so close to his they touched him as she formed her words. "And see if it doesn't haunt you with some of the same power. Maybe even more."

And then she did it—nothing more than a tender kiss, not particularly long, not particularly deep. But her hands held him with adoring tenderness, her lips, warm and dry, said a thousand silent things he hadn't heard when he'd made love to her. Her body simply leaned into his, like a flower into the wind, but he felt every gentle curve of it as though it had been a seductive caress.

He was afraid to touch her, afraid he didn't have this

slow and quiet sweetness in him. He felt it to the core of his being—a slowing of the forward thrust of his life, the turbocharge that propelled his career. The power of it startled him, and he knew without a doubt that it *would* haunt him.

He drew away before she did, just a little alarmed.

Charlotte saw the concern in his eyes and felt the smallest twinge…like the ache of a joint that predicts a storm.

"Come on." She looped her arm in his again and tugged him the rest of the way. "You can sit on the fainting couch while I find Kendra's stockings and gloves."

"The what?"

He stopped at the top of the stairs, fascinated by the endless array of wedding paraphernalia strewn about the big, open room. In one corner of the room was a desk cluttered with papers, fabric swatches, ribbons and dried flowers.

Charlotte went to it, repeating, "Fainting couch. That thing with the elbow," as she pointed to a brocade bench sort of thing with no back and one arm that curved over at a low angle. He couldn't imagine someone being comfortable in it.

He decided to look around instead. There were tables and cases all over the room that held shoes, gloves, garters, hats, jewelry, prayer books.

Hanging on hooks were ribbons in every shade of every color. In flat boxes were lengths of lace, everything from something that looked as if it had been spun in some fairyland to big, openwork lace strewn with beads.

He stopped at a rack of formal morning coats. Above it on a shelf was a top hat. He mentally scorned its formality, then, still a little drunk on Charlotte's lesson in romance, reached for it and tried it on.

Beside it on the shelf was a walking stick with an ivory head and he took that, too. Then he went in search of a mirror.

He found a gilded oval mirror over a shelf that held several silk flower bouquets and decided that he looked stupid. He gave the hat a tilt to the side. He now looked rakish and stupid.

Behind him, Charlotte felt her heart turn to sponge. The old silk top hat had turned a very modern man into a figure from the Victorian past. He held the lazy charm of the bon vivants of the period, but in his eye, under the raffish tilt of the hat, was the danger with which he loved to flirt. Charlotte found the qualities a deadly combination.

He reached up to remove the hat, but she stopped his hand from behind. She wrapped her arms around his and leaned her chin on his shoulder to study his reflection.

Derek saw the wistful, dreamy look in her eye and felt the same stab of nerves he'd felt on the stairs. But it would take a better man than he to resist a woman who looked at him as though he was what she'd waited for a lifetime.

"What is it, madam?" he asked in an affected British accent.

"It's your hat, sir," she replied in kind, smiling at his reflection. "You look very dapper."

He tucked the walking stick under his arm. "Of course. All we lords of the manor are dapper. I've just come from winning a fortune at the tables at...oh, that gambling place. What is it called? Black's!"

He saw her blink, quirk an eyebrow, then giggle. "You mean White's?"

"Whatever." He turned to catch her in his free arm and dip her backward. "I've won Paris from the French with a straight flush and they're turning it over to me tonight at Maxim's at midnight. Are you free to join me?"

She put the back of her hand to her forehead and swooned dramatically. "Maxim's? But I've nothing to wear."

"You may borrow my hat."

She laughed throatily and he leaned down to plant a kiss at the neckline of her dress.

Her eyes darkened instantly. He swept her up in his arms and carried her to the fainting couch, overwhelmed with a need to feel her in his arms with nothing between them.

Charlotte undressed him as he undressed her, then reached her arms up for him as he put her down at the base of the couch's arm. Her feet dangled over the end.

They came together explosively, out of time with the romantic atmosphere that pervaded Borrowed Magic. They climaxed together in minutes, in direct conflict with every moody little nuance in the flowered dress on the floor on one side of the couch, and the top hat and cane on the other.

Charlotte took pleasure in their passion, and the delicious abandon she'd never known until Derek made love to her. Any concern that remained from their kiss on the stairs was lost in his arms.

Now this was a love he could relate to, Derek thought as the fire inside him subsided but continued to flame, banked but still a formidable force. Love that didn't require thought or analysis, love that didn't have to be tempered or tamed, but could be given free rein to reach as high and as deep as love could go.

He felt satisfied and faintly smug.

Then Charlotte hitched her leg up against his, lifted her head off his shoulder so that his face was shielded by a canopy of hair the color of starlight. Her silver eyes went over his face, feature by feature, with a tenderness so touching he felt it physically.

And then it began again—that invasion of weakness, the paralysis of everything that had ever meant anything to him. All that was familiar was swamped by a need to simply hold her, to touch her as though she were glass— and he was beginning to think that indeed she might be. Every time he looked into her eyes, he saw himself reflected, as someone recognizable yet unfamiliar, some alter ego.

Charlotte caught that look again and this time the little ache began to throb like real pain. She pushed off him and reached for her clothes.

He tried to catch her arm but she evaded him.

"We have to get back," she said quietly. "I still have a million details to see to."

IT WAS OBVIOUS the moment Derek and Charlotte reached the Farnsworth gate that something was wrong. It gaped open, and the limo, Caleb's Cadillac and the Morreauxs' Mercedes were parked in a line on the lane just inside.

In the middle of the narrow road, everyone in the household was gathered, all talking at once. Briane, Denise and Pauline were crying.

"My father," Charlotte said, boosting herself up in the seat as Derek drove through the gate. She scanned the little crowd and couldn't find him. Had something happened to him? Is that why everyone seemed in such a dither? "I don't see my father!"

Derek reached a hand out to push her back in her seat. "He's on the other side of the Mercedes," Derek said. "There, with Trey."

Relief flooded Charlotte as she followed Derek's pointing finger and spotted her father, obviously arguing with Trey. Everyone turned as the Porsche pulled up beside the crowd.

"What is it?" Derek asked, moving to open his car door.

Caleb pushed it closed again. "Kendra's gone," he said briefly, tightly. "I need you to go to our place in Newport Beach. The rest of us are splitting up to check the mountain cabin, the tennis club, her friend Jackie in Santa Barbara."

Off to the side of the lane, Charlotte spotted Caroline with her arm around a very tense Elizabeth.

"Oh, God," Charlotte said, letting her head fall against the back of the seat. "I knew it. She misunderstood the other night."

"No." Edward came up beside Charlotte. He placed an arm around her shoulders. "Briane says Trey suggested to Kendra this morning that they postpone the wedding for a few days while he...thinks things over. She saw her leave in the Corvette about ten. She thought she'd just taken a drive to cool off."

"How do you know she hasn't?" Derek asked.

"A suitcase and a few changes of clothes are missing."

Caleb handed Derek the keys. "Call when you get there. Briane and Denise will stay here to take and relay calls. If Kendra isn't there, don't rush back. Take it easy. Spend the night. I don't want you two to be highway casualties."

Derek glanced at the clock on the dash. "I'll call you

the minute we arrive. An hour, an hour and a half at the most.''

"Drive carefully," Edward admonished.

"I should be the one to go to Newport," Trey said, joining the little cluster. "I'm sure that's where she's gone. That's where she always goes when she has to sort things out."

He looked pale and distraught, Charlotte thought. A part of her mind not concerned with Kendra's safety wondered if he'd looked anything like this when he'd left her standing at the church a year ago.

Caleb turned on him with uncharacteristic hostility. "If it weren't for your self-involvement, she wouldn't have to sort anything out. You'll stay here! One sight of you and she'll run in the other direction."

"But I…"

"Leave it, Prentiss," Edward said quietly. "Trust me that it's the smartest thing to do."

Trey turned, his face purple, his jaw set, and ran to the house.

Derek spun the little car in a tight circle and headed back down the lane.

"I *knew* this was going to happen," Charlotte said, feeling responsible. "I knew I should have tried to talk to her, but I didn't know what to say. I don't lie well, even when I'm trying to do it for someone else's benefit."

"I've seen evidence of that firsthand," Derek said, braking to a stop at the road and reaching out to pat her knee comfortingly. "Don't do this to yourself. It wasn't your fault."

"I'm sure she thinks it was."

Derek turned onto the road and picked up speed. "He

asked her to delay the wedding. He didn't show up for yours. How can she blame you?''

''She'll think I put him up to it. That I teased him into thinking he wanted me back.''

''Is that what he told you? That he wanted you back?''

At her nod, he rolled his eyes and shook his head.

She turned in her seat to ask in mild annoyance, ''You think that's unlikely? That once rid of me, a man wouldn't want me back? If so, how do you explain your own behavior?''

He smiled, unable to turn his attention from the traffic as he turned onto the main artery to the freeway.

''If I found any part of that scenario unlikely,'' he said, ''it would be the part about letting you go in the first place. In our case, I had to let you go professionally to have any chance of reaching a personal relationship.''

He sped into the traffic with impressive style and fit in neatly between a tour bus and a pickup filled with carpentry tools.

''But my reaction was for Prentiss's style.'' He shook his head over it once again. ''We have the same problem with him at the office. When told what to do, he performs very well. When left to his own devices, he can't decide which way to move because he's basically greedy. There's no gut instinct in him that makes him do one thing or the other because it feels right. He's guided strictly by being unwilling to forfeit anything while gaining as much as he can. I don't think there's a lot of hope for him. Your father puts up with him because he was about to become Caleb's son-in-law. It was only your pleas that your father not fire him after he left you at the altar that kept him on in the first place.''

''I didn't think being vengeful would help anything. He's being sent to London, isn't he?''

''The office is in good shape and it'll get him out of our hair.''

Charlotte thought about Derek's assessment of Trey's character and considered it in terms of her ex-fiancé's comparison of her and Kendra.

''He said Kendra was more beautiful than I,'' she said, ''but that she wasn't me.''

This time he did glance at her, his dark eyes running quickly over her face.

He laughed pityingly. ''Now I *know* there's no hope for him.''

Chapter Ten

It was dusk when they reached Newport Beach, a crowded shore community fronting a harbor dotted with islands and filled with pleasure boats. Charlotte lowered her window to gulp in the clean smell of the waterfront. She hoped it might revitalize her, help her think of the right thing to say if they did find Kendra.

As Derek guided the Porsche up the road onto the dune that supported the Farnsworths' glass-walled beach house, she strained in her seat to catch a glimpse of the driveway and Kendra's white Corvette.

They rounded a bend and the driveway appeared, landscaped on both sides with potted palms and boxed geraniums. There was no car.

"Her car could be in the garage," Derek said, reading her mind.

It wasn't. Derek unlocked the back door and went through the house to the garage off the kitchen. It was full of storage boxes, neatly labeled and stacked. A bicycle stood in a corner, and a surfboard leaned against the wall. But there was no car.

"She might have stopped along the way," Derek said.

"It's only an hour and a half drive," Charlotte said, guilt and distress overtaking her. She remembered in sharp detail what it was like to be hours from your wedding—though in her case it had been minutes—and discover that you weren't loved at all, that the wonderful relationship you believed you had was a source of terror for the other person. Realizing that she generated fear in someone had required more psychological adjustment on her part than being the object of pity and embarrassment.

Then she remembered the look on Derek's face when she'd kissed him on the stairs, then on the fainting couch after they'd made love. The crisis over Kendra had put it out of her mind temporarily, but now it returned to smolder inside her. In some way she couldn't understand, her tenderness had frightened him. She was suddenly very tired of men who were afraid of love.

She went back into the kitchen and searched the cupboards for coffee. Though she'd visited the Farnsworths' Bel Air home many times, she'd never been to the beach house before.

"What are you looking for?" Derek asked, leaning a shoulder against the doorway from the garage.

"Coffee," she replied coolly, succinctly.

He crossed the kitchen and opened a long narrow cupboard in the corner that held several shelves of staples. He handed her the coffee.

She wasn't surprised that he knew his way around the house. Caleb often hosted working weekends there, or mid-crisis retreats.

"Thank you," Charlotte said politely, then concentrated on filling the pot.

"How come we're not having tea?" He could guess why, at least superficially. She was in a coffee mood suddenly, edgy, anxious and, judging by the angry little V between her eyebrows, irritable.

"We'll have to stay awake to keep track of what's happening."

He reached into the cupboard for the coffee filters and gestured as though he were handing them to her. When she reached for them, he drew them back.

"What's happening with *you?*" he asked.

She looked at him blankly. "What do you mean?" she asked and reached for the filters again. He held them out of reach.

"I mean that you've had a sudden and severe change of mood. What's wrong?"

"I'm worried about Kendra," she said impatiently. "Aren't you?"

"A little," he replied, "but I'd be more worried about her if she'd married Trey tomorrow without knowing what he's really like. My guess is, she's around somewhere. She went into town for dinner." He studied her narrowly and frowned. "I have a suspicion that your change of mood has something to do with suddenly seeing this as my fault."

She didn't hasten to deny it, but simply held her hand out for the box of filters. "I think it would be best discussed over coffee."

Trouble. He handed over the box, both intrigued and concerned.

He took down cups, she poured and they sat on a deep window seat overlooking the black night and the softly rumbling black ocean. Far in the distance were the lights of what was probably a freighter.

"What are your intentions toward me?" she asked finally, stirring nondairy creamer into her coffee.

He balanced the cup on his bent knee and blinked. "Who am I talking to? You or your father?"

"My father thinks of you as the son he never had,"

Charlotte replied, forcing herself to be calm and logical despite a deep need to shout and possibly throttle him. "He'd never think to ask you. I'm just looking out for myself. I've been burned once, you know."

It took him only a moment to decide he didn't like her like this. This quiet, remote individual wasn't her. He suddenly missed the romantic who always looked just a little lost, like a woman out of time and place.

"I resent being mistaken for Trey Prentiss," he said. "I thought I'd made it clear I was nothing like him."

"You aren't," she agreed, taking a sip of coffee. She swallowed and leaned her head back against the deep window frame. "At least not visibly. But you do share something with him, don't you?"

"A company car on occasion."

She ignored his attempt at humor and said, "I'm talking about your assessment of him earlier today. You said he couldn't make decisions because he didn't want to forfeit anything while gaining everything he wanted."

He waited for her to explain. He recalled the remark, but he couldn't connect it with himself.

"When I kissed you on the stairs in my shop," she explained quietly, turning her head to look out the window as though she didn't want to look at him, "I frightened you."

"Charlie..."

"Don't try to deny it, Derek," she admonished quietly, finally leveling her gaze on him. It was grave and sad. "I know what fear looks like. I frightened Trey, too."

Derek put his cup down in a space between the cushions. It gave him time to think. He wouldn't lie, but he also couldn't explain to her what he didn't understand himself.

"Any man," he said candidly, "who denies feeling fear in the face of a relationship that addles his brain and weakens his defenses is a liar. And it isn't fear of you, it's fear of...love, I guess. Fear of not having that sweet stuff you seem to need."

She held his gaze and he saw a small glimmer of respect in her eyes. Then she lowered them, still cool, still remote.

She raised them again, and fixed him with what felt like a laser gaze. He knew he was in trouble.

"Then what is it you feel when we're in bed?" she asked conversationally. "You certainly show no fear there. What am I at that moment, if I'm not an addler of your brain or a threat to your defenses? A distraction? A toy? Just a little R and R for the brilliant young executive?"

Anger began to simmer inside him. "Have you ever felt like a toy in my arms?"

Their gazes locked. She finally put her cup down and folded her arms. "No, I haven't. But then I've discovered you're the consummate actor. You're never at a loss for the right move or the right line. I suppose this is all my fault for taking on my role too completely."

"What 'this' are you talking about?" he demanded. "To the best of my recollection, nothing has changed since we made love this afternoon, and you certainly didn't seem to feel as though you were being treated like anything less than the woman I love."

"I saw that look in your eyes again. Like when I kissed you on the stairs."

"Good God!" Derek sprang to his feet, what remained of his patience evaporating. "It seems to me you're missing an important point. If you're intent on comparing me with Trey, you might notice that I'm still around.''

He'd expected that to bring her up short, to make her look sheepish. When she held his gaze evenly, he began to wonder if they were speaking the same language.

''And what happens tomorrow, after the wedding? If there is a wedding.''

''What do you mean?''

''You've said nothing about continuing our relationship or about making it permanent. I think you're more afraid than you realize.''

Derek jammed his hands into his pockets and stalked away from her half the width of the room, then stalked back. He stopped in front of her and freed one hand to make a ''There! See!'' gesture.

''This is precisely why you don't belong in business, or maybe even in life. You assemble all available data and come to a completely erroneous conclusion.''

She looked implacably into the temper in his eyes. ''Then you were going to propose?''

''No, I wasn't,'' he replied brutally, ''because the kind of mess you had with Trey, and the kind of mess he and Kendra are now having, is what results when you try to write a contract around something as nebulous as feelings!''

''Really?'' She didn't change expression. ''Curious that it's worked for several thousand years.''

''No, it hasn't. The wedding contract is a relatively new refinement. And you call this working? A 50 percent divorce rate?''

''Marriages work beautifully when people believe in them!'' she said, standing, too. She was beginning to lose her grip on control.

''In the last century, when people followed tradition

without question. And that's the age you prefer—'' he pointed a finger at her shoulder ''—because it was a sweet, amenable time. Well, this isn't! We're a society more aware of our options. And it's simply foolish to write a contract around love. It isn't bankable.''

"Bankable?'' she shrieked, unable to believe he'd used the word. "Bankable!'' she repeated it to assure herself she'd heard it. "God, if that isn't the Cabot party line. If you can't put it in the bank and draw interest on it, it isn't worth having. Well, let me tell you something.''

She went to him, stopping within inches of his chest and straining pugnaciously up at him. "Here's a basic truth you've apparently never figured out. There are valuable things in life that *cost you.*'' She emphasized the last two words and spoke them slowly. "I know that's an alien concept for you, but it's true. They will never make you a calculable profit, because if you're lucky enough to acquire them, you have to give as much as you get. That may not be sound business, but it's life!

"And one more thing.'' She'd lowered her voice and, furious as he was, he found himself hanging on her every word. She was fascinating in a rage.

"Men and women of the last century were as aware of their options as we are. They just never considered cowardice one.''

She stormed away, leaving him alone in the middle of the dark living room.

"SHE WASN'T at the cabin or the club,'' Briane reported when Derek called the Farnsworth home. "We haven't heard from Santa Barbara yet. If she's not in Newport, that's our last hope.''

"We're hoping she just went out to dinner or something, and will be back,'' he said bracingly. He wasn't sure he believed it. In fact, he was convinced if Kendra were smart she was on a 747 right now getting as far away from Prentiss and her mother as she could.

''We'll call you if we hear anything,'' Briane said. ''Thanks, Derek.''

''Sure. I'll be in touch.''

''Any news?''

Derek looked up in surprise as he cradled the receiver. He hadn't seen hide nor hair of Charlotte in the hour since their altercation. He'd heard a door slam somewhere upstairs and thought it better not to investigate.

''No sign of her so far,'' he said. ''But they haven't heard from Santa Barbara yet.''

Charlotte stood on tiptoe to look into the freezer part of the refrigerator. She had shed her shoes, and her face had a red and puffy look, as though she'd slept—or cried.

''I've got a couple of frozen quiches in the oven,'' Derek said.

Charlotte closed the freezer door and turned to look at the stove for confirmation. There were twelve minutes left on the oven timer.

''Two for you,'' she asked wryly, looking through the cupboards, ''or is one of them mine? I thought I saw a can of asparagus in here.''

''They're both *yours*,'' he said, moving to reach into a high cupboard over the stove. ''You're the one who wants everything. Voilà.'' He handed her the asparagus.

''I don't want everything,'' she said reasonably. She'd come downstairs determined not to argue with him. She didn't want to upset what would probably be their last few hours together with anger and recriminations. ''I just can't see myself in a prolonged affair. But let's not fight about it. I'm going to magnanimously allow you one of the quiches, and half of the asparagus.''

''Thank you.''

''Don't mention it.''

''Charlie, this is nuts,'' he said, turning her away from the can opener and into his arms. ''You're imagining a problem that isn't there. We've had a wonderful few days. The rest of our lives could be as wonderful.''

She gently but firmly pushed his arms from around her. ''Not when I know you don't consider my feelings for you…bankable.''

''Maybe I don't doubt you. Maybe I doubt me.''

That seemed to shake her. She said gravely, ''Then that's even worse.''

''God, that's not what I meant!'' he said, feeling like a man on the edge of a limb he was sawing off himself. ''I meant that I've always moved too fast to slow down and think about things. It's not that my love for you isn't genuine and deep. It's that I can't imagine signing my name to a contract that's about what I feel. I've been in business long enough to know that even the most reliable numbers can turn on you.''

She pushed him gently into a chair. ''Then you have to do what you have to do. And so do I. Unfortunately that isn't going to be the same—'' she swallowed and finished a little shakily ''—the same thing.'' Then she drew a breath and went back to the asparagus.

He set the table while she served, and they sat at opposite sides of a small kitchen table and looked out at the darkness. They were silent, except to ask for the salt or the butter.

After they'd finished, Derek excused himself to take a shower. He desperately needed something to assuage his confusion and frustration. Had he made love to this woman only hours ago on a fainting couch in a Victorian loft caught on a time snag?

Charlotte made another pot of coffee, then straightened up the kitchen. She wandered out to the glass wall in the living room that looked out on the ocean and stared without seeing.

That had been close, she thought, trying to feel philosophical rather than sad. She'd almost found the right man, even though all indicators showed him to be the wrong one. He wasn't laid-back or romantic, but he made her feel very special, very right.

They could have coped with their different approaches to life, she was sure, if only he hadn't been frightened by the prospect. Well. She shook her head at her reflection. If she ever got interested in another man, she'd just have to learn to be less scary.

She reached over to turn off the light on the side table and, sliding the window aside, stepped out onto the patio. A brisk breeze blew filled with the fragrance of fall. A little chill rippled up her arms and she crossed them, tossing her hair back and out of her face.

And that was when she saw her. Moonlight shone in a bright wedge that started some distance offshore. Trapped in it, bobbing like a piece of flotsam, was a bright blond head.

''Kendra,'' she whispered to herself, then certain the figure was the missing bride, probably bent on self-destruction, she shouted as she ran to the door, ''Derek!'' she shouted. ''Kendra's in the water! Derek!''

Charlotte slipped and slid down the rocky trail to the sand. Then she ran for all she was worth, still shouting Kendra's name. The sand slowed her progress, and now on a level with the water, she'd lost sight of the figure in it.

Finally at the water's edge, she kicked off her shoes and ran into the surf. It was shockingly cold. She dove forward, lost her breath in a gasp, then swallowed a mouthful of water.

She swam powerfully but awkwardly, fear making her strokes uneven. If Kendra succeeded in killing herself, she, Charlotte, would kill Trey personally—slowly.

"Kendra!" she shouted again. "Kendra!"

A fair distance out, she stopped to tread water, hoping to spot Kendra somewhere ahead of her. But she saw nothing. A cloud had slid over the moon, and her eyes caught nothing in the direction of the ocean but absolute blackness. She turned in a circle, panic making her already labored breathing come even harder.

"Oh, Kendra," she groaned.

Behind her she saw Derek run into the water and start toward her with firm, even strokes. She started forward again, unwilling to believe Kendra had accomplished her task.

Then something rose out of the water just ahead of her. She screamed as water spewed like a fountain, then rained down on her. Images of Bitsy Tate's column carrying her gleeful obituary passed before her eyes— Once-dumped Society Woman Serves As Payback For The Sushi Craze As Shark Eats Her Raw.

"*What* are you shouting about," Kendra demanded, "and *what* are you doing here?"

Charlotte discovered that surprise was buoyant. She bobbed in the water as she stared at the shadowy features of the young woman who'd become her friend in the days they'd worked together.

Kendra appeared to be fine. Water spiked her eyelashes and made her wet hair lay back against her scalp.

The moon reappeared, highlighting her beautiful bone structure.

"I thought you were…" Charlotte, now feeling foolish, pointed out to sea. "I mean, it looked as though you might be…"

Kendra frowned, then rolled her eyes as she realized what Charlotte couldn't say. "Oh, Charlie," she scolded. "I'm mad as hell, but I am not suicidal."

Charlotte sagged with relief and swallowed another mouthful of water. Kendra held her up.

"Your parents were frantic," Charlotte said sharply. "Briane saw you tear off in the Corvette after you argued with Trey, and everyone at the house split up to try to find you. Your father sent Derek and me here."

Derek reached them, spraying them with water again as he splashed to a stop beside them. "Are you all right?" he demanded of Kendra.

"Fine," she assured him, wiping water from her face. "I just needed to get away from everyone and decide what to do. I'm amazed that didn't occur to anyone."

"You were gone a long time," Charlotte said righteously. "And the circumstances made everyone presume the worst."

"Let's talk about this on solid ground," Derek said. He pushed them gently ahead of him toward shore.

"YOU SHOULD HAVE left a note, or called when you got here." Charlotte wasn't sure why, but she'd appointed herself maiden aunt in charge of scolding.

They all sat around the Swedish fireplace in the living room, wrapped in thick robes and sipping cognac. The furniture was low, the decor white and stark. Charlotte couldn't dispel the feeling that she was in an alien environment.

"I was too angry to leave a note," Kendra said calmly, "and I didn't get here until fifteen or twenty minutes ago."

Derek frowned. "Where's your car?"

"Ran out of gas," she confessed in self-deprecation. "I didn't even check the tank when I left the house, and I drove all over the place, trying to cool off. I stopped for a cappuccino in town and sat on the sand for a long time. Then I headed here and ran out of gas about a quarter of a mile down the beach."

She downed the last of her brandy and put her snifter aside, looking suddenly tired and a little shaken. "I walked here…"

"In the dark?" Charlotte asked with disapproval.

Kendra ignored her and went on. "And all I wanted to do before I came inside was go for a swim. I thought it might loosen me up, clear my head…" She drew her knees up and rested her chin on them. Her voice became unsteady. "Make me believe it was all a bad dream."

Charlotte, sitting beside her on the floor, reached out to put an arm around her. "I'm sorry," she said. "Contrary to how this platitude usually sounds, I know just how you feel."

Kendra sniffed and raised her head to give Charlotte a grim smile. "You know, I remember how you looked that day when you came into the church to tell us that Trey wasn't coming. At first I thought you were silly to have done it. I know your father would have if you'd asked him. Or Caroline. Now I know how brave you were. And maybe even why you did it. You had to prove to yourself that you had guts even if he hadn't any."

"What are you going to do?" Derek asked.

"I don't know." Kendra wrapped her arms around her

legs and looked into the fire, her face flushed, her eyes unfocused.

"I've been thinking about going to Europe."

Charlotte sighed. "I'd love to have time for that. I think you should go for it."

"I've always thought I'd pursue my painting one day, but I've never mustered the ambition. Maybe now I'll do it."

She dropped her knees to sit Indian-style and continued to stare at the fire. "I'll live in a garret like the romantic image...." She turned to smile wanly at Derek, then at Charlotte. "But my monthly allowance will save me from romantic starvation." Her smile crumpled almost immediately and she began to cry. "I love him— the jerk!"

Charlotte helped her up to bed.

"I know you don't believe this now," she said, helping her turn down the bed, "but you'll get over him."

Kendra nodded, still crying quietly. "I think the problem is, he never got over *you*."

Charlotte straightened, coming around the bed to push Kendra into a sitting position and sit beside her.

"This has nothing to do with me," she said firmly. "He loves being in love, but he's afraid of promising anything more, so he keeps backing out. In this case, he had to find a convenient excuse to do it."

Kendra looked at her evenly. "He did try to come on to you that night in my father's study, didn't he?"

Charlotte nodded. "But it isn't because he loves me. It was because he was unconsciously setting himself up to let you down."

Kendra kicked a foot out angrily.

"I ought to drug him and drag him through the ceremony, anyway, and then make his life as miserable as he seems to think I would.''

Charlotte laughed softly. ''That does have a certain appeal. I think it's illegal, though. Europe sounds like a much more positive solution to me. Why don't you get some sleep? We'll have to be up early in the morning.''

''I know,'' she said. She looked at Charlotte, her eyes miserable. ''I hope I can be as composed as you were.''

''The minute I was finished,'' Charlotte said, ''I drove home and threw everything glass in the house into the fireplace. It was very satisfying.''

Kendra climbed under the blanket and Charlotte pulled it up over her, then turned off the light.

Charlotte stopped at the door and turned to the figure now huddled in the fetal position under the blue-and-white quilt. ''Try to think of it as a fresh start. As the first day of your career as an artist.''

''Yeah,'' Kendra said, her voice containing little enthusiasm. ''Right. Good night, Charlie.''

Charlotte went back downstairs to clean up the kitchen and found that Derek had already done it.

''How is she?'' he asked. He had changed out of the robe into jeans and a white T-shirt. He sat on the window seat in the living room, one knee drawn up, the other foot braced on the carpet while he sipped another cognac. The room was lit only by the glow from the fireplace.

Charlotte stopped halfway into the room, afraid to go any farther. She felt the pull of his attraction for her, the draw of his touch, and knew it was smarter to keep her distance.

''Tired, sad. But I'm sure she'll recover.''

Derek felt the gap between them, and knew it was wider than the space that physically separated them. Annoyed that she could be cool when he felt like raging, he said, "It wasn't very smart of you to run into the water in the dark."

That would ignite a reaction, he was sure.

She looked back at him for several seconds, her slender body lost in the voluminous folds of the robe. But there'd never been anything slender about her dignity. The duchess was back.

"I considered waiting for daylight," she replied calmly, "but I wasn't sure she could hold her breath for seven and a half hours."

Temper erupted in him, hot and quick. He swung his legs off the window seat and stood. "You had shouted for me. You could have waited two minutes!"

"If she *had* been drowning," Charlotte said, gripping control with both hands, "she could have been dead in two minutes!"

"And so could you! That would have helped her a lot!"

"It would have helped you!" she shouted at him. "My life insurance is more 'bankable' than my love. And you've got everyone convinced you're my husband. You might have been able to collect."

He grabbed the lapels of her robe before he could think twice about it and yanked her toward him.

Charlotte saw the fury in his eyes and couldn't begin to guess what would happen next. There was violence in his eyes and in his grip.

Only conditioning by a father who'd taught him to respect women, and a personal code that prevented him from hurting anyone or anything that wasn't at least as strong as he, prevented him from giving her the swat that remark deserved.

Still, he couldn't deny that he enjoyed the trepidation in her eyes just a little bit.

"You're going to pay for that, Charlotte," he said with quiet menace as he reached inside her robe.

Her hands closed on his forearms, but she couldn't stop him from cupping one hand on her hip and splaying the other against her back.

"Derek Cabot, if you dare…" she began to threaten.

"Charlie, shut up," he said, and held her immobile against him while he leaned over and kissed her. It occurred to him that he was punishing himself far more than he was hurting her, but he was driven to do it all the same.

She wriggled and struggled, and the intimate contact seemed to rob the anger from him and turn it into longing. The longing gentled his touch—and gentled her.

Then her arms were wrapped around his neck and she was kissing him as though the great gap had never opened between them. It was two days ago in the bathtub, this afternoon in the Victorian loft.

The phone rang, loud and shrilly. Derek didn't hear it for a moment, then it rang again and he felt Charlotte pushing at him.

He knew the moment he raised his head that the interruption had brought her quickly back to awareness. Her lavender-gray eyes accused him of more things than he could decipher at a glance.

The phone rang again, and he thought wryly that it was like a safety signal. Great yawning cavity, it said. Don't fall in.

Keeping a hold on Charlotte's hand, he pulled her with him into the kitchen to the wall phone. She slapped at his arm and pried at his fingers, but he held on.

It was Trey.

"I want to speak to Kendra," he said urgently.

Added to Trey's already long list of sins, destroying that fragile moment with Charlotte was going to get him murdered.

"Kendra is asleep," Derek said in a forbidding tone.

"I don't believe it," Trey said after a moment. "She just spoke to her father half an hour ago."

"That was half an hour ago," Derek replied with sorely strained patience. "Now she's asleep."

"I have to talk to her."

"It'll wait until morning."

"I have to talk to her *now*."

Derek held the phone to his chest and consulted Charlotte, who had stopped struggling.

"It's Trey," he said quietly. "He wants to talk to Kendra. He says it can't wait until morning."

She snatched the phone from him. "She's asleep after almost drowning, thanks to you!" She avoided Derek's gaze when his dark eyebrow rose to note the fib. "If you call here again before morning we won't even bring her home. We'll take her straight to the airport."

"The airport? No! Charlie, wait! I…"

She slammed the receiver with relish. Then yanked out of Derek's grip. She gave him a thoughtful, strangely satisfied little smile. "I might even join her. Good night, Cabot. Sleep tight."

Chapter Eleven

The florist was draping the iron gate with a garland of white roses interspersed with baby's breath when Derek turned the Porsche onto the Farnsworth estate.

They were halfway up the lane when everyone streamed from the house to greet them, Bitsy in the spearhead, Darby already snapping photographs.

"I'll take you around the back," Derek said, "and we'll go in through the garages."

"No, it's all right." Kendra smoothed her hair back and drew a deep breath. In the only slightly mussy white cotton pants and shirt she'd worn the day before, she appeared remarkably serene. Her hair was caught back in a loose knot, and she appeared to be precisely what she was—the product of a long line of blue blood.

"What did you tell yourself," she asked Charlotte when Derek was forced to slow the car as the Farnsworth household swarmed around it, "when you faced the church filled with people."

"That the problem was Trey's and not mine," she replied. "I was just the one who had to deal with it."

"That's good." Kendra patted her hand, then opened the car door.

Darby's camera clicked as Elizabeth enfolded Kendra

in her arms, her aquiline profile marred just for an instant with a rush of emotion. Then Elizabeth pulled herself together and held Kendra at arm's length.

"Are you all right?" she demanded quietly.

"I'm fine," Kendra replied.

Caleb came forward to take her into his arms. "Ah, Kennie," he said gruffly. "We were so worried about you."

"I'm fine, Daddy." She kissed his cheek. "I needed a little time alone to decide what to do."

"Kendra. Kendra!" Trey broke through the little crowd, fighting off Babs's grip as she tried to pull him back. "Kendra, please."

He broke free of Babs, then had to contend with Caleb, who turned to block Trey's path to his daughter.

"Daddy, it's all right," Kendra said, gently pushing her father aside and confronting Trey with a look so dispassionate Charlotte had to admire it. "What is it, Trey? I thought you were going away."

Charlotte saw the lost look in his eyes. The Kendra who'd come home was not the Kendra he knew.

"I'd like to talk to you," he said, glancing furtively at the group gathered around them. "Somewhere where we can be alone for a few minutes."

"Of course," she said. But there was condescension in her tone, not cooperation.

Bitsy, who had apparently missed the subtlety, asked, "Then the wedding's on?"

Kendra smiled her way as the crowd opened a path for her. "No, it's not. I'm leaving for Europe on an evening flight."

Trey, who'd fallen into step behind her, stopped in his tracks. She took a step back to hook her arm in his and pull him along. "Come on. We'll take a walk."

Bitsy came to stand beside Charlotte as everyone watched Trey and Kendra walk away.

"She wouldn't!" Elizabeth said on a low gasp, then turned to Caleb with a look of horror. "I finally have Trey talked around and she says she's going to Europe?"

Caleb studied her mutely for a moment, then asked quietly, "You did what?"

But the rest of their conversation was lost when Bitsy elbowed Charlotte. "Want to tell me what happened?"

Charlotte felt unutterably weary suddenly and wanted nothing more than to sit in the guest house living room with a cup of tea and go over the next months' schedule in her day timer.

"You'll have to ask Kendra that," she replied.

"She's planning to go to Europe?"

"Could be."

"But Trey's changed his mind."

"No news there, Bitsy. Trey's always changing his mind."

Edward and Caroline joined them, Edward putting his arm around Charlotte and kissing her temple. "How are you, sweets? I thought you sounded a little grim last night on the phone."

Grim? Yes. That was a good word. She forced a smile for him. "I know what Kendra's going through. I wish I could do more for her."

Caroline linked her arm in Derek's and smiled up at him with sympathy. "And how are you holding up in the midst of all this chaos? This isn't comfortable ground for a man who likes order and efficiency."

He shrugged negligently, glancing at Charlotte with turbulent brown eyes. "Charlie's converting me."

Caroline studied the look that passed between Derek

and her stepdaughter, then met her husband's quick surreptitious glance with one of concern.

"You know..." Bitsy said. Everyone turned to look at her, surprised she was still there. "If you two can't answer my questions about Kendra, maybe there's something else you can tell me."

Charlotte felt danger in her bones. Here it comes, she told herself, feeling the finger of trepidation hit every vertebra from the base of her skull to the small of her back.

Derek's arm came around her, surprisingly comfortable under the circumstances.

"What is it?" he asked affably.

"You said you were married during a recent business trip."

Charlotte felt that strum up her spinal column one more time.

"That's right," Derek replied.

Bitsy uttered a little laugh of confusion. In truth, she didn't look confused at all. She looked curiously pleased. "Well, I don't understand. I know you spent two days in San Francisco two weeks ago, and a weekend in Denver last week."

"Yes."

"Well..." That little laugh again. "It's the most curious thing. I can't find a health certificate or a marriage license registered in either county. How do you explain that?"

By telling you we're frauds, Charlotte replied to herself in a sort of repressed panic. *By admitting that Caroline, with all good intentions, placed us in this impossible position where we could do nothing but lie and deceive and humiliate everyone involved.*

She felt an hysterical giggle try to rise in her throat.

She cleared it and folded her arms in an attempt to stave it off.

Unfortunately for me, I've fallen victim to my own best performance. I'm in love with this man who rushed to my rescue, then panicked when I turned into his arms. There's an interesting parallel between Trey and Kendra and Derek and me if you were...

Charlotte's thoughts and the reply Derek had begun were interrupted by Caleb's booming voice.

"Good God, woman! I know you're expecting hundreds of people in just four hours, but the girl's had a traumatic experience. For once in your life, think about something besides yourself and how *you* will look. If she takes him back, I would say she needs psychiatric counseling, but we will have a wedding. If she doesn't, we'll send her with Henry to the airport and host a party to celebrate her good sense."

"Caleb Farnsworth!" Elizabeth gasped, her cheeks Chianti red. "What do you think...?"

"I'll tell you what I think!" he said, taking hold of her elbow and pulling her with him toward the house. "I've been itching to tell you what's been on my mind for thirty years. You're going to hear it now, Elizabeth— at high volume!"

Everyone watched in amazement as the usually gentle giant turned hostile husband and marched Elizabeth into the house. As the Morreauxs and Derek exchanged amused glances, Bitsy turned from the scene to smile broadly.

"God. This is turning into the story of a lifetime."

Caroline returned her smile with one filled with sarcasm. "I'm happy for you. Excuse us."

"Just a minute." Bitsy caught Derek's arm to stop

him from following Edward and Caroline. "You haven't answered my question."

Oh, God. Charlotte had thought for a moment there they were going to escape. The arm Derek had around her tightened as he felt her fidget.

"You didn't find a health certificate or a wedding license in Denver or San Francisco," he said, "because we were married in Massachusetts."

She frowned. "That wasn't on your schedule."

"It came up suddenly." He squeezed Charlotte to him. "We took advantage of it. Excuse us. We haven't had much sleep, and whatever happens this afternoon I'd like to be awake for it."

Derek led Charlotte to the path to the guest house and beckoned to her parents to follow. They clustered in the small living room, looking at one another in concern.

"She knows," Charlotte said, pacing a small path from the mirrored wall to the door. "I know she knows."

"She's not sure of anything," Derek said. "She'd like us to be lying, but she's not sure."

Charlotte stopped to look at him, a frail hope in her eyes. "Did you really go to Massachusetts in the past two weeks?"

He shook his head, grinning. He leaned an elbow against the high back of Caroline's chair. "No. But I wasn't specific about where we were married. She'll have to check every county before she knows for certain. By then this will all be over, one way or another."

Edward nodded from a corner of the sofa. "The important thing is not to panic. Caleb's been through a lot in the past two days. He doesn't need further embarrassment."

"So, please don't let down now, darling," Caroline

said from the chair opposite the sofa. "Keep up the pretense a little while longer, then you may berate me all you like when the wedding's over—or whatever happens."

Charlotte sank onto the sofa and let her head fall against the back. It was only ten in the morning, but she felt as though she could sleep for days. Lying was so exhausting.

She heard the silence pulse for several seconds, then her father's rumbling voice asked, "Unless pretending will be more of a problem today than it's been the past few days. You two have…a spat?"

Charlotte didn't even open her eyes. She didn't want to see the look in Derek's. A spat, indeed. "How do you do that?" she asked her father.

"I can read you like an annual report," Edward replied. "And Derek and I have a kind of mind link that happens to people who work closely for a long time. I know something's suddenly wrong between you."

Charlotte opened her eyes then to look at her father. He was so sharp, so cool. She gave a moment's serious thought to asking Derek and Caroline to leave, then climbing into her father's lap and telling him everything.

But she'd coped a year ago; she could cope today.

She made herself look at Derek. He seemed to have slipped into the mood he'd been in the morning she'd awakened him with kisses when Elizabeth and Bitsy had been at the door. His dark eyes were calm and remote.

"I can act like a devoted wife," she said, wanting to shake him out of that calm. "I was getting so into it, I almost believed it myself."

Derek heard the jibe and took it without complaint. He wasn't going to get into a battle of witty double entendres. His wit had fled, and he suddenly didn't understand anything.

"Piece of cake," he said.

Edward looked from one to the other. Caroline drew in a breath to ask a question and he silenced her with a look. Then he stood and helped her to her feet.

"As long as no one does anything radical out of a misguided sense of conscience or...anything else."

"I'm never radical," Derek assured him.

He gave him a masculine glance. "It's not you I'm worried about. Come along, Caro."

"But, Edward, I..." She gestured toward the sofa where Charlotte still sat in a disconsolate slump.

He tugged her relentlessly toward the door. "It isn't your business, my love. See you two later."

"She's been my business since the day I married you," she insisted mildly as he pushed her before him through the open door.

"You've passed the torch, Caroline."

"I have? I don't remember pa—"

Their voices trailed away as the door closed behind them. Derek locked it.

"Want a cup of tea?" he asked, heading for the kitchen.

"I'd kill for a cup of tea," Charlotte replied wearily.

He didn't even smile. "I know you'd love the opportunity to do murder, but it isn't necessary. I'll bring it."

Charlotte closed her eyes and listened to the very domestic sounds of him puttering around the kitchen. Unbidden, memories of their argument of the night before played over in her mind.

She cringed a little at her vitriolic turn of mood when they discovered Kendra wasn't at the house. Why had she turned on him like that? Certainly there was a difference between a man who admitted to feeling fear, and another who acted on it.

That kind of angry judgment was unlike her. Though Trey had hurt and humiliated her, she'd been able to be civil to him and chalk it all up to experience.

Derek she had flayed with condemnation.

She heard the kettle whistle and sat up and smoothed her hair. There was still a serious problem here, but an apology on her part was definitely in order.

Derek walked in with the cup, placed it in front of her without the twitch of a muscle in his face.

"If you're comfortable there," he said, "I'm going to sack out on the bed for an hour or so."

"Derek, I..." He straightened and met her gaze, his eyes completely blank of feeling of any kind. It occurred to her that she'd killed it. Misery as well as guilt settled in her stomach like bad doughnuts. He would probably not even hear an apology at the moment, much less accept one. "Sure," she said. "Go ahead. Thanks for the tea."

He closed the bedroom door quietly behind him. She sipped the steaming brew, a salty, solitary tear falling into it.

A SENSE OF WAITING pervaded everything. The broad back lawn that had teemed with activity while tents were set up, tables and chairs brought in, garden gatelike trellises arranged to give the vastness a definition, was now quiet. People still worked, because no one was certain yet of the ultimate outcome, but the cheer a festive wedding brought was gone.

Stepping out onto the guest house's little porch with her tea, Charlotte spotted Briane and Denise wandering among the workers, their extravagant good looks making them look like actresses hired for a play that had been canceled.

She hurried out to intercept them.

"Any news?" she asked.

Briane shook her head. "They're still talking."

Denise smiled wryly and pointed to one of the workers. He was particularly tall with well-defined pecs and slightly long dark hair. "If Kendra does call the whole thing off," she said, "I'm considering marrying him just so all this isn't wasted."

Charlotte walked with them across the rich green turf. It took an army of gardeners, she knew, to keep the grass this lush and green in the semitropical southern California climate.

Briane sighed. "I know it would be embarrassing for the family, but I hope she does go to Europe."

"She claims to still love Trey," Charlotte said.

Briane stepped into one of the garden arches and pulled the other two in after her, as though believing the wide openwork would afford them privacy.

"I would never tell her this," she said, her green eyes distressed. Her glance darted to Denise, whom she obviously had told. Denise shook her head in disgust. "But I overheard Mrs. Farnsworth talking to Trey late yesterday afternoon."

The warm morning air was still as Charlotte waited, a sense of foreboding taking over her already troubled spirit.

"Trey changed his mind because she offered him money. Big money."

"But he has money," Charlotte said.

"I'm talking high seven figures that he wouldn't have to share with four other siblings."

Charlotte digested that information while trying to decide what to do. Elizabeth had literally bought Trey for Kendra. Every instinct insisted that Kendra should know that.

"I think Briane should tell her," Denise said quietly, "but she's afraid whatever Kendra decides it would only hurt her more. Imagine your mother choosing to buy a man who no longer wants you, rather than suffer a few hours embarrassment."

Charlotte smiled thinly as she thought of Caroline, who'd had to be refrained from hiring a hit man for Trey when he'd done this same thing to Charlotte.

"No, I can't. Well. We'll just have to wait and see what she decides to do."

"Right."

Briane placed an arm around Charlotte and squeezed her shoulders. "See how lucky you were to have escaped Trey Prentiss and found your gorgeous husband?"

It wasn't difficult to dredge up a smile. Gallows humor could be powerful stuff.

"Wasn't I? I'd better get back to him. If you hear anything, let me know."

"I will." Briane looked at her watch and frowned. "It's already after eleven."

Denise added unnecessarily, "The invitations say two."

Charlotte walked back to the guest house with determination in her step. If Derek was sleeping, she intended to wake him up. She had to know how he truly felt. And she had to tell him how she felt—that she loved him more than anything.

As that thought formed in her mind, she was reminded of two days earlier when they'd first admitted love to each other. She remembered telling him angrily that she didn't intend to surrender to it. She realized now that she'd felt that way because *she'd* been afraid.

Was this the famous transference psychologists talked about, attributing your own unsatisfactory qualities to someone else?

She burst through the front door, marched across the living room and into the bedroom—to find it empty, the bed made. She went to the closet.

Loss overwhelmed her as her eyes fell on her own things—skirts, slacks, sweaters. His sport coats were gone, the colorful array of sweaters on the shelf. His shaving bag was gone from the bathroom.

She ran for the door, intent on finding him before he got away. She hadn't been gone that long and he wouldn't leave without speaking to his host and hostess, without talking to her father. She told herself bracingly that if she hurried, she could intercept him at the garages.

She tore the door open.

"Hi." Kendra stood there, still in her whites. The knot at the back of her hair was disheveled, and it looked as though her composure was, too. "Do you have time…to talk?" she asked.

No! she wanted to scream. *I don't have time. For the first time in my life I want to hurry before Derek gets away!*

But she knew the look on Kendra's face. She'd worn it herself a year ago—a hurt so deep, a self-esteem so low, logical thought simply could not function. The anguish had to be poured out to someone. Caroline had listened to her for hours.

"Of course," she said, drawing Kendra inside.

In her mind's eye, she saw Henry hand over the keys to the Porsche, saw Derek climb into it without opening

the door, back unerringly out of the garage, give Henry
a wave and turn in a tight circle, then drive away.

DEREK WAS LOOKING for anyone he recognized, but all
he encountered were the florist's staff, the caterers, the
men from the rental company that was providing the
tents, the tables and chairs. He'd tried every room downstairs including Caleb's study, and now peered around a
corner of the kitchen that was filled with the caterers'
crew.

Then he saw Babs, sitting at the butcher-block table
in the corner, sipping moodily at a jigger of something
clear. She spotted him and beckoned him over.

"Cabot," she said, her eyes perfectly sober, though
sad. "How are ya? Ever get that pretty girl to remember
she was married to you?"

He slipped into the captain's chair opposite her.
"Only once in a while. She has a selective memory."

She nodded. "Don't we all." She pointed in the direction of the caterers arranging food on trays, sliding
pans into the oven, scurrying back and forth across the
large room. "There was a time when all the women in
the family got together to do this for the bride. Not
strangers that had to be paid."

Derek nodded. He remembered his cousin's wedding.
His mother had baked for days, and she and his aunts
had met every afternoon for weeks to make her a quilt.
But he had other things on his mind at the moment to
spare too much emotion for the sad loss of the... His
mind groped for the word. Resisted the one that came
to mind. Groped again, then finally had to surrender and
settle for the only one that properly applied. Without
Charlotte, he felt a sad loss of the *romance* of things.

He suddenly realized that Babs's problems and his own might be more allied than he'd thought.

"I'm looking for Caleb," he said. "Do you know where he is? Or Edward?"

She took another small sip from her jigger. She held it up to him. "Want me to pour you one? Best medicine God ever made."

Derek shook his head. "Thanks."

Babs pointed her index finger to the ceiling. "Caleb and Elizabeth are screaming at each other in their bedroom, and I think your father-in-law is on a long-distance call. He walked outside with the portable phone."

Derek frowned and made himself relax in his chair. It didn't sound as though either man could be interrupted at the moment. He'd intended to thank Caleb for his hospitality, try to explain briefly to Edward what had gone on between him and his daughter and assure him that he hadn't hurt her deliberately, that the brief amity they'd achieved was over and the best thing he could do for both of them was take off the moment the wedding was over—or Kendra left for the airport, whichever resulted. Maybe he could be transferred back to New York. Maybe he could give Kendra and Charlotte the two tickets to Paris.

"You look like you've been hit in the stomach with a brick," Babs diagnosed. "Having more trouble with Charlotte than her remembering your name?"

He looked into the bright, wise eyes and found it easy to be honest. "Yes. Sometimes the way she makes me feel frightens me because...it's so different from anything I've ever felt before. And *that* frightens her. She thinks it means I'm like Prentiss. That I'd walk away from her one day.''

''But you married her,'' she said frowning. ''You promised to stay with her. Doesn't that tell her something?''

That was as far as he could go. He wished now he'd said yes to the drink. ''Guess not,'' he said.

Babs shook her head over the state of modern marriages. ''I think the trouble is, your generation got so into thinking about yourselves. That's good in a way. Supposed to cause less guilt, less anger. But it takes away the need to share.''

She smiled thoughtfully, memories traveling through her unfocused gaze. ''Elizabeth's father and I raised sheep. Rough life. Hard work. Lizzy doesn't like to remember that. Thinks it's dirty somehow. But it was more real than this. We loved each other, leaned on each other, took from each other and gave each other everything we had.''

She touched the bowl that sat before her on the table, the one that contained the sourdough starter she'd brought all the way from Montana, and that would *not* be used for the wedding.

''It's like this starter. You add and you take away and it goes on forever.'' She folded her arms and smiled across the table at him. ''With the new ideas about separate but equal, and your life and my life, side by side but not interfering with each other's, you never really learn what life is all about.

''In a good marriage, you borrow from each other your whole life long. If you're well matched, you've got what the other hasn't, and your partner's got what you need.'' She smiled again, a real smile that came from intimate knowledge of her subject. ''But you got to know what to do with it. You got to get it all mixed up together, you got to not hold back, and not count turns, and you know what? It'll rise for you and grow like you wouldn't believe.''

Could it be that simple?

Derek shifted in his chair. "I move fast. She likes to stop and examine every little thing. When I do that with her..." He hesitated, frustrated with the difficulty of explaining how it felt. "I get caught in the softness," he finally blurted. "I'm not sure I can ever be that way."

Babs nodded as though she understood. "I know. But you gotta give to get. It's a law of nature. Unless you're Trey Prentiss...." She made a face that told him what she thought. "And I can't think of one thing about him that's preferable to taking a chance."

Derek looked back at her, feeling a little as though he'd climbed the Himalayas and consulted the resident wiseman—or wisewoman.

He stood, leaned over her and kissed her cheek. He had a legendary reputation as a chance taker. Now was the time to live the legend.

"Thank you, Babs," he said.

She winked at him. "Sure. Hey, and if it doesn't work out, let me know. I've been looking for a younger man."

Chapter Twelve

"I don't know what to do," Kendra said, curled up in the guest house's rocking chair. "I've never had to consider anyone but myself before. I want to do the right thing."

Charlotte, holding the information Briane had learned, made herself sit quietly and listen.

"But…" Kendra sighed. "I don't know what that is."

When Charlotte offered no advice, Kendra glanced at her watch and gave her a grim smile. "Could you offer a pearl of wisdom, please? In just under an hour this place is going to be overrun with people expecting to attend a wedding." Her smile widened. "Remember what that's like?"

Charlotte laughed softly, unable to believe that just a matter of days ago the memory of her thwarted wedding still had the ability to hurt her. Had life changed that much in the past five days? Or had she changed.

"What's in your heart?" Charlotte asked. "What does instinct say?"

"Run as far away from this as you can get," Kendra replied instantly. "I just don't know if that's a healthy sense of self-preservation talking, or selfishness. Trey has hurt and embarrassed me, so it would be satisfying to show him that I can just walk away and make *him* look silly. It's tempting, but it's small. I want to be big in spirit. Like you are."

Charlotte blinked. "Excuse me? Big in spirit? Me? I was just going to vote for your plan to leave *him* at the altar."

Kendra smiled, then grew serious. "You are big. You built your own business. You came to help me even though I was engaged to the man who left you at the altar. You went above and beyond the call of duty with every little detail. You even interrupted your *honeymoon* to…"

"Stop!" Charlotte said, unable to bear another moment. When Kendra complied, wide-eyed at her unexpected shout, she added more quietly, "Stop, Kendra. That isn't true."

"It most certainly…"

"The part about my honeymoon." She sighed and let the burden slide off her shoulders. "Derek and I aren't married."

For a moment, the atmosphere inside the little guest house, as well as outside in the gardens, seemed to be absolutely still. There wasn't a sound or a movement.

Then Kendra asked quietly, "You're not? I don't understand."

Charlotte reminded her of the afternoon of her shower. "You know how our mothers have always…sort of…competed?"

Kendra nodded. "If that's what it's called."

"Caroline thought your mother was needling me because you had my old fiancé and I was still a single woman with nothing going for me, to her way of thinking. I think she's always disliked me."

Kendra frowned but didn't deny it. "I used to wonder

about that. I think it's because you've always had more
potential than I did. All I could do was look good in my
clothes and sketch things. You were smarter and more
serene. She resented you for it.''

Charlotte shook her head over the injustice of a talent
denied. ''You have all the potential in the world. She
just tried to make you another her rather than who you
are. Anyway.'' She dismissed the philosophy with a
wave of her hand. ''Caroline came to my rescue with
this announcement that I *was* married, supposedly to
save me embarrassment.'' She laughed resignedly. ''I
can't tell you the trouble it's caused. So. If I am big, it's
as a liar.''

Kendra suddenly looked more interested in Charlotte's problem than her own. ''You mean you and Derek have been sharing this guest house and you're
not...?''

''No.''

Kendra surprised her by laughing. ''Well, that's
hardly shocking in this day and age. But I can't imagine
living in close contact with a gorgeous hunk like that
and coming out with my libido intact.''

Charlotte glanced at her, then snatched the throw pillow beside her and became interested in the ruffle surrounding it. ''It isn't,'' she admitted. ''I fell in love with
him.''

Kendra frowned in puzzlement. ''That's good, isn't
it?''

''No.'' Charlotte played with the decorative stitching.
''I blew it. Things got serious, he got this frightened look
in his eye, and I climbed all over him for it and told him
it was over because it reminded me of Trey.''

''Where is he?''

''His things are gone. I imagine he is, too.''

''Charlie.'' Kendra disentangled herself from the chair and went to sit beside her. ''You sound like you want him back. Shouldn't you be going after him?''

She swallowed a pointed lump in her throat and shook her head. ''No. I'm beginning to believe I'm just supposed to plan weddings, not be in them. But the wedding at issue here is yours.''

Remembering Briane's revelation in the garden, she said carefully, ''Think hard, Kendra. Are you sure Trey's mind will stay changed? I know you love him, but if he marries you because...'' She searched her mind for a plausible suggestion that wouldn't reveal what she knew. ''Because he feels guilty for hurting you, or because he feels loyalty to your father, that wouldn't be good for either of you.''

Kendra nodded, letting her eyes close for a moment. When she opened them, Charlotte saw again how much she'd changed in the past twenty-four hours.

''I know. But I was all ready to buy a house, have babies, set up a life the way I want to have it.''

Charlotte could relate. She'd given that a little thought herself in the past few days. ''But none of that would be any good with...with the wrong man.''

''Trey told me to try to forget our conversation yesterday morning had ever happened. He said he just got a little panicky.'' She gave Charlotte a surprisingly whimsical smile given the subject under discussion. ''He tends to do that, doesn't he? But he told me he loved me, begged me to forgive him and to marry him just as though the past day never happened. He seemed so sincere.''

She shouldn't be the one to tell her, Charlotte thought desperately. It would sound vindictive and cruel coming from her. Then she decided that the real cruelty would be letting her marry Trey without knowing all the facts.

"Kendra..." she began.

A loud rap at the door interrupted her. Kendra peered through the drapes, then stood.

"It's my father," she said, smiling at Charlotte over her shoulder as she went to the door. "I guess it's time for me to make a decision."

"But, Kendra..."

"Hi, Kennie." Caleb wrapped his daughter in his arms, then smiled over her shoulder at Charlotte. "I'm sorry to break this up, but it's getting late."

Charlotte simply couldn't make herself say what she had to say in front of Caleb. *Kendra, you should know that your fiancé was bought for you by your mother. I'm sorry to tell you, Caleb, that you're married to a woman who values her social position above her daughter. Smile for Bitsy.*

"Thank you, Charlie." Kendra reached out to squeeze her hand, then walked down the lane with her father toward the big house and very probably a miserable future.

CHARLOTTE PULLED her suitcase out from under the bed and opened her lingerie drawer. She smiled over the bittersweet memory of having done this once before. Then she felt choked with tears when she realized there was no one around to stop her this time.

She gallantly folded things into her suitcase, then into her garment bag, leaving out the high-necked, long-cuffed Victorian white lace she'd brought to wear to the wedding. She said a silent prayer that Trey would be struck by lightning and zapped into a responsible and faithful husband.

DEREK WAS HEADING for the lane to the guest house when Edward intercepted him at a remarkably agile run, the portable phone in his hand.

"Derek, I need you," he said urgently.

"But I..." He pointed to the guest house where he was sure Charlotte was probably packing, ready to escape the moment the ceremony was over. The rumor in the kitchen was that the wedding was going ahead as planned.

At the other end of the estate, guests were beginning to arrive, There was a stream of cars coming from the gate, and he could see Henry and Naldo moving among them.

Edward handed him the phone. "It's London."

"But you're..."

"I know. But he says he likes your style. He wants to talk to you."

He looked toward the guest house, then back to the phone in his hand. For the first time in his career he was willing to let a multibillion-dollar deal dangle in the interest of his personal life.

He was about to hand the phone back, to tell Edward he had to speak to his daughter, when he looked up again and saw Charlie moving across the lawn, a slender vision in white, hair piled high and haloed with flowers. Briane and Denise were with her, talking earnestly, as they made their way toward the tents, the plum and purple of their dresses a warm contrast to her white.

Derek groaned his resignation. The talk would have to wait. He exchanged a frustrated look with Edward, then put the phone to his ear.

"MAYBE IF WE all told her together," Briane said as she, Charlotte and Denise fought their way past caterers streaming outdoors to the shadowy interior of the house.

"Now?" Denise whispered harshly, tapping the little diamond-studded basal of her watch. "Ten minutes before the ceremony? *You* should have told her this morning."

"I tried, but she's been with her parents for the past forty-five minutes. Now she's getting dressed."

Charlotte remembered seeing the change in Kendra's eyes from the young woman she'd been two days ago to the woman she was this morning. She'd gotten a glimpse of the real Trey. Charlotte had to believe she had reached the decision she wanted to make, the one she could best live with—whether or not it conformed with what anyone else would have done.

Elizabeth shouted from somewhere upstairs. "Briane! Denise!"

With a parting look for Charlotte that expressed their common concern, they hurried upstairs in a flurry of taffeta and tulle.

Charlotte went to the French doors beyond which men, women and children in Sunday dress took their places in the hundreds of chairs placed on the lawn.

Caroline and Edward were greeting guests and sending them on to the ushers, who urged them into the rows of chairs.

A clear image of last year at this time rose in her mind, curiously unaccompanied by pain. All she felt was a deep gratitude for the way things had turned out—up until about a week ago.

Now pain did grasp her—biting and hard. Derek was gone, and it was all her fault. She imagined this was what happened to people who judged too harshly—they ended up alone.

She squared her shoulders and prepared to slide the doors aside. Everyone would look at her. She was the tragic figure, the woman who was always the bride's assistant, never the bride.

Ah, well. If loving Derek had taught her anything, it was that she did have a taste for the daring.

She pushed the door open and prepared to step out, but was halted by the touch of a firm hand on her shoulder. She spun around with a gasp of surprise and looked up into Derek's dark eyes.

"Derek!" she whispered, sunshine bursting inside her at the sight of him. "I thought you'd left."

"Did you?" He pulled her inside and reached past her to slide the French doors closed. "Just goes to show you how wrong you can be about a lot of things."

"Yeah, well," she said, her calm composure of a moment ago dissolving under his direct gaze. He'd changed into a suit, and the white of his shirt against the dark wool blend of his jacket gave him that mysterious edge of intrigue, like a portrait in black-and-white. "I... wanted to...talk to you about last night."

"Good." He took her arm and pulled her with him. "I have a few things to say to you, too."

There were staff everywhere, coming and going with food, chairs, last-minute adjustments to flowers and decor. Derek finally opened a door through which no one had entered or exited in the past few seconds and pushed Charlotte inside.

It was a pantry. Some recent visitor had left the overhead fluorescent on.

Derek closed the door behind them and kicked a step stool up against it to prevent intrusion. Then he turned to Charlotte.

Something in his eyes alarmed her. They were dark

and bright and filled with a resolve that did not look entirely civilized. She backed away, past shelves of canned and boxed goods. He followed.

"I'm sorry I shouted at you," she said. "I hadn't reasoned out that feeling fear and acting on it are two different things. I just saw you looking frightened and that frightened me because…" She had to stop and swallow because he was still coming and she was now backed up against a shelf of onions and potatoes. A string of garlic hung above her head. "Because…I loved you so much. I think…"

He opened the buttons on his jacket and put a hand to the shelf above her head, blocking her in place. She edged sideways, and he reached his other hand up to a shelf of canned smoked oysters.

It was obvious she wasn't going anywhere. She had no other recourse but to admit the truth.

"I think I got so upset," she admitted, flattening herself against the mesh bags, turning her face sideways to avoid the look in his eyes on the chance that he didn't care, that he hadn't left simply because he didn't want to miss the opportunity to tell her what a pampered society brat she was. She swallowed again and closed her eyes. "Because I really wanted to have the wedding this time, and everything that comes after. The house, the kids, the pets, the van full of picnic stuff and Little League gear and car seats…"

He cupped her chin between his thumb and forefinger and turned her face to him. She opened her eyes. The emotion in his was so complex she couldn't read it.

"You want to know what I say to that?" he demanded.

The question had an edge of anger. Oh, God. This was it.

Without waiting for a yes or no, he lowered his head and opened his mouth over hers.

Derek let it all speak for him, the passion he'd always felt for her, steaming hot now because he'd come so close to losing her, the tenderness she'd taught him, the deep-rooted, far-reaching love that had grown so fast but felt as solid to him as the legs on which he walked.

As he kissed her lengthily, reaching deep with his tongue one moment, then lightly nibbling at her the next because his feelings were so entangled, so mercurial, he poured everything he knew about them at that moment into her. He loved her, he trusted her, he needed her, he wanted her. He would love her in return, never give her reason to doubt him for an instant, be there whenever she turned to him—during the daily struggle, and at night in their bed.

He raised his head and saw the tears on her face and the consummate happiness in her eyes.

"And furthermore," he said, his voice thick with emotion. He had so much more to tell her, but in the light of love in her eyes, words failed him. So he fell back on the language that had translated so well an instant ago.

The rattling of the doorknob finally drew them slowly apart.

"It can't be locked," a male voice said from the other side of the door. "There isn't a lock on it."

"Well, you try it then," an indignant female voice said. "Something's blocking the door."

Derek looked around them at the mundane contents of the kitchen pantry, then leaned down to kiss Charlotte's forehead and laugh lightly. "You won't be able to boast about the romantic nature of my proposal to our grandchildren."

Her arms, already wrapped around his waist, hugged him fiercely. "Romance is where you find it, in a Victorian loft or among the spuds and garlic."

He kissed the top of her head. "Then will you marry me, Charlie?"

"Yes, Derek," she replied, looking up at him, her eyes brimming with joy and promise. "The moment we get this one under way, we can plan our own."

"Then we'd better get out of here."

"Just one more kiss."

The pantry door burst open, the step stool scraping the floor as the spindly caterer and Pauline fell into the narrow enclosure. Derek, politely excusing himself, slipped past them, tugging Charlotte after him.

"Thieves?" the caterer asked Pauline.

The cook smiled fondly after them. "Lovers," she corrected.

CHARLOTTE AND DEREK saw Trey and his brother, who was serving as best man, standing at the French doors, awaiting the signal to go out onto the lawn to await the bride. They talked quietly together as Charlotte and Derek approached, Trey looking composed and in control.

"A Beamer?" Trey's brother was saying, unaware that he could be heard. "Or a Porsche like Cabot's? That's a car."

"I think I'll get a plane," Trey said, smiling as he speculated. "One of those new 31A jobs from Lear. Has the best autopilot, flight director, panel layout and nose-wheel steering system of any Learjet airplane."

"You can't fly a plane."

"I'll hire a pilot.

"It'd be cheaper to fly commercially."

"But not as cool. Charlie! Cabot." Trey smiled with

great good humor as he slid the door open for them. "Enjoy the wedding. Thanks for bringing my bride home."

"Sure," Charlotte replied, barely resisting the urge to kick him in the shin—or elsewhere. "Didn't want her to be late for the delivery."

Trey raised an eyebrow. Derek frowned down at her.

"Delivery?" Trey asked.

Charlotte pretended confusion. "I have that wrong, don't I? You're the one who was delivered, bought and paid for by the magic formula that takes all the fear away."

Trey went crimson to his hairline, like a glass filling with claret. He glanced at his brother, who looked confused, then back at Charlotte with a look of pleading.

"You didn't..."

"No, I didn't tell her," she said, making a sudden decision. Now that she knew what real love felt like, she couldn't let Kendra settle for anything less without making her see things as they were. "But I think I'll wait right here while you do. I imagine she'll be down any minute."

"I can expl—"

Charlotte stopped him with a raised hand. "Please don't try."

"You want to tell *me* what's going on?" Derek asked.

"Now *there's* a question." Bitsy Tate slipped in through the French doors Trey had opened, then slid them behind her. She looked up at Derek, a smug smile in place.

"You have *not* been to Massachusetts in the past four weeks," she said. "There is no health certificate or marriage license on file in any of the commonwealth's fourteen counties. You're going to pay for making me waste that time.''

''You did it yourself, Bitsy,'' he replied reasonably, unable to dredge up even a vague ire over the revelation that seemed imminent. Being unveiled as a liar and, to some extent, a fake seemed a small price to pay for gaining Charlotte for a lifetime. ''You could have just believed us and saved yourself a lot of trouble.''

''But you lied,'' she said self-righteously, ''and my job is to print the truth.''

''Your job,'' he corrected, ''is to ferret out every juicy little suggestion of scandal, every tender, spicy morsel you know your readers will digest with their orange juice.'' He smiled affably. ''You wouldn't know the truth unless it was embroidered with lies and illicit suggestions.''

Bitsy opened her mouth to retaliate, her fine-boned face going white and then purple. She closed her mouth and said coolly, ''You two aren't married, are you? The lovely Victorian miss and the very contemporary hunk have been living in sin in the little guest house.''

He raised an eyebrow. Her scornful glance at Charlotte finally activated his temper. ''Do you really think anyone will care?''

She smiled slowly. ''Of course they will. I'm sure they'd love to know that beautiful Charlotte Morreaux isn't married *this* time, either.''

Charlotte caught Derek's arm as he took a step toward the reporter.

''It seems to me,'' Trey said calmly, ''that this presents us with a new opportunity to come to terms, Charlie.'' He looked out at the large crowd of people waiting for the wedding to begin. Many of them had been at her almost-wedding. She knew in their hearts they'd probably sympathized with her position, but they'd eagerly gossiped about it for days anyway. She'd found it unsettling then to know that any given hour of the day someone was discussing her failed love life and her humiliation.

Curiously that didn't seem to matter now.

She smiled up at Derek. "Do you care?"

"Not a damn," he replied, "but you..."

"Don't give a damn, either. Trey Prentiss, you are such a lowlife they should make a place for you beside the escargots. And Kendra should know that. Then you are welcome to walk out there with Bitsy and announce our depravity to the world."

The conversation was arrested by the beginning strains of "The Wedding March." Then there was the sound of a door closing upstairs.

"Well. That's us." Trey grinned at his brother, then winked at Charlotte. "Better think twice, Charlie." And he walked out, followed by his best man, to take his place beside the nearest trellis arch.

The atmosphere was heavy with tension, the music beyond the French door growing insistent. Happy for the diversion, Charlotte, Derek and Bitsy turned to watch the bride descend.

Chapter Thirteen

Everyone took a step back in surprise as Elizabeth appeared at the top of the stairs, a handkerchief pressed to her lips. She came down slowly, a feverish but unfocused look on her face, one hand clutching the hanky, the other hand on the gleaming mahogany banister steadying her progress.

Her beaded lavender jacket over a slim skirt flattered her figure, but lent a curious color to a face gone almost green.

"Elizabeth?" Bitsy asked, following her a few steps and getting no sign that she'd been heard or seen. "Elizabeth, what is it?" Elizabeth walked on as though in a trance.

"You may as well get it from me, Bitsy," Kendra said, appearing at the top of the stairs.

Everyone stared. It was easy to presume what had upset Elizabeth. Kendra was not wearing the white Victorian pinafore dress that had begun this whole charade. She wore a bright yellow suit and carried a tote bag. She was obviously dressed for traveling.

Caleb followed her down the stairs, carrying the rest of her bags.

Outside, the strains of "The Wedding March" continued to play in counterpoint to the little drama unfolding in the rear foyer.

Out of the corner of her eye, Charlotte saw Trey, straining to see into the house. But she was too pleasantly surprised to enjoy his concern.

"I'm not getting married today, Bitsy," Kendra announced calmly. Charlotte could see evidence that she'd been crying, but judging by the resolve in her manner, some decision about her future had permanently replaced the tears.

"The story's really too sordid for your column," Kendra went on, "although you could get Mother's version from her. I really don't care. I'll be touring Europe."

Bitsy looked a little avid, as though unable to wait to get to her laptop.

Kendra turned to Charlotte. "I heard you refuse Trey's offer to be silent." She hugged her. "Thank you. Dad had just told me the truth."

Caleb set her bags on the floor and shook his head grimly. "I didn't even know what Elizabeth had done until we got into a quarrel when you brought Kennie home this morning."

Kendra wandered to the door where the crowd was beginning to grow restless.

"I think we have to give them *something*," she said over her shoulder, a smile playing at her lips. "This could turn ugly if we don't handle it correctly."

"What do you have in mind?" Bitsy asked.

Without replying, Kendra slid the glass door open and beckoned to Trey, who was now looking decidedly uncomfortable.

The music stopped abruptly. He sent a quick glance at his brother, one at the crowd, gave them his endearing,

212 The Unexpected Groom

apologetic smile, then loped across the lawn to the French doors.

"Kendra!" he gasped as he slipped inside. "What are you doing in that suit? Why..."

She stopped him with a very dignified but very final, "Trey, please. I know everything." She studied him a moment, as though looking for some sign in him of the man she'd loved, then sighed, apparently prepared to accept the truth that he'd never existed. "The kindest thing I can do for you at this moment is allow you to escape with some modicum of dignity. My father will explain to your family."

Trey looked around the little group in disbelief, that innocent surprise still in place on his perfect features. "Kendra, you misun—"

"Or," she suggested with a smile, "I could have Derek and my father escort you out."

The French doors slid open and Trey's brother looked Kendra up and down in her suit, then studied the hostile faces on the rest of the group and frowned at his brother.

"Is it off?" he asked.

Trey's answer was to stalk off in the direction of the front door. After a moment's hesitation, his brother followed.

Kendra dusted her hands, that unhappy task taken care of. Then she turned to Charlotte and Derek.

"I know just what'll save the day."

Charlotte, bursting with pride for her, hadn't a clue what she was talking about. "What?"

"Do you know that they *aren't* married?" Bitsy asked, "that they've tricked you and your family and everyone out there who was at the shower and who read my column?"

Kendra dismissed her with a swish of her lustrous blond hair. "Of course, I knew."

"You—?"

"I knew," Kendra repeated, then approached Bitsy with the same smile she'd given Trey. The older woman looked back at her warily. "But I wouldn't like to read it in your column. In fact, if you're tempted to write it, anyway, or to reveal the grisly details about Trey my mother will probably tell you, you might recall the night we went to the Karaoke bar."

"The bar?"

"Yes. You don't remember the second half of the evening, do you?"

"I...I..."

"If you recall, Briane was photographing the evening." Kendra put a companionable arm around Bitsy's shoulders and walked her a few steps in the direction Trey had taken. "I have photographs of you onstage doing a most interpretive version of 'After the Loving' with the drummer."

Bitsy made a little choking sound.

"And you were wearing your Saturday panties on Thursday. I'm sure the *Herald* could do a lot with that." Kendra smiled again. "Do we understand each other?"

Bitsy could only stare.

Kendra gave her a squeeze. "Good. Thanks for coming." She pushed her gently toward the front door.

She turned back to Derek and Charlotte and Caleb. "Now where was I?"

Caleb gave her a bear hug. "God. I didn't even suspect what you were made of, girl. You were about to save the day."

"Oh, right." She pushed the French doors wide, everyone in the chairs sat straighter and strained to see.

She slipped one arm in Charlotte's and the other in Derek's. "Follow us, Daddy. We're going to need you."

"I'll be right behind you."

The orchestra struck up "The Wedding March" one more time. She silenced them with a wave of her hand.

"Let me do the talking," she said, leading them toward the trellis arch, smiling at the hundreds of guests.

That was easy to agree to, Charlotte thought. If what she thought was about to happen was truly about to happen, she wasn't sure she could speak, anyway.

Kendra stopped before the stunned minister, still smiling. She stepped out from between Charlotte and Derek, then pushed them together until they were arm in arm.

"There," she whispered with satisfaction. "Don't you love it when things work out right." Then she faced her guests and cleared her throat.

"You've probably guessed by the way I'm dressed," she said, "that I'm not getting married today."

The low murmur that had greeted their walk to the trellis arch turned into a strengthening roar. She waited until it subsided.

"I apologize for keeping you waiting like this, and for the change in plans. Trey and I have had a change of heart," she said graciously, "but my parents had planned a lovely afternoon for you, and I'd like you to enjoy it, anyway. Toward that end, I've enlisted the help of Derek and Charlotte Cabot." She slanted them a wink that encouraged them to stay with her.

"Since they sneaked off to get married without us, I thought it only fair that they renew their vows today, since we have everything else in place."

There was a smattering of applause. Leading it were Caroline and Edward in the front row of chairs.

"Good. I'm glad you agree." She turned to her father. "Daddy, will you be best man for Derek?"

Caleb nodded with a smile. "I'd be honored."

She turned to beckon Edward, then Briane and Denise, who'd been waiting at the other end of the lawn for the bride to appear. They ran up the aisle to take their place behind Charlotte while Edward stood beside Caleb.

"But I don't have the renewal ceremony with me," the minister whispered in concern. "It isn't the same as…"

"Just do the wedding one," Kendra whispered back. "No one will know the difference."

Everyone on the lawn fell silent. The only sound was the drone of bees and the very small sigh of a breeze.

For an instant, her face sobered and she looked unutterably sad. Then she shook off the mood and said with satisfaction, "There." Then she hugged her father and turned for the house, shoulders square, step even.

The minister cued the orchestra and, once again, they struck up "The Wedding March." Charlotte saw the poetic irony in it as Kendra marched away to the melody.

Then, certain Kendra didn't require another moment's concern on her part, Charlotte turned her attention to the minister as he began the wedding ceremony.

She glanced up at Derek, who smiled down at her with an intimacy that made her feel as though they stood alone together despite their considerable audience. Everything inside her brightened and intensified.

She knew it was visible in her eyes—the rightness of this—Charlotte and Derek, the Duchess of Winter and the man who'd brought the thaw.

Derek felt swallowed in her gaze, welcome, caressed, shown the truth of everything she believed. *I am yours,* she told him silently, *and you are mine. From this day forward. Forever.*

He lost the thread of the minister's words for a moment and leaned down to kiss her with all the sweetness he'd learned in her arms, to let her know that she could expect it, that there would never be anything they couldn't share as she'd once thought.

"Ahem." The minister cleared his throat, glanced surreptitiously over their heads at the smiling audience and said under his breath. "That comes later. Pay attention."

He continued the ceremony, having to ask their names when they reached the vows. They spoke them so loudly and clearly that most of the audience thought the conviction in their voices came from having done this before so recently.

He finally pronounced them husband and wife, and Charlotte turned into Derek's arms. The afternoon breeze billowed the lace of her skirt, and fluttered the lock of dark hair on Derek's forehead.

A bird sang, the guests applauded and she could hear Caroline crying. Sunlight streamed on them through the latticed arch. She'd have been shocked had anyone pointed out to her that she was more aware of the reality of the moment than the romance.

Derek saw the breeze flutter a tendril of her hair and the baby's breath caught in it, saw the sunlight silver her eyes, so filled with love, and thought he would never forget the romance of their wedding day.

She pulled his head down to her and whispered, smiling, "Only a romantic would have done this, Derek. I've converted you, haven't I?"

He looked deeply into her eyes, love so strong inside him it was almost pain.

"The thing is," he whispered, "with us, romance is reality."

Epilogue

"I look like a truck wearing black stockings." Charlotte stepped back from the mirror in the hope that lengthening her reflection would slenderize it.

Derek walked behind her, affixing jade cuff links to his dress shirt, and stopped to evaluate her criticism. She wore a black crepe tent dress and black shoes with a low wedge heel. Pinned to her shoulder was the Victorian gold-and-enamel heart-shaped brooch he'd given her when she'd told him she was carrying their child.

She'd cut her hair short, a decision they'd argued over and he'd thought he'd won—until she came home with it cropped to her chin.

For a moment he'd been horrified. So many of the wondrous moments of his life had been spent all entangled in her hair. Then he'd seen the sparkle in her eyes, the beautiful definition of her chin and jaw, the graceful exposure of her neck, and he'd had to admit that he liked it.

Today he thought he'd never seen a more delectable, exciting woman in his whole life. He wrapped his arms around her and pulled her back against him to tell her so.

"You do not look like a truck. You look like a woman eight months' pregnant."

"I look like a truck eight months' pregnant." She waddled off to the bathroom. "I'm not going."

He didn't panic. After a year and a half as her husband, he knew how to deal with this mood. He tucked his shirt into his pants and fastened on the elasticized bow tie. "What do you want me to tell everyone?"

"The truth," she called, now out of sight.

"That you're feeling too fat to be seen in public?"

She came to the doorway, her shoes off, a lipstick in her hand. She frowned. "I'm sure you could put it more diplomatically than that."

He shrugged into his formal jacket, looking at her reflection just above his shoulder in the mirror.

"Kendra," he rehearsed, "I'm so sorry, Charlotte couldn't come to the opening of Paris Tout Partout, even though she promised when we bumped into you on our honeymoon that if you went to work and put a collection together she'd get all her friends to come and buy. She likes to look perfect, you know, like a genuine Victorian, and now that she's carrying my son, she doesn't like to be seen looking less than svelte." He paused to add significantly as he buttoned one button. "Even though she looks more beautiful than I've ever seen her."

She padded toward him in her stocking feet. "I did get a lot of people to come."

"You think they'll be as confident about buying if you're not there?"

"We might not feel confident about buying. We still don't know if she's any good. The stuff just came off the plane this morning and was hung this afternoon."

He caught her reflection and asked quietly, "Is that the point?"

She wrapped her arms around his waist and leaned against him. He felt the mound of her stomach against the small of his back and wondered if there was a more delicious feeling in the whole world.

"You're sure I don't look ugly?" she asked.

He reached behind him to tug her around in front and into his arms.

"You look absolutely gorgeous," he said with complete sincerity. "And you promised me this evening. The Butler wedding took so much of your time I've hardly seen you this past month."

That had the predictable result. Using guilt against her was shameless, he knew, but she needed to relax, and he knew she'd do it for him before she did it for herself.

He enticed her further with a few gentle strokes in the middle of her back. He took advantage of the opportunity to nibble on her neck. "We'll spend some time at the show, buy something even if we don't like it, then stop at Spago's on the way home for a late dinner, and when we get home I'll give you my famous back rub before we go to bed."

He knew he'd won when he felt her sigh and rest her weight against him. "As I recall," she said dreamily, "it was one of your back rubs that turned me into a truck in the first place."

THE GALLERY WAS FILLED with Kendra's friends and family and all of Charlotte's conscripts. And judging by all the red Sold dots on the title boxes, no one would have to be bullied into buying.

Charlotte was not surprised. She stared openmouthed at the impressive collection of French city and pastoral scenes.

She supposed the style might have been called impressionist, although what little she knew about it brought to mind pastels and subtlety and a looseness that suggested rather than portrayed line and form.

The latter quality fit, but these colors were primary and bold and evoked strong feeling. Mood seemed to predominate rather than atmosphere.

Kendra greeted them just inside the gallery. In a sleek red dress that clung lovingly to every line and stopped mid-thigh, her hair in an elegant French twist, she looked like a woman in love with and in charge of her destiny.

She squealed in delight over Charlotte's girth and wrapped her in a hug. Then she drew back to look at her.

"How dare you wear that dress," Charlotte said in laughing indignation, "when I can't even get Derek's sweatshirt over my stomach."

"She exaggerates," Derek said, kissing Kendra's cheek. "She's now using most of my upper-body wardrobe. How are you? You look wonderful."

"I *am* wonderful." She raised a hand above the crowd to beckon to someone across the room. "In fact, I was thinking just this morning that Trey Prentiss was the best thing to happen to both Charlotte and me."

At Derek's and Charlotte's raised eyebrows, she explained simply, "He brought you two together and was responsible for my going to Paris. Antoine! Over here!"

A man just Kendra's height with thick, wavy auburn hair and a bright red moustache and beard materialized out of the crowd to slip into her extended arm. She gave him a resounding kiss.

"Antoine, these are my friends, Derek and Charlotte Cabot. Remember I told you they had my wedding instead of me? Cabots, this is Antoine Badineau, the most gifted sculptor in all of Paris."

He reached a hand out to Charlotte, and then to Derek. "I am delighted to meet you," he said in charmingly accented English. "Only a friend of *la belle's* could decipher such a sentence. 'They had my wedding instead of me.'" He repeated with a shake of his head. "In any other circle but Kendra's—" the *r* rolled on his tongue deliciously as his eyes rolled toward her "—it would not make sense. But I understand. She has bent my reality."

As a newcomer joined their circle to claim Kendra's attention, Antoine pulled them aside.

"Have you seen the pieces in the anteroom?" he asked, leaning closer to be heard in the growing crush of people. At the shake of their heads, he led them toward the back of the gallery. The crowd and the din were thinner here. He swept a hand to encourage them inside. "I believe there is a portrait of the two of you here."

"A portr—?" Charlotte began to ask in surprise, but he, too, had been claimed by a guest. She turned back to the room and saw it immediately.

Derek was already moving toward it, a large canvas depicting a summer lawn and garden and rows of chairs and women in hats and men in light-colored suits.

Dominating the painting were the figures of a woman in a high-collared white dress with wispy flowers in her hair, and a man in a dark suit bent gently over her. A minister garbed for ceremony faced them.

Derek put an index finger to the title box beside it. "Charlotte's Wedding," he read.

Charlotte lost herself in the painting. She experienced a reprise of everything she'd felt at that moment—all the love and hope and promise, all the wonder that it had all turned out so beautifully, after all.

She turned to Derek, wanting to tell him what she felt,

but she didn't have to—the same emotions stood out clearly in his eyes. He kissed her quickly, then left the room and reappeared with the gallery owner, who placed the Sold dot on the box.

When the owner left, they stood back arm in arm to study themselves.

Suddenly an arm came around each of them, and a short figure in a crocheted shawl over a brown shirtwaist peered between their shoulders.

"Babs!" Charlotte said, reaching back to draw her into the middle.

Babs inclined her head toward Charlotte's swollen stomach. "I see you finally remember your name."

"You bet."

"And you." She looked up at Derek. "You took my advice, didn't you? You borrowed the magic."

He shook his head as he squeezed her closer. "No, I think this time I own it."

Make-Believe Mom

Chapter One

Barbara Ryan studied the can of garbanzo beans on her desk and waited for inspiration to strike. Nothing happened.

She rolled her chair backward to the wall of her small cubicle in search of a different perspective. There had to be one. Successful advertising worked on one of two basic principles—creating an image for the product, or motivating the consumer to action.

Two hours ago she'd tried to imagine mobilizing consumers into an army on the march for garbanzos, but she'd decided to attempt to give the bean charm and appeal instead—to create the image. The entire staff of Cheney & Roman had gone to lunch, and she was still sitting there, staring at the twelve-ounce can.

She tilted her head and wiggled the pencil caught between her fingers, trying to relax and encourage thought to flow. But the sounds of construction from the opposite side of the office challenged her ability to concentrate.

Barbara put on the ear protectors that had been provided by the management when work had begun a week ago and tried to concentrate on what she'd learned about garbanzos. They were also called chick-peas. Chick-peas. She had an instant mental image of a cuddly chickpea emerging from an egg and weaving around on little chick feet.

She groaned, mentally erased the thought and tried again. Nutlike flavor, good in minestrone and Spanish stew. A garbanzo with castanets!

Get real, Ryan, she told herself firmly. Garbanzos could get her out of the copywriting bleachers and into the game. She could get one of the more stylish accounts, gain some attention, take a step up the rickety corporate ladder. *Think!*

The health aspect of beans was important. And healthy eating had snob appeal for young and old alike. Maybe that was it—a doctor in pristine whites, his stethoscope around his neck, standing in the rice and beans aisle of the grocery store, extolling the virtues of the bulbous little bean.

The muted but still audible sounds of hammering and ripping provided a very appropriate background for such an awful idea.

"Barb, here's the dress!"

Carol McDonald stood breathlessly in the doorway of Barbara's cubicle and held up a long plastic dress sleeve with the name of a chic boutique emblazoned on it. Underneath was a silky dark blue dress that shimmered even in the dim light of her tiny office.

Barbara gasped as she reached across the small space and lifted the plastic wrapper. Tiny beads sparkled like the night sky.

"Are you sure you want to lend this to me?" she asked, as Carol perched on the end of her desk. "I'll be wearing it to a dinner, and I'd die if anything happened to it."

Carol was a tall redhead whose desk in front of the boss's office was covered with photos of her two-year-old. She waved a careless hand. "I haven't worn it since I got pregnant with Casey. I hate to leave her at night when I've been gone all day, so Jerry has to entertain his clients without me. But you have a man to impress. Try it on."

"Good idea." Barbara indicated her doorless office and the racket coming from the ladies' room, where the crew was ripping up old plumbing. "Where do you suggest I do that?"

"In Mr. Cheney's office." Carol tugged Barbara out of her chair and turned her bodily in that direction.

Barbara resisted as Carol pushed. "I can't do that. His office is locked and I…"

"Of course you can. He's out of town until tomorrow afternoon. The office is empty, he has a floor-to-ceiling mirror in his private bathroom, and you happen to be on personal terms with his secretary." She batted long eyelashes dramatically as she pointed to herself with a graceful index finger. "Come on. I'll let you in."

"Carol—"

"Ryan, tonight you're going to meet the man and woman who gave birth to the man you're dating. Why you're dating him is a mystery to me, but that's your business." Carol ignored the roll of Barbara's eyes and went on. "Trevor is handsome, he's successful and he's…sort of…"

"Intelligent and kind," Barbara put in as Carol groped for words.

Carol retrieved a key from the middle drawer of her desk and grinned at Barbara. "I was going to say stuffy."

Barbara nudged Carol in the backside with her knee as her friend unlocked the door. "He's not stuffy. He just takes his work very seriously."

"Barb, he gave you an *IRA* for your birthday. He even thinks of *you* in terms of money. I think you should throw him back." Carol pulled her inside and closed the door.

"He is not a fish, Carol. He's a man. And he's entitled to his eccentricities. Given his work, he probably thought an IRA was a very special gift."

Carol eyed her steadily. "You were disappointed."

"I was...surprised."

John Cheney's office was large—but functional, rather than elegant. Neat piles of mail, faxes and telephone messages sat atop the desk along with the usual pencil cup, an assortment of framed photos, a call director and a calendar.

The chair was high-backed brown leather, and a small matching sofa sat under a window that looked out onto the port of Portland. The office was quiet as a tomb.

Carol opened a door that led into a spacious bathroom complete with the full-length mirror she had promised.

Barbara stood on the threshold and peered into the bathroom. It was done in black and white and had a tub, a Jacuzzi, a shower and a sauna.

John Cheney did seem like the kind of man who expected his conveniences. Barbara had never spoken to him, except on her first day six months ago when Carol had taken her on a tour of the office and introduced her to the partners.

Hal Roman was short and a little paunchy and always smiling from ear to ear.

By contrast Cheney was tall, dark and gorgeous. She remembered that he'd stood to lean across his desk and shake her hand, and she'd felt his energy and the impact of his gaze. All the women in the office whispered about his good looks, but she found them almost too wolfish for comfort.

He had the honey-colored eyes of a wolf, a strong, straight nose and a smile as ready as his partner's—except that his was more feral.

She'd been happy to learn that Hal Roman oversaw the employees, while John Cheney dealt with clients.

"I'm starved," Carol said, handing her the dress. "Shall I run down to Rubio's and bring back soft-shell tacos while you're changing?"

Barbara hugged her with her free arm. "Please. And thanks for taking most of your lunch hour to go home to get the dress."

Carol dismissed Barb's gratitude with a wave of her hand.

"That's what friends are for—to come through for you when the cleaners ruins your favorite frock."

Barbara closed the door behind Carol, hung the dress on a hook on the door and pushed off her black flats. She unpinned the loose knot of her hair, then pulled the teal and fuchsia sweater over her head. Seeing her reflection in the mirror, she laughed. She looked like a warning against using the wrong shampoo.

She slipped out of her slacks, folded everything on the closed commode, then pulled the plastic sleeve from Carol's dress. In the bright fluorescent light of the bathroom it glittered like an angel's garb.

Barbara stepped back and simply admired it. It would be snug, she guessed, and would reveal a little bosom. She felt a thrill of excitement.

She was taking a step toward the dress, arms raised to reach for the hanger, when the door burst open.

JOHN CHENEY dropped his briefcase and jacket on his desk, pulled at his tie and headed for the shower. As he pushed his way into the bathroom, his mind was filled with all the details he had to put together for his upcoming impromptu appointment.

A startled little scream stopped him in his tracks. He was completely shocked to find himself with a fragrant, half-naked young woman in his arms. He stared into dark brown eyes and at a stream of dark hair and was about to decide he could happily adjust to the situation when she leapt backward.

She collided with the towel rack, and a thick black bath sheet slithered to the floor.

"Oh, no," she said, rubbing her shoulder with one hand while reaching for the towel with the other—keeping her eyes on him all the time as though she expected him to pounce. "Mr. Cheney, I'm so sorry!"

Even before she used his name he realized she worked for him. He guessed it was the way she was dressed—or *un*dressed—that had confused him.

This was Ryan from Domestic Products. The young woman who'd saved Barnett's hide with the charter boat slogan. Usually all he saw of her was the dark coil of hair at the back of her head and the square, slender shoulders facing her computer terminal.

He'd had no idea what he'd been missing.

Those ivory shoulders were anything but stiff in the cap sleeves of a low-cut black silk teddy. Her small high breasts appeared above the towel she clutched as she took a startled breath. She had straight hips and the thighs of a young man's dreams. They emerged from the high French cut of the teddy, leading his eyes down to shapely knees and long calves that ended in a trim ankle and the incongruous note of teal blue socks.

Barbara's breath caught in her throat. Surprise, embarrassment and the warm sensation of John Cheney's hands on her bare arms combined to stall her brain.

She tried to think. She didn't intend to lie about how she'd gotten in here, but she had to cover for Carol. And now that her employer had gotten over the initial shock of finding a woman in his bathroom, a suspicious frown was forming between his golden eyes.

He appeared even taller without the pulled-together look a jacket gave a man, and the stark whiteness of his shirt against his tanned face and hands was dramatic.

She watched one of those hands now as he reached behind himself for the door handle, to close and lock the door. Her heartbeat accelerated.

John had to push away the thought that her white skin and black silk outfit made her look as though she'd been designed to be placed just where she stood—just for him—and made himself think about what her presence here could mean. New-Age Advertising had underbid them on several new accounts in the past few months and he and Hal were getting suspicious. The bids and the proposal were so close that they would have to have had inside information on the Cheney & Roman plans.

"Let's determine why you're in here," he said, folding his arms, "before we decide whether either one of us is sorry about it."

Barbara blinked, not entirely sure what he was suggesting. Did he think she'd lain in wait for him in her underwear?

She dropped one hand from the towel and pointed to the dress hanging behind him on the door.

"Carol is lending me that dress for a party tonight," she explained with a swallow. "I was trying it on."

"This office was locked," he said sternly.

"Yes, but you were supposed to be away until tomorrow," she stated reasonably. "And the bathrooms aren't usable for a few days. I apologize. I used poor judgment."

"You must have also used a key," he said implacably. "The door hasn't been tampered with."

That was safe enough to admit. "Yes, I did."

"And where did you get it?"

"From Carol's desk."

"She keeps it locked."

"She'd stepped away for coffee. Mr. Cheney…"

He put his hands in his pockets and asked quietly, "What did you expect to find in my office?"

"A mirror!" she replied a little loudly, patience thinning. "Do I look as though I'm dressed for industrial espionage?"

He wasn't sure what to think. Carol usually guarded the privacy of his office as though she were armed. On the other hand, Barbara Ryan's dark eyes reflected embarrassment and impatience, but not guilt.

"I'm sure," he said, fixing her with those wolf's eyes, "that espionage of all kinds is often conducted just this way. A man comes home to find a beautiful woman among his things, and she makes him forget to wonder what she's doing there."

Barbara, unsettled by the notion that she was capable of disorienting him, dropped the towel long enough to pick up her pile of clothes and cover as much of herself as she could. It wasn't much.

"But you didn't forget to wonder, did you?" She gave him a cool, affronted tilt of her chin. "First you suggested I was here to somehow ensnare you, and then you as much as accused me of looking through your office."

"Did you?"

"No! Now, if I'm fired, I'll leave. If I'm not, I'd appreciate it if you'd let me pass so I can get back to work."

"Without trying on the dress?"

She groaned. The dress. She'd almost forgotten the damn thing.

He relented, convinced she was innocent of everything but wanting to use his bathroom. He would have to speak to Carol about keeping a closer eye on her keys. Or maybe he wouldn't. This had certainly brightened a dull, working weekend.

"Very well." He stepped aside and opened the door. "But I'd have liked to see you in it."

Barbara sailed forward, eyes averted. He caught her arm, his grinning glance running the length of her. "Maybe you'd better put something on before you go out there."

She pulled away from him, then stopped in the middle of his office and backed away from him toward the door. "Everyone's at lunch," she said, anxious to get away. "I'll dress in my cubicle."

Then without warning the office door burst open, and a man with a wide smile walked in, saying in a booming but cheerful voice, "Hey, John. I know we're early but I have to handle hospital rounds for...ah...oh!"

The man stopped short, his hand still on the doorknob, when he caught sight of Barbara's skimpy attire. Another man coming in behind him collided with his back, and they were pushed four steps farther into the office as the four people behind *him* slapped into each other like dominoes.

Five figures fanned out around the first man to see what had stopped him. In her embarrassment, Barbara noticed only two details. One of the group was a woman. And they were all wearing clerical collars.

She didn't even wonder what the clergy was doing here, or why they'd descended on her en masse. She just knew this day was developing into something that made garbanzo beans seem as usual as white bread. She considered doing herself in with an airbrush or by drinking the art department's coffee.

Everyone stood in silence. Barbara could imagine how lewd this must appear to the men and woman of the cloth. She opened her mouth to explain, hoping something would come out.

John found himself more amused than horrified. Ryan was clutching her clothes to her, her cheeks pink, her eyes closed. He imagined she struggled over forming an explanation.

He, on the other hand, rarely found it necessary to explain himself. But this was a touchy situation. Cheney & Roman had a lot to lose if Daniel Burger and his group misunderstood this interesting tableau.

As Ryan opened her mouth, apparently ready with the explanation, he took action. He walked past her to the man who'd led the assault on his office.

"Daniel!" Barbara watched her employer shake the first man's hand with every appearance of hospitality. "Welcome to Cheney & Roman."

Daniel looked doubtfully from Barbara to his host. "Hello, John. I'm...sorry. I had a scheduling change this morning and, since you were fitting us in on a day when you aren't supposed to be here, anyway, I thought you might not mind if we arrived fifteen minutes early." He looked guiltily at Barbara. "It seems that wasn't a good idea."

Cheney laughed lightly. ''Well, you did catch us a little off guard.''

Barbara, still clutching her pile of clothes to her, felt a stab of alarm when he turned to her with a smile and extended his hand. Taking it would have meant freeing the shoes that she held atop the pile. Instead, she went hesitantly toward him, sure he was about to explain to his guests how she'd broken into his office, taken over his bathroom and caused this embarrassing little debacle.

That wasn't what he did.

It wasn't even close.

John Cheney wrapped an arm around her shoulders and pulled her to his side. Then he inclined his head and kissed her—briefly, quickly, but with the ease of a man who had the right. She was too surprised to object.

''Gentlemen,'' he said, ''Mrs. Gordon, may I present my wife, Barbara. Darling, this is...'' He went down a list of names and church affiliations, but she didn't hear a thing. She was too busy smiling and trying not to undermine his deception by letting her mouth fall open.

By the time he finished introductions, she could see the cleverness of his ploy. Of course. His wife. She had to applaud his quick thinking. Certainly even the clergy couldn't condemn a man's lust for his own wife in his own office.

''We've only been married a short time,'' he said, apparently trying to give the fiction substance.

Barbara accepted that she'd gotten him into this and owed him a good performance. She looked up at him with a reverence she was sure they'd understand. And she took a little satisfaction in the fact that he seemed surprised by her cooperation. ''And he's been away for several days. He got back just before you arrived, and I'm afraid I tried to distract him from business.''

The man he'd called Daniel fixed her with a confused smile. "But we met him at the CC breakfast this morning."

"CC?" she asked in a small voice, wishing she hadn't decided to be heroic.

"Daniel and his group," Cheney explained, looking pleased that her effusion had almost thwarted her, "are the board of directors for the Cooperative Churches. I came back from Denver a day early to attend their breakfast and get a feel for what they're looking for in their ad campaign. You remember. I explained when I called you last night."

"Oh, yes," she said a little too brightly. "Right!"

"Our discussion this morning went so well that I suggested we meet here after lunch so I can show them exactly what we can do for them."

She nodded and saw her opportunity to recapture her role. "So my plan to meet you here and charm you into coming home early was a bad idea."

John was intrigued to see that she was good at this, fast on her feet. And despite the urgency of the moment, he couldn't help but stop and consider what they'd be doing right now if that look in her eye were genuine and she *had* intended to charm him. Then he had to let the thought go. The distraction was too great—and too dangerous.

A gleam in his eye told her that her rejoinder had been a good move. He kissed her temple. She noted abstractedly that his lips were warm and dry. "It was a great idea," he said in a low, suggestive tone. "Just one we'll have to pursue later. Maybe you'd better get dressed."

She smiled apologetically at the group, which now looked at her indulgently rather than critically. "I've enjoyed meeting you," she lied. "I'll just slip out when I leave.'' She smiled up at Cheney, thinking something more might be required in front of their audience. ''I'll see you at home,'' she said softly.

She saw the challenge in his eyes, felt the slightest pressure of the hand that now held her elbow. She tipped her face up. He intercepted her lips with his, gave her one heartfelt kiss that completely upset her equilibrium, then walked her to the bathroom, pushed her gently inside and closed the door.

Barbara locked herself in and fell against the door, gasping for air and praying for her emotional and physical balance to be restored. She was going to kill Carol.

She knew she was flirting with fate, but she took an extra moment to slip on the blue dress. She stood on tiptoe to create the impression of wearing heels and turned to study her reflection—and remind herself what had started all this in the first place.

She was going to meet Trevor's parents. The very thought calmed her. Trevor was potential husband material—steady, reliable, calm. So Carol insisted he was stodgy. That wasn't a bad trait. Barbara's father had been a flamboyant architect with all the excitement in his life anyone could want—and none of the stability. He'd always been somewhere across the globe or deep in a creative frenzy whenever she needed him. He was now working on a shopping complex in Tokyo, and her mother had married a doctor.

The dress was beautiful, and what was even more important, it made *her* beautiful. It clung everywhere, the long column of shimmering silk dramatizing her height and highlighting her slenderness. The low, draped neckline suggested but did not display cleavage.

This wasn't the style of dress one would normally wear to meet a man's parents, but Trevor would be receiving an award at a formal dinner and they were flying in from Palm Beach.

She studied the low neckline in concern for a moment, wondering what his parents would think. Then she laughed softly as she quickly but carefully pulled the dress off. Even if they disapproved, their thoughts would probably be mild compared to those of the clergy on the other side of the door.

Barbara groaned aloud as she hung the dress again and pulled on her clothes. If her cheeks weren't still hot pink, she'd be wondering if that whole fiasco had ever happened.

Of course, that was the story of her life—good intentions that went awry, innocent adventures that had a way of turning on her. Well, she'd escaped this one unscathed, and she was grateful to be getting out with her skin—even though everyone had seen it.

Her mother insisted it was because she was like her father that trouble always found her. She wanted so much to prove that wasn't true.

It was time to get serious. She loved her job, and she fully intended to one day be invaluable to Cheney & Roman. But she wanted a home and children, too. She wanted life insurance and a station wagon to drive the kids to ballet and tuba lessons. She wanted to buy in family-size quantities and learn to use leftovers.

She brushed her hair, freshened her makeup, tossed the dress over her arm and squared her shoulders. "All right," she told herself aloud. "They're going to be deep in a marketing discussion. Keep your eyes front and your pace quick, and you're out of here."

She had so convinced herself a hasty retreat was possible that when she opened the door to find everyone in the office staring at her, it stopped her cold. Every occupant of the six chairs pulled in a semicircle around Cheney's desk studied her with eerily intense concentration.

Her "husband" sat on the corner of his desk, his jacket tossed back on his chair, his tie pulled away from his throat. She saw a kind of amused resignation in his eyes and felt her heart sink to her stomach. She didn't know what that look meant, and she was sure she didn't want to know.

"Well." She smiled brightly, carefully avoiding her employer's eyes as she backed across the office. "Have a lovely afternoon, everyone. I have places to go and people to see."

She sailed as far as the door, under the steam of determination. Then John Cheney said her name.

"Barbara."

It was nothing, just her name. But she'd been Barb since childhood. Friends called her Barb. Trevor called her Barb.

The rolling syllables of her full name rode off Cheney's tongue like some mystical spell—as though he'd called to something inside her attuned to the lyrical sound. She turned.

He smiled and beckoned. "Can you stay a minute? Daniel has an idea he'd like to run by you."

She didn't like the sound of that at all. She had no idea why; she just didn't. But seven pairs of eyes were staring at her, and John Cheney's were trying to tell her something.

Intrepidly, because she felt she owed it to him to play her "wifely" role until these people finally left, she hung the dress hanger on the hat rack by the door and went to the edge of desk he'd cleared for her beside him.

The moment she was seated, Daniel Burger rested an

elbow on the arm of his chair and leaned toward her. "My colleagues and I," he said with that ever-present smile, "want to launch an advertising campaign that will bring young people back to the church."

She nodded, trying to sound knowledgeable without encouraging what he had in mind—at least until she knew what it was. "I believe that's already a trend, isn't it?"

He bobbed his head from side to side in a gesture that was indeterminate. "If it is, it isn't moving fast enough for us. Attendance is way down in most churches." Everyone nodded.

Barbara felt Cheney's arm come around her to settle carelessly across her shoulders. She got the impression it was intended to hold her in place. She braced herself.

"Your husband likes our plan," Daniel said. "And we hope you will, too."

"But I have no say in campaign devel—"

"You would in this one."

She refused to ask the logical question, afraid of the answer. He gave it to her, anyway.

"Because we want to find a couple that typifies the young American family, to show them in all their worldly pursuits, in their home, with their children, at their leisure—" His voice quieted. "In their obvious delight in each other."

She began to see it coming and decided Cheney had known what he was doing when he'd put his arm around her. Given the opportunity to bolt, she would be in Kansas by nightfall.

Daniel's voice regained its firm tenor as he went on. "And show them at worship so everyone can see that a man and woman in tune with the world they live in still have room for God in their lives.'' He smiled beatifically. ''We think you two would be perfect!''

Chapter Two

A portly man with thick white hair leaned forward. "John and the twins have been coming to St. Bonaventure's since I arrived two months ago." He gave her a questioning smile. "But I haven't seen you with them, Mrs. Cheney."

Her brain crowded by panic, Barbara tried desperately to think. Admitting that she didn't go to church would probably get her out of this dangerous situation, but it would also scotch the deal for Cheney & Roman.

"I've been spending weekends with my mother," she said. The lie came out smoothly, despite the turbulence inside her. "She hasn't been very well."

The priest frowned in concern. "Perhaps I should call on her."

"She's beginning to improve," Barbara said quickly, brightly, wondering what her very healthy Methodist mother would do if a Catholic priest appeared at her door, offering to comfort her in her illness. "She's able to get around now."

The priest nodded. "Well, the offer stands."

"Thank you, Father."

"Will you do it, Barbara?" Daniel asked. "John thinks all our ideas can be incorporated into the campaign, and we're excited at the prospect. We'd intended to simply hire models—until we saw the two of you together. You're a handsome couple and very much in love. That'll shine through with complete honesty.''

The only woman among them shook her head. She had short, fair hair and, Barbara had noticed, a perpetual frown. ''I have to object once again. I think we'd be safer with models.'' She cast a swift glance at Barbara that registered disapproval. ''Granted, they seem very much in love, but if they quarrel, that will also come through with complete honesty.''

''That's not a problem, Joanna,'' Daniel said. ''Lovers can quarrel and still care deeply for each other. Disagreement is healthy. People understand that.''

Joanna sat back quietly without further comment.

''Of course, we don't want you to feel coerced into agreeing to do this,'' Daniel said. ''It'll mean someone from your staff and one of our representatives, living with you, photographing you, observing you, for the next few weeks. You should know that.''

John turned slightly to flip the pages of his calendar on the desk behind him. ''We have a conflict at the end of next week. It's my parents' anniversary, and we'll be spending a few days there.''

Father O'Neil slapped Daniel on the shoulder. ''That would be perfect. Three generations celebrating together, showing how we can live our own lives and still be drawn back to the family that nurtured us.'' He beamed at Barbara. ''One of our most important messages is that love once given can be carried down the generations.''

Barbara was truly beginning to feel like a fraud. What had begun as a harmless and very temporary deception was assuming potentially lethal proportions. She had to do something.

John had little trouble seeing the tension in her smile.

"Can we talk about this before we decide?" she asked.

He squeezed her shoulders, applying as much pressure as reassurance. "Of course. Daniel, I'll call you in the morning with our decision. If this doesn't work, I'll have an alternate plan in place in time for you to start this project at the end of the week, anyway. Meanwhile, my partner will show you some of our previous campaigns so you'll be able to see firsthand what we can do for you."

John picked up his telephone and asked Hal Roman to show the group around. He appeared instantly; the short, round embodiment of good cheer. Shaking hands with the group, he did a double take at the sight of John with an arm around a copywriter he knew his partner seldom saw.

"Daniel," John said to Hal, "wants to use Barbara and me as the models for their campaign."

Hal raised an eyebrow. "You and...Barbara?"

John nodded. "Barbara's a little reluctant." He squeezed her to him in a show of husbandly tolerance. "We're still jealous of our privacy. Nauseating newlyweds, you know."

"Newlyweds," Hal said slowly.

John replied with the slightest emphasis, "Right."

Barbara knew that word around the office was that John Cheney and Hal Roman were so successful because they read each other's minds and, creatively at least, they were in perfect sync.

Hal nodded a little vaguely, treading carefully.

''When you called me about this after your breakfast meeting, you said to round up some models.''

Daniel beamed. ''Then we arrived a little early and walked in on John and Barbara...and saw how much in love they are, and got the idea to use them instead.''

Hal looked blank and a little desperate.

''We'll talk it all over later,'' John said briskly. ''Right now I'd appreciate it if you'd show them some of our past print and broadcast campaigns before they leave.''

''Ah...right, sure.''

Daniel stood and the rest of his group followed. He shook hands with John, then Barbara.

That close to him, her hand locked in his large, firm one, Barbara saw wisdom, strength, compassion and determination in the minister. She wondered if he saw the truth in her.

''All I ask,'' he said quietly, as John saw everyone else to the door, ''is that you understand that we don't want to invade your privacy, we just want to show people what you have and convince them that they can have it, too. And that we know Who can help them find it.'' He placed his other hand atop their joined ones and pressed. ''Goodbye.''

When the door closed behind the Cooperative Churches members, Barbara faced John Cheney in the middle of his tobacco brown carpet.

He guessed by her mutinous expression that she was about to refuse to cooperate. He couldn't let that happen. He wanted very much to keep Daniel Burger and his group happy, and he wasn't averse to doing something good for himself at the same time. And Ryan was the most interesting woman to cross his path in a long while.

The prospect of several weeks spent in intimate circumstances with her certainly brightened his horizon.

"I won't do this," she said, as he walked slowly toward her. "It would never work. And I'm practically engaged."

He caught her arm and pulled her gently with him toward the leather sofa before the window. "How can you be 'practically' engaged? Either you are or you aren't."

She placed a knee on the sofa and sat facing him, an elbow on the back. She kept her expression firm. "I've been seeing someone for almost a year. I couldn't possibly pre—"

John sat in the same position, the knee of his pin-striped pants just an inch from her woolen slacks, careful not to touch her. "Has he asked you to be his wife?"

"Not yet, but his parents are—"

"Then, you're not engaged."

She expelled an impatient puff of air. "All right, if you want to be technical, my feelings are engaged, even if my person isn't. I cannot pretend to be your wife for this ad campaign. Trevor is…"

"Trevor?" He raised an eyebrow and bit back a smile. "Very dramatic name. Was that dress intended to push him over the edge into matrimony?"

"No," she said tightly, obviously irritated.

John could see she didn't like to be teased.

"No," she said more quietly. "It was intended to replace my dress that was ruined by the cleaners. I hadn't time or money to buy one suitable, so Carol…"

"Suitable to what?"

"Suitable to the awards dinner being held in Trevor's honor this evening at the Downtown Hyatt. So Carol is lending me her dress."

He nodded dryly. "Right. Carol. Incidentally, she explained to me how you got into the office. It was noble of you to take the blame." While Barbara had been in the washroom, he'd made a quick trip to Carol's desk to ask her to bring coffee for his guests, and she'd explained everything. It touched him that Barbara had tried to protect her.

"Well…" She imitated that dismissing wave of Carol's. "I know she shouldn't have done it, and I didn't want you to fire her or anything."

He shook his head, negating that possibility. "I couldn't function without Carol. But I'd have thought someone so concerned about a friend would extend that concern to the problems caused by her unauthorized use of my office."

"I was in your bathroom," she reminded him quietly, "not your office."

"In your underwear." He used the same controlled tone. "In which my potential client saw you and would have assumed the worst had I not intervened."

"I was about to explain," she said defensively. "It would have absolved you of blame and cleared up the entire misunderstanding."

He smiled, thinking he had her. "Do you think for a moment they'd have believed you were in my office to try on a dress? Mrs. Gordon, particularly?"

Barbara opened her mouth to assure him that they would have, then closed it, knowing they wouldn't. The scene had been just too incriminating.

"Since you don't seem to have a conscience," he said, "I have to insist that you pretend to be my wife for this campaign."

"Mr. Cheney, I know nothing about you," she protested in desperation. "I mean, I've heard Carol talk about your kids, but I don't even know if you're widowed, divorced—''

"I'm neither," he replied. "I guess I'm what you'd call an unwed father." His smile was ironic. "I lived with a woman who became pregnant with my child. Well, we thought it was a single child at the time. She didn't want it, but I did, so I took care of the expenses, then took the babies."

Barbara was completely surprised. She was sure that situation happened rarely. Even men who were willing to take financial responsibility for an out-of-wedlock child were usually eager to have the woman, or some adoption agency, assume personal responsibility. She shook off a mental image of little wolf cubs.

"Daniel said we'd be studied and photographed for two weeks. I'd have to…to…"

"Move in with me," he provided, his gold eyes steady as he watched for her reaction. "Eat with me, sleep with me."

"That's out of the question."

"I'm afraid it's the only answer."

She folded her arms stubbornly. "I accept that this is all my fault, but, much as I love my job, I'm not willing to climb into your bed to save the company."

He nodded affably. "That's fine, as long as you convince the CC representative, and the camera, that you've done it."

"I don't think a woman can fake the wifely glow."

The telephone rang and he ignored it. His smile was wicked and slow. "Let me take you close enough that you'll imagine what it would be like. That might be enough to fool them."

She stared at him a moment, as though trying to decide whether or not he was serious.

He pressed. "The Cooperative Churches promises to be a lucrative account for us. If the Northwest campaign works, they intend to present it to their national board. And you can't dismiss the worthiness of the issue. This account would give us national prestige."

"Then, let them do it with models."

"They want us."

"But, we're a *lie*. You don't think the camera will pick that up?"

"No. We're simply an untried element." He smiled, the dangerous gold eyes going over her, then settling on her mouth. "Had I gotten to know you before this forced us together, I'd have made a point of knowing you better, and by this time you wouldn't have to fake anything with me. Anything at all."

Her balance tottered dangerously again. She fought to hold on to it. "I don't *think* so. I'm engaged, remember?"

He shook his head. "He hasn't asked you, remember?"

The buzzer sounded on his call director. He pushed himself off the sofa and leaned over the desk.

"Yes, Carol?" he asked into the speaker.

Carol's voice, sounding subdued, replied, "It's your daughter, Mr. Cheney."

"Thank you." He pushed the blinking light and picked up the reciever. "Hi, baby. What is it?"

Barbara stood to leave, but he put a hand out in a halting gesture. Frustrated, she wandered around the office while he talked.

"Yes, I missed you, too. How've you guys been?" He listened for a moment, then Barbara saw him put a hand to his eyes and shake his head. "No. No. Jade, you weigh less than seventy pounds. You can't have an

ATV. No, Joe isn't getting one, no matter what he told you.'' He shook his head at Barbara as he sat on the edge of his desk. ''Yeah, I know. Well, I'd move to Jurassic Park with the other dinosaurs if it really existed. Ask Libby if she needs anything from the store on my way home.'' He waited a moment. ''All right. I'll be there in about an hour. Love you, too. Yeah, sure. Put him on.''

John made a helpless gesture with one hand, then returned his attention to the phone.

''Hi, Joe. Yeah. No, well, you know how women are. You have to be specific.''

He grinned at Barbara when she sent him a cool look.

''Well, next time explain that it's a plan and not a reality. I'm not sure you could ride an ATV all the way to Boston, anyway. All-terrain vehicles are only off-road, you know, and you might have a problem when you get to the Rockies. Well, get a map out and we'll plan it after dinner. Right. Love you, too. Bye.''

John hung up the phone, still smiling. Barbara could see that the feelings that prompted the smile also lit his eyes and lent him a tenderness she hadn't seen before. She found herself speculating on the private life of the paradoxical John Cheney. For an instant she even entertained the notion of becoming a part of it, if only temporarily. Then she shook off the thought, remembering how easily she got into trouble.

''That remark about knowing women sounded to me as though you're raising a little chauvinist,'' she scolded gently.

He nodded with a laugh. ''He does have tendencies that way, but his sister thinks of herself as a cross between George Custer and General Patton, so they'll cancel each other out when they grow up.''

He sobered, she squared her shoulders, and they studied each other in silence for a moment. Then she asked without preamble, "What if I refuse to play the part of your wife?"

"Then," he said with a reluctant sigh, "I guess I'll have to stop playing the part of your employer." He didn't want this opportunity—personal as well as professional—to slip away.

Barbara required several seconds to understand what he meant. Then she examined his studiedly innocent expression and asked pointedly, "You mean you'd fire me?"

"I mean," he replied, his wolf's eyes not quite carrying off the ingenuous gaze, "I'd have to conclude you don't have the interests of Cheney & Roman at heart."

She refused to give him the satisfaction of her indignation. "That's harassment."

He did not appear intimidated. "Of an employee whom I found inside my locked office in my absence."

Now she didn't care who saw her indignation. "I explained that! I took nothing and damaged nothing!"

"You were in your underwear, Barbara."

She doubled her fists in frustration. "Fine! Then you're free to take me to court, and *you* can explain to the CC why you lied to them about my being your wife. *I* was going to tell the truth!"

He shook his head with that same expression of regret. "Then I'd lose a client and you'd lose your job, probably your reputation and very likely the proposal you seem to feel so sure is in your future. If I were you, I'd give it all a second thought."

"My answer," she said firmly, "is no! Would you like me to clear out my desk?"

"I'd like you to think about it overnight."

"I don't have to."

"Good. I'll call Daniel in the morning and tell him you've agreed."

"But I said—"

He opened his door and was pushing her gently through. He peered around the corner to speak to Carol. "Get Morgenthaler on the phone for me, please. And get me a double cap."

"Right." Carol picked up the phone.

"Mr. Cheney…" Barbara caught his shirtsleeve, trying to stop him as he stepped back into his office.

He looked down at her fingers clutching his shirtsleeve, then into her eyes. She freed him immediately.

"Morgenthaler on the phone," Carol said.

He grinned. "I rather like the idea of you clutching at me. Excuse me. I have a call." And he closed the door.

Barbara turned to Carol with fire in her eyes, but her friend cradled the phone on her shoulder and made a cross of her fingers to hold her away.

"Hi," she said into the receiver while smiling at Barbara. "This is Carol at Cheney & Roman. I need a double cappuccino for Mr. Cheney. Chocolate on the top. Right. Thanks."

As she hung up the telephone, she handed Barbara a paper bag. "Your taco," she said. "Eat, you'll feel better. I know, I know…" She raised a restraining hand as Barbara prepared to tell her what letting her into Cheney's office had caused. "He told me briefly what happened, when he stepped out to ask me to get the CC's coffee. I'm sorry I insisted you use his bathroom, but look at how it turned out."

Carol was beaming, Barbara noted, as though what had happened had been somehow positive.

"I'm *not* going to do it. Trevor wouldn't like it, I couldn't possibly pull it off, and someone would surely find out and we'd all be in worse trouble. It's an absurd idea."

Carol sobered. "Barbara. You're responsible for his predicament."

Barbara narrowed her eyes. "*Who's* responsible?"

Carol stood to follow her as she stalked back to her cubicle. Carol stood in the doorway and leaned a shoulder against the opening.

"He and Mr. Roman have worked so hard for this contract," she said gravely. "But the CC was having difficulty getting everyone to agree. When they called while Mr. Cheney was gone, I told them how to reach him in Denver. Unfortunately, he made the plans to come back a day early and neglected to tell me. I guess inviting them back here was all very impromptu."

Barbara delved into her paper bag, took a sniff of cold taco and tossed the bag and its contents away. "Very unfortunate for all of us. But I can't help it. If anyone should pretend to be his wife, it should be you."

Carol came to lean against the lineup of print ads Barbara had tacked up on her corkboard wall. "We need this account, Barb. Cheney & Roman's reputation for integrity and excellence has earned them more local work than we can manage, but they need national exposure. If this account works locally, they'll go national with it."

"He explained that to me."

"Then how can you say no?"

"Because it would take two weeks. *Two weeks* of living with him in intimate circumstances, being with his children, pretending to know things about him I don't know, being photographed…"

Carol nodded calmly. "His kids are great, he lives in a Georgian mansion in the woods that has every convenience a woman could want, and he's not all that complicated."

Barbara sighed, feeling control slip away from her. "All men are complicated."

Carol shook her head. "Men who think of everything in terms of money are complicated, maybe because the dollar goes up and down, and the exchange rate is always changing. Men who think in terms of people are more instinctive and honest. You're afraid of him because he isn't stodgy."

Barbara frowned her disapproval of the suggestion. "If I were afraid of him, it would be because he introduced a complete stranger to a client as his wife."

Carol went on as though she hadn't spoken. "Because inside you is this free spirit who comes up with brilliant, hooky ideas that are wild and wonderful. But you're afraid to indulge yourself completely, afraid of what might happen, afraid you'll turn out to be like your father. So you choose a stodgy man you don't love but who you think centers you and provides you with balance."

Barbara put a hand over her eyes. "I'm not paying seventy-five dollars an hour for this, am I?"

Carol ignored her. "I think you should just let loose. Stop holding back. Do this! Get a dose of John Cheney and give him a dose of you before you tie yourself forever to Trevor Wentworth."

"Trevor," she said loyally, "is a won—"

"I know. And duller than ditch water. And he gave you an IRA for your birthday. Think about it." Carol stood and turned to leave, then stopped in the doorway and turned to whisper, "Imagine what it would be like to make love for the rest of your life with a man who keeps a portable umbrella in his briefcase.''

"In today's world," Barbara said pontifically, "there is nothing wrong with stability."

Carol expelled a little sound of impatience. "Don't you read the headlines? In today's world, there *is* no stability. Preparing for it isn't a virtue, it's an error. But it's your life. Have fun tonight."

CECIL AND OLIVIA Wentworth reminded Barbara sharply of the models in a bulk fiber ad she'd seen recently in a women's magazine. The stiffly handsome white-haired man and the coolly attractive gray-haired woman had been obviously chosen to assure the consumer that even elegant suburbanites reached for their product.

Barbara smiled as Cecil talked on about his stock portfolio, but she'd tuned him out some time ago. He was a handsome, older version of Trevor. His wife and son were focused on his every word. In their obvious enjoyment of each other, they seemed to have forgotten she existed. But she was more relieved than hurt.

She found herself looking out onto the sea of small tables and wondering what everyone else was talking about. She knew this sudden irreverence was directly linked to this morning's episode and her conversation with Carol. Those few moments of drama made a detailed discussion of stock premiums seem very tedious.

As her eyes surveyed the room, they stopped at a beautiful brunette in white, who was laughing as she leaned closer to speak to the man in a tuxedo opposite her. He laughed heartily in response. It was John Cheney!

"Barb!" Trevor said sharply, righting her water glass. He handed his mother a linen napkin to catch the water that was drenching her bread plate and utensils and dripping into her lap.

"Oh, I'm sorry!" Barbara's heart thudded uncomfortably as she added her own napkin to the flow. The Wentworths weren't smiling.

"What did you say about chains?" Trevor asked with a frown as a waiter hurried over to place a napkin under the puddle and distribute fresh linens around the table.

Barbara saw Cecil and Olivia exchange a quick glance, then smile politely. They probably thought she had quirky plans for later and disapproved. They didn't like her. She'd suspected their disapproval when Olivia's frowning glance kept coming back to the blue dress. Trevor's mother wore fashionable, silk, loose-legged pants and a short jacket. Very chic, very sedate, very similar to the attire of half the women in the room.

"Chen—*ey,*" she corrected. "John Cheney. My boss." She pointed across the room, trying to appear casual about the situation. "Right over there with the woman in white."

"Ah." The woman turned in their direction. Trevor smiled and waved. "Sandra Ryder," he said. "Manager of our Yachatz branch."

The woman waved back, then Cheney, following her gaze, noticed Barbara and waved also. She returned the greeting, then quickly gave her companions her full attention.

This evening wasn't going at all the way she'd hoped. She wanted her feelings for Trevor to quiet the temptation to take part in Cheney's scheme. She wanted to feel the comfortable security Trevor always instilled in her. But he was completely absorbed in his parents.

The awards ceremony was brief. Trevor was presented and applauded, then gave a speech in which he praised his colleagues and introduced his parents. Cecil and Olivia waved as though they were royalty.

Trevor was given a brass plaque and tickets for two to the Cayman Islands. "As a bonus—" the president of the bank who made the presentation smiled at Trevor "—we're giving you the next two weeks off to get in some deep-sea fishing. Our limo will take you to the airport."

There was more applause. Then the ceremony was concluded.

"The Cayman Islands!" Cecil said with the first glimmer of enthusiasm he'd shown for anything that did not involve money.

"Cecil is an acknowledged deep-sea fishing expert," Olivia told Barbara. "He gets hundreds of dollars to go out on a charter."

Of course. Barbara suspected money had to be involved somehow.

"Tell you what, Dad," Trevor said as they inched their way through the departing crowd. "I'll take you with me. We'll take off together in the morning."

Barbara saw Cecil's eyes express the same surprise she felt, that she hadn't been asked to accompany him. She couldn't have gone, of course. She had to come up with a slogan for garbanzos. But she felt there was a revelation for her in the fact that he hadn't even considered her.

"Barb's hip deep in putting a campaign together for some little client," Trevor said. "She doesn't want to go fishing. And Mom was going to leave tomorrow to spend some time with Aunt Rose in Seattle, anyway. What do you say?"

"Well…" Cecil made a pretense of looking to Barbara for approval.

She smiled sweetly, resolve hardening inside her. "By all means. Have a wonderful time. Trevor's right. I have work to do."

JOHN SAW HER across the crowded lobby, standing out like a moonbeam among the tailored evening suits that seemed to be this fall's fashion code.

That glorious hair was piled on her head in a slightly more complicated do than she wore to work, but he considered it a travesty, anyway. Confining hair like that was tantamount to caging a raven. And the dress. It outlined her slender curves and dipped just low enough over her bosom to force him to control a reaction inappropriate to the time and place.

Trevor Wentworth had an arm around each of his parents while Barbara led the way through the crowd. To John, who studied every aspect of the human personality in his work, the image spoke volumes. He wondered if Barbara had any idea. Barbara didn't seem as though she'd had a pleasant evening with the Wentworths. And she didn't look like a woman thrilled at the prospect of two weeks in the Caymans.

The perverse demon in him he sometimes couldn't control—and often chose not to, anyway—turned him in their direction.

Sandy tried to hold him back. "What are you doing?" she demanded in a whisper.

He had told her all about the morning's episode over dinner. "Indulging myself. Just keep smiling."

"Johnny—"

But he'd already caught Barbara's eye, and he saw something akin to a challenge in her expression. He expected her to panic as he approached, suspecting he intended to spoil her evening. But she didn't. She even met him halfway.

"Barbara," he said as they came together in the middle of the lobby while the crowd funneled through the doors. She looked truly exquisite, and he marveled that Trevor Whoever wasn't touching her possessively to tell the world she was his. "You look illegal in that dress."

He saw that his compliment startled her. Trevor didn't react. John was disappointed. Had someone said that to his woman, he'd have decked him.

John put an arm around her shoulders and drew her with him as the crowd surged forward. "Barbara, I'd like you to meet my sister, Sandra Ryder. Sandy, this is Barbara Ryan, one of my copywriters."

Sandra reached around him to shake Barbara's hand. The crowd had now spilled onto the street, and John pulled them against the outside window of the hotel as people rushed by them. The night was chilly, and the clean smell of rain mingled with car exhaust and ladies' perfume.

Barbara looked from John's face to Sandra's and found a resemblance in the glossy dark hair and the strong bone structure. But Sandra's eyes were blue, softening to prettiness the dramatic features she shared with her brother.

"Hello," Barbara said, warming to her easy manner. Then she smiled up at her employer as Trevor and his parents caught up with her. "Mr. Cheney, I'd like you to meet my friend, Trevor Wentworth, and his parents, Cecil and Olivia Wentworth." She turned her smile on the three. "This is John Cheney."

John offered his hand to Trevor, who shook it, smiling pleasantly.

Olivia said pointedly, "I was about to look for a policeman. I thought for a minute you were kidnapping her.'' Trevor and his father seemed to miss the tension.

John, his arm still around Barbara, admitted frankly, ''I'd like to.'' His glance down at her was significant. ''I don't know what I'm going to do without her while you whisk her off to bask in the sun of the Cayman Islands.''

''Actually...'' John saw a complex collection of turbulent emotions flash in her eyes. Then she said with all evidence of amiability, ''Trevor's taking his father with him. They're leaving in the morning.'' She looked casually up into John's surprised face. ''And you wanted me to help you with that special project.''

Olivia turned to Trevor with a raised eyebrow.

''The garbanzo thing,'' he said. ''I told you about it when I picked you up at the airport.''

John looked into Barbara's eyes, wondering if she meant what he thought she meant. He saw vague hurt, singular determination and a gleam of daring that beckoned to his own streak of recklessness.

''All right,'' he said. ''We'll start on it first thing tomorrow.''

''John!'' a familiar booming voice called from several yards away. ''Barbara!''

Everyone turned toward the sound. A man appeared out of the crowd, hands in his pockets, collar turned up against the cold wind, not quite obscuring the clerical collar.

''Hi, kids!'' Daniel Burger greeted them warmly. ''How's my favorite couple?''

Chapter Three

Barbara, who never went to church, prayed for divine intervention. And she didn't care what form it took. Earthquake, hurricane, anything to forestall the impending disaster.

John felt his senses sharpen and the adrenaline begin to flow. This was as close as the average businessman ever got to living life on the edge. Something primitive in him responded to the danger.

He tightened his grip on Barbara's shoulder as he reached past her to shake Daniel's hand.

"Daniel, our favorite client. What a surprise," he said with real sincerity. "What brings you to the Hyatt?"

"Nothing." Daniel pointed behind him to the Gothic church in the middle of the block across the street. "Just on my way home from work."

Barbara launched into introductions, hoping to divert him from saying anything that would suggest further that she and John were man and wife.

She introduced Trevor's parents first. When she got to Trevor, she noticed that Sandra had placed herself directly beside him so that she looked as though she accompanied him.

Barbara guessed John Cheney had confided in his sister. "Trevor Wentworth," Barbara said quickly, "who received an award tonight for Banker of the Year."

Daniel looked duly impressed, and Trevor duly modest.

"And Sandra Ryder. Well…" She tried to draw Trevor away to put an end to the conversation.

But Daniel asked hopefully, "Have you given any thought to our campaign?"

Barbara bit back a gasp, then played every word over in her mind and realized there was nothing incriminating in it.

"She has," John replied. "And she's agreed to do it."

"Wonderful!" Daniel boomed. He smiled approvingly at him. "You're a lucky man to have a woman like this." Then he smiled at the group, apparently failing to notice the collective look of confusion, then started away, turning to wave. "I'll be in touch in the morning. God bless you all."

Barbara was frozen to the spot. John gave her shoulder a final squeeze, then, directly under Trevor's and his parents' gazes, he leaned down to kiss her cheek.

Barbara's heart, just beginning to slow its panicky pace of a moment ago, began to pound anew. She felt the angular smoothness of his jaw against her cheek as he held her to him one danger-defying moment longer. Then he straightened and smiled at the Wentworths as he took Sandra's hand and pulled her toward him. "Cheney & Roman *is* lucky to have Barbara. One day she's going to be the best copywriter in the business. Nice to meet all of you. Have a wonderful trip." He winked at Barbara. "See you in the morning."

Barbara felt the breath rush out of her like air out of a punctured inner tube. Apparently accepting John's careful twisting of Daniel's remark, and ignoring the kiss, Trevor pointed his parents to the parking garage and caught Barbara's hand to tow her after him as he followed.

"WELL, WHERE IS SHE?" John paced from the door to the window in his office as Carol walked in with a steaming paper cup.

"She'll be here, Mr. Cheney." Carol placed the cup on his desk. "I told you she said she had an appointment and would be a little late. But she knows the cooperative will be here at eleven."

"It's ten fifty-five."

"But she's dependable. You know that. Here. I took the liberty of ordering you a double cap. Have a swig."

The telephone rang, and Carol ran out to her desk to answer it. John picked up the hot cup and downed several swallows. He didn't know why he was edgy. This was just a meeting like hundreds of other meetings he'd held during the lifetime of his advertising firm. He knew how to make a confident presentation and how to convince a shaky prospective client that he and Hal would give him the best ad campaign this side of BBD&O.

He'd just never done it as a married man before, and he'd feel a hell of a lot better when his "wife" arrived.

The door connecting his office to Hal's opened, and Hal peered around. "They here yet?"

The sound of Daniel Burger's booming voice came through the open office door. John looked up to see him striding toward him with the full complement of Cooperative Churches representatives.

"Right on time," John said. "You ready with the schedule?"

Hal stepped into the office and closed the door, wav-

ing a manila folder. "Ready." Then he looked around
with a frown. "Where's Ryan?"

John groaned, put his cup down, then went to the door
to greet Daniel, wondering how to explain that he'd mis-
placed Barbara.

"Good morning," he said with smiling confidence,
shaking hands as the group trooped through the door.

The last member of the party slipped a slender hand
in his and stopped the greeting in his throat.

In a pine green dress that clung to her bosom and
waist, then flared at her knees, Barbara looked like
something just plucked from the woods behind his
house. Her cheeks were pink, her eyes dark, her hair—
short!

Before he could stop himself, he said accusingly,
"You cut your hair!"

Her eyes widened at his remark, and he realized what
he'd done. As her husband he was probably supposed to
know she was having her hair cut.

To his surprise she looped her arms around his neck
and stood on tiptoe to kiss him. "Good morning, darling," she said, in just the right husky tone of affection.

John forgot his displeasure as her lips closed over his
warmly, but too quickly. She was soft in his embrace,
and his body seemed to find her nearness and the quick
touch of her mouth sufficient to warrant a reaction.

She pulled out of his arms and turned to smile at Daniel and his companions. "We argued about this last
night, and I suppose he thought he'd won. I felt shoul-
der-length hair would be neater for the photographs. But
John didn't want me to trim an inch." She looked up at
him, teasing and challenging him to assume his role.
"Don't you like it?"

John laughed, but one of his hands at her waist

pinched her lightly. He turned to the priest. "Isn't there something scriptural about a wife obeying her husband?"

Father Mike, a head shorter than John, grinned at him. "There is, but I wouldn't try to use it in an argument. There are at least as many references that tell a man to cherish his wife and make her happy."

"With a woman," Daniel said, chuckling, "making her happy usually involves giving her what she wants."

"A woman's hair should be long," Joanna Gordon offered abruptly from her chair near the desk, her perpetual frown in place, "so she can tie it back. Or short, so it doesn't get in the way." She patted her own closely cropped blond hair, then indicated Barbara's. "That length will take time and effort."

For a moment all the men frowned at Joanna. Then Hal stepped forward, placing a folder on John's desk and opening it.

"We *have* planned a busy itinerary, but it won't be so bad that you'll have to tie your hair back for wind resistance, Barbara." He pointed to the long list with the tip of his felt pen.

"I thought we'd start things off at home after lunch, since you two are in the habit of taking Thursday afternoons off." He smiled at the group as he explained. "I'm sure being followed around will take a little adjustment, and it seemed easier to begin at home where they're most comfortable."

Everyone listened to Hal intently, except Barbara, who looked up at John in horror. *She* would not be more comfortable at John's home. She'd never been there. She'd hoped they would begin in the office where *she* felt comfortable.

Under the guise of kissing her ear, John whispered,
"Steady. It'll be all right."

Barbara, rubbing cold hands together, wondered what
had happened to the confidence with which she'd awakened this morning. After Trevor had driven her home
the night before, never mentioning John's suggestive behavior, but talking instead about the impending fishing
trip with his father, she'd decided it wouldn't be difficult
to give her all to John Cheney's plan.

But now, confronted with the reality of it, she began
to see all the pitfalls, to wonder if her "wild streak"
was finally leading her into something fatal to her mental
and emotional health.

"So you'll be photographing them yourself?" Daniel
asked Hal.

Hal nodded.

"Good." He smiled, apparently pleased. "And who's
writing copy?"

"Barbara and I are," John said. At her look of surprise, he shrugged. "Who knows us better than we do?"

Indeed. She half expected lightning to strike him. Apparently so did Father Mike. He suggested with a smile,
"Well, we know Who does, but He's not writing advertising copy at the moment."

Daniel laughed. "Good point, Michael. The cooperative has decided to send two representatives along," he
told John, Hal and Barbara. "Father Mike, because he's
the most enthused about what we want to do with this
campaign, and Pastor Gordon, because she has the least
faith in it. We thought that would help give us the best
balance."

Barbara nodded, privately thinking that no combination of two people could have made the project more
difficult for her—John's new priest, who was better ac-

quainted with him than anyone else in the group, and would naturally be a more discerning judge of *her* performance as his wife, and the only woman among them, who clearly didn't like her, didn't believe in the project and would be more difficult to deceive because of her mistrustful attitude.

She wondered if it was moral to pray for help in executing a deception.

"Then the three of us will move in with you tomorrow for the next few weeks," Hal said with a confident smile directed at Barbara, "and let the rest of the scenario develop naturally, depending on what you have planned."

"Didn't you just say we're all going to the house this afternoon?" She hoped for a reprieve.

Father Mike nodded. "But I have a late-afternoon appointment I couldn't change, and Joanna has a dinner meeting. We'll come to the office in the morning to watch you at work, then we'll move in with you tomorrow night."

"If we're going to catch your afternoon off," Hal said, "we have to get this one, because next week you'll be getting ready to go to John's parents, and the following week, we'll already be wrapping up."

She smiled her understanding while thinking privately, *Rats. No reprieve.*

There was a rap on the office door, and Carol walked in with a tray filled with orange juice.

"A toast to the project," John said as she distributed glasses.

"To love," Daniel said, raising his glass. Barbara resisted until John put his arm around her and pinched her again. She lifted her glass beside his. "In its many beautiful forms. May it take over the world."

A resounding Amen followed the toast.

Daniel placed his glass on the wet bar in the corner. "I'd like to confer with Father Mike and Mrs. Gordon before you get under way."

"Use my office," John said promptly. "Hal and Barbara and I will wait for you at the elevators."

The three left the office, closed the door behind them and found themselves confronted with employees looking up expectantly from desks, peering around cubicle walls, stopping in the process of message and mail deliveries.

John gave them a thumbs-up, then had to stop spontaneous applause with a quick, "Shh!"

"We'll fill you in," he said quietly, "at the next staff meeting. Back to work."

"*I* like your hair," Hal said to Barbara as they stood in a circle with John near the elevators.

Barbara remained close to John unconsciously, his size and solidity providing reassurance at a time when she was wondering what on earth she'd agreed to do. "Thank you," she said with a nervous smile. "I wish I'd had my head cut instead. Off."

John put an arm around her, feeling the little tremor of nerves under the chic little dress. "You're doing fine. But, in the future, don't make big decisions without consulting me."

She gave him an impatient look, but she didn't move away. "It's my hair. Having it cut was hardly a big decision."

"It was when it affected the roles we're playing," he insisted. "You surprised me, and I looked as though I didn't know what you were up to."

"Then you'll have to be on your toes, won't you?"

she challenged. "I think surprise is a basic part of the husband-wife dynamic. The successful ones, anyway."

She was probably right, but he didn't appreciate being called to task on it. "We have to work together," he said, "if we're going to succeed."

"She did her part." Hal punched the Down button as the cooperative streamed across the office toward them. "Her remark about you thinking you'd won the argument saved your hide."

John turned to Hal with a critical frown for which he got only a bland stare in return. Then the members of the cooperative were upon them as two elevators arrived. John, Hal and Barbara headed for one along with Father Mike and Mrs. Gordon, while Daniel and the other members wished them luck and called their goodbyes as they took the second one.

Barbara, trying to make conversation as the doors whispered closed, asked Hal, "What precisely did you want to photograph at home?"

"I think it'll all look most natural if you just follow your usual routine," he replied.

"All right." John leaned against the elevator's oak bar and pulled Barbara into his arms. "Our usual routine in the elevator is to steal a kiss."

Surprise parted Barbara's lips and allowed him to kiss her soundly. For him it began as payback for cutting her hair, then for teasing him about almost dropping the ball in the office. But as she clutched at the back of his jacket with one hand and held his shoulder with the other, suddenly everything changed.

He experienced the same sensation he'd felt in his washroom when he'd opened the door and found her suddenly in his arms. It felt right. He heard a click as a light flashed near his face.

The elevator jolted to a halt on the bottom floor, and he pulled away, perplexed. Barbara, eyes startled, looked at him as though she, too, felt something that unsettled her. There was another click, another flash of light.

"Well," Hal said, shouldering his camera as he leaned against the doors to hold them open. When the priest and the minister had passed him, he winked at John and Barbara. "I'd say we're off to a good start."

BARBARA HALF EXPECTED to see Scarlett O'Hara flirting with the Tarleton twins on the veranda of John's Greek Revival mansion. Graced with Doric columns wrapped with mimosa, it stood in antebellum splendor in the middle of a plush green lawn.

"Geez Louise!" Barbara breathed, unable to stop herself from staring, though she knew Hal followed in his van with Father Mike and Mrs. Gordon. It wouldn't do to have the mistress of the house staring at her own home. "What is this doing in Oregon?"

John offered her a hand, then concerned by her distraction, caught her waist instead and swung her down.

"I bought it from a man who came from Louisiana. He wanted something to remind him of home. I got it for a steal because it was a little big for the average home buyer."

Barbara wandered toward the porch steps, still staring. She looked at the deep veranda with its comfortable-looking, natural wicker furniture, at the many windows flanked with simple black shutters, then inhaled the mimosa and felt its sweetness flow deep inside her.

"A *little* big?" she asked. "You and the children must get lost in it."

He shook his head. "I wanted something that would give the kids lots of room—inside and out. My parents

live in a big old farmhouse on the beach where Sandy
and I grew up. I remember feeling myself stretch as I
grew older because there was room to run, room to get
away from everyone else if I felt the need, room enough
that I never felt confined.''

For the first time since John had pulled up in front of
his home, Barbara was more aware of him than the
house. So that was how a nimble mind developed—open
space with room to grow. She remembered her struggles
with the garbanzo beans account and smiled privately.
She'd grown up in a low-ceilinged condo tucked in with
thirty other residences, moved into a dorm room with
four other young women and now lived in a small apartment in a forty-eight-unit complex.

John opened the door and ushered her inside. She had
a quick impression of parquet tiles and a stairway worthy
of Scarlett when John pulled her into the living room. It
was done in shades of blue with white woodwork.

''You have to loosen up,'' he said quietly but urgently. ''You look at me as though you're terrified. Mrs.
Gordon's going to catch that.''

She shook off the hand that held her arm. ''Of course
I'm terrified. This was a ridiculous idea. I don't know
why I ever thought we could make it work.'' She turned
to look nervously through the lace sheers to the driveway. ''We shouldn't be talking about this, anyway.
They're right behind us.''

''Hal was stopping for gas,'' John said, taking her arm
again and turning her to him. ''We *can* make it work.
You just have to start acting like a wife.''

''I'm trying!''

''I know. And you're fine when you initiate the action.
It's when I do and you have to react that you panic.''

That was true. His touch, his eyes, reached something

inside her Trevor hadn't tapped in almost a year of keeping steady company with her.

She nodded, shaking her hands as though that could
magically loosen her whole body. "You'll have to forgive me," she said wryly. "I've never had a husband
before."

"That shouldn't be a problem," he said, "if you just
relax and let yourself be honest. You like it when I touch
you. Let that show."

She opened her mouth to deny it, then changed her
mind. It would be futile. That moment in the elevator
had proven that. Still, there was a considerable difference between sexual attraction and husband-and-wife familiarity.

"It's hard to even imagine being your wife," she admitted with a little frown, "when I don't really know
you at all. It's hard to look like the woman you love,
when I don't know—" She stopped herself, feeling as
though she'd stepped onto quicksand.

John saw the solution as starkly simple—and too
tempting to ignore. "Kiss me," he instructed.

"Mr. Cheney, that isn't—"

"Don't call me that," he ordered softly, firming his
grip on her. "It's John. Or whatever wifely endearment
you'd like to create yourself. Now, kiss me. It'll tell each
of us a lot about the other."

"You kiss me," she argued, her eyes looking everywhere but at his mouth. This was different from the
experience in the elevator. This one was calculated. "It's
your idea."

"All right, but you'll have to be quiet."

"I'm never quiet. It's a problem I've had since childhood. I chatter when I'm ner—"

He placed a hand at her back and pulled her to him.

She came up against him, breast to ribs, thigh to thigh, and felt every thought in her head dissolve.

He studied her for a moment, a small pleat of concentration between his eyebrows. As he lowered his head, hers rose of its own accord.

Their lips met in what she supposed to be the spirit of exploration. It took him one second to show her that he did nothing so tentatively. He was confident, decisive and wordlessly authoritative.

He cupped her head in one hand and took her mouth with a tenderness that drew a response right from the heart of her.

John felt her lean farther into him, felt her lips part and her hands move gently up his back. The cool silk of her hair spilled over his hand.

He kissed her as a husband would, possessively and passionately, tongue dipping into her mouth, hands moving over her in ownership.

Barbara had never been touched with such competence. Even as his hands wandered boldly over her and his kiss went farther than a first kiss should have, she understood he was simply showing her how the woman he loved would feel.

She struggled to hold on to the reserve that put a cap on the famous Ryan wild streak. But her reserve was frail stuff compared to John's artful assault. She felt it strain and stretch.

John was aware the instant she put up her defenses. One moment she was pliant and mobile in his arms, and the next she was stiff and still.

He drew away slowly, pulling himself together. Deep inside he felt the stirring of something he hadn't known since the days before Gracie, when he'd believed in a good woman, children around his dinner table and love that grew with the passage of time. He stared down at Barbara in suspicious surprise.

Barbara didn't have to wonder why he was frowning. Their bodies had been entwined when she'd felt it—a small shower of sparks as though something had shorted out.

Even as she took a step back from John Cheney, she knew that demonstration kiss had fused something in them, connected them to one another in a way neither had expected. She felt as though she stood with her toes over the edge of the Grand Canyon.

Chapter Four

"Just pretend we're not here," Father Mike said with complete conviction that that could be done. He sat on a chair by the white marble fireplace.

Joanna Gordon sat in a chair on the other side, her watchful, suspicious eyes making any kind of pretense difficult.

"Just do what you do," Hal said encouragingly. He was testing the light as he moved around the sofa on which he intended to photograph John and Barbara.

His subjects studied each other warily. John tossed his jacket aside, pulled his tie and shoes off. Barbara quickly decided that if he went one step farther, she was out of there.

"Barbara and I take Thursday afternoons off," he said, "because it's the only day of the week where we can be alone together at home. The kids are at school or, in the summer, at day camp, and the housekeeper takes a few hours off." He settled into a corner of the sofa, one knee bent, his stocking foot propped on a cushion. He reached for Barbara.

Certain she would not survive this, Barbara slipped out of her shoes and curled up next to him. He put his arms around her and pulled her firmly against him until she had to rest her head on his shoulder to be comfortable.

"We talk about how the week's going...how we feel." John stroked her arm as she lay stiffly against him. He entwined his fingers with hers and rested them on his knee. "Nervous, darling?" he asked, his tone gently indulgent.

"Yes, I am." She resented his calling everyone's attention to the fact, but she knew she hadn't been hiding it from anyone. The best she could do was make her discomfort seem like camera shyness. "John's the showman in the family," she said. "I prefer to be behind the scenes. He once even modeled for a Mr. Saturday Night ad."

She blessed her own nosiness in going through old Cheney & Roman portfolios when she'd first joined the company. That was a genuine touch.

At least, she hoped it was. She seemed to be losing her grip on the situation. All she was aware of now was John Cheney's body surrounding her—arms and legs providing a strong barrier between her and the woman she'd been only this morning. That, coupled with the memory of his kiss, was serving to undermine her concentration.

John felt her stiffen further, though she seemed to be trying hard to play her part. He kissed her temple, a reward and a display of encouragement for their audience.

Hal stood at the foot of the sofa and shot repeatedly.

"Did I tell you your Kate Cunningham wardrobe arrived?" John asked her.

Barbara, afraid to believe what that remark suggested, turned to look at him. "No," she said cautiously.

"Yes." John turned to the priest and Mrs. Gordon as

Hal moved around the sofa to reposition. "Kate Cunningham is an Oregon designer winning national accolades. She's also a client of ours. She called yesterday after Barbara left the office to see if she'd be willing to wear her fall collection. She wants it to be seen by other businesswomen."

Barbara's smile was wide and genuine. She lusted after the Cunningham clothes when they were brought into the office to be photographed. Hal focused and shot.

For the first time Barbara was unaware of him. "Really?" she asked.

"Really," John confirmed. Of course, *he* had called Kate, but the result was the same.

Barbara sat up and turned toward him, her knees folded under her. Hal shot again.

"The *whole* collection?" she asked, ingenuously wide-eyed.

"Down to belts and shoes."

She stared at him, then laughed softly. "Wow."

John put a hand to her hair, touched by her delight. The gesture was genuine. Hal's camera clicked.

"How are you adjusting to the children, Barbara?" Father Mike asked. "It must be different having to deal with two ten-year-olds after being single."

Barbara relied on what Carol had told her and what she'd overheard when John had spoken to his children on the phone. "They're wonderful," she said. "I have a lot to learn, but they're patient with me." At least, she hoped they would be.

"You mentioned an office in your home," Mrs. Gordon said, apparently having had enough of the cozy sofa scene. "May we see it?"

Hal took more photos of John and Barbara looking over an ad layout on his desk. It happened to be the Kate

Cunningham fall catalog, and Barbara became excited and animated. Hal went into action.

Later she made a pot of coffee while Father Mike and Mrs. Gordon sat at the table, watching. Finding the countertop coffeepot was easy, and John, behaving like a helpful husband, brought her filter, coffee and cups. She gave him a grateful glance.

Hal, the priest and the minister left as Libby, John's housekeeper, arrived home.

Barbara saw her smile politely at the departing trio and hurry into the house, as though anxious to avoid contact.

When they'd waved goodbye to their guests, John and Barbara found Libby in the kitchen.

She introduced herself to Barbara, then studied both of them with a frown. "I want you to know right now that I'm really terrible at this sort of thing. I blush when I lie.

"I once tried to hide twenty dollars from my husband, rest his soul, when we were first married and scraping for every penny. There was this gray felt cloche hat and…well, I guess that isn't important. But the deceit lasted all of ten minutes before I burst into tears and confessed everything."

Barbara liked her already. She was tall and pretty and impeccably groomed. She guessed her age at early sixties. She hooked an arm in hers and tried to lead her toward the back door. "Good. Neither am I any good at deceit. Let's run away together—a sort of Thelma and Louise of the Coast Range."

"Who?"

John moved to cut them off.

"I thought women in the nineties were more adventurous and invincible than ever before," he scolded.

"We can do this if the two of you would just show a little spirit."

He brought them back to the middle of the oak and white kitchen. Libby gave her employer a maternal look. "Lies are not an adventure. Lies are a trap."

John nodded. "In most cases, but I explained about this, Libby. The lie began to save Barbara's reputation, then the whole thing got beyond our control. But if we all do our share, it'll work out."

Libby studied him without response.

"The children are willing to do it," he said reasonably.

"That," Barbara said, "is because they're not old enough to see the pitfalls. They probably think it's a game."

"Actually, they're thinking of it as a stage play," Libby said. Then she added for Barbara's benefit, "They were both in *The Nutcracker* last Christmas. We talked about it over breakfast this morning." She sighed grimly. "I'm reluctant to say they think it will be fun. Well, Joe does, anyway."

Barbara nodded. "Figures. That's the little chauvinist, right?"

John closed his eyes and drew a deep breath, anxious to put an end to the women's reluctance and assure himself of their loyalty.

"What if I promise you your heart's desire if you cooperate?" he asked Libby.

She began to shake her head before he'd even finished. "No. I don't have to be bribed. I'll do it for you and the children because you're as dear to me as my own. I just think you're looking for trouble. This whole thing seems to have the potential for—"

"Your own Harley," John said baldly.

For a moment Barbara thought he'd lost his mind, trying to force cooperation from a woman in her sixties with a high-rolling motorcycle. Then she saw the look on Libby's face.

"Oh, Mr. Cheney. Certainly you don't mean—?"

"I do, Libby. All the extras. Everything you want. Yours when the Cooperative Churches signs the contract."

Fascinated, Barbara watched the flush of pleasure on Libby's face, the dreamy glow in her eyes.

John put his hands on the woman's shoulders. "So, will you put your heart into it for me? Will you make Father Mike and Mrs. Gordon believe that Barbara is my wife and that we're as in love as you and Peter were?"

Barbara saw resolve take shape in the midst of that dreamy glow. "I will," Libby said. "I'll do it."

"Good. Will you excuse us? I haven't had an opportunity to show Barbara around yet."

Barbara saw one large comfortable room after another: dining room, kitchen, library, the office in which they'd spent half an hour, spare bedrooms, the children's bedrooms. She noted absently that despite the fact that one child was a boy and the other a girl, their rooms were very much alike, decorated in clowns and primary colors. They had dozens of shelves literally packed with toys, deep, walk-in closets that held more clothes than she would ever own, artfully constructed bunk beds that also boasted storage, and windows that looked out onto the deep green woods at the back of the house. These were truly privileged children.

Something about that tugged at her.

John closed Jade's bedroom door and opened another across the wide, carpeted hall. He urged Barbara into an enormous bedroom, somewhat separated from another room about a third the size by two Corinthian columns, each spaced about five feet from the wall at each side of the room.

A king-size four-poster covered with a thick, quilted chocolate brown spread stood against one wall in the bigger room. A matching dresser occupied another wall, a chair stood near the bed, and a wide trunk rested at the foot. A window seat with brown plaid cushions stretched from the big room into the smaller one.

In it was a small sofa, a television, a wet bar and a fireplace. Barbara had never seen anything like it this side of *House Beautiful*. And it was more than size and the careful choice of furniture and appointments. The house had warmth and charm. To prevent herself from succumbing to it, and to show him that she wasn't affected by it, she turned and placed her purse on the foot of the bed. "I get the bed. You get the sofa."

He smiled, and she had a suspicion he saw through her pose. "A very unimaginative arrangement, but, sure, why not?"

She climbed onto the foot of the bed and kicked off the green flats that matched her dress. "And I want you to know that I can't be bought off with a Harley." She bounced a little on the bed—or tried to. He apparently preferred a firm mattress. He moved to the foot of the bed and leaned his shoulder against the post. She frowned up at him in genuine confusion. "How did you know Libby wanted a motorcycle—and *why* does she?"

He smiled, and this time the gesture expressed fondness. "Her husband was in the Coast Guard and owned a serious hog. Whenever they got time away from the children, they rode off on it to be alone together. She has fond memories of riding on the back of it on the open road. She still has their helmets in her rooms."

Barbara absorbed that information in wonder.

"What's yours?" he asked.

She looked up. "My what?"

"Your heart's desire."

She leaned back on an elbow, and said candidly, "Leftovers."

He sat on the trunk, braced a hand on the footboard of the bed and repeated flatly, "Leftovers."

She nodded, tracing the star-shaped quilted pattern in the spread with an index finger. "When I was a child, there were never leftovers because my mother cooked only for the two of us. I never have leftovers because I buy individual microwavable meals, or individual salads or portions of things from the deli." She shrugged her shoulder. "I want to cook for six people and have lots left over." She sighed, then heard her own words suspended in the air and thought how silly they must have sounded. She smiled a little sheepishly and sat up. "I don't know. Leftovers seem like a friendly, family thing to me."

John was both pleased and saddened by that little glimpse of vulnerability. "Where was your father?"

She slipped off the bed and into her shoes. "He was an architect in great demand. He spent most of his time in exotic locations, and my mother finally filed for divorce when I was in high school. I think he's building apartments in Tokyo right now."

John heard loneliness and loss in the quiet tone of her voice. He wanted desperately to erase it.

"Leftovers I could provide, but technically it would be Libby doing it, and I think asking you to give this your all should cost me, personally."

"Good point." She went to the window that looked out onto the lawn, the road that wound to the highway and the purple mountains in the distance. Then she wandered toward the open bathroom door.

John stood and followed her, thinking how strange it felt to have this graceful young woman in his bedroom. He hadn't brought a woman home since the children had been old enough to ask questions.

Barbara emitted a squeal of surprise. "Whoa. Three people could bathe in that tub at once."

She walked into the beige-and-gold bathroom, with its double-size step-in tub with whirlpool jets. There was a large shower, a simple oak shelf filled with fat towels in shades of brown, and a fireplace.

"Oh," she said softly, delighted to find that among the towels were two cats, curled up side by side. One was black and white and was lying on his back, two front paws stretched over his head. The other was a fat, gray tabby wound into a tight C. Barbara laughed and reached out gently to stroke each furry body. The black one stretched then settled back into place. The striped one began to purr.

"The contortionist is Walter," John said. "The one with the eating disorder is Hillary. I know it probably isn't cool to have them sleeping in the clean linens, but they show up in the damnedest places and always together."

"They're wonderful," she said, still stroking. "I always wanted pets, but I've never lived where they allowed them. Are they related?"

"No. Jade found Hillary in the woods behind the house. Joe brought Walter home. One of his schoolmates was moving and couldn't take the cat, so Joe made a deal with him. He gave him his Nintendo, and he got Walter.''

Barbara's eyes widened. ''His Nintendo? I've never really seen one in action, but don't little boys revere them above all else?''

John nodded and led the way back into the bedroom. ''Joe will never be a businessman. He thinks with his heart. He isn't quite the unsalvageable chauvinist you imagine him to be.''

From downstairs came the slam of a door that reverberated through the house like a gunshot. Then a voice shouted, ''Dad?''

''Up here!'' John replied. Footsteps pounded up the stairs like Hannibal's army, then two short, dark-featured gangly children appeared in the doorway.

Barbara's first thought was that they were much too small to have made all that noise. Then she wondered which was the girl and which was the boy. They were dressed similarly in blue shorts and matching T-shirts imprinted in gold with the name of a summer day camp. Both had short dark hair, wide gold eyes, and the healthy glow of well-loved, well-cared-for children.

One walked to Barbara with an interested smile, and the other went to place arms around John and study her with open suspicion. The gesture said more clearly than words could have that Jade was placing herself between Barbara and her father.

The boy offered Barbara his hand. ''Hi, Mom,'' he said with a cheerful grin. ''I'm Joe.''

Barbara laughed and shook his hand. This was no ordinary ten-year-old boy. This was the wolf cub she had imagined earlier, who'd obviously inherited his father's intelligence and ready humor. ''Hello, Son,'' she teased.

"Have you done your homework and taken out the garbage?"

"No, no," Joe said. "You're supposed to ask me if I've had a good day and offer me cocoa and cookies."

Jade leaned her head against her father's flat stomach and sighed. "He's so stupid. He thinks it's gonna be fun to make believe we have a mother."

John stroked the glossy dark head. "It will. We're going to do a lot of fun things together, and Uncle Hal will be with us a lot of the time. Then we're going to Grandma and Grandpa's for the anniversary party and to spend a few days."

Jade was noncommittal on the activities, but not on what she thought of Barbara. "She doesn't even look like a mother."

"Yes, she does," Joe defended quickly. "She looks like Lane Prather's mom."

"Lane Prather's mom is a model. But she's always gone. Who wants a mother like that?"

Barbara could only side with her on that one. "Maybe you could tell me what you want in a mother," she said, "and I'll try to behave that way for the next two weeks."

Jade unwound her arms from her father's waist and faced Barbara. "That's the thing about mothers. You don't have to tell them things. They know everything before you say it, like when something hurts or you need new underwear."

Joe rolled his eyes. "She acts like she knows what it's like to have a mother."

"I do," Jade said, eyes darkening with emotion. "Becky and Ginger Goodrich talk about their mother all the time. And when I sleep over, she kisses me good-night and checks on me during the night and fixes things

I like to eat.'' Her eyes swung to Barbara. ''That's what a mother does. And a lot of other things you probably don't know.''

''Jade.'' John's voice held quiet censure and a suggestion of warning. Then he turned to Joe. ''Why don't you take Barbara down to the kitchen and see if Libby will give both of you cocoa and cookies. Then you can help her bring her things in. But leave the big bag. I'll get it.''

''Right.'' Joe took Barbara's hand and drew her toward the door. ''Come on, Mumsy. I'll tell you all about what *I* want in a mother. You don't happen to have an ATV, do you?''

The door closed behind them, and John coaxed Jade toward the window seat. The mid-afternoon sun was warm and bright. He drew the miniblinds and sat sideways to face his daughter as she plopped down on a cushion, arms folded in disgruntled displeasure.

''I don't like her,'' she said, second-guessing the reason for their private conference.

''You made that plain,'' he said, his tone mild but scolding. ''She's a guest in our home, helping me with a special project. We talked about this last night.''

''I know.'' Jade pouted and looked out the window. ''I just don't like her.''

''You don't know her yet.''

His daughter looked at him with an expression that startled him. His endearing tomboy had suddenly become very feminine. ''She's pretty,'' she said, her tone suggesting condemnation.

John frowned. ''Yes, she is. Is that bad?''

''It's not right for a mother. You should have picked somebody else.''

''I explained to you what happened. It had to be Barbara because she was involved in the whole thing. Why isn't it right for a mother to be pretty?''

Jade turned her gaze to him. ''Pretty mothers don't stay.''

''What do you mean?''

She gave him a long-suffering sigh, as though wishing she didn't have to explain *everything* to him. ''Pretty mothers are models and actresses and news ladies on television. They're never home. The other ones that aren't those things have affairs with other men, then they get divorced, then they end up moving away and the kids have to go, too, and only get to see their dads at Christmas.''

John saw genuine concern in her eyes and couldn't for the life of him imagine where it had come from. The night before, when he'd explained everything, both children had thought the pretense would be fun. Joe apparently still thought so, but Jade was suddenly as reluctant as the other two women involved.

He pulled her into his lap and wrapped his arms around her. ''Baby, nothing like that is going to happen to you. We're just pretending all this, remember? It's make-believe. Barbara's going to be with us for two weeks, then it'll be just us again.''

He felt her small body relax against him as she expelled a deep sigh. ''I know. But I still don't like her. She's too pretty for a mother. Mrs. Goodrich is a little bit fat, and she wears sweatpants, and her hair's short and a little messy.''

John hugged her, understanding her fascination with Elaine Goodrich. He'd been room ''mother'' with her the previous year. Her warmth and her kindness were unconditional, and she made the best brownies west of the Rockies. But he'd discussed their situation as a motherless family with the children several times in the past, and they'd never seemed as though they felt deprived. He wondered if it was the sensitive preadolescent stage that had brought on Jade's preoccupation with mothers, or if there was something else at work here.

"All right," he said. "You don't have to like Barbara, but you do have to be polite to her. She's doing this as a favor to me, so I want to make it as easy for her as possible. Okay?"

There was a martyred sigh, then a reluctant "Okay."

"Good. Now let's go see if we can get in on the cookies and cocoa, too."

Jade leaned into him as they headed down the hallway to the stairs. "She's not going to make me do chores and wash behind my ears and stuff like that, is she?"

"I do that all the time."

"I know. But you belong to me. Or I belong to you. Which is it?"

"We belong to each other, I think."

When they reached the stairs, Jade took his hand and they started down. "How do you suppose she gets her hair to do that?"

"Do what?"

"Curl under at the bottom just a little bit."

John heard the reluctant interest in her voice. Maybe she wasn't quite as hostile as she pretended.

"I don't know," he replied. "Why don't you ask her?" In truth, he'd wondered himself how Barbara did it. When her hair had been long, it had been stick straight. Now, it looped under just above her shoulder as though it had been carefully molded to do that—yet it moved freely and glistened in the light. Women and girls, he decided, were filled with mystery.

Chapter Five

"So, tonight, are you guys going to practice being married?" Joe asked. He stood in the middle of the master bedroom in cotton pajamas decorated with dinosaurs.

Barbara turned from hanging a yellow sundress in the closet, her mouth open in momentary dismay. John stood behind him in the doorway, a steaming mug in his hands. His grin was in appreciation of Barbara's confusion.

Barbara sent him a dismissing glance, then concentrated on the child. "Ah...well...we have a lot to learn about each other in a short time."

"He's pretty much a nice person," Joe said, "as long as you do what he tells you, don't shout at anybody and don't tell lies."

Barbara's dark eyes slid back to John's, at that, in silent accusation. *The last part of that rule doesn't apply to you?*

John walked into the room and put a hand on his son's shoulder. "Thanks, Joe. I appreciate the recommendation. Ready for bed?"

"Yeah." Joe reached up to give him a hug.

John held the boy to him and offered the mug to Barbara. "Libby thought unpacking might be thirsty work." Then he wrapped both arms around the child and held him for a long moment. "Got your paints for art class tomorrow? Fed the cats?"

"Yep. I came to see if Barbara wanted to practice tucking me in."

John looked up at her over the boy's head, gold eyes filled with challenge.

"I'd love to," she said. She put the mug on the bathroom counter, then followed Joe out the door as he called good-night to his father.

"You pull the blankets up," Joe said in knowledgeable tones. "If it's been a day when I've done something you don't like, you sit on the edge of the bed and explain to me what it was. You're supposed to look...." Unable to decide on the proper word, he recreated the expression instead. He drew his eyebrows together and pursed his lips. "Then you tell me you love me, anyway. If it's just an ordinary day, you hug me, tell me you love me and remind me that tomorrow I have a dentist appointment, or you're going to be late from work so we're going to McDonald's for dinner."

"And how do you know so much about mothers?"

"Justin Goodrich is *my* best friend."

Of course. The redoubtable Mrs. Goodrich. Dutifully Barbara leaned down to hug him and was absurdly happy when he hugged her back. "I'll be home on time to meet you tomorrow afternoon because your father will be bringing home Father Mike, Mrs. Gordon and your Uncle Hal."

"They're going to live with us for two weeks."

"Right."

"It's exciting, isn't it?" Joe asked. "Like a play. Only *we* know what's going to happen because we're in it. I'm going to write them when I grow up and live in New York."

"That sounds very exciting. But I don't think that's a good place to have an ATV."

He blinked. "Well, everyone who lives in New York has a summer place in Connecticut. That's where I'll ride it."

"Of course. Well. Have I taken care of everything?"

"You have to pull the blankets up one more time and turn out the light."

"Got it." Barbara did as he instructed. "Good night, Joe."

"'Night, Mom," he replied.

Barbara was both pleased and concerned by his easy performance. She found Jade's door partially open and went inside to dose herself with the child's stabilizing skepticism. A Beauty and the Beast night-light glowed near the bed, illuminating the child propped up against her pillows.

"Hi," Barbara said. "I'm on a tucking-in practice run. Can I do it for you?"

"Daddy already did it," Jade said, pulling her blankets a little higher.

Barbara considered forcing the service on her in the hope of relaxing the child and herself, then decided that could be fatal to any future cooperation between them.

"Okay," she said, turning to the door. "Good night. See you in the morning."

She was in the hallway when Jade called, "Wait!"

Barbara stepped back into the doorway. "Yes?"

There was a moment's silence, then Jade asked, "Can you close the closet door?"

Barbara performed the service, remembering that as a child she'd also been convinced that an open closet door would admit nameless monsters into the room. She closed it firmly. "Anything else? Glass of water?"

"That glass of water stuff is just something you see on television," Jade informed her, curling onto her side. "Usually mothers don't like you to drink anything after you go to bed so you won't…you know…have an accident."

"Oh. Right. Sorry." Barbara tucked in the blanket where it had pulled out at the foot of the bed. "See you in the morning. Good night, Jade."

"Yeah," she replied.

In the master bedroom, Barbara found everything she'd brought with her put away, including the suitcases, which John was placing on the top shelf of the closet. He tossed up the last bag, then closed the door.

"I put the pink silk thing on the counter in the bathroom," he said. "Your toiletries are in there, too."

"Thank you." She felt a sudden, edgy nervousness as they faced each other in the middle of the room. It was dark, lit only by a small tulip lamp near the chair, and the corners were filled with shadows.

It was night. And she was about to share a bedroom with a man with wolf eyes and a lethal smile.

As she usually did, she confronted the fear head-on. "The children are settled," she said. "And I think we should settle a few things, too."

He looked more intrigued than annoyed. "Sure," he said. "I'm listening."

"Okay." She drew a breath for steadiness. "I understand that we have to share these rooms because we don't want Father Mike and Mrs. Gordon to see us coming out of separate bedrooms. And I will trust you to stay on your own side."

"My clothes," he said, his eyes blandly—suspiciously—innocent, "are in the closet on your side."

"Then I'll trust you to be a gentleman."

Despite himself, he could not sustain the innocence. A grin broke and the wolfish eyes gleamed. "Then you'll be disappointed. I gotta be me."

"John—"

He laughed softly. "I'm sorry. You looked so pious I couldn't help myself. For a woman who broke into my office and confronted me in her underwear, I thought you'd have a better sense of humor."

She turned her back to him, patience strained. "I thought anyone developing a campaign for a group of churches would have a better sense of decorum."

"You consider sexual attraction in poor taste? We're supposed to personify a happy husband and wife. We'll do a better job if we live the part."

She shook her head at his blatant attempt to manipulate her into his trap. "Good line, Cheney, but it won't work." She walked toward the bathroom, pulling the pins from her hair. "I'd never fall in love with a man like you."

He wandered after her, stopping in the doorway to lean his shoulder against the jamb. He couldn't deny a stab of hurt feelings. "Why not?"

She pulled the rubber band off her ponytail and combed the knot of hair out with her fingers. "Because you think everything's funny. You're always working things to your advantage. And you travel."

He looked at her reflection in the mirror as she brushed her hair. "Traveling is a vice? I do it for business."

She nodded, delving in her makeup bag for cold cream. "I know. My father traveled for business. The trouble was, my mother and I were at home. Eventually we learned to live without him because he was never there for us. I want a man who stays put, who'll be there. And one who isn't in advertising.''

''What do you mean? You're in advertising.''

''Precisely my point. No offense, but you're an advertising genius. You dramatize and sell a product. You spotlight all its good qualities and make all the bad ones go away.'' She spread her hands to indicate that she'd stated her case. ''Advertising makes us lose our grip on reality. How can we be trusted to know what's real and what isn't—particularly how we feel?''

He found that to be an interesting argument and liked what it suggested about her. ''You mean, you're falling for me beyond the boundaries of your role as my wife?''

She glared at his reflection. ''No. But I imagine it could happen to a less cautious woman.''

''So you've chosen this Trevor Whoever as the kind of man you want?''

She gave his reflection a scolding look as she found a jar and turned the lid. ''He doesn't travel, and he's not in advertising. And his name is Wentworth.''

John came into the room and caught her right hand before she could dip her fingers into the cold cream.

''You might want to rethink that,'' he said.

He'd caught her other hand also, and her back was trapped against his chest. She was sharply aware of his warmth and muscle and the faint, citrusy scent of his after-shave. He seemed to be possessed of some invisible snare that stole around her and held her immobile.

''Why?'' she asked, her tone quarrelsome.

''Because,'' he answered softly, leaning down to plant a kiss just under her ear, ''Trevor is traveling. He's in the Cayman Islands—with his father.''

He caught her eye again, and for an instant, his gaze held no amusement. Then he leaned down to place his cheek against hers. The suggestion of a beard chafed her soft skin. "But I'm here. And I'll be just a few steps away all night long." He kissed her temple and freed her hands. "Good night. I'll be in the office downstairs for a few hours. If you need anything, hit the intercom."

Barbara stared at herself for a moment after he was gone. Her eyes were wide and a little shaken, her lips parted in surprise. Her cheeks were flushed, the one he'd rubbed against a little brighter than the other.

John Cheney, she thought, was like a sudden shock to her system.

"Yo, Mom!" Joe greeted her as he ran past her chair on the way to catch the bus that took the children to their day camp. He kissed her cheek and gave her shoulders a squeeze. "Don't worry about tonight when the church people come. Jade and I are ready."

She hugged him, grateful for his cheerful presence. "Good. I'll follow your lead."

Joe moved to hug his father. "See ya, Dad. Tonight, can we talk ATV?"

"Sure."

"Are you gonna say no?"

"Of course."

Joe smiled winningly. "I'll feed it and take it for walks."

"Cute. Go."

Jade paused in front of Barbara's chair. Barbara waited for her to speak. When she didn't, Barbara smiled and squeezed the little girl's arm gently. "Have a good day. I appreciate your wanting to help me pretend to be your mother."

Jade was frowning now. "How do you do that?"

"Do what?" Barbara asked, sure she was being accused of some terrible misdeed.

Jade put a small, short-nailed forefinger to the wave that fell from Barbara's side part and curled under just above her shoulder in a soft curve. "That curl."

Surprised that her interest was personal and purely feminine, Barbara had to restrain herself from offering an overly enthusiastic reply.

"A curling iron."

Jade nodded, still studying the wave. "Ginger has one. I don't."

Barbara said casually, "You're welcome to borrow mine."

"Come *on!*" Joe reached out to grab his sister and pulled her along with him toward the door. On the way he rolled his eyes at his father. "Curls. Geez. Who'd want curls?"

The door slammed behind them. Libby cleared their plates from the table and poured more coffee. Barbara shifted a little nervously in her oak, ladder-back chair, wondering what had ever possessed her to agree to this scheme. It suddenly seemed impossible.

John put down the financial page and placed a hand over hers. "It's going to be fine. You will be fine. Now, eat your omelet. You're going to need your strength."

She pushed her plate away. "I never eat in the morning."

He pushed it back. "That's a bad habit. You have to set a good example for the kids."

"The kids," she said, pushing the plate away again, "are gone."

"Eat the toast," he coaxed. "Bread is the staff of life."

She sighed. "Man does not live by bread alone. Let's

not start quoting Scripture to each other. That would be overdoing it. What are we doing today?''

''We're going to put together the Baker Street Bookstore's campaign. Hal thinks it would be good to see you and me at work on developing a slogan and the copy.''

Barbara tried to forget that she'd been alone in her cubicle when her brain had been frozen on a campaign idea for garbanzo beans. She hated to think what having three people staring at her, waiting for her to come up with something brilliant, would do to her creative ability.

She winced. John grinned. ''It'll be fine. I work well under pressure—and, come to think of it, so do you. You saved Barnett with the copy for Churchill Charters' ad.''

Barbara blinked, surprised he knew about that.

''I know what's going on,'' he said. ''I'd come in late one night to finish up a presentation to Petrie Shoes and saw you hard at it in your cubicle. I stopped in the doorway, intending to say hello, but you were so deep in concentration I didn't want to disturb you. Then I saw the copy flow right off your fingers onto the screen. You had kicked off your shoes, as I recall, and had your feet up on the desk and the keyboard in your lap.''

''I don't suppose Barnett gave me credit for it.''

''Never mentioned you.''

She shook her head and shrugged with reluctant acceptance. ''That's the lot of mid-level women in corporate America.''

''Not at Cheney & Roman,'' John said. ''Barnett's moving to production next week.''

Barbara stared in surprise.

''We gave him the option of moving to production or taking a hike. He chose to stay, but I'm sure it's just until he lines up another job.''

"I'm sorry."

"You shouldn't be. Come on. We have to get going. Take the toast with you."

Barbara took the triangle of wheat toast with her to make him happy—and because he'd backed her even before he'd needed her for this project. Something about that warmed her and made her want to cooperate even in this small way.

It didn't, she told herself firmly, mean anything else.

"WE COULD PLAY on the obvious Baker Street connection to Sherlock Holmes," John said from the depths of his high-backed desk chair.

"Right. That's what comes to mind first." Barbara stopped pacing across the office and stopped at the bar to pour a cup of coffee. "I was thinking of playing off *baker.* You know, cooking and heat and time running out. 'You'll find potboiler mysteries, sizzling romance, recipes for dinner and for life at Baker Street Books.' Something like that."

John raised an eyebrow and nodded. "Or we could mess with the alliteration—Baker Books believes in Brontë, Beethoven, brownies, behavior, birthday cards, bookmarks and..."

He stopped, floundering for an ending.

Barbara put the coffee cup in his hand. "Don't they have a coffee bar?"

"Yes, they do."

"Then..." She repeated part of his list. "Behavior, birthday cards, bookmarks..." Then she added triumphantly, "bagels and brews!"

Hal cheered for her, Father Mike laughed his approval, and Mrs. Gordon remained completely unmoved.

John put his cup on the desk and pulled her into his

lap. She landed with a little squeal of surprise and a protest on the tip of her tongue. His eyes warned her to remember they were being watched.

She decided quickly it was in both their interests for her to play along. The sooner Hal got his pictures—and he was snapping madly now—the sooner this would be over. Besides, she wasn't entirely uncomfortable.

The shoulder of John's white shirt was soft under her hand, and its just-laundered fragrance mingled with his after-shave. His gold eyes were both amused and respectful, and his smile was warm and genuine. She found it very hard to hold out against it.

She collapsed against him with a giggle. "I know, I know. You'd like to spend hours praising me and rewarding me, but we're supposed to have this ready by Friday."

"Bagels and brews," John repeated. "That's brilliant. I completely forgot the coffee shop element in all this, and that's important. Now, what'll we do for artwork?"

Barbara smiled at Hal, pleased at being able to put him on the spot. He'd been ruthlessly photographing them all morning. "That's Hal's department, isn't it?" she asked.

"Easy," Hal said. "They have an alphabet header at the front of each aisle. We'll photograph the *B* in front of the long aisle, caption with your brilliant copy, then say something about when the reader is finished with that, there are twenty-five more letters in the alphabet."

"Then they can start over again," Barbara said, sitting up in John's lap as inspiration struck her. She placed her hands on his shoulders and added with enthusiasm, "because Baker Books believes in bringing you bestsellers and bargains before any other bookstore..." This time she floundered, then added shamelessly, "...in the bicinity."

The groan was communal and even included Joanna Gordon.

Father Mike patted the empty cushion beside him on the leather bench. "Come and sit, Barbara." He laughed. "I think after a joke like that you need a confessor."

The afternoon went on in the same spirit. John and Barbara exchanged ideas, jokes and laughter and by mid-afternoon had the outline of a solid campaign. Hal photographed the process. Father Mike observed with interest, and Joanna, with jaded suspicion.

"Where are you going?" John asked Barbara when he returned from taking a client's call. He arrived back in time to see her shoulder her purse and snatch a file off her desk. Hal had taken Father Mike and Joanna with him to the darkroom.

"The children come home at three," she reminded him, reaching into her middle drawer for a yellow pad.

"But Libby's always there."

Barbara stacked her few burdens in the crook of her arm and straightened to face John. "Every working mother in the world would like to be there when her children come home from school or, in this case, day camp. If I truly *were* your wife, I'd have that option and I'd take it. I'm sure our observers know that."

John couldn't argue with her. "Then, I get a kiss goodbye," he said.

She smiled sweetly. "No, you don't. They're in the darkroom. We aren't being watched."

"Don't look now," John said, focusing somewhere over her shoulder, "but they're at the light table with Hal, probably looking over today's shots."

Barbara groaned and grimaced.

"Now, come on," he chided gently, pulling her loosely into his arms. "It isn't that hard to kiss me, is it?"

It wasn't. And that was the problem.

Without waiting for an answer, he tipped her chin up and put his lips to hers, his touch light as down and twice as gentle. She found herself leaning into him, enjoying his tenderness but craving his possessive touch.

"You did well today," he whispered, then kissed her earlobe, causing a ripple that ran all the way to her toes. "Professionally *and* theatrically." He placed his lips to the other side of her face and nipped gently at her other lobe. "You're a quick thinker, Barbara. And a good sport."

She rubbed her cheek against his and felt the suggestion of late-afternoon beard. It was a delicious rasp against her own smoothness. She found herself wondering what it would feel like against the bare skin of her shoulder, her breast.

She pushed away from him and cleared her throat. "That ought to be convincing enough," she said and turned to leave. The first thing she noticed as she walked out of her cubicle and onto the floor was that there was no one at the light table. There had never *been* anyone at the light table. She turned to John, indignation flushing her cheeks.

He winked. "Gotcha," he said, walking away. "See you at dinner."

Barbara would have followed him and told him what she thought of his tactics, but one of the copywriters was already running toward him, waving a sheet of paper.

BARBARA SAT in the middle of the bed, looking through a box of costume jewelry she'd brought with her, hoping she hadn't forgotten the crystal star she always wore on her black dress, when Joe and Jade appeared in the doorway.

"Yo, Mom!" Joe said, putting a knee on the trunk where his father had sat the night before. "How'd it go today? Did you make everyone believe you're married to Dad?"

"I was pretty convincing," she said, pushing the box toward Jade as she noticed her interest in it. "But I think Mrs. Gordon doesn't quite believe us."

Joe nodded as though he knew all about her. "The grumpy lady."

Barbara straightened and said in mild reproof, "I don't think she's grumpy, she's just...I don't know. Lonely, maybe. Did your father say she was grumpy?"

"Uncle Hal did. He called Libby just now to tell her Dad said they'd be half an hour later than usual. Libby told me." He pushed to his feet and went to the door. "It's time for Combat reruns. Want to come watch?"

Barbara shook her head reluctantly. It was the first time in the last few days she'd been invited to do something rather than been coerced. "Thanks. But I have a few more things to put away."

With a blown kiss he disappeared into the hallway then thundered down the stairs like a three-hundred-pound tackle.

"A mother," Jade said judiciously, sitting on the edge of the bed and fingering the things in the box, "is supposed to meet us at the bus so we're not stolen by a crazy person."

"But your father let you go to the bus on your own this morning," Barbara said, carrying her things to the dresser. She peered into the small drawers at the top for a place to put her box. They were filled with socks, handkerchiefs and a black velvet envelope she guessed held cuff links or tie tacks.

"That's because Becky and Ginger's mom waits there with us in the morning." Jade pulled open the sock drawer, then a wider one at the bottom that held underwear and methodically dropped all the socks into the other drawer.

Barbara, realizing she was probably being too hopeful, took the small action as a gesture of friendship.

"Thank you," she said, trying not to frighten the child with effusive gratitude. "Well, as I said last night, I have no kids of my own, so I'll need a little help figuring out what to do."

"First of all," Jade said, following Barbara back to the bed, "you never call us 'kids.' You say 'my children,' like it's a holy word or something." She closed her eyes and said it reverently, enunciating and rolling the *r*. "I'm not sure why, but Mrs. Goodrich always says, 'my children,' and she's about the best mom around."

Mrs. Goodrich again. Barbara sat on the bed, and seeing Jade's eyes go to the small pile of jewelry she'd left there, she scooped it up and offered it to her. Jade cupped both hands and took it.

"What makes Ginger and Becky's mom the best?"

Jade studied the crystal star, the gold hoops with three little crystal drops, the jeweled watch Barbara never wore to work. "One day," she said absently as she studied each piece a second time, "she chased the school bus down and got out of her car at a red light with Ginger's lunch 'cause she'd forgotten it. Ginger forgets everything. Mrs. Goodrich comes to all the volleyball games, she sews their Sunday clothes, and she makes the best brownies."

Jade sighed and held up the gold hoops. "I wish I had a pair of these."

"They are pretty, aren't they?" Barbara said. "But I think they'd be a little big for you. Smaller earrings would be nice, though, if you had your ears pierced."

"Dad won't let me." Jade handed the sparkling little pile back to Barbara, then added with a reluctantly accepting smile, "He says I'm perfect just the way I am."

Barbara smiled. "Well, that's true. But I think men don't always understand that women who are already pretty like to wear things that make them feel even prettier."

Jade looked at her closely. "Yeah," she said after a moment. "Do you really think I could use it?"

Barbara was momentarily lost. "Use what?"

"Your curling iron."

"Oh. Yes, sure. It's in the drawer in the bathroom."

Jade stood and put a hand shyly to her hair. "Do you think my hair's too short to make curls?" The gesture was purely feminine and Barbara felt something connect between them.

"No. Come on." Barbara headed for the bathroom and waved for her to follow. She pulled the tool out of the drawer. "Here it is."

Jade stood beside Barbara at the counter and looked at her in the mirror, raising a finger to point at the wave that fell from her side part. "I'd like to let my hair grow until it could do that." Then she smiled as Barbara plugged in the curling iron and set the control.

Barbara felt as proud as though she'd personally brought peace to the Middle East.

Chapter Six

"Look, Mom! Dad's home." Joe made a dramatic production of his father's return. Barbara decided she would have to discuss with Joe the power of subtlety.

Mercifully, Father Mike and Joanna Gordon didn't seem to notice his center-stage behavior.

Jade, hair frothy with curls, elbowed Barbara. "You'd better kiss Daddy hello," she whispered. "And call him 'sweetheart' or something."

Reluctant but resigned, Barbara went to John while Joe playfully sparred with Hal.

"Hi, darling," she said, her eyes warning him not to take advantage of her approach. "How was your afternoon?"

He pulled her into his arms and kissed her soundly, his firm grip reminding her not to struggle. When she looked up at him with disapproval, his golden gaze flashed and he dipped her backward, kissing her again. The priest and the children laughed, Hal focused and shot, and Mrs. Gordon looked away in apparent disgust.

"Good," he said, lifting her upright. "How was yours?"

"Fine." Her eyes promised revenge even as she smiled for the observers and tucked her arm in his. She hated that he could put her in a dither so easily when she was trying so hard to lend her performance some semblance of style.

"We curled my hair," Jade said, putting her thumb and forefinger to a short ringlet. "Do you like it? Isn't it pretty?"

John looked down at his daughter and put a hand to the curly mass atop her head. "It's very pretty," he said. "But, then, you'd be very pretty without hair, never mind without curls."

Jade laughed and went to show Hal.

Barbara saw John's gaze wander after her with a mystified frown. She recognized the look as a father's first realization that his child was female, and would one day be taken from him by another male.

He looked so startled that Barbara found herself assuming her role as hostess with the gracious hospitality of the real Mrs. Cheney—had there been one.

"Welcome, Mrs. Gordon," she said, smiling determinedly into the woman's grave expression. The day before, she'd looked around the house with awe and interest but had now settled into her customary displeasure with almost everything. "Jade will show you to your room. Take as much time as you need to freshen up. We'll serve dinner when you're ready. Father Mike."

Barbara extended her hand to the priest, ignoring John's raised eyebrow at her assumption of control. "I understand you're fond of pasta, so I asked Libby to prepare chicken fettuccini for you." Actually, Libby had conceived the idea herself, but Barbara felt sure she wouldn't mind the fib in the interest of adding convincing texture to their deceit.

The priest sniffed the air and made a sound of approval. "Wonderful. I'm so looking forward to our adventure here. In fact—" he looked around, nodding "—I think I'll forget my vow of poverty and speak to the chancery about remodeling the rectory in this style."

Barbara laughed at his joke and hooked an arm in his. "Just in case that doesn't work out for you, I hope you enjoy your stay with us. Joe will show you to your room, and we'll bring your bags right up."

As the boy and the priest disappeared, Barbara turned to face a grinning Hal. "I suppose," he said, "I'm expected to find my own way up since I'm often part of the furnishings around here."

"Not until you've helped me bring the bags in," she said, smiling uncertainly. "Was I convincing?"

Hal pulled off his jacket and tossed it on a hallway bench. "I'd have sworn you've been married to John and mistress of this house for a decade, anyway."

"The story I gave Father Mike," John said, "was that we've been married just a few months. That's why the passion is so fresh."

Barbara followed as John and Hal strode out to the car. "You don't think passion lasts ten years?"

John opened the trunk. Hal pulled out the priest's single black suit bag. "He doesn't think anything lasts ten years. You'd have to have known Gracie to understand."

"Gracie?" Barbara took a tote bag John handed her.

"The children's mother," John replied, pulling out the remaining two bags and closing the trunk. "She went in more directions than the wind—and in a mere fourteen months. But enough about that. We're doing well. Just keep it up and Cheney & Roman will have a national reputation by January."

LIBBY LOOKED NERVOUS. Barbara, warming to her role, caught the cook-housekeeper's eye and gave her an encouraging smile.

The fettuccini and marinated vegetables were like ambrosia to Barbara. She had seconds and praised Libby with lavish compliments that were completely sincere—and contributed, she was sure, to their little scenario.

"Mom thinks I should have my ears pierced," Jade announced when Libby served baklava cheesecake.

John turned away from an ad layout Hal was illustrating on a napkin and focused on his daughter with a carefully noncommittal gaze. Then he transferred his attention to Barbara, a trace of censure in his expression.

"Really. Did you tell her how I feel about it?" he asked mildly.

"Yes." Jade continued to eat, as interested in her food as she was in the outcome of the discussion. "I told her you thought I was too young and that you didn't like the idea of me making a hole in my ear, anyway. She said we should talk to you about it."

Hal took a photograph.

John turned to Barbara. *This is it,* she thought. The nitty-gritty they're looking for. The family dynamic at work.

"My opinion," she said, "is that it isn't disfiguring. Earrings can be a lovely enhancement to a woman's impression. It's true that she's young, but there are very small earrings for girls her age. She can graduate to something bigger when she gets older."

"Can I, Daddy?" Jade pressed.

"Mom and I'll talk about it," John said, his eyes telling Barbara they would indeed discuss it. She refused to be concerned. This had all been his idea. She was just doing her part. She might as well take it a step further.

"I think we should redecorate her room, too," Barbara said. Jade looked up at her in pleased surprise. John's gaze swung slowly back from Hal's sketch. It told her clearly not to push. She ignored it. She found it stimulating to suddenly be the one in a position of power, such as it was.

"She's too old for clowns and primary colors. Now she needs something she can grow with. Flowers and feminine colors." She turned to smile at Joe. "And you're probably ready for revolutionary soldiers or signal flags, aren't you?"

"Yeah," Joe agreed heartily. "I'd like something with bikes and babes on it."

John put a hand to his eyes. Father Mike laughed, then quickly sobered when Joanna gave him a frown of disapproval.

"I'll bring home a wallpaper sample book," Barbara said, heroically holding back her own laughter. "There's a paint and wallpaper shop just around the corner from the office." She smiled broadly at John, who had lowered his hand to his mouth, where it rested casually, as though he were merely considering the situation. But Barbara knew he was annoyed. "What do you think?" she asked him.

"Is that important?" he asked easily, a trace of humor in his tone. To those around the table it sounded like playful banter.

Barbara was completely incapable of suppressing the little demon at work inside her. "Of course it is, darling. You know I never go ahead with anything unless I'm sure you disapprove."

As Hal choked, she laughed and punched John's upper arm. "Just kidding. Of course it's important. We'll talk about it later. Shall we clear the table and talk business, or would you like to move to the living room and watch a movie or play a board game?''

''WHAT IN THE HELL do you think you're doing?'' John demanded in a loud whisper.

Barbara had put the children to bed hours earlier, and their guests had finally retired after a lively game of charades.

John confronted Barbara at the foot of the bed. ''For a woman who had difficulty getting into the role of wife and mother, you've suddenly found your stage feet with a vengeance.''

''It was all very harmless,'' she explained calmly, now feeling a little guilty about the pleasure she'd taken in rattling his hold on their shaky situation. ''Jade was looking through my jewelry and saw my earrings—''

''I don't believe,'' he said with paternal authority, ''that a ten-year-old girl needs pierced ears.''

''It isn't a case of need. It's a case of exploring her femininity in a way that's virtually harmless. Women wear adornments to give themselves and their men pleasure—it's been the way of the world since Eve.''

''I don't want you countermanding my rules for the children.''

''I didn't—''

''You've never been a parent so you don't understand this,'' he said, ''but parents discuss things before taking issues in dispute to the children. That way you don't hurt and disappoint them unnecessarily.''

She nodded impatiently. ''I appreciate that. But you've never been a *mother* so you don't understand *this,* but mothers and daughters talk, and they share things it's difficult for a man to understand. You have an absolutely delightful and charming son…and a lovely little girl that you're trying to make into another boy.''

''I'm not—''

''Then why is her hair cut just like his and why does she wear the same clothes?''

''It was not deliberate. I didn't—''

''Notice. I know. But I'm a woman, and I did notice. She's a girl, and it's important that her life contain feminine things. That was all I meant when I suggested earrings.''

John wasn't sure why he was so rattled. What she said was perfectly reasonable. Libby had made the same point to him not that long ago. He'd taken no action then because he wasn't sure what to do. He didn't intend to get married and provide the children with a mother, and hiring a nanny wasn't a solution he could live with.

He'd explained about their mother when they'd first asked five years ago, making it clear that she had thought them beautiful and lovable, but had other things to do. He, on the other hand, loved them with a fierceness that nothing else in his life could have replaced. They had accepted it with the ease of children secure in their position. Or so he'd thought.

But there had to be something behind Joe's exaggerated eagerness to play the part of Barbara's loving stepson and Jade's capitulation from suspicion to adoration.

And it had all happened in the space of a day and a half.

''Look,'' he said. ''Don't turn my life upside down, all right? Just do your job without getting in too deep.''

Needing action of some kind, Barbara took the bed covers and yanked them back. ''Another thing that's escaped your notice is that wife and mother are not surface jobs. Good ones tend to get a little involved in their duties.''

"Just remember that you're acting."

"So are you," she said. "Like a jerk. Now if you'll excuse me, I'd like to go to bed."

John considered retreat the better part of valor. While she was in the bathroom, he pulled out the sofa bed and made it up. Then she marched past him with an icily polite good-night, a trail of some floral fragrance in her wake wrapping around him. He noted broodingly that she'd brushed her hair and that it, too, floated out behind her.

He stood under the shower for a long time, hoping to loosen the tightening muscles in his neck and back. What was wrong with him? Things never got to him, particularly things that had a funny side like this farcical little adventure with the Cooperative Churches and a beautiful woman. No woman had gotten under his skin since Gracie.

Well, it wasn't his fault. He turned off the shower and yanked a gold towel off the rack. She was the one presuming too much. True, he'd asked her to put in a convincing performance, but he hadn't asked her to arrange his life as a real wife would. He hadn't asked her to interfere with his children.

Or to look and behave with such fascinating womanliness that he began to feel that his life lacked something important.

He stepped out of the stall, the faintly antiseptic smell of his no-nonsense soap mingling with what remained of the floral scent of hers. He toweled himself off roughly, yanked on his pajama bottoms and opened the door.

The coolness of the bedroom, also laden with her floral scent, slapped his face and naked chest. He needed a brandy, he thought, snatching his robe off the back of the bathroom door. He had a feeling Joanna Gordon, if she was still wandering around, wouldn't appreciate meeting his bare-chested body.

Barbara lay quietly on her side as he left the room.

Hal, in a brown cotton robe so new it still wore creases in a square pattern from the packaging, stood at the stove bobbing a tea bag up and down in boiling water.

"Tea?" John asked in disbelief, going to the cupboard where he kept his small store of alcohol.

Hal seemed surprised by his scornful tone. "I needed a brandy, too, but I'm trying to stay in character. You'll notice I even bought a robe."

John filled the bottom third of a balloon glass with the gold liquid, then went to the stove and topped up Hal's cup with it. "This account is important," John said, toasting him with his glass, "but it's not worth our emasculation."

Hal followed him to the table against the window and sat across from him with a cautious smile.

"Emasculation? That's an interesting word for you to use—I mean, with your new marital status and all."

John swallowed half the contents of the glass and waited while it burned a trail down his throat to his stomach and settled there like a friendly little fire.

"She's messing with things that aren't her business," he said, his voice faintly scorched.

"She's only doing what you asked her—what you practically coerced her into doing. And she's doing a damned good job if you ask me."

"I didn't."

"Well, I'm telling you, anyway. Jade's hair looked

great, and I hadn't really thought about it, but maybe it is time you redid her room. She and Joe weren't even here yet when we put up the clown wallpaper, remember?''

John turned to him with a pointed look. "Of course I remember. She's *my* daughter."

"It doesn't diminish your performance as a father because Barb saw something in Jade that you missed."

John further sharpened the pointed look. "Jade's hair and Jade's room are none of her business."

Hal shrugged a shoulder. "I suppose. But didn't you see Jade glowing at the dinner table? She's a great kid, always has been, but tonight she felt...pretty. You could see it in her."

"She's beautiful," John said, downing the rest of the glass. "And not because Barbara curled her hair."

There was a moment's heavy silence, then Hal said slowly, carefully, "You know, you can let her be a girl, and she won't turn into Gracie on you."

Hal's incisive, insightful observations were what made him a brilliant photographer. And that same quality made him tough to take as a friend because he had no qualms about telling someone precisely what he saw. The desire to punch his lights out was almost overwhelming to John.

"You're a pain in the butt, Roman," John said candidly.

Hal grinned. "I strive to perfect all my abilities. So, what are we doing tomorrow?"

John sighed, wishing he were going to a ball game, or on an all-male camping trip. He felt a desperate need suddenly to get down and dirty in a strictly-male environment. Instead, he faced many hours with Barbara and the children. "We're taking the kids to the zoo."

Hal nodded approval. "It's hard to get a bad shot with kids and animals. In fact, I think I'd be hard put to get a bad shot of Barbara anywhere, doing anything."

John slapped his glass on the table and stood. "Well, don't sit drinking juiced-up chamomile all night. The kids'll be up early. Good night."

John pushed through the swinging door into the darkened living room, missing Hal's grin.

THE BEDROOM WAS DARK and smelled of roses when John walked silently toward the sofa he'd made up.

"John?" Barbara's voice called quietly.

He turned toward her, wondering if the subdued tone meant something was wrong. "Yes?" He stopped at the foot of the bed.

She sat up in the shadows, her fragrance moving with her. It wound around him and seemed to tighten his chest.

"I'm sorry I overstepped," she said. "I was a little giddy with success and got carried away. I'll be careful in the future."

John felt his chest tighten further. Other parts of him also felt constricted. He moved until he could reach the tops of her covers.

"No need to apologize," he said, noting that his voice, too, sounded choked. "I'm not used to sharing my children and I was too touchy. Don't worry about it. Go to sleep."

Barbara leaned back against the pillows and enjoyed the sensation of being tucked in by strong, sure hands. No wonder Joe and Jade knew all there was to know about it.

Then John placed a hand on her pillow on either side

of her, and breath and thought whooshed away. He leaned down and kissed her gently.

"Good night," he said, his voice like velvet in the dark.

Certain a pounding heart would not be conducive to sleep, she curled onto her side and bade him good-night as he went toward the sofa.

CHILDREN RAN on batteries, Barbara decided. No, that was wrong. They were plugged into some permanent source, and even in the event of a power failure, they had some kind of backup system. She'd never seen such physical or vocal energy in her life.

In the back seat of Hal's station wagon, between John and Father Mike, Barbara struggled to appear coherent, but she hadn't slept well, and she'd been jostled awake at 5:00 a.m. by the twins bearing a glass of orange juice and an itinerary that could not be filled in a week, much less a day.

Though belted into the wagon's middle seat, Jade and Joe talked incessantly, turned toward her as much as their confinement would allow. Joanna, in the front with Hal, had turned the radio up but it hadn't discouraged them.

John, used to dealing with their energy, and looking relaxed in loose, stone-colored slacks and a matching cotton-knit sweater, smiled at her. Last night's argument, then the gentle kiss that ended it, had changed something between them. She couldn't analyze it precisely, except to know that their relationship had taken another step— and that it was somewhere beyond pretense.

As Hal and Joe exchanged little-known facts on elephants, Barbara laughed softly. "I'll wake up any moment now, I promise. I've always thought myself extremely virtuous to bounce out of bed at seven when I'd really love to sleep until ten. Five o'clock is a lot to ask of a died-in-the-wool sack rat.''

John put an arm around her and pulled her closer to him. ''Close your eyes. You can doze for about fifteen minutes.''

She tried to protest, but he pulled her back. ''Take advantage of the opportunity. It won't come again until after dinner.''

With a grateful little sigh, she pressed her cheek into the cozy hollow of his chest and shoulder and closed her eyes. The way she felt now, she wouldn't last until lunch.

As John and Father Mike talked quietly over her head, the children still chatting with Hal, Barbara absorbed the physical impressions of her position as sleep crowded in. But she had only a moment to feel the warmth and solidity and the firm protectiveness of John's arm around her before her eyes fell closed.

She awoke with a start and sat up. The station wagon was still and empty. She leaned down to peer out the window and saw that they were in a parking lot, surrounded by hundreds of other cars. Just ahead was a line of ticket booths and turnstiles. Barbara turned slowly, knowing she hadn't been left alone.

John sat beside her, or almost under her, in the corner of the back seat. His gold eyes were calm but a little less amused than usual. He put a hand to her back and rubbed gently. ''Awake, now?'' he asked.

His touch, though tender, created a sensation of heat.

''Yes,'' Barbara answered breathlessly, aware of the sudden electricity in the enclosed space, the sudden rise in temperature, the sudden shortage of air. ''Where is everyone?''

"I sent them on ahead. I wanted to give you a few extra minutes." Then he pulled her slowly back to him, turned her so that he could cradle her in his arms and look down at her. Barbara saw a vee of concentration between his eyebrows, as though he were about to do something that required consideration. "And I needed a few extra minutes myself."

"Why?" she whispered, not because she didn't know the answer, but because she wanted to hear it—or, in this case, taste it.

He couldn't wait another moment. He'd endured a long night of knowing she was just across the room, then sat quietly in this seat while she slept against him, trustingly secure, unaware of the hormonal riot taking place within him, demanding some satisfaction.

But as her limpid brown eyes looked up into his, as they roved his face, every bit as eager for what was about to take place as he, it was no longer satisfaction he wanted but a sincere communication, an exchange of thought and emotion that would tell her all the things he couldn't say.

Her lips were soft and warm, faintly minty, and the scent of roses invaded his senses as she wrapped her arms around his neck and drew herself up to meet him.

He braced a foot on the floor, supporting her against his thigh as he felt the mind-bending touch of the tip of her tongue against his lips.

Barbara felt his mouth open over hers, and his tongue meet hers in a battle that began gently, then seemed to escalate to a life-or-death struggle. He took everything she offered, then encouraged her to offer more.

His hands moved over her with such strength and confidence, it didn't occur to her to resist. And he seemed to be leading in a direction she wanted very much to explore.

John felt her small breasts through the light knit of his sweater, beaded tips letting him know he was not alone in the sudden conflagration taking place inside him.

The high-pitched laughter of children passing by on their way to the ticket booths finally drew them apart. Barbara pushed against John's shoulders, trying to force herself back to the here and now and the task at hand—putting in a convincing performance as husband and wife. She smiled wryly at the realization that they'd done just that, but without their audience.

John, his hands still bracketing her waist, felt weak with the struggle to bank desire, to remember that the present circumstances were too complicated for him to make love to Barbara in the back seat of Hal's station wagon.

He tucked Barbara's errant wave behind her ear and raised an eyebrow at her smile. "You're thinking that was wasted with no one to see it."

The wolf eyes saw everything, she thought, but they sometimes interpreted what they saw incorrectly. It gave her a very small boost of confidence.

She braced a foot on the floor and swung off his lap and onto the seat beside him. She took her purse from the opposite corner and reached in for her hairbrush.

"I did think it ironic that we did our best work without an audience." She put the purse aside and gave him a knowing glance as she drew the brush through her hair. "But I never once considered it a waste." She dropped the brush in her purse and smiled brightly. "Ready?"

"No," he said, reaching for her as she opened the door and leapt out. He wanted to know precisely what she meant. But she was halfway to the ticket booth before he managed to lock the car and set the alarm.

He found her standing sheepishly aside as the growing line of visitors purchased their tickets.

"No cash," she said, hooking her arm in his.

"Hmm." They took their place in line and inched forward. "You run away from me one moment, then expect me to cover your expenses the next."

She rolled her eyes. "It's a measly few dollars. You gave Libby a Harley."

"Libby didn't tell me she enjoyed kissing me—just before she ran away from me."

Barbara frowned at him. "I didn't tell you I enjoyed kissing you."

"Well, not in so many words. The meaning was the same."

It was futile to deny it. She wouldn't have fooled him, and she certainly wouldn't have fooled herself. She was falling for John Cheney. And he knew it.

She skirted that issue. "You'll have to stake me to a bag of peanuts, too, and fish to feed the seals."

He bought two tickets, then hooked an arm around her as they entered the zoo. Exotic sounds and pungent smells filled the air. A warm effervescence filled her being.

"I wish I'd known how demanding you are before I proposed," he teased.

She laughed up at him, finding it perfectly natural to loop an arm around his waist. "I don't think 'Do it or I'll fire you,' can be considered a proposal, even among the most tolerant of women."

The click of a camera shutter betrayed Hal, watching them from behind a directional sign.

"Good one," he said, joining them to form a threesome as they started off toward the aviary where they could see the children, Father Mike and Joanna. A breeze rippled the small pond on their right. "You guys are getting pretty good at this. I had no idea what good actors you are."

"You think we're pulling it off?" Barbara asked.

He shrugged. "Father Mike believes it. I'm not sure about the reverend Gordon, though. She keeps watching you when she thinks you're not looking. I think she's waiting for you to slip, or break into a nasty quarrel."

Hal changed lenses as he spoke, then moved ahead of them, walking backward and focusing on them as they strolled down the shady lane.

"Be careful," John warned, laughing as Hal almost collided with a stroller. Fortunately the toddler was not in it, but pushing it. He giggled as Hal struggled for balance and finally remained upright. "That'll look good on the SAIF report. 'Photographer's leg broken when he fell over a baby stroller. The loss of his ear and right arm were the result of a roll into a lagoon of crocodiles.'"

As he spoke, a croc raised its head from the peaceful stretch of water beyond the fence. Enormous jaws revealed long, lethal teeth, then snapped shut with a force that made Barbara shudder.

The children ran to meet them and they began a leisurely and systematic study of every creature housed at the zoo. The children, fascinated by everything, slowed to a studious pace. They took turns reading every sign aloud and asked a million questions, some the adults could answer, some that required a perusal of the brochure and some which John promised to look up when they got home.

At a vendor's stand they bought hats that were com-

prised of fabric animal fronts and backs attached to baseball caps. Father Mike, sporting the fangs and rattles of
a snake, frowned when Joanna chose a simple, utilitarian
sunshade.

Joe and Jade, pleading starvation, dragged John toward a food vendor. They all ordered foot-long hot dogs
and curly fries, except for Joanna, who settled for a tuna
salad sandwich and a cup of coffee.

They sat at a picnic table in the shade of an exotic
tree and devoured their sandwiches as though they'd
been starved. Father Mike told tales from his seminary
days, and Hal talked about some of the more amusing
clients Cheney and Roman had dealt with when they'd
first opened the office.

Barbara noticed that Joanna almost smiled once, then
stopped herself, glancing around quickly as though to be
sure no one had seen her near lapse. When her eyes
caught Barbara's, they held for one moment, dark with
envy, then went back to her sandwich. Barbara found
herself wondering just what the woman's childhood had
been like, or what her ex-husband had done to her to
create such a cautious, suspicious woman.

"You know what?" Joe asked under his breath. He
stood next to his father, elbows leaning on an outer fence
looking through an inner fence which surrounded a number of lions.

John's eyes were on Barbara, wandering down the
lane with Father Mike and Joanna. Hal stood aside,
changing lenses.

"What?" he asked absently.

"You wouldn't be able to live here," Joe said.

That brought John's attention back to him. "Really,"
he said. "Shortage of legs? No tail?"

Joe shook his head. "No mate. Everything here is male and female. They're all in families."

John was shaken by that observation. "Well, you know, families take all kinds of different shapes today."

"Yeah," Joe agreed readily, but he pointed to the lioness leaning languidly against her golden-maned mate. "I know. The world's different today and all that. But it seems like when nature does it, there's always a mom and a dad. Like, maybe that's the way it's really supposed to be. Unless somebody dies or something and then you can't help it. But if you get to choose the way you want it, it works better if there's a mom and a dad."

John always dealt honestly with his children and faced their problems head-on, no matter how uncomfortable it might be for him. And it certainly was this time.

"Do you feel deprived because you don't have a mother?" he asked. "Tell me the truth, now."

"Deprived," Joe repeated thoughtfully. "That means like I'm missing something?"

"Exactly."

"Well, yeah. I mean, I've always felt like that a little bit because most other kids at school have a mother, or a stepmother, sometimes both. But it was always okay because we seemed to have more fun than a lot of them. And none of them got anything from their moms that you didn't give us—except maybe brownies."

John was tempted to smile at his son's thorough exploration of the subject, but he sensed it was too important.

"And that's changed somehow?"

"Well, maybe a little." Joe spoke reluctantly, as though he were being careful of John's feelings. "Except for the brownies and some little stuff, I didn't really notice it much. Until Barbara moved in with us."

"But she's only been here two days."

"I know. But I saw it right away. Didn't you? It's like everything's a little…softer or something. I like it when she hugs me."

John had little difficulty relating to that.

"When you hug us, it's like having a bodyguard. You feel like if somebody that strong loves you, nothing can happen to you. But when she hugs us, it's very soft and I smell flowers. It makes me feel like the world is a very nice place."

Joe took a step closer to him and looked up at him with that killer smile that was one day going to make a young woman give up everything she had to follow him.

"The best part about it is that when you put it all together, a kid with a father *and* a mother feels like life is really neat and you'll always be safe in it."

John pulled Joe close to his side and kissed the top of his head, completely at a loss for a response. Joe had put forth the best argument he'd ever heard for the traditional family—at least, from a child's point of view. He was grateful the boy hadn't applied any pressure on him to change things.

Then Joe completely dissolved that easy thought by adding, "So, we think it'd be neat if you married her."

Chapter Seven

"Daddy! Come here!" Jade ran out of the building, took her father and her brother by an arm and pulled them back with her. "You have to see this, Joe! It's a nursery."

Joe resisted, frowning at his father as Jade dragged them. "You mean plants and stuff?"

"No, *babies!*"

Relieved to be able to avoid a discussion of why he would never marry, John smiled bracingly at his son. "Humor her. I know it isn't the snakes, but I bet you'll enjoy it."

John certainly did. The moment his eyes adjusted to the quieter lighting, his eyes fell on Barbara cuddling a fuzzy, blue-eyed tiger cub. It nestled against her shoulder, contentedly drinking milk from a bottle she held to its mouth. Hal was taking pictures as the priest looked on fondly.

Barbara turned to smile at John, apparently enjoying the experience as much as the cub seemed to. "Isn't she beautiful?" she asked. "Jade and I are plotting to kidnap her and take her home with us."

"She's only three weeks old, Daddy," Jade said, reaching up to stroke the cub. "Her mom is sick, so they have to take care of her in here.'' She pointed to a pen in which another cub about the same size lay fast asleep. ''This is her brother.'' She shared a look with Barbara. ''Looks like all brothers are the same. All they do is sleep and cause trouble when they're awake.''

Joe, stroking the spotted back, turned to make an ugly face at her. ''And all sisters do is eat. Is her mom going to get better?''

The uniformed young man standing by nodded reassurance. ''She just got a little run-down and needed time without her cubs.''

Joe winked at Barbara. ''I'm glad that doesn't happen to you, Mom.''

Barbara took the impromptu dramatics with an appropriate smile. ''Thank you, darling. Here, Joanna. You haven't had a chance to hold her.''

Joanna protested and took a step backward, but Barbara placed the cub in her arms. It reached greedily for the milk as Barbara passed the bottle along, also.

Joanna seemed nervous, then relaxed as the cub settled comfortably in her arms and continued to eat. She glanced at Barbara with a hesitant smile. ''She likes me.''

Barbara heard a wealth of revelation in those simple words. They expressed surprise, even disbelief. And she guessed that Joanna's suspicion that she wasn't liked ran to people as well as animals. The puzzle of the grim Reverend Gordon was coming together, Barbara thought.

''You're going to develop into a very social little being,'' John said as the cub was later passed on to him. The cub didn't seem to mind as long as the milk came along, also.

John enjoyed the weight of the small, sturdy body and

the silky texture of its fur against his hand. But mostly he enjoyed the way Barbara leaned into him to stroke the cat. Its bright blue eyes watched her as it guzzled milk.

"I think she knows me," Barbara said seriously. "I think she'd like to come home with me."

"And what will we do with her in six months when she weighs several hundred pounds?"

Barbara grinned at him flirtatiously, enjoying the moment. "She could sleep at the foot of our bed."

He smiled indulgently at her. "You thrash around too much. What if you kicked her while she dreamed about chasing antelope? We'd have to call you No-Feet Francie."

She was surprised that he'd noticed her restless sleep from across the room.

John handed the cub to the attendant and thanked him. "I think I'd better get my girls out of here before the cub turns up missing."

Barbara and Jade walked out ahead of him, hand in hand. Joe followed with Father Mike, and Hal with Joanna. John trailed along behind in the nature of an observer.

His daughter had certainly done an about-face where Barbara was concerned, and his son was completely smitten.

It was obvious she had the priest convinced she was married. Joanna was the only holdout that he could see, and even she seemed to be softening just a little.

John realized with reluctant acceptance that he was Barbara's most genuine conquest. Though he'd found her beautiful and fascinating from the beginning, he'd looked on this whole thing as a lark, a way to get Cheney

& Roman national advertisers. He'd thought it could be entertaining as well as profitable.

But he could feel his attitude changing, and he wasn't sure what it meant. Or why it concerned him. It wasn't that he found it comfortable to have her around. He didn't. He was sharply aware of her every moment, and she made him think about things he thought he'd long ago decided upon. Like the fact that he had never let a woman as deeply into his life as he'd allowed Gracie.

Yet Barbara poked and prodded at his emotions in little ways—some that touched him and some that annoyed him. Either way, they *affected* him, and he didn't know what to do about it. So he found himself kissing her when they didn't even have an audience. And he found himself admitting to her that she intrigued him. What was wrong with him? What had happened to his resolve? Emotionally what he was doing was akin to ripping off his bulletproof vest. He had to be crazy.

Then she turned, still holding Jade's hand, and let everyone else in their group go past them to the snake house. She waited until he approached, then hooked her free arm in his.

"You have to keep up, John," she teased, loud enough for Joanna to hear as the woman glanced surreptitiously over her shoulder. "We'd hate to lose you."

"I had you in my sights," he said, then leaning down and giving her a swift, hard kiss. Because Joanna was watching, because he didn't want Barbara to feel smug about teasing him—because he had to. Then he pinched Jade's chin and pulled her to his other side and led them into the building.

Joe was so fascinated by the snakes that John stayed right behind him, afraid he'd find a way to reach inside the displays for closer contact. He fielded dozens of questions, and it wasn't until they were almost finished that he realized Barbara, Jade and Hal were missing. Leaving Joe under the priest's watchful eye, John stepped outside, expecting to find them sitting on a bench. He didn't.

He looked up then down the long, narrow lane to the other exhibits, telling himself that they were safe as long as they were with Hal. But what if they weren't? What if they'd wandered off separately? What if—?

Then he caught a glimpse of them through the trees. Temper flared, then relief calmed it. And the sight he saw as he cleared the leafy barrier banished the last trace of anger.

Barbara and Jade stood atop a low stone wall surrounding a pond. Mallards paddled around in the midst of many exotic ducks, and several species of geese and swans. Hal was taking photographs.

The ducks swam to the other side of the pond and Barbara followed them along the wall, arms held out gracefully for balance. Jade came up behind her, looking more like an airplane than a bird, and, running too fast, collided with Barbara's back.

There was a little screech, and a mad flailing of arms. John headed for the pond at a run. Hal fell into step beside him as Barbara and Jade caught hands, tottered for one unsteady moment, then splashed into the water. Ducks of all kinds skimmed the surface of the pond, moving in the other direction, flapping and squawking their complaints.

Barbara and Jade surfaced together like a pair of mermaids, Barbara with a water lily on her shoulder. Seeing the water was only to Jade's waist, John slowed his steps, then planted a foot on the stone wall and looked at them with severity. For all of two seconds.

They were laughing so hysterically he had difficulty holding back his own smile. He held a hand out to Jade. "Out of there," he said. "I imagine we'll be asked to leave very soon, anyway."

John placed his dripping daughter on her feet on the outside of the wall, then reached in for Barbara. She came onto the wall like Venus rising out of the ocean, water streaming from her beautifully outlined form in wet cotton.

She laughed as she placed her hands on his shoulders for balance. "I'm sorry. There were little ducklings against the wall that we couldn't see very well without climbing onto it. I didn't think—" Her smile changed suddenly to a look of concern. "That wasn't very motherly, was it?" she whispered as he swung her to the ground. "I set a bad example. Do you think I gave myself away?"

He relented with a smile. "I don't think so," he said under his breath as the rest of their party came running. "I'm sure there are mothers who lead their children into mischief. And they know that you're new at this mothering business."

"I DIDN'T KNOW zoos had nurses," Joe said. "Do you think it's in case a lion bites your arm off or something? Or a bear reaches over the fence and grabs you?"

"I think it's more likely," Father Mike replied, "they have a nurse on hand if someone falls and skins a knee or forgets to wear a hat and feels dizzy."

"Oh." Joe seemed disappointed, then smiled at the crocodile hat he held in his hand. "How could somebody forget to buy a radical hat like this?"

As the rest of the group compared hats, Barbara sat wrapped in her blanket, afraid she'd ruined the entire scheme. Father Mike didn't seem to have noticed anything, but she'd gotten a definite look of disapproval from Joanna. Then a lingering gaze of what seemed to be confusion.

She's convinced I'm a fraud, Barbara thought. She isn't sure, but she'll find a way to *be* sure before this is over—if it isn't already.

"Warm enough?" John asked, pulling her closer with the arm he held around her. Except for that instant of censure at the wall, he'd been the consummate husband and father, indulgent yet concerned.

"I'm fine," she lied, then leaned into his shoulder and closed her eyes.

"You're a little green around the gills," Hal observed through the rearview mirror.

"People don't have gills," Joe corrected.

John laughed. "You must have missed your mother's episode in the water. Seriously, Barbara. Are you all right?"

She sighed. "My stomach's a little upset, that's all."

"She had two ice-cream sandwiches and *three* Slurpees," Jade reported, as though she considered that an impressive accomplishment.

"And she finished my popcorn," Joe added.

Father Mike shook his head pityingly. "And my curly fries. Perhaps I should administer the Last Rites as a precaution."

Barbara glared at the priest with one eye as everyone laughed.

By midnight she thought he might be right. Miserable with nausea, she climbed stealthily out of bed and stood still for a moment, listening to John's even breathing across the room. He was still asleep.

Briefly she entertained the thought of what she would do if John Cheney truly were her husband. She would climb into bed beside him in search of body warmth and comfort. She would hook an arm around his waist and press her ailing stomach to his warm back....

Deciding she must be approaching delirium, she tiptoed to the door, opened it soundlessly and stepped out into the hall. The house was dark and quiet.

She looked in on the children, found them both fast asleep, then went downstairs to the kitchen in search of a cup of tea to quiet her stomach.

She boiled water in the kettle and removed it from the burner before its whistle could disturb the household. She brewed something with wintergreen that she found in a tin and went to the table to sit.

She was half-finished and feeling only marginally better when a movement beyond the window caught her eye. Even before she could become alarmed, a masked and pointed little face peered in at her at the bottom of the French doors. A raccoon!

Barbara knew Libby saved table scraps for them. She slid the door aside and watched her visitor scamper back to his companions eating from the big bowl left near the woods.

She sat on the bench on the deck, watching the gray and black of the nocturnal raiders in the moonlight. Their long-fingered paws handled the food with almost human dexterity, turning it and washing each piece in a bowl of water Libby also left for them. Their masked faces were so beautiful and so mysterious in the balmy night, she put her mug aside and enjoyed their potluck celebration. It occurred to her how idyllic this setting was and how different from her apartment in town with its traffic fumes and noise.

"Haven't you had your fill of animals today?"

John's voice startled Barbara out of her nature study, and she sat up guiltily. "I'm sorry I woke you," she said as his tall form filled the doorway, blocking the light from the kitchen. "I just couldn't sleep."

He nodded. "Too much junk food and too much excitement. Come on. I have a cure for that."

If ever she'd heard a dangerous proposition, Barbara thought, that was it. He came to stand before her in a knee-length terry robe, his bare legs apart, his bare feet firmly planted. And he offered her his hand.

It would be reckless to take it. They were alone in the middle of the night with a force between them that sizzled with a glance, crackled with a touch. John's wolf eyes suggested all kinds of things that could be fatal to a woman searching for a steady, reliable man.

Contrary to every logical thought in her head, she placed her hand in his. She could almost hear her mother saying, "No surprise, Barb. You have your father's wild streak."

John led Barbara to the canopied lawn swing, sat in a corner and pulled her down beside him and turned her into his arms, encouraging her to stretch her legs out. The raccoons turned in unison to watch them, then, deciding they posed no threat, turned back to their banquet. The clean scent of dewy grass filled the night.

"This usually works with the kids," he said, cradling her against him and rubbing her back. "You're probably just tense from the strain of acting all day long. And on top of two ice-cream sandwiches, three Slurpees, the rest of Joe's popcorn—"

"Please," she interrupted, a hand to her stomach, "it doesn't help to catalog my sins. I can't believe how ready the kids were to rat on me."

"Lesson number one in parenting," he said, a smile in his voice. "Never trust a child to be discreet."

Barbara concentrated on the strong, soothing hand running up and down her spine and couldn't imagine why she felt safe. She was in a vulnerable position with a man with whom she'd shared eager kisses and an intimate embrace.

But she felt tenderness in his touch, concern in his demeanor. She leaned her weight against him and closed her eyes. "I'm sorry about the pond," she said softly, sleepily.

"Don't worry about it." His hand moved up to stroke her head. "Jade thought it was great. And I'm grateful you chose the duck pond rather than the croc lagoon."

She smiled against his chest as she felt all her limbs grow heavy. "I do have that much sense."

"That's a mercy."

Sleepy thoughts of the pond turned into drowsy images of the ocean. "I wonder what Trevor's doing?" she thought aloud.

"Fishing," John replied as his hand continued its gentle journey from the base of her spine to her shoulders. "With his father."

Barbara felt sleep inching up her body. "He—" she yawned "—would never feed raccoons."

"Why not?"

"Don't know. He doesn't even have a dog or a cat. And you know what?" She flung an arm around his neck and pulled herself up a little higher, searching for that comfortable hollow in his shoulder. She felt his breath against her forehead as the edges of her world began to blur.

"What?" he asked in a whisper.

"If I told him...my stomach was upset..." She

yawned mightily and had to hold on to the thought as it began to slide away in the mellow darkness overtaking her. "He would have…given me…an antacid tablet."

John was beginning to think he could use one himself. Barbara fell asleep, her curled fingers against the side of his face, the silk of her hair against his chin, the scent of roses driving him wild.

Every nerve ending in his body quaked with longing. He was getting in deep—he could feel it. Like a riptide, Barbara's quick wit coupled with her sweet softness were shaking his footing, threatening to take him under.

Normally he wouldn't be concerned. He'd always been a strong swimmer. But right now he seemed to be losing the will to escape. Her slender body, molded against him in nothing but a thin cotton nightshirt, made him feel possessive and protective—and very willing to let himself be drawn into even deeper water.

BARBARA WOKE to the feel of sunlight on her body. Eyes closed, she enjoyed the warmth on her face for a moment, then turned into the pillow, unwilling to relinquish sleep for another day of pretending she didn't care for John while acting as though she did.

Then she caught the tang of citrus in the pillow and sat up abruptly. She'd fallen asleep last night against the fabric of a robe that had carried the same fragrance.

The door across the room opened and John appeared in a T-shirt and gray slacks, his hair wet and smoothed into place, his smile warm and…knowing?

"You slept with me," she accused quietly, pulling the blanket up to cover her nightshirt.

He went to the dresser in a corner of the room and pulled out a graphite-colored cotton shirt. He glanced at her as he reached into the drawer where she kept her jewelry. Then, remembering his socks had been relocated, he opened a lower drawer and pulled out a pair.

"I did. You fell asleep outdoors, if you recall." He smiled and pushed the drawer closed. "Ardor kept me warm for a while, then I was afraid we'd both catch cold so I brought you inside."

"And took advantage of the situation."

He sat on the edge of the bed and pulled the socks on. "Actually, you're the one who took advantage. You had your arms around my neck and wouldn't let go. So I took the only gentlemanly course left me and stayed with you."

Memories came back to her of the lulling sway of the swing and his hands stroking her back. She remembered feeling comfortable and secure—and very, very sleepy. She also remembered hooking an arm around his neck and feeling his breath against her forehead. He was probably right, and she'd left him little choice in the matter.

John stood and turned to face her, pulling on the shirt as he pushed his feet into gray loafers. "Afraid Trevor Whoever won't like it?"

"Wentworth." She corrected him out of habit, then leaned back against the pillows with a frown. "No, he doesn't have anything to say about it."

John raised an eyebrow as he buttoned the shirt. "If I knew the woman I cared about and with whom I'd been intimate spent the night in another man's arms, I'd have something to say about it, no matter how innocent it was."

Barbara crossed her arms over the spread and focused on his golden eyes. "Trevor and I haven't been intimate."

His hands froze for an instant on the last button, then

he buttoned it and tucked the shirttails inside his pants, laughing softly. "I knew the guy didn't have a pulse."

"He's asked," she said, before he could think otherwise. "I've just refused."

"Asked?"

She gave him an impatient look as he went to the bedside table for his keys and wallet. "Men don't just take today, or hasn't that message gotten to sophisticated bachelors?"

He dropped the keys into his side pocket, then placed the wallet in the inside pocket of a jacket flung over the chair. "I've never *taken*," he said, emphasizing her word, "even before the message circulated. But I've courted, charmed and generally seduced. It's made me crazy to stand near you. I can't imagine keeping company with you for months and not taking the relationship further."

She tried not to be pleased, but couldn't help it. "Maybe I didn't want to take it further."

He sat beside her on the edge of the bed and looked directly into her eyes. "Well, maybe you'd want to with me."

She would. She did. She returned his steady gaze with her own and admitted quietly, "Yes. I would." But she had to remember her tendency to trouble. "But I'm careful because I tend to behave on impulse. I mean, witness the fact that I am here today. Anyway, I promised myself I would take great care that I had the right man before I made love with him. Love has too many consequences."

He couldn't deny that. He was raising two such consequences right now. Still, it sounded like a cold-blooded approach to such a warmhearted emotion.

"I think if you loved Trevor," he said, "your attitude

would be different. You might still want to be cautious, but you'd find a solution to the dilemma damn quick.''

"Like what?''

"Like marriage.''

"I thought you didn't believe in marriage.''

He sighed and stood, reaching for the jacket. "So did I.''

She knew she was out of line to ask, but the words formed before she could stop them. "You've finally forgotten Gracie?''

He considered her a moment, then leaned over her, gold eyes bright, and kissed her slowly. "No," he said finally. "I got acquainted with Barbara.'' Then he straightened and said briskly, "You'd better move it if you're coming.''

She sat up, trying to behave normally while thoroughly shaken. "Where?''

"Church," he replied. "It's Sunday. I think Father Mike will expect you.''

"Why didn't you tell me?'' she demanded as she leapt out of bed and ran to the bathroom.

John stared after her, groaning as her rounded form in the T-shirt and her long, slender legs disappeared behind the door.

BARBARA HAD NEVER attended church regularly, but she was sure a woman wasn't supposed to think about men while listening to the homily. Several times she pulled her mind away from thoughts of John to the ceremony surrounding the ancient rite of the Mass. But several times she found herself standing when everyone else was sitting, or continuing to kneel when everyone else had stood.

Jade, who'd appointed herself in charge of Barbara's

progress through the unfamiliar routine, alternately pulled and pushed her, offering cues under her breath.

Father Mike greeted them in front of the church after the service.

"I'm going to miss spending the day with you four." He pulled Jade and Joe into his embrace and winked at John and Barbara. "I have to be on the job on Sundays. But be sure to tell Libby I'll be back in time for dinner. I understand we're having cheese enchiladas. I'm delighted that you came, Barbara. I take it your mother's improved."

She nodded truthfully. "My mother's great."

"Good. Well, I'll see all of you tonight."

The children pleaded to have breakfast at a fast-food restaurant.

John winced and turned to Barbara for support.

But Joe wrapped both arms around her. "*Please,* Mom. They have these great hash browns in a little patty, and muffins and pancakes and all kinds of great stuff."

Jade worked on her father. "And we're going to be gone all afternoon. You won't have to put up with us while we're at Uncle Hal's nephew's birthday party. So you should spend some quality time with us this morning—having breakfast where *we'd* like to go."

"Or you'll feel that guilt stuff parents get," Joe warned.

John looked at Barbara, who was biting back laughter. "Did you ever hear such skillful manipulation?"

She hugged Joe and shook her head. "No. I think it should be rewarded with a fast-food breakfast."

"Then you owe me an elegant lunch," he said.

"Me? I'm not the one manipulating you."

"No, but you've obviously thrown in with them. All right. In the car."

"I hope Uncle Hal gets up in time for the party," Joe said from the back seat as John pulled away from the curb. "He was still sleeping when we left."

"Mrs. Gordon says he's a heathen," Jade announced from the other corner. "She was walking by this morning when Joe opened Uncle Hal's door. She was getting ready to go to her church. I think she likes him anyway, though."

John found his daughter's face in the rearview mirror. "Why, Jade?"

"Because she blushes when he talks to her. And she watches him."

"She watches everybody," Joe said. "She reminds me of a spy. Like she's just waiting for me to do something wrong—like call Mom Barbara instead of Mom. Then she could tell the…the…"

"Cooperative," John provided.

"The cooperative, not to give Dad and Uncle Hal the account."

"I don't think she's that bad," Barbara said. "She just had an unhappy life and it makes her kind of…" She thought carefully for the right word and finally used the only one that fit. "Well, maybe she is grumpy. So we should do our best to be nice to her."

The car fell quiet, then Joe's voice piped up, "I'll bet she gives grumpy sermons."

Chapter Eight

John waved Hal and the children off just after noon, then went back into the house to find Barbara coming down the stairs in jeans and a soft pink blouse that was frothy and erotic at the same time. He felt his mouth go dry.

"Ready?" he asked.

She stopped one step up, putting them eye-to-eye— except that she didn't seem able to look into his.

"I thought I'd spend the afternoon at my place...you know...catching up on laundry—"

"Libby did it yesterday. All your things are in a neat pile on the bed."

Her glance bounced off him, then wandered to the ceiling as she smiled artificially. "I have to check my answering machine—"

"You did that with your remote this morning."

"Pick up my mail—"

"Carol did that for you. I saw you put it in your brief-case at the office."

She finally met his gaze with an impatient frown. "I have things to do, John. I have a life—a *real* one."

"I think you mean," he said, placing his arms gently at her waist, putting him less than a fraction of an inch away from her, "that *this* one's getting too real for comfort."

She pushed at his shoulders, unwilling to let him close that quarter inch. "John, please don't tell me what I mean."

He held firm, neither retreating nor advancing. "Then you tell me what you mean."

"I mean..." she began with a great head of steam, then looked into the bright gold of his eyes and had to close hers. She finally admitted ruefully, "I mean that this one's getting too real for comfort."

He closed the small distance between them and simply held her. "You don't really want to miss our first chance to just be ourselves together," he coaxed, "without children or observers?"

She wrapped her arms around his neck and leaned her forehead against his. "I don't. But what if we like it?"

"Come on," he chided gently as he held her closer. "We already do. There's no going back." He lifted her off the step and held her against him, a strong arm cradling her bottom, the other hand tangling in her hair as he kissed her.

Barbara was robbed of her ability to reason, much less resist.

He eased her down to the carpet, letting her slide along his body, torturing both of them with the passion that flared between them. He'd told her he would never "just take," but he'd be damned if he'd let her deny what she felt for him. He was satisfied to see that her eyes denied nothing.

He combed her hair back into order with his fingers. "I thought we'd have lunch in Old Town, do a little antique shopping or jewelry shopping, or whatever kind of shopping you prefer, and maybe have dinner and go dancing.''

That sounded safe enough, she told herself. Although she knew better.

''Okay,'' she said. ''I'm ready.''

OLD TOWN was a wonderful collection of Italianate buildings converted to shopping malls. Quaint specialty shops had been incorporated into the turn-of-the-century atmosphere of what had once been the center of Portland commerce.

Barbara could not believe that John was willing to wander into shop after shop while she examined the wares and dawdled over interesting displays. Trevor hated to shop.

She tried on a broad-brimmed hat decorated with beads and buttons; the brim was held back at the front with a phony pink stone set in gold filigree. It made an impression of junky elegance.

John bent his knees to smile at her reflection in the square mirror over the little vanity placed in a corner of the shop.

''Is it me?'' Barbara asked, turning this way and that.

''More so than the monkey hat we bought you at the zoo yesterday. Do you like it?''

''I love it. But do I need it?''

He frowned at her. ''That's the last question you should ask yourself when you really want something.''

She turned to him in disapproval, her luminous complexion sparkling under the gaudy jewels on the hat.

''You've obviously never been down to your last three dollars and forced to make a decision on whether to buy lipstick or a hamburger.''

''That's true. But some things feed the soul, and I

firmly believe you have to nourish it as well as the body to remain healthy. Particularly when your livelihood depends on your creative spark. Let's buy the hat.''

Barbara caught his wrist as he would have signaled for the clerk.

"*I* will buy the hat."

"Barbara—''

"Look," she insisted under her breath, "you can throw your weight around in front of Father Mike and Mrs. Gordon, but not when we're alone."

He leaned over her and said quietly, "But we're not alone. The clerk goes to St. Bonaventure's."

Barbara rolled her eyes at his ploy. "She does not."

"John!" A plump, white-haired woman heaved into view, stopping Barbara's words in her throat. She wore a hat similar to the one Barbara sported. "And this must be your wife. Father told me about her this morning after Mass. I'm sorry I missed you both."

"Darling," John said, placing a hand on Barbara's shoulder, sending her a laughing glance in the mirror. "I'd like you to meet Nancy Webster. Nancy, this is my wife, Barbara."

"Well, where have you been hiding, you pretty thing?" Nancy asked. "John and I worked on the roofing fund together. He never said a word about you."

"We haven't been married very long," Barbara said, her voice a little feeble as she donned her role again. "And my mother's been ill, so I've been spending most weekends with her and haven't gotten to church."

"Well, I'm delighted to see that he has you. A hunk like that shouldn't be alone, particularly with children."

Barbara avoided John's eye in the mirror and smiled. "So am I. And he was about to buy me this hat."

Nancy clapped plump hands together. "Wonderful

choice. Shall I box it for you, or would you like to wear it? It's perfect with your shirt.''

Reckless with relief because Nancy seemed satisfied with her paltry explanation, Barbara made a quick decision. ''I'll wear it, thank you.''

John and Barbara had lunch on the top floor of an old bank turned mall. Under an arched window that showed sunlight gradually being lost to cloud cover, they ate salads with cheese bread and shared a split of chardonnay.

''Gracie never wore hats,'' John said as he passed her the olives from his salad. ''She thought they were pretentious.''

Barbara looked up, surprised that he'd brought up the subject. He usually backed away from a conversation that involved Gracie. The obvious reason now was that he wanted to talk about her. She tried not to appear as though she wanted to know.

''Well, Trevor doesn't like hats on women. He says they're conspicuous.'' She smiled, letting him know he could continue or not, whatever he preferred. ''Maybe we should introduce him to Gracie. Want my boiled eggs?''

''Sure.''

The careful transference of a dozen slices of egg from her plate to his took another moment. Then John took a sip of wine and asked candidly, ''Do you want to hear about her?''

''Do you want to tell me?'' she asked.

''No. But I feel as though I should.''

''Well, don't.'' She dribbled dressing over her salad with a teaspoon. ''Even if we...if this...'' She sighed, not quite sure how to define what they had together. ''I mean, we won't, because we're not right for each other.

But if we were, I wouldn't have to know your secrets. Just that that was a part of your life you'd put away.''

"That's a very sane attitude," he said with an appreciative nod, "but I have the children I made with her. That keeps her a part of my life even though I haven't seen her since the morning she delivered them.''

Barbara started to speak, but didn't know what to say. Such a reaction to giving birth was so alien to her that she couldn't quite absorb it.

"They look a little like her. Jade, particularly, of course, when she smiles. And they ask about her from time to time. But they've never seen her. I didn't give them a photograph, so she remains a little out of focus. I think that's better for them, at least while they're growing up. What they decide to do when they're adults is up to them.''

"What made you keep them, John?" she had to ask. "I mean, you had to know it would be difficult, sometimes close to impossible to raise two babies without a mother.''

"They're mine," he said simply. "They were conceived in love, at least on my part.''

"I'm sorry it didn't work out.''

He shrugged. "It was a hard lesson to learn, but those are the ones we remember best. She was so full of life, such a wonderful free spirit.'' He sighed, as though still trying to banish the ghosts of that relationship. "Trouble was, when the time came to make a few important life decisions, we couldn't agree. Despite our precautions, she became pregnant. I wanted to get married. She had plans for a career in fine art and wanted to terminate the pregnancy. So we made a deal. I paid the expenses and set her up in a studio for a year, and I got the baby.'' He grinned as he made the correction, "Babies. They didn't see the second one on the ultrasound until she was six months along.''

''Women who don't want babies,'' Barbara said, ''shouldn't raise them to please someone else. Everyone suffers.''

''Absolutely.'' His answer was swift and firm. ''I just couldn't love a woman who felt that way. Anyway...'' He leaned back in his chair and stabbed a bite of salad. ''She said she didn't want contact after they were born, and she's held to that. And that's the Gracie story.''

A cloud had moved over the sun and now freed it again, pouring bright light over their table under the arched window.

''But you vowed never to marry.''

He put his fork down, then leaned toward her on folded arms, his smile warm, his eyes free of any thought of Gracie.

''Then I met a woman who considers me a completely unsuitable husband, and I suddenly find myself determined to change her mind.''

Happy to see him free of his troublesome thoughts, she smiled. ''Do us both a favor,'' she said, ''and don't try.''

''Because I travel?''

''Partly. And because I'm looking for someone more serious.''

''Serious?'' he repeated disparagingly. ''You mean like Trevor Whoever who *didn't* take you to the Caymans, who gave you an IRA for your birthday, who isn't in advertising, who wouldn't feed raccoons and who'd soothe your nerves by giving you an antacid? That's not serious, Barbara. That's dead.''

She couldn't help the laugh that erupted. And as it did she remembered that Trevor had never made her laugh and that she hadn't thought about him, except the few times his name had come up in conversation, since she'd moved in with John and his children.

John's eyes went from the laughter in hers to the sparkling hat she wore. "I'd hate to think that you'll never get to wear that hat in the future."

"I'll wear it." She studied the bright green bib lettuce and the fat shrimp on the end of her fork. "I know Trevor isn't what I want in a man, either. I think I mistook dullness for seriousness."

That comforted him. He knew Trevor Whoever wasn't right for her the moment he saw him, but it relieved him to hear her speak the words.

In truth, John was far more serious than she gave him credit for. And he was about to turn all that seriousness toward changing her mind about him.

They walked all over Old Town, arm in arm against the cooling afternoon. They bought cappuccino and cranberry *biscotti* at a coffee bar and looked in shop windows as they drank and dunked the crisp cookie.

They bought dinosaur T-shirts for the children and one for Libby that said Motorcycle Mama.

Barbara laughed as they put their purchases in the car. "When are you buying her the Harley?"

"It's on order already," he said. "Her family's having a reunion in September down the coast. They're all into bikes. She'll be able to arrive in style."

They locked the doors, then crossed the street to methodically canvas the shops on the other side.

"I was so surprised that her heart's desire was a motorcycle," Barbara said. "She looks like such a conventional, mature woman."

He hooked an arm around her shoulder, and she reached up to thread her fingers through his.

"That's because you're stuck on 'seriousness' as important in a relationship," he said. "And because you have a warped notion of what's real and what isn't. Her husband was hardworking but fun loving, and they had a great life together on his bike."

"You think she'll be able to handle one on her own?"

"She used to. When her children were home, she had her own bike, and one of the girls rode behind her, the other with her father. When the girls were both married, it was cozier for them to go to one."

Barbara tried to picture the romance of such an adventure and couldn't. She sighed. "I'm glad Libby was so happy. But my idea of a vacation would be in the passenger seat of a Cadillac or, at worst, a comfortable Jeep."

"I'll remember that," he said. "And where do you envision yourself on a honeymoon?"

"Not the Caymans."

"No."

She played the game. "Maybe...Canada. Lake Louise, that area. It's supposed to be so beautiful."

"Good choice. I've been there."

"Of course." She gave him a teasingly superior glance. "You're a man who travels."

He pulled her to him and squeezed until laughter bubbled out of her.

"THE DIAMOND HORSE CAFE?" Barbara stared out the car window at the blue-and-white neon sign. She heard loud country-western music coming from inside when a couple opened the door and walked in. She frowned at John. "When you said dinner and dancing, I thought—"

"I know. *Serious* stuff." He followed her gaze to the

groups and couples hurrying into the low structure. "But it's time you loosened up."

She turned to him with a sound of dismay. "I've never done a line dance in my life!"

He pulled the keys from the ignition. "Neither have I. But the Diamond Horse is a good client of Cheney & Roman. We should patronize them."

"We can't," she said, as though certain she had an irrefutable argument. "We don't have boots."

He shook his head in mock disappointment. "You'd let a little thing like that prevent you from having a good time?"

She gave him a fastidious look. "I prefer to be appropriately dressed for all occassions. And when I look ridiculous, I never have a good time."

"All right." He turned to her and pulled her toward him, enfolding her hands in his. "Close your eyes."

"John..."

He leaned over to kiss them closed. Lost in the gesture, Barbara sighed and absorbed the sweetness of it, keeping her lids lowered.

"Good," he said, giving her hands a little squeeze. "Now, imagine yourself in the middle of a dance floor with a faceted light rotating overhead and couples dancing in a circle all around you."

She sighed. "Okay. I'm in the middle of the floor."

"Imagine there's a man beside you."

She hesitated just a moment. "Okay."

"Who is it?"

She focused on the face, but she didn't really have to. She was already familiar with the feelings John's very nearness evoked in her—even in her thoughts.

"You," she replied honestly.

Then she felt his lips on hers sweetly, tenderly.

"That's for giving the right answer," he said. "Okay, now focus on us standing together. What are we doing?"

Eyes still closed, she smiled as she related what she saw. "We're laughing."

"Of course. Now focus on you. What are you feeling?"

That required a little exploration. She drew deeper into herself and was surprised to discover that under the little protective shield of caution and "seriousness," she felt eager, adventurous…brave.

She parted her lips to explain and couldn't quite believe it.

"What do you feel?" he prompted.

She sighed, let the shield fall away and opened her eyes to admit with a smile, "Fearlessness. And my toe was tapping to the country music."

The gold in his eyes brightened as he put a hand to her cheek. He grinned. "I'm sure you grasp the metaphor at work here."

She turned her lips into his palm and planted a kiss there.

John felt his spine turn to oatmeal.

"That standing beside you will dissolve all my inhibitions," she whispered, "and erase my fears?"

He pulled her into his arms and kissed her again, slowly this time and with tender care. "Right again," he said finally. "And it will also make you realize that you're wrong about our work warping our reality. What you feel is real, isn't it?"

She concentrated on herself and realized, heaven help her, that it was. "Yes, but—"

He placed a finger on her lips. "Don't qualify it. Let it be what it is." He kissed her again, then reached beyond her to open her door.

THE OWNER of the Diamond Horse, a tall, lanky young man in fringed white, complete with boots and rhinestones on the band of his hat, came to their table to welcome them.

In the middle of the floor, long lines of revelers danced in complicated patterns, shouting and clapping to the music. A jaunty tune spoke of love found, then lost, then found again. Overhead, the faceted light John had placed into her imagination flung diamonds across the room as it turned. Barbara felt a little as though she were afloat in the Milky Way.

She was surprised to discover that the lanky young man, Colorado, had a broad New York accent.

"Cowboy clubs aren't a matter of heritage," he said with a wide smile, "they're a matter of spirit. Even though I grew up in an apartment in Manhattan, I was alway dreaming of leading a cattle drive across the plains."

He swept a hand toward his enthusiastic clientele. "They don't do that anymore, of course, so moving a partying crowd east and west across my dance floor was as close as I could come. So, you two want to try it?"

John raised a questioning eyebrow at Barbara.

She braced herself. "That's why we're here."

Colorado gave her a hearty slap on the back as he pushed away from the table. "That's the kind of woman that won the West. Where'd you find her, John?"

"In my bathroom."

"'Scuse me?"

"It's a long story. I'll tell you about it at the wedding."

Barbara turned to John with a scolding look.

Colorado looked from one to the other. "I take it you haven't told *her* about the wedding yet."

"She's balking," John said, grinning in the face of her displeasure. "But I'm tenacious."

Colorado smacked him on the arm. "And that's the kind of *man* that won the West. Come on. I'll get a partner, and just follow us."

It seemed hopeless. Barbara no sooner got the hang of one series of steps when they launched into another in a different direction. She and John were constantly stepping on each other's feet or colliding with their neighbors, who took it all in laughing good spirits.

Colorado and his partner, a shapely, leggy blonde in a snug blue blouse, short blue skirt studded with rhinestones in the shape of a horse's head, and dyed-to-match boots, linked arms with them and led them with expert, confident movements.

Then they moved away to help another group of newcomers.

"We can do this," John said, finding a place on the end of a line and trying to fall into step. Barbara, her eyes on the lineup of boots, missed a sudden turn to the side. Her body moved in the wrong direction, stopping John's momentum. They fell to the floor in a laughing tangle.

John propped his elbow on the scuffed hardwood floor and grinned at Barbara, who lay on her back beside him, breath coming in giggling gasps.

"Of course, no matter how intrepid we are," he said gravely, "there's the possibility that this simply isn't our style."

Barbara sat up to tug her shirt down. "I hope that isn't true," she said. "I'm really getting a hankering for a pair of boots like Kitty's."

He sat up beside her. "A hankering?"

She nodded. "Though I grew up in a little resort community in Washington, my heart was always leading a cattle drive across the plains.'' She gave him a dry glance, then nudged him in the ribs with her elbow. ''It's just that my feet don't understand that. Do you think we could just grab a burger somewhere and listen to music from a jukebox?''

John could not remember a moment when he'd been happier, when life seemed to hold more promise, when every moment seemed as satisfying as it did now.

''We can do anything you want,'' he said with a seriousness so sudden and intense that it communicated itself to her and made her realize that she'd been looking in all the wrong places for the stalwart, steady man of her dreams.

She got to her feet and reached down for him. ''Then let's go. I also have a hankering for onion rings and a caramel-dipped ice-cream cone.''

''You have to promise me you won't say *hankering* anymore,'' he said, using her hand only for balance, but appreciating the way she took a firm stance and put muscle behind the yank that brought him to his feet.

''I have a powerful hankering,'' she said deliberately, her grin a challenge, ''to burst through saloon doors and cast a steely sweep of my eyes along the bar. I'd like to swagger across the floor in my lavender boots and—'' She punctuated whatever was coming next with a stab of her fist in the air.

John caught her wrist and pulled her after him. ''I'm getting you out of here before you try to make an arrest.''

She faked a frown. ''You're no fun.''

He grinned wickedly as he took his jacket from the back of his chair and handed her her purse. ''I can be, I assure you. All I need is the chance. Come on.''

"Isn't Libby expecting us for enchiladas?" Barbara asked suddenly as John pulled into a brightly lit drive-in. "Remember? Father Mike said..."

John shook his head as he pulled into a spot. "I told her not to expect us. Hal will be there with the kids, so we're not really needed."

He placed their order with a girl in a cheerleader outfit and rollerskates, while the sound system played music from the sixties.

Barbara unbuckled her seat belt, slid down in her seat and closed her eyes with a contented sigh. "I know it's only been a few days, but I feel as though Wednesday was a year ago."

"Time accelerates when we're together," he said, turning to lean against the window. "A lot of things accelerate. My heartbeat, my pulse..."

She heaved a gusty sigh and stretched languidly. "I know. I'm such a sex goddess."

"How does a sex goddess get away with eating onion rings?"

"We don't kiss anyone."

"Ever?"

"Not after onion rings."

"I see."

She sat up, opening her eyes. "I still don't know what to do about the garbanzos."

"No problem," John replied. "I didn't order any."

"Very funny. I'm talking about the account."

"I know. But that's a forbidden subject on a Sunday evening. Do you think Mrs. Gordon is sweet on Hal?"

Barbara turned in her seat and tucked her feet up under her. "I haven't noticed, but then I've been so concerned about my own performance, I haven't paid much attention to anyone else's. But I don't think she's quite the hard case she'd have us believe she is. I think she's been hurt.''

John nodded, remembering his own pain with a wry smile. ''That can make you cranky.''

''Has Hal...noticed her?''

He shrugged. ''He's usually very private about the women in his life, but he told me that he deliberately tried to distract her on the way home from the zoo after your spill into the pond.''

''Because he's your partner. He has as much at stake if you lose the account as you do.''

''Maybe I'm crazy, but I thought it was more than that. I can tell when he...connects with something, when he sees beyond what's apparent. He sometimes does that with a product when we're developing ideas. He spaces out, then he comes back with this resolution in his eyes. He did that while we were talking about Joanna.''

Barbara smiled, the subject of Joanna just too complicated for consideration when she was in such a mellow mood. ''The children certainly love him.''

''No surprise. He's been there for them almost as much as I have. He's painted nurseries with me, walked floors with them when the kids were colicky or teething, he's bandaged them up, consoled them, played with them, scolded them. He couldn't mean more to us if he truly were my brother.''

There was a sudden grating sound as the skating carhop arrived. She placed the tray on the lowered window, took John's money and made change, then skated away with all the grace and style of an Olympic contender.

John passed Barbara a hamburger and a lidded paper cup.

She took a big bite of the sinfully, deliciously fatty concoction, then moaned in approval as she ate.

"This whole teen experience," she said after swallowing, "of burgers and fries wasn't prevalent when I was in school. We were all into health and fitness, eating salads and tofu and exercising with our Jane Fonda tapes until we dropped."

John toasted her with his paper cup. "What made you come to your senses?"

"An inherent love of fat and sugar, I guess. May I have an onion ring?"

"No," he said, concentrating on his sandwich.

She expected him to admit that he was teasing and capitulate. When he didn't, she tried to reach past him for one. He caught her wrist and gently put her hand back in her lap.

"I said no." He spoke with a gravity that made her suspicious.

She tried to probe for a motive. "Do I have to wrestle you for it?"

He didn't even consider before shaking his head. "Interesting as the possibilities are, there, no."

"Ask nicely?"

"You already did, and I said no."

"You certainly don't want me to grovel?"

"Of course not."

"Then why won't you share one with me?"

He sipped from his cup and swallowed. "Because of your rule," he said.

For a moment she didn't know what he was talking about. Then she remembered her earlier joke about being a sex goddess, and her rule about not kissing after onion rings.

She wrapped up her burger and placed it carefully on the cup holder on the floor, putting the cup in the hole beside it. When she looked up at him, his eyes were alive with mischief and interest.

"I could take them from you, you know," she challenged, sitting on her knees and facing him.

He put his food aside as she had done and met her gaze evenly. "I'd like to see you try."

He'd never meant anything more sincerely in his life. He'd been reining himself in all afternoon. He couldn't wait for body contact with her.

Barbara glanced at the bag of onion rings on the tray perched on the window. The only way to reach them was to lean over him. It was time, she knew. They'd been dancing around it all afternoon, coming in close and backing away, connecting, then pulling apart, afraid that what was already fragile might be broken by a sudden move.

But she'd been living with the need for it all day. And he'd made it obvious that he had, too.

"Maybe," she said, scooting toward him until her knees were right beside his thigh and she could place her arm around his neck, "we're ignoring another solution here."

She could see splinters of brown and green in the eyes watching her, see that confident tilt of his brow almost before it happened, feel the heat that emanated from his body, the rocklike shoulders under her arm. She had to concentrate to remember what she was doing.

"What's that?" he asked, sitting quietly docile, but dangerously alert.

"Peaceful negotiations," she said. "I give you a kiss, then you give me an onion ring."

He held her away with a hand to her shoulder when she would have leaned down to offer her part of the bargain.

"No deal," he said. "I'd get only one kiss *before* you get the onion ring, then none after."

She rolled her eyes and, using his shoulders for leverage, boosted herself into his lap. "Then what's your solution?"

"We've already discussed that," he said, determinedly stubborn. "You get no onion rings."

"Really." With a superior glance, she reached over her shoulder to the shelf, snatched the bag, and tried to escape across the front seat with it.

But he already had her in his grip, and she dropped the bag on the floor as he prevented her escape by yanking her toward him. "Really," he said. "You'll notice that you still don't have them. So I get a kiss now and the promise of more afterward at every stop light between here and home, in the driveway, on the porch, and upstairs—" His voice dropped to a whisper that suggested the meaning behind his words. "When everyone else has gone to bed."

She wanted desperately to make love with him, but she knew it would negate all the care she'd taken thus far.

"But it's…asking for trouble."

"I know," he whispered, kissing her earlobe. "But expecting to live your life without trouble is far less realistic than writing advertising slogans."

His kisses traced the line of her jaw. When his hand slipped under her blouse, she felt the world spin. "John," she said breathlessly.

In a matter of seconds she felt as though she'd never had a grasp of reality. His lips moved on hers, reshaping her thoughts, her plans, her fondest wishes for solidity in her life. His tongue delved deep inside her, searching for the love she wanted to hide from him. He kissed her until that love flowered between them, too bright, too alive to ignore.

And all the time his hand caressed her softness, sculpting it to his touch. She leaned into him, whispering his name again.

"Yes," he said softly. "You're mine. It doesn't matter whether you admit or deny it. You belong to me, and I belong to you."

She had no clever argument with which to fight him, no brilliant plan to disarm him. The hard truth was that he was right.

And she'd forgotten why she'd ever thought otherwise.

Chapter Nine

It began to rain. Large drops plopped onto the windshield, blurring the neon lights into a bright riot of pattern and color as John drove home.

He and Barbara leaned toward each other at every red light, sometimes kissing, sometimes simply looking into each other's eyes and seeing things that hadn't been there the day before, things that were the product of this day's honesty.

At home, they stood in the darkness of the garage and held each other. John kissed her, then reached into the car for her hat and placed it on her head.

A short, covered walk connected the garage to the back porch, and they stopped again under the light to drink in the glow in each other's eyes. Then John took her hand and urged her inside.

They found Hal alone in the kitchen, reading the Sunday paper at the table and sipping brandy. His gaze went from John to Barbara then back to John as though he saw something he wanted to confirm with a second look. Then he nodded and smiled, his eyes moving up to Barbara's hat.

She resisted an impulse to hide behind John, certain the weight she felt on her head wasn't whimsical milli-

nery at all, but her feelings for John, gathered into a
formidable little pile and tied with a bow.

"Good day?" Hal asked.

"Great," John replied. "You?"

"Nerve-racking. Remind me never to volunteer to
play bouncer at a kids' birthday party again. Your children are asleep, by the way, having consumed a dis-
gusting amount of food."

John grinned. "Thanks for taking them. Father Mike
and Joanna get back okay?"

"In time for dinner. They've both retired for the night.
Libby, too. The weekend answering service called. Bentley-Bowles left an urgent message about some new company they've acquired. I tried to call them back and got
their weekend answering service. I told them we'd be in
touch tomorrow morning."

John groaned. "Why do we get all the clients who
love to work on Sundays?"

"Just lucky, I guess." Hal looked from one to the
other again with a small smile. "Don't sleep too late.
Libby promised eggs Benedict for breakfast."

Barbara said good-night politely while reading the
speculation in Hal's eyes.

She and John looked in on the children together, then
walked into John's dark, cool bedroom. Rain tapped
lightly against the windows and the roof and made little
whooshing sounds in the trees behind the house.

John reached for the light switch, but Barbara caught
his hand. She didn't want to shed light on anything. She
wanted to capture the dark velvet of the moment and
react with the reckless impulse she was tired of denying.

She loved John Cheney. What had begun as deceit
seemed to have turned into the single most important
truth of her life. She didn't care that he traveled and

solved everything with a grin. She wanted him more than anything.

John turned the hand she'd caught so that he could capture hers. He felt hers trembling. It started a tremor in him he tried desperately to steady.

"What is it?" he asked, using his free hand to slowly remove her hat and put it aside.

She came against him in the darkness, one hand moving inside his jacket to the back of his shirt. His body reacted as though she'd touched naked flesh.

"Love," she whispered, her eyes luminous in the darkness as she said in awe, "John, I'm in love with you."

He crushed her against him, their combined heartbeats quickening the tempo of the quiet night. "Barbara," he said softly. "I've been waiting for you for a long time."

"Oh, John." She heaved a ragged little sigh and pulled away from him.

John felt a moment's concern, certain she'd decided loving him was not a sound decision after all. Then she put her hands to the lapels of his jacket and pushed it from his shoulders. He let it fall to the floor.

She worked on the buttons of his shirt, and he tried to unfasten hers, but the buttons were too small for his large fingers. So he tugged the blouse out of her jeans and she opened the top two buttons, then raised her arms to let him lift it off.

The white of her silky bra shimmered in the darkness. He placed his hands gently over her, and she closed her eyes, leaning into him. He heard her shuddering breath.

Barbara felt the electric sensation of his touch from the tips of her breasts to the soles of her feet. He pulled her to him, caressed her bare shoulders and waist with hands that were strong and sure, then unhooked her bra and pulled her away to slip it off.

The moment she was free of it she went back into his arms, pressing her breasts against the jut of his ribs. His groan and her sigh merged in the quiet room.

He lifted her onto the bed and unbuttoned and unzipped her jeans. He slipped his fingers between the silk of her skin and her undies and pulled down. She lifted her hips to help him then sat up to reach for him as he tossed jeans, panties and shoes aside.

He went back to the mattress with her, his knees straddling her waist as her hands crept up between his undershirt and his skin. The sensation was so intense, he felt as though he could discern her very fingerprints against his body.

He yanked the shirt off and braced himself as she unbuckled his belt, unbuttoned the waistband of his slacks and lowered his zipper. His body began to riot.

In moments he'd shed his slacks and briefs, then he braced his hands on the mattress as she drew them down.

"I love you," he said urgently. "Did I tell you that?" He couldn't remember. His thoughts were spinning.

"You did," she said, putting her lips to his chest and kissing a line across his shoulders. "Right after I told you I love you."

"I don't think the word is strong enough." He enfolded her in his arms and stroked every silken curve and hollow of her back. "What I feel is like—like dynamite in a teacup." His touch became more urgent. "Impossible," he said breathlessly, "to contain."

Barbara suspected her body temperature had reached a combustible level. The movement of his hands over her, touching, shaping, teasing, was acting like a match to her own explosives. Everything inside her was racing, smoking.

He turned her onto her back and leaned over her, opening his mouth on hers as he swept his hand down her stomach and dipped gently inside her.

She moaned against his lips. Her body opened for him, strained against his touch, quaked madly with the quickening of the moment.

Barbara swept her hand down his side, over his hip, then to his manhood.

Her small, firm hand ignited the dynamite, destroying the teacup, the very world he lived in, and flinging him out into the universe. He rose over her just in time to take her with him. They clung together in an orbit around the perfect world each had wanted and never hoped to find.

Landing safely, each thought separately, was going to be the only problem.

BARBARA STEPPED out of the shower into John's waiting arms with a little shriek of surprise.

"I'm drenched," she warned, pushing halfheartedly against his naked body with one hand as she stretched her other hand just short of the towel rack.

"Doesn't matter," he said, nuzzling her neck. "I'm not dressed."

"You should be…getting dressed. The alarm rang fifteen…minutes ago. John, it's Monday."

"I heard the alarm," he said, reaching beyond her straining hand for the towel and drying her back with it as he continued to kiss and nip at her. "I don't care what day it is. Where's your sentimentality, anyway? This is all so familiar, Barbara. This is how we met."

Barbara had to work to form words as he rubbed the

towel over her bottom and the backs of her thighs. "I was not naked," she denied. "I was wearing a teddy."

He made a wolfish sound of approval. "I remember. It's imprinted on my mind."

"The children will be up soon," she cautioned as he began to dab at her breasts with the towel.

John looked into her eyes and saw the same desire and awe that he'd felt last night. He hadn't imagined it. She loved him, too.

Barbara watched him toss the towel aside and pull her to him with all the fevered burning emotion that had surrounded their union the night before. She felt the heat rise in her again, bringing her back to that same burning recklessness that made her see and feel only John.

"Then we'd better hurry," he said. He swept her up in his arms and turned sideways to pass through the door into the bedroom.

Barbara was fascinated that it could all be new again this morning when they'd made love three times during the night. Though his touch had become dearly familiar, and she realized she could feel it on her even when he drew his hands away, the style with which they came together now was different.

Out of necessity he moved quickly, but remembered every little detail he'd learned about her during the long night. He brought her quickly to gasping, greedy madness, then entered her with a swift thrust that sent both of them into a little corner of heaven.

"YES," JOHN SAID into the portable phone as he tried to button his shirt with one hand. It wasn't working.

Barbara, clad in a white blouse with a ruffly jabot and a half-slip, came to brush his hands aside and help him.

"Hal told me you called," he said, running a knuckle over her cheekbone. "I read about the acquisition in the *Wall Street Journal.* Congratulations."

Finished buttoning his shirt, Barbara tried to walk away, but he caught her hand and pulled her back. She gave him a scolding smile, pinching the side of her slip between thumb and forefinger then indicating the closet to explain wordlessly that she had to finish getting dressed.

She heard indistinguishable conversation on the other end of the line as John nodded. Then he slipped his hand into the elastic waist of the slip and tugged down.

She slapped at him and he raised an arm in theatrical defense while saying in the most polished business voice, "Of course. We'll want to move on that right away."

Smiling, Barbara went to the closet and pulled on a simple, pin-striped skirt. She wondered if Bentley-Bowles's new company would mean a temporary halt to the development of the cooperative's program. When Cheney & Roman developed a new campaign, John worked tirelessly with the client, according to Carol, inspecting all their products and listening to all their ideas. This part of a project would not allow the observance of Father Mike and Pastor Gordon.

Bowles's offices, she knew, were in one of the new buildings by the river, so even if John had to be out of the office during the day, she'd still have him at night. And right now she wouldn't complain about anything that lengthened this time they had together.

"No, I don't know a lot about them," John said into the phone, wandering across the room to the window. "Rubber products, I believe the article said. Everything from bar mats to parts for the F14."

Barbara pulled her matching jacket out of the closet and looked around the room for her purse.

"I missed that part," John said. "Where is their plant?"

Barbara heard the small silence and knew instantly what it meant. She turned from her search behind the chair next to the bed, hair rumpled, and looked into John's eyes.

His gaze held hers steadily. "Rhode Island," he said. "You couldn't have acquired something in Washington or California?"

Barbara heard the laughter on the other end of the line and wanted to throttle John and the president of Bentley-Bowles.

She calmly resumed her search. So much for her cozy little scenario of John coming home to her every night. He was going to be thirty-three hundred miles away.

"Yes, I can," John was saying. "I can lay a good foundation in a few days, but I have to be home for a personal obligation at the end of the week. If necessary, I'll return later for details." He listened for a moment. Barbara felt his eyes follow her around the room as she lifted the dust ruffle and peered under the bed. "Good. I'll leave this afternoon and be there first thing in the morning."

She saw nothing, not even dust. She surfaced, her hair falling over her eyes, to find herself nose to lens with a camera. Hal, one knee braced on the foot of the bed, took the picture.

She gave him a moue of disapproval. "Is nothing sacred?"

He shook his head. "Your door was open and I saw that you were dressed, so I followed the cats in." He pointed to the tuxedo and the tabby who must have wandered in while she was distracted by the search for her purse. They were curled up together on John's pillow. "I figured you might pay me to destroy that shot. All photographers have a blackmail file for when times get lean."

She pushed him aside and went past him. "I don't think Mrs. Gordon would approve."

"I believe she considers me a lost cause, anyway."

Barbara passed John, still on the phone. He reached out to touch her cheek. Hal photographed the action.

Barbara drew away without meeting John's eyes to check the bathroom. The spark with which she'd awakened this morning was sputtering dangerously, and she wanted to keep the feeling to herself until she understood it.

She heard John terminate the call, then palm down the phone's antenna. Then he demanded of Hal, "What are you doing in our bedroom?"

"It's on our schedule of shots," Hal replied. Barbara heard the rustle of paper. "See? Right here. 'Preparation for work.' What'd Bentley say? You off to the new company?"

"Yeah. It's in Rhode Island."

Hal whistled. "You need me?"

"No. You'd better make sure everything runs smoothly here. We'll go back together after I figure out what they want. Now, will you beat it so we can finish getting ready?"

"Right."

The bedroom door closed.

Barbara was now in the closet, checking the cedar shelves, parting clothes to check the floor.

"I'll be home by Thursday," John said from right

behind her. When she didn't reply, he reached in and pulled her out.

"Yes, I know," she said and moved past him to check underneath the nightstand.

"Barbara," he said, his tone exasperated. He pulled her to her feet and lifted her chin until she was forced to look at him. "Don't confuse me with your father. I'll be thinking about you all the time I'm gone."

She sighed and raised her hands to his arms. "I know. I understand that you have to go."

He sat on the edge of the bed and pulled her onto his lap. "Then, what are you upset about?"

She looped her arms around his neck and ran her thumb gently along his jawline. "Because I woke up, still glowing from making love with you—and then there was Hal with his camera, and I remembered that we're just like the actors in the coffee commercial."

"You know that isn't true," he said, squeezing her to him. "It began that way, but now it's real."

She looked into his eyes, hers wide and troubled. "Do you know what's real? How much of this is what you feel for me, and how much is just advertising entangled with your home life? Is this just my wild Ryan streak kicking in, loving the danger, wanting to stretch it to its limit?" Her voice quieted and she lowered her eyes. "Do you really love *me,* or do I just represent the rounding out of your family Gracie couldn't provide?"

"I do not," he said firmly, "have you confused with Gracie."

Perhaps he didn't; she didn't know. The theatrics and the reality were hopelessly entangled and winding tighter.

"I think we should slow down," she said gravely, "until we're sure what we're doing."

"*I'm* sure," he said, tipping her backward in his arms and placing her on the mattress. "And I'm not going to leave room in your mind—or your body—for doubt." He reached under her and unzipped her skirt.

She pushed ineffectually at his hands. "Your trip will give us time apart to think."

"That's right." He pulled her skirt and slip off. "But I'm going to think about you," he said, curling his fingers into the waistband of her panties and hose. "And I'm going to make sure you think about me."

In less than a moment he made it impossible for her to think at all.

Chapter Ten

"No." Joe smiled at Barbara as he shouldered his back-pack.

"You don't want to come with us to the airport?" she asked, mystified by the children's casual attitude about their father's impending trip.

In a rare show of brotherly assistance, Joe held Jade's pack for her to slip into.

"Dad goes to the airport all the time," Jade said. "And the day camp's going to OMSI today."

Of course. The Oregon Museum of Science and Industry. No child would want to miss such an adventure.

Joe studied Barbara a moment, then put a comforting arm around her shoulders. "You know Dad always comes back, Mom. And he brings presents every time. We should send him away more often."

John, who'd just come in from the veranda with the paper, swatted him with it.

Joe laughed and reached up for his hug. "Have a good trip, Dad. You think you'll have time to look for Captain Kidd's gold? It's supposed to be buried in Rhode Island somewhere, according to the treasure book you bought me."

"Jamestown," Jade informed him.

John shook his head regretfully and leaned down to wrap Jade in a bear hug. "Sorry. I'll be pretty busy in Warren. Take good care of Mom for me."

"Don't we always?" Joe smiled, pleased with himself and his continued performance. He seemed never to miss a cue.

Barbara saw John fight the smile. "Yes, you do. Promise me you won't take her to any bike shops and make her test-drive an ATV."

Joe pretended indignation. "You think I'd do something like that behind your back?"

"In a minute."

Joe turned to Barbara with a sigh. "Don't you hate it when he reads your mind?"

Her nod was sincere. "Every time. You guys have fun. I'll see you this afternoon."

Jade looped her arms around Barbara's neck and hugged. She wasn't the consummate actor her brother was. Barbara knew the gesture was sincere. She held the child an extra moment.

"Have a good day, darling."

Jade whispered in her ear, "Ask Daddy again if I can get my ears pierced."

Barbara caught John's curious glance. "I will," she promised Jade. "Don't wander away from the group at the museum, and stay with your brother."

Jade looked at Joe with a grimace. "I wanted to have fun."

"Now, be nice," Barbara scolded quietly.

"Yeah." Joe led the way to the door, Jade following. "I'm nice to you."

"When?" Jade demanded.

"Did I let the zoo keep you when they thought you were funny-looking enough to put in a cage? No. I told

them you were my precious sister and I— Oof!'' His
voice and what sounded like a fist hitting flesh were cut
off abruptly as the front door closed behind them.

The adults around the table, even Joanna, laughed.
Father Mike shook his head at John. ''I don't know if
that boy's going to become president of the United
States or end up in some prison.''

John groaned. ''I know. Barbara and I have opened
an account for bail money just in case.''

JOHN SAW genuine distress in Barbara's eyes as he stood
at the boarding gate and kissed her goodbye. Father
Mike and Joanna looked on while Hal moved around
them, taking pictures.

''I'll call you every day and be home for dinner
Thursday night,'' John said, holding her. ''You could
pack for us so that we can start for my folks' early Friday morning. You know where I'll be,'' he reminded,
''so call me if you want to.''

''Okay.''

She forced a smile, surprised that a lump had risen in
her throat. What was wrong with her? The man was
going to be gone for three days. Certainly she could deal
with that without becoming emotional. But it was difficult. He'd become so important in her life. And the lovemaking that had caused them to be late to breakfast
made her miss him already.

Then she remembered her promise to Jade.

''I told Jade I'd ask you again about having her ears
pierced,'' she said.

The attendant called for final boarding.

''You think it's all right?'' he asked.

''Well…yes,'' she replied. ''I don't think it would do

her any harm, and it might boost her feminine image of herself.'' She lowered her voice and added for his ears alone, ''But she's not my daughter.'' That sounded like an untruth, somehow. Joe and Jade had become as important to her as their father. ''At least, not really.''

She walked him to the ramp as the attendant called his name.

''Well, she's going to be,'' he said, ''so do what you think is best.''

''John—''

He stopped to give her one quick and final kiss and a warm smile. ''I'll trust you to do what's best for my daughter, if you'll trust me to be a great husband.''

She knew how he loved his children and knew he didn't give his trust lightly where they were concerned. She didn't see how she could withhold her own.

''Deal,'' she said. Then she blew him a kiss as the attendant said his name with a new tone of desperation. ''Go, before you're forced to chase the plane. See you Thursday.''

She felt the world close up when he disappeared from sight and told herself sternly that she was being a ninny. She was a competent woman who'd gotten along just fine on her own since she'd gone away to college, and there was no reason she wouldn't be just as fine until he returned.

And she was. She took her entourage with their sympathetic glances out to lunch, then they returned to the office where everyone down to the mailboy was careful to call her Mrs. Cheney.

Hal took Father Mike and Joanna off to the photo lab, and Barbara settled into John's office with her garbanzo folder, determined to come up with an idea. But she didn't. All she did was stare at her cross outs and scribbles and think about John.

The children didn't seem to notice particularly their father's absence, except that they ran to the phone when it rang and remained near her every moment they were home. She couldn't decide if they were fulfilling their promise to John to take care of her, or hoping to find in her that edge of security that seemed to be missing in his absence.

Too wound up to sleep the second night because she'd dealt successfully with a client for whom copy had been promised but not delivered, she pulled John's robe on over her nightshirt and wandered into the kitchen. His citrusy fragrance clung to it and made her feel less lonely.

The children and Father Mike were asleep, and Hal had accompanied Joanna back to the manse because of a plumbing emergency. The house was strangely silent.

Barbara had missed John's phone call to the office, and felt both enervated and depressed. She thought a cup of tea and half an hour of raccoon watching might help her sleep.

Then she heard humming from the open door beyond the kitchen that led to Libby's two rooms, and went to investigate. She found the housekeeper polishing a shiny red and silver helmet with a screaming eagle on it. It seemed so completely at odds with the flowered wallpaper, the quilted bedspread and the chenille robe she wore.

Barbara stopped in the doorway and smiled. "Getting ready to ride your own bike again?"

Libby's eyes glowed. "Yes. These have served as flowerpots long enough." She indicated the second helmet that had yet to be polished. A perky philodendron stood in it. "I sold the bikes when my husband died because it all seemed too scary to me on my own. But Mr. Cheney's offer of the bike made me realize that you can be afraid, or you can be alive, but it's hard to be both simultaneously." She winked at Barbara. "At least, if you want to have any fun or accomplish anything. So I'm going to our family reunion next month, and I'm going to let my son-in-law introduce me to a retired highway patrolman he's wanted to fix me up with for the past six months. Romance is in the air. You and Mr. Cheney have inspired me."

"We're acting, Libby," Barbara reminded her.

Libby looked up from her task, met her gaze with a quietly direct blue stare, let it slip to the oversize robe she wore, then went back to polishing. "Acting like you're in love?" she asked. "Or acting like you aren't?"

Damned if I know, Barbara thought. It was becoming difficult to keep track of the situation.

She took a course parallel to the question. "I'm going to make tea," she said. "Want some?"

"Just made myself a cup. If I'd known you were up—"

"That's all right. I need something to do. Can I have a ride when your Harley comes?"

"First thing."

The ring of the telephone competed with the shrill whistle of the kettle a few moments later. Barbara felt her heartbeat accelerate as she picked up the portable, certain it was John. "Hello?"

"Barbara." His deep voice melted over her, warm and soothing. "My calls kept missing you today."

"I'm sorry," she said. "I was busy being Wonder Woman."

"So Hal told me. You actually got a team together

and wrote the copy for the spot—and convinced him it was good—in an afternoon?''

''It's the kryptonite.'' She laughed. ''It keeps me running.''

''That was the Man of Steel not Wonder Woman.'' His voice had softened and she heard his smile.

''They were lovers, I'm sure,'' she said, moving to sit at the table with her mug of tea. ''I've thought so since I was ten.''

''You're supposed to have a magic belt or something.''

''Bracelet,'' she corrected. ''How is everything going in Rhode Island?''

John leaned back in the conference room chair and propped his feet up on the long table now empty of everyone but him. ''Lonely,'' he admitted, picturing her in his mind in the middle of his bed. He'd longed for her since he'd looked into her eyes at the airport and knew she already missed him. ''I never got lonely until you. I missed the kids, of course, but that's not the same.''

She was dissolving into a puddle of emotional and physical need. She tried to think of something perky to say, but what came out in a husky, desperate little voice was ''I miss you, too.''

John let the words wash over him like balm. ''Are you in the bedroom?'' he asked.

''No, the kitchen. At the table, drinking tea.''

''What are you wearing?''

Understanding that he was creating a mental image of her, she smiled as she replied, ''Your robe over my nightgown. I cut quite a dashing figure, I assure you.''

''*My* robe?'' he asked softly. ''Shall I speculate why you're wearing it?''

"No," she said, taking her tea and moving into the dark living room, knowing Libby's door remained open. "I'll tell you why." Safe in a big chair in a shadowy corner, she indulged herself, coaxed by his voice and by the aching hunger for him it aroused in her. "Because the scent of your after-shave clings to it, and having it against my skin makes me feel as though you're in it and your arms are around me."

"Barbara." His whisper was husky and low, but she heard it clearly. "In my heart they are. My arms are tightening around you and I'm pressing you close."

He bridged the distance of a continent, and Barbara felt him, corded muscles contracting around her until she truly believed she sat in his lap in the chair.

John heard her hungry sigh, closed his eyes and felt it against his throat. "Only forty-eight hours," he said, his voice weighted with desire and frustration, "and I'll be there."

The conference room door opened, and a dozen men dressed casually for a long night of business streamed around the table. More reluctantly than he'd ever done anything, John lowered his feet to the floor and prepared to tell Barbara that he had to hang up.

"Remember that I love you," she said softly, hearing the buzz of conversation behind him. "And I'm waiting for you. Bye, darling."

"Barbara—"

"I know you can't say anything—"

"The hell I can't," he disputed. "I love you, too. Keep the middle of the bed warm." She heard distant male laughter, then the honeyed sound of his voice again. "Bye, Barbara."

"Bye, John."

Barbara hung up the telephone and heard the bridge

that had connected her to John break apart in the sudden silence. She was alone, and he was three thousand miles away.

Loneliness washed over her again.

Then she also remembered the rich sound of his voice promising to be home, telling her to keep the bed warm, and suddenly she didn't feel quite so solitary.

She sat up in the chair and examined the feeling with wonder, trying to analyze the lightness she felt, the subtle feeling that she'd rid herself of a cumbersome weight.

She realized what it was. Reality. With John more than three thousand miles away, she'd felt his love for her as though she'd been in his arms. And she'd telegraphed her own feelings across the miles. Theirs was no staged affair. They were in love.

The light of truth went on, brightening her shadowy little corner of the living room.

"Mom?"

With the sound of Jade's voice she realized that it was no mystical light, but the simple application of fingertip to light switch. Jade stood in the doorway to the living room in a faded green, Princess Jasmine nightshirt. She rubbed her eyes, a spike of hair standing up on the back of her head.

It had worried Barbara for several days that the children called her Mom so easily. Tonight her concern seemed to recede.

"Was that Daddy?" Jade asked sleepily.

"Yes." Barbara opened her arms to her, and Jade curled into her lap without a second thought, gangly legs hanging down. "He's anxious to come home."

"I know. When I talked to him this afternoon, I told him we're having my ears pierced tomorrow." Jade sighed contentedly, then giggled. "He said not to let them do my nose by mistake."

Barbara laughed, too, knowing she'd live the next two days for the moment he walked in the door.

"You're going to like Grandma and Grandpa," Jade said. "Daddy told them all about everything, and they said they can be pretty good actors, too."

"That's lucky," Barbara said with more enthusiasm than she felt. What would two fine, upright citizens think of the woman found almost naked in their son's office washroom? And if they were able to accept how that had come about, what would they think of her willingness to pretend to be John's wife, stepmother to his children and to share his room and eventually his bed?

It occurred to her that he may have spared them that detail, but certainly the rest of her activities were suspect enough that they would wonder what kind of creature their son had taken up with.

"We're going to have a clambake," Jade said, her voice fading, "and we're going to have to help Aunt Sandy decorate the church hall. Fortieth anniversaries are very special."

Barbara stroked her hair. "Yes, they are."

"I didn't think I was going to like you," Jade admitted sleepily. "I didn't think good mothers were supposed to be pretty." She snuggled closer. The early-August night was warm, but the air-conditioned house was cool.

Barbara rubbed the child's bare arms. "You have a lot of ideas about mothers," she said quietly. "You sort of gave me my training."

Jade closed her eyes and smiled. "Most kids' mothers train *them*. Now the other kids are jealous of us."

"The kids at school?"

"Yeah. Uncle Hal gave us a picture of you to show

them 'cause they didn't believe us. *Nobody* has a nice mom that looks like you.''

Prudence would have required that she remind Jade that the situation was make-believe and temporary, but it truly didn't feel like it at the moment, and it didn't seem fair to bring the child back to reality when she was about to drift into dreams.

The front door burst open, jarring Barbara into sitting up. Jade had fallen asleep.

The sound of high heels, clattering into the hallway was followed by the closing of the front door and another, heavier tread.

''Joanna...'' Hal's exasperated voice drifted out of the hallway toward Barbara, but he and Joanna were still out of sight.

''I was *not* shouting at the plumber.'' Joanna's voice followed Hal's, high and ragged with uncharacteristic temper. Barbara had seen her suspicious, tense and judgmental, but she'd never seen her angry.

''You're shouting now.'' Hal's voice was quiet and controlled.

''I am not! I'm speaking loudly enough so that you can hear me! I told you I didn't need you to come with me to the manse. I told you I didn't need your help! I told you I could deal with the plumber without your interference, and when he walked out, I told you I didn't want you to call him back! That I would call someone else! But what did you do? Everything I told you *not* to do!''

There was a long, pulsing silence. Then Hal's voice said, ''You know, if you don't want to find yourself a lonely old lady, you'd better improve your attitude.''

There was a sputter of indignation.

''The plumber was doing the best he could while

standing in six inches of water. When he asked you to stay out of the kitchen, I'm sure his concern was for your safety and not that he didn't want to avail himself of your divinely inspired advice. The way I understand it, clergy are supposed to help people, not lord it over them. That's God's job.''

"Don't tell me my job." Now there was flame and fury in her voice. "You're a heathen!"

"I'd be willing to let you convert me if you could prove to me that you know something I don't.''

"Thank you, but I tried that once. It doesn't work. Good night, Mr. Roman.''

"I thought God encouraged that seven-times-seven forgiveness thing!" Hal called after her as she ran up the stairs. A door slammed on the second floor.

Hal turned into the living room, stopping wearily, hands in his pockets. Then he saw Barbara and the sleeping child.

"I'm sorry," Barbara said with a sheepish smile, indicating Jade. "I was an unwilling but captive audience.''

Hal came toward them slowly. "It's all right," he said. "I deserve to be publicly scorned and humiliated for falling for Reverend Dragon Lady.''

"Hal," Barbara admonished gently.

He leaned down to scoop the child out of her arms and led the way to the stairs. "Father Mike tells me she fell in love with a two-bit criminal she met while counseling at a county jail. She married him, and he ran off two weeks later with most of the church treasury. She's embarrassed and bitter.''

"Understandably," Barbara said softly as she followed him upstairs.

He placed Jade in the middle of her bed and stood

aside while Barbara pulled up her blankets and tucked her in.

"Bitterness is never understandable," he said. "It's destructive. She needs to start over."

Barbara turned to him, her own newfound insight helping her see what he felt. She smiled and urged him out into the hall. "Haven't you ever heard of the 'catching more flies with honey' theory?"

He heaved a big sigh. "There's so much in this world for a clod to know. Scripture, platitudes..."

"You'd be perfect for her. But go gently. You've let her know you're no pushover, and that's fine. Now show her that you have a gentle, caring side that will never hurt her the way her husband hurt her."

He leaned against the wall, glancing toward the other end of the hall and Joanna's room. He shook his head, then raised a hand to rub the center of his brow. "The woman gives me a migraine. She judges everything and everyone so harshly."

"Wouldn't you, if the person you thought you loved wanted only your access to a large amount of money?"

"I guess so," he admitted after a moment. He straightened and kissed her cheek. "Thanks for listening."

"Anytime."

Barbara watched him walk away, a not very tall, sturdily built man miserable with love. She found herself smiling. Love, she thought, should come with assembly instructions.

She peered into Joe's room and found him fast asleep on his tummy, Walter on his back, Hillary draped over his head on the pillow. Her heart swelled with affection.

She closed the door and went back to her empty bed—

missing John desperately, but not quite as lonely anymore.

JOHN FOUND BARBARA and his children sitting in the middle of the front lawn on a red-and-white checkered tablecloth, apparently having a tea party. But he didn't recognize the blue willow pot and cups.

Father Mike and Joanna were absent, but Hal knelt a small distance away, shooting the event.

They ran to greet him with flattering enthusiasm, literally pulling him out of the car and across the grass to the picnic. Jade and Barbara hugged and kissed him, Barbara's eyes looking into his and telling him how much she'd missed him, how much she longed for the moment they could be alone together.

Joe hugged him, then punched him in the arm. "I'm glad you're here, Dad. These two are getting really girlie on me."

Hal framed the four of them with his camera as, arms around each other, they sank to the tablecloth. Hal looked grim, John thought. Before he could speculate why, Jade scrambled to sit directly in front of John and hold back the short sides of her hair.

"I'm losing the light," Hal lied, getting to his feet. "See you guys at dinner."

"Notice anything different?" Jade asked, turning her head from side to side.

Tiny little star-shaped earrings studded her earlobes. Barbara had told him last night on the phone that Jade had taken the piercing heroically and was dutifully following some turning and cleaning regimen.

He cupped her face in his hand and had a startling revelation of the woman she would become—a miraculous combination of her mother's mouth, his eyes and hair, and an air of competent femininity that reminded him of Barbara.

She had curled her hair again and put on a blue sundress and her Sunday shoes.

"I like your earrings," he said. "You look beautiful."

She threw her arms around him and hugged him fiercely. "Thanks for letting me do it, Daddy."

"You're welcome."

"Do you want some tea?"

"Ah...it's not that chamomile stuff, is it?"

"It's orange cinnamon. We got it from Barbara's when we went to get the teapot."

Jade poured and Barbara explained as she helped him pull his jacket off. "Jade thought a tea party would be a good way to celebrate her new look when you came home, but Libby told us you don't own a teapot. I did."

Joe leaned against him while munching on a peanut-butter cookie. "Do you believe choosing to own a teapot, and not having an ATV? I don't understand it."

"Women are an enigma," John assured him, accepting his tea from Jade.

"What's that?"

"A puzzle. If it's any comfort, there are presents in my briefcase."

"All *right!*" Both children ran for the car, Jade momentarily forgetting her new dignity as she pushed Joe out of the way to reach the door first.

John turned to Barbara with a look half questioning, half amused. "The earrings were going to improve her feminine image of herself, did you say?"

She nodded without apology and picked a cookie from the plate in the middle of the cloth. "Today's woman fights for what she wants. It's part of her feminine makeup."

His wolf's eyes, suddenly focused on hers, sharpened her attention.

"Are you willing to take up arms?" he asked softly as the children started back toward them at a run.

"Duel…after children's bedtime," she said quickly. "Bedroom. Be there."

Certain his heart was going to beat itself to pieces, John gave her a look that accepted the challenge. Then he concentrated on his children to avoid anticipation apoplexy.

Joe exclaimed over the model of a sleek sailboat, patterned after one of the many elegant boats that sailed at Newport. Jade squealed over a pair of small gold earrings in the shape of scallop shells and gave him another hug. Barbara opened her foil box and found a gold filigree bangle bracelet.

She looked up at him, her eyes bright with pleased surprise.

"Wonder Woman," he said, "should have a bracelet." He helped her with the clasp, then brought her fingers to his lips. "Thanks for taking care of things while I was gone."

"Grandma called," Jade said excitedly, squeezing between them to pour more tea. "She said everything's ready for us. And Aunt Sandy said to tell you she bought the tickets to Hawaii, and she doesn't think Grandma and Grandpa suspect anything. They just think we're having a party."

"Great," John said. "I can't believe we're really going to pull this off."

Joe made a scornful sound, then slurped inelegantly from his cup. "Why?" he asked. "When we've tricked everybody into believing Mom's Mom—even her."

Chapter Eleven

John was almost surprised to find Barbara sitting in the middle of the bed wearing nothing but her bracelet.

He'd been afraid that while he took care of last-minute phone calls after the children were in bed, she would recall Joe's remark about tricking everyone into believing Mom's Mom—even her, and her fear would be revived that they were playacting, confusing fantasy with reality. Or that she might have remembered that she hadn't wanted a husband who worked in advertising and traveled, and would forget to keep the appointment.

But she was there like an apparition, the contour of her body a graceful, ivory shape in the darkness.

She lowered one foot to the floor, presumably to come to him, but he stopped her.

"Please don't move," he said, overwhelmed with the sylphlike S curve of her body in the shadows, thinking that artists agonized to put beauty on canvas, or to sculpt it, and couldn't approach what nature created with an offhand genetic configuration—woman at her most perfect.

He sat before her, putting a hand to her face, afraid to believe what he'd read in her eyes this afternoon.

She put her fingers to his cheek and smiled. "I

know,'' she whispered. "It just...came to me after I spoke to you on the phone Tuesday night. I love you because you're not like my father at all. You travel because you have to, not because you're running away. And when I heard your voice, I felt as though you were right here with me.''

"I was," he said. "I will always be. This is where I belong.''

"Yes.'' She pushed up the simple T-shirt he'd changed into after dinner and pulled it off him. He lay back as she unbuttoned and unzipped his shorts and swept them down his legs. She folded them and reached to place them over the chair, but he sat up, reached an arm around her waist and pulled her back to the bed.

She fell onto him with a little peal of laughter. "I thought you were being awfully docile.''

"I've dreamed about you for three days and nights," he said, sitting her astride him, "awake and asleep. I'm not going to wait while you tidy up the bedroom.''

"I dreamed of you all the time, too." She lay against him, delighting in the way his bone and muscle supported her softness and took it into the concavity of his stomach, the hollow between his ribs.

John felt the tight tips of her nipples against his chest, the downy gate of her femininity against his lower abdomen, inviting him inside.

He groaned softly. She moved tauntingly against him and slipped her body downward, offering just what he was afraid of rushing.

She dotted kisses down the center of his chest, making his already-eager body quake with wanting her. She hadn't even reached his navel when he caught her waist and raised her over him.

Her hands braced against his upper arms, Barbara took

him inside her and closed around him like a morning glory enfolding the evening.

They moved together in the eternal rhythm, turning in time with the universe. Pleasure tightened their orbit until they reached a pulsing center of waiting, reaching, wanting—then fulfillment burst upon them like a cosmic explosion.

Hands laced together, they felt the flash between them, lighting their world.

"Are you all right?" he asked, holding her tightly to him. She was shaking. He pulled the blankets up over her.

"I think so," she said. "Isn't it a little scary that we have that kind of power? Did you feel it?"

He laughed softly. "I imagine Mars felt it." He pulled her down beside him and tucked the blanket over her shoulder. She relaxed against him, flinging a knee over his thigh. "This is as real as it gets."

She kissed his chest, then ran her fingertips lightly over him, loving the suedelike texture of his skin. Then she held up her wrist, dangling the bracelet so that he could see it. "Maybe it's magic."

He pulled her up closer so that he could reach her lips. "The bracelet isn't magic," he said. "The woman is."

Barbara kissed him again, then settled back on his shoulder.

"Jade said you explained everything to your parents," she said lazily after a while.

He kissed the top of her head. "Right."

"Did you tell them what's happened to us?"

"That we've fallen in love? Yes."

That wasn't what she'd meant, but it would do for now. She was suddenly very spent, and it seemed better to let tomorrow take care of itself. She hooked an arm around John's chest and went to sleep.

TOM AND EDIE CHENEY stood "on-stage" on the porch of their home like a pair of Broadway veterans, waiting for their cue. As John turned his Safari into their driveway, Barbara could see by their smiles that they were eager to become part of their son's "John married Barbara" production.

Tom Cheney was several inches shorter than his son, with a thick gray mustache that matched the little fringe of hair around his head, and a comfortable paunch.

Barbara pegged Edie Cheney as the obvious source of her son's good looks. She was tall and slender in white jeans, a chambray shirt knotted at her waist. Graying dark hair was caught back in a bun, around which she'd tied a red bandanna.

They hurried down the steps of the old beach house with its broad front porch and sea grass growing up to the steps. The sun was high and warm, and the coastal wind blew gently around them, perfumed with the fragrances of places beyond the horizon.

Edie opened her arms to her grandchildren with a warmth that was generous and genuine. Then she reached for Barbara. But Barbara saw her careful scrutiny in the few seconds before Edie took her into her arms.

"Hi, Mom," Barbara said, hugging her lightly, afraid not to embrace her, for the sake of appearances, but also afraid that too emphatic an embrace would offend her. She looked like a woman who chose her friends carefully.

"Barb," Edie said with a smile, keeping an arm around her as she reached for her son.

John came into her arms. "Hey, Mom," he said, enfolding her and Barbara in a bear hug. Then he said softly into her ear, "What do you think?"

"The priest'll be a piece of cake," she replied under her breath. "But the woman looks like a hard sell."

John pulled away and introduced their guests. As his mother greeted them, he moved to embrace his father, bringing Barbara with him.

"How's my favorite daughter-in-law?" Tom asked, kissing her cheek.

"Fine, Dad," Barbara replied, trying desperately not to sound as shy as she felt. "I've been looking forward to your famous clambake for days."

"I'm ready," he said. Then he added quietly to his son as Edie and Father Mike laughed over something, "Good going, Son. How's it all coming together?"

"So far, so good."

"And you?" Tom asked Barbara. "Are you holding up okay? This guy's always got a scheme."

Hal was embraced by both of John's parents as though he were an important part of their lives.

Barbara found herself wishing she were, too.

The children led the way inside as Edie followed with Joanna, Tom with Father Mike. Barbara tagged along, arm in arm with John and Hal.

"You're doing beautifully," John told her. "Just keep it up."

"I've decided," Barbara said, "what you can give me as a bonus for doing this. *My* heart's desire."

"What's that?"

"I want your father to adopt me."

JOHN HUNG THEIR CLOTHES in the small closet that had been his until he'd graduated from college. Barbara placed underwear, socks and foldables in the drawers of a mirrored maple dresser.

The wallpaper was a soft pattern of yellow roses on a vine, growing randomly around the room. John saw Barbara looking at it when he went back to the bed for another collection of hangers.

"When this was my room, the wallpaper was signal flags. I think they redecorated so I wouldn't be tempted to move back."

His task accomplished, John closed the closet door and fell onto the bed beside the suitcase they'd shared.

"My father can't adopt you," he announced, lying on his back and stretching both arms out.

"Why not?" Barbara slipped the empty suitcase under the bed.

John caught her arm and pulled her down beside him. "Because that would make us brother and sister. I think you should just settle for me."

She affected a stubborn look. "I like your father."

"My mother's tougher than she looks," he warned. "And she's very proprietary about her family."

"Then what makes you think she'll let me have you?"

"Two very good reasons. First, you're everything she's been trying to get me interested in for years, and second, she has nothing to say about it."

She hooked an arm around his neck and rested her head on his shoulder, a curious feeling overtaking her. She felt the warmth and happiness in this house, saw in Tom's and Edie's faces that they adored their son and his family and would do everything in their power to help him. But a nagging sense of foreboding tapped at her awareness.

She wondered if it was because she found it difficult

to *pretend* to be a family in the presence of such a fine example of one.

She tried to share that thought with John, but she wasn't sure he understood.

"That doesn't make sense," he said flatly, "because the 'fine example of a family' that you're talking about *is* the family you're pretending to be a part of. Anyway, I thought we'd concluded that we've all stopped pretending."

Then he reached under her cropped top, unhooked her lacy bra and banished all suggestion that their relationship was anything but real.

JOHN'S SISTER, Sandy, and her husband, Kyle, arrived for dinner with a new baby girl and a lively two-year-old boy. Edie immediately went off to the kitchen with Kristin, the baby, followed by both the twins. Tom brought out a pedal car for Sam, who pedaled in one door and out the other as though it was a well-established route.

Kyle, Barbara learned, owned a small construction company, and Sandy had met him when he'd gone to the bank to open an account. He was quiet and easy-going, a contrast to his vivacious wife. He managed to draw Joanna into conversation.

Hal spent the early part of the evening taking photographs. After dinner he played with Sam, patiently rolling a colorful rubber ball back and forth across the carpet.

By that time John had Kristin on his hip and was expertly refilling drinks while the baby clung to his arm. Barbara heard baby giggles when he disappeared into the kitchen. His competence with children was both touching and intimidating to a woman who'd had so little experience with them.

She passed a dish of foil-wrapped chocolate mints to her right and found herself looking into Joanna's grave profile. She was watching Hal and Sam laughing together and battling for the ball, now behind Tom's chair, amid gales of laughter.

Despite the seriousness of Joanna's expression, Barbara saw vulnerability in it, and she probed her mind for something to say that would reach her. Over the past few days she'd begun to avoid conversation with her because it usually led to criticism or condemnation of something or other.

But Joanna surprised her with a heartfelt sigh and a quiet revelation. "I used to want children."

For an instant Barbara was at a loss. That was the first personal thing Joanna had ever revealed about herself. With everyone's attention on Hal and Sam, she struggled to generate conversation.

"Don't you still?" she asked finally. "I mean, a woman in her early thirties is much too young to give up on the idea."

Joanna turned to face her, and Barbara had another glimpse into her character. She was just another woman, flattered for being taken for several years younger than she was. She even smiled. It made a world of difference in her face, Barbara saw. She looked approachable, pretty.

"I'll be thirty-eight in November." Then a small frown pinched away the smile. "I...I don't have the temperament for marriage. A strict childhood, a sheltered adolescence and most of my young adulthood spent in divinity school left me—" She parted her hands in a gesture of helplessness. "Well, I don't understand how the game is played. I'm too direct and honest, and…a bad experience has made me…distrustful of men.''

''Hal's as worthy of trust as any man I know,'' Barbara said.

Joanna folded her arms and crossed her legs. ''I'm not interested in Hal.''

''I don't believe that for a minute,'' Barbara replied evenly, ''and I'm sure you know he's interested in you.''

''He doesn't even go to church.''

''He'd never hurt a soul, and he's one of the kindest, fairest bosses I've ever worked for.''

Joanna turned to her in confusion. ''I thought *he* worked for *you?*''

Panic clutched at Barbara's throat, and she forced herself to be calm, to think. No harm had been done. It was a small slip that could be easily rectified. But the knowledge that she could blow the entire complicated scheme in a heartbeat unsettled her so completely that she stammered.

''I…he…well, I met John when I came to work for Cheney and Roman, and…ah…Hal was my boss.''

''I see.'' Joanna seemed unaware of her confusion and accepted the explanation without question. She turned her attention back to the man and the little boy. ''I think he tries deliberately to upset me,'' she said.

''Because you treat him as though he isn't worth your notice.''

''Because *he*—'' Joanna began defensively.

''I know. But that leads to a vicious circle. Isn't your job to convert the heathen and bring him to the light? I happen to know he's looking for direction in his life, for stability and…family.''

Joanna turned to her again. ''He is?''

"He is."

"Barbara, can I see you for a minute?"

Barbara looked up to find John standing over her, a look in his eyes she couldn't quite define. She felt trepidation. He'd overheard her conversation with Joanna.

He smiled questioningly at Joanna. "Would you mind holding Kristin for a few minutes? Sandy's in the kitchen with Mom, and Kyle got a call on his pager. But one of them should be back in a minute."

"Well, I don't…I'm not… Okay." Her attempt to refuse the baby was nipped by Kristin's excited gurgle and the extension of both arms to Joanna.

John took Barbara by the wrist and walked her off into the kitchen. Edie and Sandy, stirring some kind of seasoning into a giant bowl of popcorn, looked up in surprise.

"'Scuse us," John said. "We're going into the laundry room."

"The laundry room?" Barbara asked.

John kept pulling her through the kitchen and into a small dark room on the other side. "It's the only place to have privacy without going upstairs."

"Put the towels in the dryer while you're in there!" Edie shouted.

John flipped on the light and closed the door. A harsh fluorescent tube revealed the standard white washer and dryer, and a table that held a stack of folded laundry and several magazines. A collection of children's toys was under the table.

John lifted Barbara onto the dryer, braced his hands on either side of her hips and frowned into her eyes.

"You heard me put Joanna on to Hal, didn't you?" she asked guiltily.

He raised an eyebrow. "No."

She uttered a gasp and raised both hands in dismay. "Then you heard me almost slip, didn't you? Didn't you?"

He frowned. "No. God, what have you been up to?"

"Well, Joanna said how she was distrustful of men and I said that Hal was trustworthy, that he was the kindest, fairest boss. Then she said, 'I thought *he* worked for *you?*' And I thought, Oh, God!" She mimicked the feeling with a strangling hand to her throat. "So I—!"

"Whoa. Whoa!" John pulled her hand down and held it in his, the other resting soothingly on her thigh. "Start over and tell me slowly."

Barbara drew a breath and recounted the first part of her conversation with Joanna.

John listened intently, then shrugged. "It sounds like you covered yourself, and it was a very small slip. I don't think it was enough to worry about."

"But it made me realize how easily it can happen," she said, placing her hands on his shoulders and fidgeting with the collar of his shirt. "I mean, after being so careful, after the kids turning in stellar performances and getting your parents and your sister involved. I almost blew it with a careless—"

He put a hand over her mouth. "Nothing happened," he said. "Everything's fine. We'll just think of it as a reminder to all of us to be more careful."

She sighed, unable to shake the on-the-edge feeling of how close she'd come to ruining everything. "Okay."

"Okay. And what was that about turning Joanna on to Hal?"

"Oh." She was happy to discard the thought of disaster in preference to considering the possibility that something could develop between Hal and Joanna. "Remember I told you last night about the fight Hal and Joanna had?''

He nodded.

''Well, Hal was really depressed because he truly feels something for her, so I suggested he try to be kind and gentle with her, instead of reacting to—you know how she gets.'' Before he could nod or shake his head, she went on. ''Well, tonight she said…'' She told him about Joanna's revelation about children, her admission that she knew she was difficult, and, Barbara's suggestion that she remember her calling and help Hal find stability and direction in his life.

John frowned. ''Is he looking for those things?''

''Isn't everyone?''

He hunched a shoulder. ''I don't know. You seem to think it's important, but a lot of us like to kind of, you know, live a less structured life.''

''Structure is important for children.''

''Hal doesn't have children.''

''Joanna would like to have them.''

John had no idea where to go with that or how to win if he continued to argue with her. Not that winning was on his mind at the moment—about the argument, anyway.

Barbara asked in concern, ''If you didn't hear me slip, and you didn't hear me encourage Joanna to work on Hal, then why did you drag me in here?''

He tucked a hand under each of her hips and pulled her toward him. She wrapped her legs around him and grinned with sudden understanding.

''It's been two or three hours since I've kissed you,'' he said, teasing at her lips with his.

''Barely one,'' she said, looping her arms around his

neck. "You caught me in the pantry when your mother sent me for Sam's teething cookies."

"It seemed like three hours. So kiss me now."

It wasn't difficult to give the kiss everything she had. It rose out of her so eagerly—passion, generosity, real, unadulterated love.

John took with greedy urgency, then gave back in equal measure. He gave her all the fire that warmed him, the power that sustained him, the light that had brightened every little corner of his life since the day he'd found her in it.

Barbara felt a little stab of alarm she hid from John with a crushing embrace. There was such a thing as happiness so complete that it couldn't be, wasn't there? One heard about it in torch ballads and read about it in novels of misbegotten love.

This was like that—born of an accident, too good to be true. And the line between success and failure was razor thin and just as lethal.

John felt the desperation in her and wasn't sure what it meant. Unless it was the fear she'd obviously felt at having come so close to tipping her hand to Joanna with a careless remark.

He held her tightly, then pulled her away to look into her eyes. "Everything's going to be fine," he promised. "Joanna didn't notice anything, and if you've put her on to Hal, she'll have other things to think about. We're going to do this."

She smiled, more than ready to believe him. "Right."

"Now, you're going out there," he said gravely. "Tell them you think you're having a sudden attack of malaria and you need to lie down. As your attentive husband, I'll have to go check on you, and we can—"

She rolled her eyes. "Where would I have gotten malaria?"

"You worked on the tropical tanning oil ad copy, didn't you?"

She took his face in her hands and shook her head over the pitiful suggestion. "Do you think anyone will swallow that with your wolf eyes gleaming so wickedly?"

He stared at her, shamelessly intrigued. "Wolf eyes?"

"You have wolf eyes. No woman has ever told you that?"

"No. Well, maybe we could tell them that *I* was outside bringing in wood and was bitten by a wolf. Yes, that's good. And you, as my attentive wife—"

She shook her head. "You don't bring in wood in the summer, there probably isn't a wolf within hundreds of miles, and we're staying with the party until every last guest has retired and every last dish has been dried and put away."

"And you once accused me of being no fun."

There was a rap on the laundry room door. "Dad?" Joe's voice called, then added in tones of confusion, "Are you doing laundry now?"

John dropped his forehead on Barbara's shoulder. "I'd sell him to M.I.T., but I just know one day he's going to do something brilliant and I want to be around to live on his residuals. Yes!" he shouted toward the door. "I'm putting towels in the dryer for Grandma."

"We're choosing up teams for Balderdash," Joe said urgently. "Grandpa wants you on our team 'cause you lie better than anybody." There was an exaggerated whisper. "And he doesn't even mean the…you know— the thing with Mom."

With a groan John straightened, yanked the door open

and pulled his son inside. "Don't talk about that out loud!" he warned.

"I was whispering," Joe said, lowering his voice to demonstrate.

"Joe, I heard it through the door."

"Well, only Grandma was around. I wanted Mom for our team, but I think it's gonna be one of those girls against the boys things. Are you coming?"

Joe lifted the washer lid as he spoke. Then he frowned at his father. "The towels are still in here. What're you doing, anyway?"

Then he looked from one to the other and grinned. "Oh. So, should I tell Grandpa you'll be a while or what?"

John grabbed him teasingly by the neckline of his Trailblazers T-shirt and pulled him to him, saying with mock ferocity, "You know I could trade you to gypsies for an ATV I could ride myself."

Joe, hanging dramatically from John's hand, grinned up at him. "You wouldn't do that."

"Oh, no?"

"Who'd set your digital watch when we change back to standard time?"

Barbara held back a guffaw with a hand over her mouth. Joe made the best of the moment with an innocent look that reminded her of the one John used on her to good advantage.

John's laughing gaze shifted to her. "I could make you part of the trade and ask them to throw in a TV/VCR combination."

"Who'd program Monday-night football for—? Never mind." Joe stopped and lowered his eyes when John's gaze snapped back to him.

"Give it up, Dad," he recommended. "You need us

both. Jade, however, is another story. With her gold earrings, we could get a good price for her.''

Tom appeared in the doorway. ''Are we going to do laundry,'' he asked, ''or beat the women at Balderdash?''

Barbara leapt off the dryer and began to pull the towels out of the washer. John caught the wet laundry as she tossed it to him.

''Let's go! Let's go!'' Tom prodded them like a coach, until everyone was gathered around the dining table and the game—except Hal and Joanna, who sat side by side on the sofa, holding sleeping children and discussing the turbulent situation in Moscow.

Barbara smiled across the table at John, happier than she recalled being in a long, long time.

Chapter Twelve

When Barbara awoke shortly after 9:00 a.m., it sounded as though all the activity was already outdoors. She found Sandy alone in the kitchen, putting beer in a cooler filled with ice. Raucous male laughter came through the screen door from the beach at the front of the house.

"Good morning," Sandy said, looking fresh in a mint green T-shirt and matching shorts.

"What's going on?" Barbara asked.

"They're getting the pit ready for the clambake." Sandy went to the coffeepot and poured a cup, handing it to her. "The digging is becoming some kind of male rite or something. They're all trying to outdo each other. Trust me. Tomorrow morning they'll all be in traction."

Barbara laughed and sipped her coffee.

"Don't tell me Mom's competing?"

"No, she's on the porch shucking corn. But Jade was outshining Joe when they sent me in for beer. Joanna's on the porch, wrapping potatoes in foil."

"Can I help you carry that?"

"Please."

Barbara took one handle of the cooler and followed Sandy onto the porch. Edie called a cheerful hello, and

Joanna was…laughing!…at the antics going on near the pit. Hal now stood waist-deep in the hole, shoveling up damp sand.

The men, including Father Mike, were shirtless, that very action seeming to make them half a step lower on the evolutionary scale than they'd been around the dinner table the night before. Their hair was wet and sandy, their backs sweaty, their voices loud. Piled on the sand beside the pit was a mound of stones and a pile of seaweed.

Joe stood in the shallows, hunched over something in a tidepool.

"That'll do, Roman," John called to Hal from the rim of the pit. "Jade can finish that rocky corner you're having trouble with."

"Yeah!" the child called, scrawny in a neon-flowered bathing suit bottom and a T-shirt.

Hal leaned on his shovel and squinted up at John. The sun was already high in a sky so blue it almost hurt to look at it. "Come down here and say that."

John leapt gracefully into the hole, prepared to take the shovel from Hal. But that wasn't what he wanted. Hal tossed away the shovel and assumed a combative stance. "Come on. Two falls out of three."

John looked up at the men peering with interest into the pit. They hooted and hollered. John looked back at Hal.

"Hal. Buddy," he said with exaggerated amiability. "I must have a foot on you."

"You do," Hal said, puffing out his chest and strutting across the hole. His friends howled. "And right now it's in your mouth. Can you take me down or not?"

John folded his arms and studied him. "Hal, I'll hurt you, you know I will. Remember the time you called

Nolan Ryan an old man? It took you three days to fight your way out of the Dumpster.''

''I've been going to the gym.''

''To pick up girls. You have to work out when you go there or it doesn't help. You're sure you want to do this?''

Hal opened his mouth to reply, but Sandy shouted, ''Beer's here!''

The men around the pit immediately lost interest in the squabble and went to the cooler. Hal grinned at John. ''We'll do it tomorrow. Two out of three. First thing.''

''Right.'' John scrambled out of the hole and reached for Hal. ''But after we come back from Mass, so I can pray for you before I kill you.''

Barbara was in a state of mild shock. She'd never seen John like this, nor had she ever imagined that the man in a three-piece suit with negotiating skills the UN might have admired could look so downright earthy.

Grungy sex appeal usually did nothing for her. She appreciated elegance and style. But this was something else. An appeal that was simply basic and unrefined, and captivating to a woman who'd grown up safe and ''serious,'' because of the danger it posed.

With an arm on Hal's shoulder, John headed for the cooler, then noticed her standing aside. He yanked a beer out of the ice, touched his sister's bare arm with the cold can and darted away when she raised her hand threateningly. Smiling broadly, he hooked an arm around Barbara's neck and walked her toward the water.

She tucked her thumb into the waistband of his shorts and leaned into him, so happy she felt she might burst. His shoulder was sandy against her cheek, and he smelled of salt and ocean and man.

He reached around her with the can to pop the top,

then took a long swallow. "Good morning," he said, planting a kiss in her hair. "Want a sip?"

"Thanks. I've got a cup of coffee in the kitchen. I haven't had breakfast yet."

"Mom always has a stash of scones in the freezer. A minute in the microwave and they're great."

"Thanks. Everything okay this morning? No breaches in our security that you've noticed?"

He took another long swallow and shook his head. "No. You?"

"No. In fact, I don't want to alarm you, but Joanna was on the porch laughing when Sandy and I carried out the beer."

"That's the beach for you. Mellows out everyone who walks across the sand and is forced to slow down."

She smiled up at him, hearing a note in his voice she hadn't heard before. "*You're* not thinking of slowing down?"

"Maybe," he said, turning his strong profile to the horizon where sky and ocean met in glittering brilliance. He turned back to her, his eyes as burnished as precious coins. "We're getting married next week. Did I mention that?"

She stopped in the damp sand, her mouth agape. "No. You didn't."

He nodded, staring at the top of the can he held. "I've been thinking about it." He looked out at the horizon again. "We won't be lying to anyone anymore—most of all ourselves. The kids will be thrilled and I—" His eyes came back to hers, full of love and promise. "I'll have *my* heart's desire and do my best to fulfill yours. We'll do it when we get back to Portland to make us quickly legal, then we'll come back here to do it with ceremony when there's time. So what do you say?"

The casual stance he affected, waiting for her reply, was difficult to maintain. He wanted to shake her and plead with her—tactics he wouldn't discount if she made it necessary.

But she didn't. She put both hands to his chest, then around his waist. "I say, 'I do!'" she replied, laughing.

Nothing in his life had ever felt this good, this right, this perfect. He lifted her up against him and laughed with her, turning her in a circle as cool water lapped at his ankles and the receding tide pulled at him. Her bracelet bumped against his chin as she framed his face in her hands and lowered hers to kiss him.

He felt a new, indefinable something in her, that somehow made sense for all its lack of definition. Maybe that was trust, he thought, the acceptance of feelings that made rightness out of what reason might consider nonsense.

He kissed the swell of her breast against the neck of her tank top. "I love you, Barbara," he said.

She wrapped her arms around his neck and held, filled with feelings so strong she simply hadn't the words for them. Except the ones he'd used. "I love you, too. But that seems to say so little."

"Not to me it doesn't. To me it's everything."

John went back to help the men line the hole with stones and build a roaring fire in it. Sandy explained that it would be allowed to burn for several hours, then they would place seaweed in the bottom, cover that with chicken wire and add another layer of seaweed.

"Those aren't razor clams," Barbara said when a large potful of very small clams that had been soaked in brine was placed on the seaweed. Razor clams were long and slender and slightly curved, like the old-fashioned straight-edge from which they'd taken their name.

"They're littlenecks from New England," Sandy explained. "Dad has them flown in by the local fish market. They're much more tender."

Tom added potatoes and corn and a dozen chicken halves, then another layer of clams. A final layer of seaweed was placed over the top, and the pit was covered with a tarpaulin weighted down by stones.

"Isn't it exciting?" Jade asked, hunkering down between Barbara and Sandy near the pit. "I wonder if the Indians cooked this way?"

Sandy shrugged. "I'm not sure. But the colonists did."

Barbara put an arm around Jade. "I know what you mean. It's nice to know we can do things without fancy appliances and electricity, isn't it?"

Jade nodded, then grinned. "But I'd hate to have to give up your curling iron."

Barbara laughed, and the three went back into the house to help Edie with lunch, since the clambake wouldn't be ready until dinner.

THE SKY WAS INDIGO, the day at the very edge of dusk and slipping into night. Stars were visible, and a cool wind had risen, causing them all to run into the house for sweaters.

The leftover food had been taken in, and a pot of coffee brought out and settled on a grate, placed over a new fire in the pit.

John held Barbara and Jade in his right arm, with Joe leaning against his left side. He studied his mother and father, sitting back-to-back, humming to the strum of Kyle's guitar; Sandy, a hand on each baby asleep on either side of her, her loving eyes watching Kyle as he hummed; Father Mike, a little apart, staring at the stars and probably communing with God; and Joanna, with her mind undoubtedly on things very unsecular as she and Hal leaned tête-à-tête, whispering in the light of the fire.

He thought about gratitude. He was a lucky man. He'd thought he had everything when his world had been simply him and the children. Then he'd found Barbara and learned that there was more—and that it, too, could be his. He felt more complete at that moment than he'd ever felt in his life.

Barbara decided that everything was going to be just fine. Every reservation she'd held had been erased in the course of the clambake, the volleyball game, the long swim with John and the hour they'd stolen in the middle of the afternoon when the children had been asleep.

For the first and only time in her life, she'd benefited from the wild, impulsive streak she'd inherited from her father.

"Daddy?" Jade asked lazily.

John touched her hair with the hand that held Barbara to him. "What, baby?"

"Did you think this would ever happen?"

"The clambake?"

"No, this." She pointed an index finger along the four of them. "Us. That we'd find a mom in your bathroom at work?"

For a moment the danger of the question asked in open company didn't even register with him. He was busy thinking that he hadn't thought this could happen, that in his wildest dreams he hadn't imagined himself this happy.

Then Joe reached across him to smack his sister's arm and Barbara stiffened against him. His mother, father and sister straightened slightly in alarm. Kyle dropped a note, then picked up smoothly. "I forgot," Jade whispered, her eyes wide with guilt and worry.

But Father Mike was still staring at the stars, and Joanna seemed to have completely forgotten anyone existed but Hal.

"It's all right," John said, and ruffled her hair again. But the incident reminded him how impatient he was growing with the whole deceit.

What had begun as a challenge, and as a way to get to know Barbara, was now chafing his reality. His life had become what he'd been pretending it was, and the possibility of being found out, however remote it was, threatened everything.

He couldn't wait to get Barbara back to Portland and marry her. If anything parted them now, he didn't know what he would do. She'd become far more important to him than a national advertising schedule. She'd become...his. Like Jade and Joe, she was part of the fabric of his being, and he would destroy anything that threatened to touch a single thread.

Barbara tilted her head back to look into his eyes. "What are you thinking?" she asked.

He told her, thinking she should know how rooted his feelings were.

She kissed his chin, her eyes fierce in the firelight, telling him her feelings ran as deep. That relaxed him, somehow.

"RED AND SILVER?" John looked up at the crepe paper streamers that Sandy and Barbara held from wall to wall. They stood on ladders on opposite sides of the church basement, awaiting his approval. He winced, wondering how to put it delicately. "It's a little...gaudy."

Retribution struck immediately in the form of a wrapped roll of streamers to his head.

Kyle, standing beside him, gave him a pitying look. "I thought you understood. When you have an opinion that differs from Sandy's, you keep it to yourself."

"Stupid me."

"We have to decorate with red," Sandy decreed from her perch, "because the fortieth wedding anniversary is ruby."

John amended his position. "It's stunning. I love it. But why didn't we just reserve a restaurant?"

Kyle yanked on him just in time to prevent his being struck by the second missile.

"Because Mom's worked with St. Bonaventure's Auxiliary for thirty-three years, and they wanted to do this for her. A few of the ladies even volunteered to take our children home after dinner and sit with them until we get home from the party. I explained all this months ago. But, does anyone ever listen to me?"

"No," Kyle said.

"No!" Sandy answered her own question, missing her husband's quietly spoken reply. "So I'm forced to explain things over and over." Tacking her end of the streamers in place, Sandy reached for a red honeycomb bell she'd placed on the ladder's pail rest and missed, knocking it to the floor. She looked down at her husband and her brother and pointed. "Would you get that for me?"

The men looked at each other and shook their heads.

She raised an eyebrow, apparently refusing to acknowledge mutiny. She pointed again. "The bell."

They looked at each other again and gave her the same wordless reply.

"Guys," Barbara said, still holding her end of the

streamers against the wall, afraid to lose the drape they'd
worked so hard to achieve. ''My arm's about to fall off.
Get the bell.''

''Sorry,'' John said, folding his arms. ''It's the principle of the thing.''

''There are no principles involved with crepe paper.''

''There are principles involved in men and women
working together,'' he said patiently. ''Like mutual respect and cooperation. So far we've experienced very
little of that from the two of you. It's been 'set up the
tables, carry in the chairs, get the centerpieces out of
Kyle's truck.' And now it's 'get the bell.' And all that
without a please, a thank-you or a cup of coffee.'' He
heaved a loud, high-pitched, dramatic sigh. ''We're not
taking it anymore. Are we?''

He turned to Kyle for confirmation.

''Ah...''

John's gaze sharpened. ''Are we?''

''No,'' Kyle agreed, clearing his throat. ''Of course
not.''

Sandy gave Barbara a dry look. ''I know what this is
all about,'' she said. ''It's because we wouldn't open the
box of donuts until everything was done.'' To the men
she added, ''I told you we'd have coffee when we're
finished.''

''And we're telling you,'' Kyle said, moving to the
foot of the ladder, ''if you want the bell, come down
and get it.''

Barbara saw the electricity arc between them. They'd
been like a pair of giddy teenagers all morning. She
imagined it was a rare treat for them to be together,
without babies, for three or four hours. Father Mike and
Joanna had volunteered to baby-sit while Tom and Edie

relaxed and prepared for their big evening. Hal was supposed to be along later to photograph the decorating.

"Kyle, hand me the bell," Sandy challenged.

Kyle rested his hands on his hips. "Come and get it."

Sandy made it to the fifth step from the bottom when Kyle caught her thigh and her waist and swung her off the ladder. She squealed and landed safely in his arms. She smiled complacently. "Wouldn't it have been easier to hand me the bell?"

He tilted her backward, holding her waist to him with a muscular arm as her head swung toward the floor. She screamed his name, laughed and threatened, to no avail.

"Say, 'We're breaking for coffee,'" he ordered, "'and the men get the first pick of the donuts.'"

"We're not finished!"

He dropped her another inch and she screamed again and capitulated. "We're breaking for coffee!"

"And the rest of it."

"The apple fritter is mine!" she insisted defiantly.

"Ah, 'scuse me," John said, getting down on his haunches beside her. "But I want the fritter."

"Over my dead body!"

John looked up at Kyle. "Go ahead and drop her."

"Oh, this is good," Hal said, winding his way toward them among the tables and chairs. He made an adjustment to his camera lens and focused. "This will make my fortune. This is the cover of *Sex and Sensitivity* if ever I saw it." He snapped the shutter and moved around.

"Hal Roman," Sandy threatened, torn between laughter and indignation, "if you dare take a—"

"Sandy, please. Don't distract me." He got down on his knees, turned sideways, leaned precariously on an elbow and focused on her red face. "Smile."

"It's a matter of principle," Kyle said, ignoring her as she pounded on his shin with a doubled fist. The shutter clicked.

"It's a matter of an apple fritter," John corrected.

"Not anymore."

Barbara, who'd been virtually ignored since the fracas began, came out of the hospitality room's kitchen with a cup of coffee in one hand and the apple fritter with a large bite missing from it in the other. "Let her up," she said.

Kyle swung Sandy to her feet, then held her with both his arms around her waist as she adjusted to being upright again. "I'm sorry I had to do that," he said, "but you were getting a little bossy."

John straightened, grim purpose in his eyes as he started toward Barbara. "That was my fritter," he said.

She shrugged a shoulder. "Now, it's mine."

He quickened his step. "That's where you're mistaken."

She turned with a scream and headed back toward the kitchen. Hal followed them, camera in hand.

"It was so good of you to give up your morning to make this place so beautiful," Edie said, her eyes dreamy with sentiment as she surveyed the room. A sea of snowy white table covers were decorated with silver candlesticks and red candles surrounded by dried rose petals. Across the room the streamers hung, beautifully draped, complete with bells. John, Barbara, Sandy and Kyle looked at one another and shared the joke. "What are children for?" John asked.

Hal took Tom and Edie aside to photograph them against a draped window. Edie wore a scarlet dress

bright with sequins, and Tom wore a tux with a red
cummerbund and red rose boutonniere.

"I want a dress just like that when we're married forty
years," Barbara said.

John put an arm around her and watched his happy
parents pose. His heart felt too big for his chest.

"By then, a few of the Paris designers will probably
be clients of Cheney & Roman. Who would you like to
dress you?"

"Actually, I think I'll stay with Kate Cunningham.
This is one of hers." Barbara did a small pirouette in a
simple but clingy dress in a shade of royal purple that
pinked her skin and brought out the darkness of her eyes.
The soft knit clung to every curve and flared out saucily
a few inches above her knees.

Desire bored into John's middle like a fatal wound.

Then Barbara caught his arm and pointed to the door.
"Guests. Come on, we're on."

"IT'S GOING PERFECTLY," Sandy said to Barbara. They
stood together on the sidelines after dinner had been
cleared, the tables folded away to make a space for dancing. Then she asked, as though needing reassurance,
"Don't you think so?"

Barbara put an arm around her and squeezed. "I do.
You've done a wonderful job of coordinating everything. And dinner was delicious. Those auxiliary ladies
are worthy of the Cordon Bleu."

Sandy heaved a satisfied sigh. "I've been so worried
about it. I wanted it to be special, because Mom and
Dad are so special. Father Mike's blessing was beautiful."

"He's grown very fond of them in just a few days,"

Barbara said. "So have I. They've even loosened up Joanna."

Sandy grinned. "I think Hal's had a little something to do with that, too."

Barbara didn't doubt that for a moment. When the Cheneys had all left for Mass that morning, Hal had driven off with Joanna to her church services.

Sandy tugged Barbara out a side door into the parking lot. She leaned against a pillar that supported a covered walkway and said gravely, "The twins love you."

Barbara nodded. "I love them."

"They've never even seen their mother."

"John told me."

Sandy shifted her weight and hooked an arm around the pillar. "I think all three of them, the twins *and* John thought they were fine just as they were. Then this whole crazy thing happened, Johnny dragged you in, and suddenly they all realized that a successful, well-rounded family needs a wife and mother in it."

"That was lucky for me."

"You've helped Jade become a little girl, not just Joe's twin. Joe thinks you're the most wonderful mother a kid ever had, and John has a light in his eyes that went out when Gracie kept her promise and never did come to see her babies. We voted informally last night, after you and Johnny went to bed, and you're in."

Over the last few days Barbara had watched the efficient Edie and the funny but competent Sandy at work and had only one concern. "But I tend to act on impulse. Recklessness isn't a good trait in a mother, is it?"

Sandy laughed aloud. "It should be a requirement! It takes a love of danger to find the balance between keeping them safe and letting them explore." Then she smiled gently and led Barbara toward the door and the

sounds of music and laughter. "Jade told me how the
two of you fell in the water at the zoo. She thought it
was the greatest thing that ever happened to her. According to her, nobody else's mom, except some lady
named Goodyear—"

"Goodrich," Barbara corrected.

"—Goodrich, ever has fun with her kids, and doesn't
yell at them when they get dirty or wet. Just relax and
be Barbara. That's the best thing you can do for anybody."

"What are you two doing out here?" John asked as
he stepped outside, followed by Kyle.

"Girl talk," Sandy said.

"Uh-oh." Kyle frowned at John in the wedge of light
from the open door. "That means they're tearing us
apart."

"Maybe they were saying something good."

"Get serious."

"Okay." John folded his arms and blocked the doorway. "What, precisely, were you talking about?"

Sandy went to Kyle and looped her arms around his
neck. "I was telling Barb," she said, "how lucky I was
to find you in this world full of yuppies and no-brainers.
How you meet my every need, emotional and physical,
and that when you're not standing me on my head,
you're the best husband any woman ever had. Want to
dance?"

Kyle swallowed and ran a splayed hand up and down
her spine, his eyes devouring her. "That's not what
comes to mind, no."

"It'll be a nice setup for later," Sandy said, nipping
at his lip.

He expelled a breath. "Then let's do it."

John stepped aside to let them into the room, then

braced a hand across the doorway when Barbara tried to follow.

"And what were *you* talking about?" he asked.

She smiled up at him and wondered if this was what it was like to crawl into an earthen den and see the wolf in the shadows. All that was clearly visible were eyes, bright and golden and watchful.

She put her hands to his face and pulled it down to her, opening her mouth to welcome him. His tongue dipped gently inside her with that confident possession that was always in his touch, his eyes, his kiss.

She drew away to nip along his jawline. "I told Sandy how much I love you and the children and that I'm determined to be the best thing that's ever happened to all of you."

She kissed him again and felt his passion ignite.

"Just one thing," she said.

He raised his head warily. "What?"

She grinned. "Next time you go for donuts, buy two apple fritters, or we'll fight to the finish over it every time."

He laughed wickedly, remembering how he'd chased her into the rose garden behind the hall that morning and kissed her into relinquishing half of the fritter. "That could be a good thing," he said.

THEY DROVE HOME with Tom and Edie in the back seat, still staring at their tickets to Hawaii.

Kyle and Sandy followed with Father Mike, Joanna and Hal.

Barbara leaned against John's shoulder, too happy to speak. She couldn't wait to get home, to get into their room, into their bed and into his arms.

John suddenly leaned slightly forward to peer through

the darkness with a frown. "Who's that on the porch?" he asked.

"Where?" Tom and Edie leaned out the same window as John turned into the driveway, pulling all the way in to leave room for Kyle to park behind him.

Barbara straightened, only half-interested, sure it was probably someone who hadn't made it to the party leaving a gift.

Then the headlights of the car almost up against the porch picked out a male figure sitting halfway down the steps, a hand shielding his eyes from the blinding lights.

Barbara gasped, her heart leaping into her throat. Trevor!

Chapter Thirteen

"So, it's true!" Trevor walked down the porch steps like a king descending the steps beneath his throne.

Barbara stood in the middle of the walkway, thinking that she'd almost forgotten what he looked like and that she hadn't thought about him in days.

Then she began to wonder frantically what she could say or do to prevent imminent disaster. Tom and Edie were out of the car behind her, and behind them she heard everyone else come forward.

She wasn't sure if the impression was truly physical or simply psychological, but she felt them pressing closer to see and hear.

Then John walked around the front of the car and up the steps.

"Come inside, Wentworth," he said, taking Trevor's arm and turning him toward the house. "I'd like to talk to you."

Barbara thought for a moment that the ploy would work, that John would get him into the house before everyone followed, explain the situation, earn his sympathy and send him out the back door, never to be heard from again.

She should have realized that was a naive notion.

Trevor aimed a fist at John's face. John blocked it neatly and turned him, twisting Trevor's arm behind his back. Barbara saw Trevor's awkward movements, then looked into the bloodshot eyes directed at her and realized he was intoxicated.

Kyle leapt up the steps to help John with the intruder. "Who is this clown?"

The front door opened and two gray-haired women, one small and frail and the other tall and sturdy, frowned at Trevor. "He says his name is Wentworth, and that he's engaged to marry someone named Ryan, who's supposed to be at this address. We tried to tell him that there was no one here by that name, that everyone staying in this house is named Cheney, but he wouldn't listen. He insisted, so we told him he had to wait out on the porch."

"She," Trevor said, pointing his free hand at Barbara, "is Barbara Ryan. My fiancée!"

John tried to haul him up the stairs, but Father Mike stepped out of the group and moved toward him. "Wait, John. He's probably just confused. She's not Barbara Ryan, young man. Her name is Barbara Cheney. She's married to this man." He pointed to John. "John Cheney."

Trevor, unfortunately not drunk enough to have difficulty connecting information, studied Father Mike. "You're on the Cooperative Churches deal, aren't you?" he asked.

Father Mike frowned, looking puzzled. "Yes. But how do you know?"

"Because I went to Cheney & Roman on Friday, trying to find Barbara, and got the runaround from the staff.

"They said she was on vacation for a couple of weeks, but no one knew where. But a man named Barnett happened by and told me there was a whole scam going down about *Mrs.* Cheney, and if I wanted to know more about it, I should meet him there Sunday, so we could talk with no one around. He said he owed Barbara. So, I met him there at noon and he told me everything.''

''Young man—'' Father Mike tried to reason.

''Father,'' Trevor said, ''unless these two were married in the last week—and I know you've been with them day and night during that time—they're not married. If you've watched them walk into the same bedroom together, they're what your people would call 'living in sin.'''

Barbara felt an arm come around her, and she looked into Edie's smile. ''Let's all go inside and talk about this,'' she said, hooking her arm into Father Mike's as they passed him. ''Come on, Father. We'll clear up everything inside.''

''We?'' he asked.

She nodded. ''I'm afraid we're all conspirators in this. Come along. Come on, Joanna.''

Dispersing everyone to chairs, and dispatching Sandy to put on a pot of coffee, Edie hugged the two ladies from her auxiliary who'd watched the children and denied entry to Trevor Wentworth. They seemed reluctant to leave, looking back into the living room with great interest and asking questions as Edie pushed them firmly out the door.

Barbara sat in a big, old, overstuffed chair, dealing with guilt, embarrassment, anger at Trevor and her own stupidity for once having been interested in a man who could delight in revenge, and the desperate wish that things could have turned out any way but this way.

It's divine intervention, she thought. They'd tricked the representatives from a group of churches. How else could it have ended? She considered her earlier thought that everything was ending so well and couldn't help the glint of dark humor that crossed her general despair. Her mother had been right after all.

Though John had started this, she'd gone along with it and fallen in love, so that her performance was that much more convincing. If anyone was to blame for the completeness of the fiasco, it was she.

John saw the look on Barbara's face and resisted the temptation to shove Trevor Wentworth through the bay window. Instead he took pleasure in pushing him into a corner of the sofa where one of his mother's friends had forgotten a knitting project, needle protruding handily from the work.

Trevor yelped satisfactorily. John yanked him up, again, removed the knitting to the coffee table and pushed him down again. His father, taking the chair that matched the sofa, sent him a silent look filled with approval and amusement.

John sat on the arm of Barbara's chair, trying to reassure her with his eyes. But her gaze met his briefly, told him she loved him, then slid away filled with guilt and remorse.

Briefly, without much adornment, he told everyone gathered in the living room what had happened. He began with his appearance at the prayer breakfast that fateful morning and ended with assuming responsibility for bullying Barbara into cooperating.

"I told her she'd be fired if she didn't help me," he said. "I told her it was her fault and that she owed me. That's the only reason she did it."

"No, it's not," she corrected him. Her eyes met his, but with a cool resolve he wasn't used to seeing there. It unsettled him. "I did it because the night before, I'd worn a special dress to Trevor's awards dinner. He barely noticed it, and when he was given a trip to the Cayman Islands and chose to take his father, never once considering to take me, I realized we weren't after the same things. So I decided to take part in John's campaign for the cooperative.''

''You're saying what you were after with Mr. Wentworth was a trip to the Cayman Islands?'' Joanna asked, a vague edge to her voice. Barbara saw Hal, seated beside her, turn to look at her.

''No,'' Barbara replied. ''I was looking for a husband. When I realized he'd take his father to such a romantic spot to go fishing, I saw that he wasn't thinking of me in terms of a permanent relationship.''

''But I was!'' Trevor insisted, the picture of affronted dignity. ''I came home early from the Caymans to ask you to marry me.''

''Fishing must have been bad,'' John said.

Barbara ignored both of them.

''Something about John touched the reckless streak my mother always warned me about,'' Barbara went on. ''I wanted to be part of the scheme and see if we could carry it off. Not because I wanted to deceive anyone, but because Cheney & Roman is a good employer, and I wanted them to get ahead. The entire staff does.''

''So, you're telling us you had noble reasons,'' Joanna challenged.

Barbara shook her head. ''No, I'm telling you I had selfish reasons, and they were my own. John had nothing to do with my decision.''

''He says he threatened you with dismissal,'' Father Mike reminded her.

''He didn't mean it. He demoted the man who gave Trevor this information, because he tried to take credit for work I'd done. He wouldn't have fired me. He's fair.''

"He demoted Barnett," Trevor said, "because Barbara *told* him Barnett had stolen her idea."

Barbara turned to Trevor, anger rising in her like a cleansing force. "And you believed that? That I would take credit for someone else's work?"

"Of course! The slogan he wrote was for a charter boat service. What do women know about that? What do *you* know about that?"

"I researched it," she said coolly. "And I wrote it while he was at a Mariners' game the night before deadline."

"The point," Joanna said, "is that you were hired to portray—or rather to *be*—the quintessential American family with a grip on its spirituality and a foothold in the secular world. And you lied." The last was delivered like a verdict.

"Not for very long," John said. "I fell in love almost immediately. She followed soon after. We are the quintessential American family you describe—it just isn't completely official yet."

"Meanwhile, you've—" Joanna waved a hand in the direction of the stairs, indicating, Barbara was sure, the bedrooms.

"Yes," John replied without hesitation at the same moment that Hal groaned, "Joanna!"

Joanna turned to Hal, her cheeks pink, her eyes snapping with anger and something deeper that caused Hal to frown.

"Don't give me that righteous groan," she said, getting to her feet and pulling herself up until her shoulders were square and her indignation apparent. "I'm beginning to understand everything. You were part of it, too, weren't you?''

''What do you—?''

''Father Mike swallowed all of it right away, but I thought I detected something,'' Joanna said. ''A shyness in the way Barbara looked at John when he wasn't watching, a subtle something in the way he looked at her—as though he wasn't entirely sure of her. Those didn't seem like the qualities of a loving husband and wife, intimately familiar with one another.'' She gave the pair an accusing once-over, then glowered at Hal, who stood beside her. ''So, you were to provide the distraction, weren't you? Keep the suspicious one busy so that she doesn't notice she's being hustled.''

Hal stared at her, grimness overtaking his puzzlement.

''I dragged Hal into this,'' John said to Joanna, ''just like I dragged Barbara. And there was no plan to 'distract' you.''

Joanna looked from one partner to the other, then settled on John. ''I find that difficult to believe, particularly from you. If you'll excuse me, I'll say good-night. And I think it only fair to warn you that I'll be calling Daniel in the morning and telling him what we've learned.''

Father Mike stood and called after her.

Joanna turned at the stairs. ''Good night, Father. My mind is made up. Yours should be, too.''

Everyone stared at everyone else. It was over. The elaborate charade had been shattered by Trevor's sudden and unexpectedly ardent turn of mind. Or bad fishing. Barbara wasn't sure.

At the sound of a slam upstairs, Tom rose from his chair, pulled Trevor to his feet and walked him to the front door. ''I believe you've done what you came here to accomplish,'' he said. ''You're no longer welcome here.''

''But I—she—'' The door closed on his stammered justification.

Sandy and Kyle went upstairs to claim their sleeping children. Hal, after a thorough study of the toe of his shoe, sent a dark gaze up the stairs, then followed it.

Sandy, holding Kristin, wrapped an arm around Barbara as they gathered at the door. ''Remember what I told you,'' she said quietly. ''This doesn't change that. Wentworth's always been very self-absorbed. He's no great loss, Barbara.''

Sandy hugged John and kissed his cheek. ''It's all right. You did the best you could in a difficult situation and it didn't work out. So what? Tomorrow IBM will be knocking at your door. And the important things you gained through this are still yours.''

''Right.'' John kissed her forehead, then the baby's, and walked them out to their car.

Kyle grinned at him in the light from the porch. ''If you get desperate, I can always use someone on my second crew.''

John punched his shoulder. ''Get out of here. We're leaving in the morning, so we'll be in touch.'' He closed the car door and waved as Kyle backed out of the drive.

In the living room, John found Father Mike on the sofa with Barbara. He heard puttering in the kitchen and guessed that his parents had made themselves scarce.

''When can I marry you two?'' the priest asked as John settled beside Barbara.

Surprised by the question, John turned to Barbara. He didn't like the concern he saw in her eyes. He looked back at the priest. ''We were planning on the middle of the week, soon as we have the health certificate and the license together.''

''Good.'' Father Mike smiled from John to Barbara. ''I know the world doesn't consider this much anymore, but nothing gives marriage the solid foundation as vowing before God that you'll love each other forever, and asking for His help to keep the promise. I know you think you already have it all.'' His smile broadened. ''But wait. Just wait and see what His blessing will do for you. Well.'' He stood. ''It seems the party's over, doesn't it? So I'll say good-night.''

''Father.'' John stopped him with a hand on his arm. ''Thank you for understanding. The afternoon that the cooperative walked into my office and found Barbara there, I didn't really know her yet, so I thought the most important thing in my life at that moment, was securing your account.''

The priest shrugged. ''Once, in the seminary, I solicited help from a fellow student for a theology test—during the test.'' He smiled self-deprecatingly. ''I'd studied hard, and I have the heart of a priest, but the brain of a mule. Anyway, I was discovered and invited to the theology master's office. He told me I'd be doing an extra tour of duty in the kitchens and that I would have to retake the test. Not because I'd sought help, he said, but because I'd sought help in the wrong place.'' He smiled again, cheerfully, this time. ''See you in the morning.''

John ran a hand down his face, feeling as though he'd just been chastened by God, Himself.

Barbara stood beside him, and he took her in his arms.

''You okay?'' he asked gently.

''I don't know,'' she said. ''I almost can't believe it's all over. I'm sorry.''

He shook her gently. "Don't be. The important part isn't. We're getting married this week."

Barbara kept her reservations about that to herself. The evening had been too traumatic all around as it was.

John led the way into the kitchen in search of his parents. He found them sipping coffee in a corner, talking quietly.

"I'm sorry your anniversary celebration was spoiled," he said, wrapping his arms around Edie. Tom pulled Barbara into his.

"Don't be silly," Edie said. "It was a wonderful evening. We have tickets to Hawaii and enough money to live like royalty for a month." Then she pulled away to ask him seriously, "Could you use a loan?"

John laughed. "No, the business is in good shape—even if this doesn't work out. We were looking for the benefit to our image almost more than to our bank account.

"Can you guys gather up Kyle and Sandy and the kids and come up for a wedding in the middle of the week?"

Edie beamed. "Of course we can!"

There were more hugs, more assurances.

"Sometimes things that seem the worst turn out to be the best for us," Tom said philosophically. Then at John's raised eyebrow, he added with a grin, "Or some tripe like that. The important thing is you were honest in the crunch. That's all the world asks of a man."

JADE AND JOE were sitting on the foot of the bed when John and Barbara walked into the bedroom. They were wide-eyed and wary.

"We heard everything," Joe said.

Jade's lip quivered. "What's going to happen?"

John opened his mouth to reply and found that Barbara was taking charge. She sat between the children and gathered them close to her.

"We're going home in the morning," she said, "and we've probably lost the account, but your father and I are getting married during the week."

John leaned a hip on the dresser, pleased but surprised by her simple explanation. He'd thought he'd seen hesitation, second thought, in her eyes.

Joe, also, looked surprised, then he smiled broadly. "Excellent!" he said.

Jade, who never trusted as easily, asked carefully, "And you're staying?"

Joe rolled his eyes. "No, dummy. They're getting married, then Mom's leaving to go with that geeky guy." He turned to give Barbara an incredulous look. "How could you have liked somebody like that?"

Barbara ignored him, apparently concerned with Jade's insecurity with the situation. "I'm staying."

"Our other Mom," Jade insisted, "didn't even want to see us."

John straightened away from the dresser at that, a dark line between his eyes.

"Nobody told me," she explained. "I heard Aunt Sandy and Grandma talking about it once."

He opened his mouth to speak, ready with a long list of reassurances, but again Barbara forestalled him. She pulled the children closer and said in an easy manner, "There are people in the world who just don't relate to other people. They can be very nice and very interesting, but when you need them, they don't notice it because they spend most of their time thinking about and looking for what *they* need.

"My dad was like that."

Both children looked at her in amazement. John saw the strong bond already forged among them strengthened further.

"The trouble was, he stayed and tried to be a father but it really didn't work because there were other things he wanted to do more than that. Your mother knew she would be that kind of parent, so she didn't stay. She made room for someone else to come in who really wanted the job."

Jade smiled for the first time. "You."

"Right."

Her doubts disintegrated, Jade kissed Barbara, then her father and went off to bed. Joe did the same, then stopped at the door with a hand on the knob.

"It's going to be hard to sleep," he said.

"Don't tell me." John went to him. "Because you don't have an ATV to dream about."

Joe shook his head. "No. Because Uncle Hal and Mrs. Gordon are screaming at each other in the room next door."

John peered into the hall and, sure enough, the sound of loud, angry conversation filtered toward them. Then the door opened and Hal stormed out. There was the sound of feet pounding down the stairs and across the living room.

John decided grimly that his friend had it rough. It didn't seem to him as though loving Joanna Gordon held a lot of promise for a man.

John shooed Joe out the door. "Now you ought to be able to get some sleep."

Joe peered back around with a winning smile. "You know, an ATV to dream about was an excellent—"

John put a hand to Joe's shoulder and pushed until he could close the door.

Then he turned to find Barbara sitting moodily in the middle of the bed, wearing the same removed expression she'd worn before they'd found the children in their room. She looked pale now in the bright purple dress.

He approached the bed with caution. "What?" he asked.

She parted her lips to answer, then closed them again and shook her head. Then she raised both hands in a gesture of desperation. "I don't know. It's all so complicated."

He sat facing her, a foot braced on the floor. "I might be able to follow," he said, his voice dry, "if you go slowly."

She gave him a lethal look. "This is not the time for your brilliant adman wit. I don't know what to do here."

"Where?"

"Here," she replied impatiently. "In this relationship."

She was getting testy. He wasn't sure if that was an improvement over that removed look or a worsening of the circumstances.

"You just told my children what you were going to do," he said. "You told them you were marrying me."

She nodded, her gaze unfocused. "I had to. They need to know their world is secure."

He didn't care for the turn this was taking. He studied her, trying to find a thread of reason to pick up. He finally gave up.

"I don't understand," he admitted.

She focused on him as though he interfered with whatever else was being worked out in her mind. "I can't let them down. That would be devastating to them. Besides, I love them. I couldn't bear to be without them."

That was good—sort of.

"And I'm…incidental to that?"

She treated him to another exasperated look. "Of course not. I love you." Then the look softened, became a little desperate and slid away. "But I'm worried about us."

Now he was growing impatient. "I love you, you love me, together we love the children. What's to worry about?"

"I can't forget that this all came about because I let myself into your bathroom." She climbed off the bed and reached for the nightgown she'd tucked under her pillow. She didn't look at him. "And if this has a bad effect on Cheney & Roman, which it's bound to have, I'm afraid one day *you* won't be able to forget it, either."

"Oh, please." He stood and pulled at his tie, feeling suddenly as though it were the noose at the end of his rope. He'd had a rough evening, and he selfishly wanted to hear her confidence, not her doubts. "If you've run out of enthusiasm for this relationship, please don't blame it on me. I am not now nor have I ever been the kind of man who blames someone else for his predicament. I told Daniel you were my wife, and that's what precipitated this whole thing. In which, I might add, I've had a hell of a lot of fun."

"I should have refused. I should have foreseen—"

"Barbara." John yanked at the buttons of his shirt as she balled the nightgown in her hands. "I'm not asking you to be my conscience or my fortune-teller or my business-of-life consultant. I take my own chances. If you want to gamble with me, fine. If you don't, I won't make you stay. I'm going to take a shower."

Women! he thought as he stood under the spray of lukewarm water. Even the good ones were enough to drive a man to desperate measures.

He stayed under the water until he felt some semblance of calm, then reached through the curtain for a towel to wrap around his waist. Then he yanked a hand towel off the rack and buffed his hair, now calm enough to realize it probably hadn't been wise to tell her he wouldn't make her stay. The way his luck was running... He stepped out and walked into the bedroom.

He knew instantly that she wasn't there. He stood still for a moment, feeling the serrated edge of bitter anguish and disillusion. He had to lean against the dresser and put a hand to the pain. It flowed out from his gut in waves, radiating to every corner of his being.

He'd claimed to be a man who assumed the blame for his mistakes, he thought, through the grinding blur. This is what he got for giving her a choice.

Then a quiet and very familiar feminine voice said, "I'm right behind you, Cheney."

He spun around, joy instantly dispersing the pain. She stood there in the nightie, arms folded over small breasts almost visible through vanilla lace. The joy was doused as temper erupted inside him like a fountain of flame.

"You *hid* from me?" he demanded in disbelief.

She stood her ground. "No. I went into the bathroom to talk to you just as you stepped out of the shower with a towel over your head and walked in here." She yanked at the towel that had slipped to his neck and took both ends in her hands.

"Don't you ever minimize my concerns," she said, "by telling me to get over them or get out."

He had to lean down to allow her control of the towel, yet the look in her eye was fascinating. This was a side of Barbara he hadn't seen before. It was a darker variation of the firm way she'd dealt with Jade and Joe's fears.

"I did not tell you to 'get out,'" he said, repeating those words with the scorn they deserved. "I told you I wouldn't make you stay."

"So I thought I'd let you see what your life would feel like without me."

She saw instantly that had not been a wise thing to say. He straightened, snapping the towel out of her hands. He yanked it off and tossed it aside. Then he swept her off her feet and carried her to the bed, his eyes dangerous. "Then maybe you'd like to feel what it's like to toy with a man's affections."

"I did not—" He dropped her in the middle of the pillows, and the single bounce terminated her denial.

"You did," he said, his expression without one betraying hint of humor. She felt a niggle of concern. "You stayed behind me as I walked into the room so that I would think you'd gone."

She sat up in a huff, determined to make him listen. "I wanted to get your attention," she said. "I wanted you to realize I'm important to you, to take me seriously when I tell you I'm a little worried that the way this all started may…make it hard to hold."

"You are important to me," he said angrily, "and do *you* listen to *me* when I tell you there's nothing to worry about? That I'll love you into eternity whatever the hell happens to the business or to us? No."

Barbara found that she could not ignore such emphasis. He leaned over her, eyes blazing, shoulders bare, and she accepted once and for all that he was right. She'd seen his shoulders slump when he'd thought she was gone, heard the low, strangled sound in his throat as he leaned against the dresser. The picture had been clearer than a look at his face.

"Okay, okay," she said gently, planting a kiss on his

shoulder. "I'm sorry. The evening was kind of a shock and I got a little panicky."

She undid the tuck in his towel and hitched a leg over him.

John saw nothing after that but the wave of her hair falling over his face and her lips coming at him. Then she was atop him, containing him, and everything he knew for certain fled his mind, except her love.

Chapter Fourteen

"Where's Hal?" John, packing the van to leave for home, took the bag his father handed him and tucked it into a corner. "Where's his bag?"

"He left after you and Barbara went to bed," Tom said, holding out empty hands. "That's the last of it."

John closed the tailgate and frowned at Tom. "What do you mean, he left? In what? We all rode together."

"A cab. Said he had things to do."

John would have closed his eyes and taken a moment to collect himself, but there wasn't time. Joanna had informed them at 8:00 a.m. that she'd spoken to Daniel Burger, and he and the other members of the cooperative would be meeting them at the office at noon. It was now after nine. If he was going to have time to drop the children at home, he had to hit the road.

He'd have preferred to have his friend and partner at his side when he faced the cooperative, but he understood Hal's anguish over Joanna. And Hal wasn't the one who'd gotten them into this; he was.

"All right," he called to the subdued little group exchanging hugs and handshakes in the driveway. "Let's go."

"It's going to be fine," Edie said as she held him to

her when everyone else was in the car. "I feel it. Father Mike's on your side."

John shook his head. "Thanks, Mom, but the cooperative's decision on anything has to be unanimous, and they'd rather change plans than lose a member. I blew it."

"Hindsight's twenty-twenty," Tom said, giving him a bear hug. He had to admit it felt good. "Brave people look ahead."

John smiled at him as he pulled away. "You're full of philosophy lately."

Tom put an arm around Edie. "Comes from living with your mother. I find I have to get philosophical about a lot of things."

The drive home was eerily quiet. Father Mike played word games with the children, but Joanna sat alone in the middle seat, face set and hurt.

Late summer traffic was thick on the coast, and John found himself less patient than usual. He had to admit he was worried. The reputation of Cheney & Roman was on the line. Now that he and Barbara had settled things between them, he allowed himself to worry about the business.

When he stopped at a lineup of cars waiting to merge off a beachfront road to the highway, Barbara leaned sideways in her seat and reached out to turn his face to her. She kissed him gently. "I love you," she said.

He felt something relax inside him. He was grateful that, at least, was settled.

THE CHILDREN BOLTED from the van at the sight of a helmeted figure on a motorcycle, circling the front lawn. He had to take a moment to watch and smile.

"Libby's Harley came!" Barbara exclaimed, leaning

over him to peer out the window as the bike turned in their direction, the children following. Then Barbara sobered and looked into his eyes. "But the deal…"

John shook his head. "She did her part. Life's too short to belabor the fine print. Here I thought I had everything, then I found you, and now I probably only have fifty years to enjoy you. I should have looked for you sooner."

Barbara kissed him soundly. "I'll make the fifty years so great you won't think anything's missing—even time."

"Hi! Welcome home!" The visor on the helmet went up and Libby's face beamed at them. "It came this morning!" she shouted, probably still hearing the roar in her ears. She reached in to hug her employer, bumped her helmet on the roof of the Safari, then laughed as she pulled it off. She reached in again and gave him a resounding kiss on his cheek. "Thank you!" she gushed. "I've had the best morning!"

Father Mike hung out the side window, crowding a grumpy Joanna to the other seat.

Libby waved at him, then frowned at John. "But your mom called and said—" She spotted Joanna in the middle seat and stopped.

"It isn't over yet," John said. "And anyway, the bike's yours. Just keep the kids off it, okay? We should be home for dinner."

"Right." She walked the bike backward like a veteran of the road. "Good luck!"

CAROL MET THEM at the elevator and dispatched another secretary to take Father Mike and Joanna to the conference room. She held John and Barbara back and walked slowly between them toward the big double doors.

"We held our own staff meeting this morning," she said softly as watchful eyes looked up from scores of desks and offered encouragement. "And we want you to know you have our vote as the best ad team in the business, whether or not the cooperative gives you theirs." She stopped at the doors and added with a hand on her hip, "Unless losing this account results in a loss of revenue and a dip in salaries. Then we're all out of here."

John gave her a hug. "What a devoted crew."

"Good luck," she whispered.

John pulled the doors open and stepped into the room before Barbara, ready to protect her an extra moment against the assault of the cooperative's disapproval. But they were all crowded at the end of the table, poring over something he couldn't see. Daniel sat at the head of the table, and Hal leaned over him, pointing.

Only Joanna stood aside, her arms folded, her lips pursed.

Barbara physically pushed John out of her way and stood beside him. "What's going on?" she whispered. "What are they looking at?"

"Gallows plans?" he guessed. Then he walked into the room. "Good afternoon, gentlemen."

"John." Daniel looked up from the table, an indeterminate look on his face. He was without his customary smile. Then he flashed it briefly. "Barbara. Come and join us."

John approached the table and saw photographs, some taken as recently as the day before. Hal must have been up all night developing them. John looked up at his partner for an explanation.

Hal shrugged a shoulder. "I couldn't sleep so I came home early to have at least part of a presentation ready."

John walked around Daniel's chair to study the shot he was inspecting so closely. It was one of the group taken at the airport when Barbara had seen him off to Rhode Island. Love brimmed in her eyes and shone blatantly in his.

Daniel picked up several more. One was of Barbara and Jade, balanced like ballerinas on the wall surrounding the zoo's duck pond. In the next they were wet as a pair of seals as they surfaced, looking at each other and laughing. There was a third of him, trying desperately to look severe and failing, as he hauled them out.

"If we were going to do this," Daniel said, selecting another photo he'd placed at hand, "this would be the centerpiece. It says everything."

Barbara went around to look. It was a photograph taken the night before at his parents' party. They were slightly out of focus in the background, looking toward him and Barbara, who were standing on opposite sides of the children. Jade and Joe were in an animated conversation, and he and Barbara were simply smiling at each other, he in his suit, she in her slim purple dress.

They weren't touching, except with their eyes. That indefinable something that binds man and woman for a lifetime was as clear between them as if it had physical substance.

Barbara's arm stole around his waist. John wrapped an arm around her shoulders and looked up at Hal, a catch in his throat. His friend looked both proud and miserable.

"Sit down, please," Daniel said briskly, gesturing toward chairs. "We have to decide what to do here. The cooperative must vote."

John led Barbara to a chair. This was simply a formality, he knew. He'd heard that remark, "If we were going to do this,'' the choice of words suggesting he'd decided not to.

Barbara cleared her throat and took her courage in her hands. ''Reverend Burger, I know Joanna told you that we tricked you, and we don't deny it, but I think you should hear our—''

Daniel silenced her with a look. ''I had a telephone call this morning from John's mother and another from John's sister, filling me in on 'the other side.''' His voice emphasized the words. He smiled thinly. ''I was also stopped first thing this morning by John's secretary, who was chosen as spokesman for your staff. She regaled me for twenty minutes with a litany of your virtues, John, and Cheney & Roman's refusal to take alcohol or tobacco clients, their improved health-care policy for employees, profit sharing, fully equipped gymnasium.''

''The point,'' Joanna said, taking a chair at the end of the group, ''is that they lied to us and misrepresented all the qualities we were hoping to tap with this campaign.''

''The point,'' Hal said, taking the chair opposite her, ''is that your hurt feelings, your belief in your own fabrication, and your inability to loosen up because you can't forgive yourself for one mistake, are coloring your judgment, Joanna.''

''Hal,'' John said quietly.

Hal ignored him. ''You told me the night of the clambake that you regretted doubting them in the beginning, that the beach had given you a new perspective on everything.''

''We've been deceived,'' Joanna said to Daniel.

Daniel nodded. ''I believe there's been a deception here, all right.''

Barbara took John's hand under the table, squaring her shoulders.

"But I believe *we* were not the victims of it," Daniel went on. He held up the photo taken at the anniversary party. "John told us—or, rather, I believe I assumed—that he and Barbara were passionately in love. Is there anything in this photo that would cause you to doubt the truth of that?"

Members of the cooperative looked at one another. Joanna tried to speak, but Daniel interrupted her. Hal smiled at John and Barbara.

"Joanna tells us they weren't married when we walked in on them that afternoon. I've explained to you what Edie Cheney and Sandy Ryder told me about the incident. John wanted our account and did his best to save the day.

"I believe the most obvious deceit here was between these two when they told themselves they were acting. Does that look like acting?" He held up the airport photo.

Barbara turned to John, who squeezed her hand but remained calm, listening.

Daniel turned to Joanna, studied her for a moment with a smile Barbara thought was almost apologetic. She had only a moment to wonder what it meant. Daniel picked up another photo and passed it down to her.

"And my companions and I are victims of another deception, Joanna, if you want us to believe that you haven't fallen in love yourself—with the man who took that photograph."

Barbara strained to see as the photo was passed to Joanna. In it, she sat in the shallows in a pair of John's mother's cutoffs, her calves and feet bare, her short hair ruffled, her smile wide and free—and all for the man shooting the picture. Hal.

Joanna tried to push away from the table, but Hal was around it and behind her, blocking her in place with his arms on either side of her. "You have to vote before you leave," he said.

"I ask you to do what you believe to be best," Daniel said. "Our votes are required to be unanimous, but we have high hopes for this project, and we want everyone to believe in it, if we proceed."

Daniel began to poll. There were five out of six ayes when the vote reached Joanna.

"Can you fault them for falling in love," Hal asked softly, "when you fell in love yourself?"

Joanna held herself stiffly away from him. "That was before I knew you'd used me."

"I didn't use you," Hal insisted gently, sincerely. "I fell in love with you."

"Hal," John said quietly, "I don't think you can influence a vote like that and expect it to have any binding—"

"This whole thing is about truth, isn't it?" Hal said, unmoved by John's mild censure. "Aren't we searching for the truth, Joanna? Do you love me, or not?"

"The truth," Barbara said to Joanna, "is that Hal was already in love with you the night the manse's plumbing burst. He asked me for advice after your quarrel that night. I'm the one who suggested he get to know you better, try to learn what you needed. It was no trick."

Joanna turned slightly in her chair to look over her shoulder at Hal. Her eyes were wide and suspicious and spilling tears.

Hal pulled her out of her chair and into his arms. "I love you, Joanna. I declare it in front of the cooperative of churches and my business partners. Would a lying man do that?''

Daniel asked calmly, "Your vote, Joanna?''

"Yes!'' she cried, turning to sob into Hal's shoulder. "Yes!''

There was a shriek beyond the double doors, followed by the sound of a general commotion. Daniel looked at John.

"My secretary, I believe,'' John said.

"Well.'' Daniel and his group stood. Daniel shook John's hand, then Barbara's. "I believe this is going to be a happy association. Father Mike tells me he'll be marrying the two of you this week.''

"That's right,'' John said. "You're invited to the wedding—all of you.''

"We'll be there.'' He indicated Hal and Joanna, still holding each other and talking quietly. "We may have to schedule two.''

While John and Barbara walked Daniel and the co-operative to the front doors, Carol sat sedately at her desk, and all heads were bent industriously over drafting tables and computer terminals.

The moment the doors closed, pandemonium broke loose. Barbara leapt into John's arms, triumphant shouts filled the room and papers and streamers flew in the air. Pizza and champagne were delivered, and the party lasted until dinner.

Hal and Joanna had already left, arm in arm, smiles blinding, when John fell into the chair behind his desk and pulled Barbara into his lap.

"Do you believe this happened?'' he asked her lazily.

"Yes,'' she replied, leaning her head on his shoulder. "It was a miracle, but these people deal in miracles. That's their business. We're going to have to get used to that if they're going to be our clients. And used to it on a national level.''

"It was Hal, loving Joanna," John said, holding Barbara close and thinking how completely her love affected him, inspired him, renewed him.

Barbara, who'd once sought to replace love with order and system, held fast to the man who'd changed her life. "That's what I just said," she told him. "Love is the miracle.''

Epilogue

St. Bonaventure's was filled with flowers.

"I've never seen so many people," Edie said, peering from the vestibule into the body of the church, "at a wedding that was planned in five days!"

Barbara, in an ivory tea-length gown, thought that no one was more surprised than the bride herself. The pews were filled with many of John's friends, all the Cheney & Roman employees, many of their clients and Libby's family, who'd arrived the previous evening on motorcycles.

Barbara's mother was in the front pew, and her stepfather stood a few feet away talking to Tom and waiting to escort her up the aisle.

Her father had called from Tokyo to congratulate her, wish her well and tell her that a snag in the construction of the apartment complex he'd designed precluded his coming for the wedding.

She couldn't deny that part of her had hoped against hope that he would come to give her away. But another part of her looked around at her mother and stepfather, at Jade and Joe, the children who'd been hers almost from the moment she'd met them, at her new in-laws and at John, the man who'd made her dreams real, and could feel no disappointment. She lacked nothing that was important to her.

Jade put her basket of rose petals aside and fluffed the ruffled sleeves of Barbara's dress. "You look great, Mom," she said. "Dad'll faint when he sees you."

Barbara smiled, having difficulty imagining John in a faint. "You look beautiful, too," she said.

Jade picked up her basket and ran rose petals through her fingers. She frowned up at Barbara. "You know, it's weird that they let you litter in a church."

Carol and Sandy, Barbara's matron of honor and bridesmaid in different shades of yellow, emerged from the dressing room.

Carol smiled at Barbara's hat. "Your chapeau is dynamite."

"The rose was my idea," Sandy said with no attempt at modesty.

Barbara touched the broad-brimmed hat, the front pinned back to the crown with a champagne rose from her bouquet. "Is it straight?"

"It's perfect."

"All right. Groom coming through." There was a sudden commotion of protest as John and Joe forced their way into the little cluster of women.

"John!" Edie said, trying to push him away. "It's bad luck for you to see the bride before—"

"I know, I know." He fended her off gently. "But it's an emergency."

"What?" the five women demanded in unison.

He flashed a disarming smile. "I missed her." He took her hands and pulled her into a corner with the children.

"Everything okay?" he asked, his eyes going over every beautiful detail of her glowing face, her soft shoulders, and the subtle swell of bosom disappearing into the ivory silk.

"Everything's wonderful," she said, thinking deep down how absolutely true that was. "But I'm glad you missed me."

He was breathtakingly handsome in a dark suit and a paisley bow tie that had been a gift from Hal and Joanna, who would be married the following week.

Joe, beside him, also wore a suit for his role as a groomsman. But the more formal clothing did not diminish the devilish glint in his eyes.

"Uncle Hal tried to tell him you were fine," he said, "but he had to see for himself. Now we're probably gonna have bad luck or something."

John, his eyes still looking into Barbara's, shook his head. "Not a chance. We're charmed. Or, I suppose Father Mike would call it 'blessed.'" He leaned forward to kiss her gently, careful of her hat. "We just came to tell you that we love you. And we're so grateful that you belong to us."

Jade, always cautious, reminded him, "You told me that we belong to each other."

He touched her hair in its coronet of yellow roses. "You're right."

Her heart full enough to burst, Barbara placed an arm around each of the children and leaned toward John.

He wrapped them all in his embrace, emotion crowding his throat.

"John!" Edie whispered. "Father's calling for you."

"Be right there." He gave Barbara one last look that said everything she would ever want to know about his love for her.

She squeezed his hand. "We are blessed," she whispered.

''John!'' Edie's whisper was desperate.

Everyone scattered: John and Joe to run around to the side entrance to take their places at the altar with Hal; Edie and Tom to take their places; Carol, Sandy and Jade to line up at the door as the music began.

Barbara stood with her stepfather in the wide doorway as the women began the procession, and Jade followed, ''littering'' the carpeted aisle with rose petals.

The church seemed to burst with music, flowers, smiling faces waiting for her and the rampant joy of a happy wedding.

It was like a dream, she thought, starting up the aisle. But she couldn't imagine a dream that could compare with her reality.

Middle of the Rainbow

Chapter One

"Do you, Patrick, take Regina to be your wedded wife? To have and to hold from this day forward, for better, for worse, for richer..."

Patrick let his mind wander as the judge droned on in a voice too loud for the stuffy little office in which the wedding was taking place. He didn't want to hear the ceremony, anyway. If he didn't listen, taking the vow wouldn't be a lie.

He tried not to look at Regina. Though he'd only known her forty-eight hours, she had a way of turning those large gray eyes on him and interrupting the impulses from his brain, of affecting his body's processes.

He felt her shoulder bump against his upper arm as she shifted her weight, heard the rustle of something silk under the soft blue dress she wore, filled his nostrils with her musk-and-magnolia scent with every breath he drew.

He'd come to Los Angeles to meet Wyatt Raleigh, single-minded in his purpose. He hadn't expected the solution to his financial problems to be a wife.

Patrick became suddenly aware that the room was silent and the judge was watching him expectantly. Beside him he felt Regina shift again. Behind him he heard the subtle cough of Paul Sinclair, his best man—the person who'd gotten him into this. He realized what they waited for.

"I do," he said firmly, clearly. He wasn't going to worry about it. She'd been as up-front as he had and they'd struck a deal.

Regina shifted again, this time losing her balance and falling hard against his arm. As the judge instinctively reached out for her, Patrick caught her hand and steadied her with an arm around her waist.

She glanced up at him with a wry little smile. "Sorry," she whispered, her eyes catching his for an instant before turning back to the judge.

"Do you, Regina, take Patrick for your wedded husband, to have and to hold from this day forward, for better..."

Get a grip! Gina warned herself. *You made a deal. So it all seemed less bizarre four days ago in your father's house than it does this morning in the judge's chambers. Remember that you'll get what you want, and that's what's important.*

As the judge's voice registered somewhere beyond her awareness, Gina tried to be comforted by that knowledge. But comfort had completely eluded her from the moment she'd read Patrick Gallagher's file.

She'd seen immediately that he was unlike anyone in her family or circle of friends. There was energy in the way he moved, excitement in his eyes.

He was perfect. But now as he stood beside her, tall, broad...and proprietary, she wondered if she'd gotten in over her head.

PATRICK COULD FEEL her losing her nerve. The hand he held was shaking. He firmed his grip, wanting to get through this before she changed her mind.

The outrageousness of the deal they'd struck had hit him that morning when he'd been shaving, but he had too much to lose…and a roll of the dice was worth the gamble.

IT HAD ALL BEGUN as a request for a loan from a financier with a reputation for bold investment. Of course, approaching Wyatt Raleigh had been Sin's idea. Patrick could only blame himself for forgetting that anything involving his buddy, Paul Sinclair, deserved careful consideration. But he hadn't had time.

He'd driven from Candle Bay, Oregon, to Sin's place in Malibu. He'd have preferred to fly, but driving his long-bed truck would allow him to pick up the double oak doors for the hotel's main entrance from a Southern Oregon craftsman.

"Why don't you just let *me* lend you the money?" Sin had asked as they'd had drinks on a redwood deck overlooking the ocean while a colorful sunset bloomed out of it.

They'd had that argument three days earlier on the phone. "I told you. If I lose everything, I don't want it to be your money."

"It wouldn't matter."

"It would to me."

Sin glanced away from the horizon. "It's only money, Pat," he said with a grin.

Patrick laughed. "Spoken like a man with an endless supply. Thanks, but I'll take my chances with Wyatt Raleigh. He knows I'm coming?"

Sin nodded. "I confirmed this morning."

The following afternoon, Sin's classic Pininfarina had

wound its way into a hilly, wooded area that had surprised Patrick with its rustic remoteness. Sin had dropped him off in front of a modern, multilevel house fitted on a slope like an angular bird. ''Be back for you in a couple of hours,'' he'd said. ''Good luck.''

A small brunette in an apron answered the door. She studied Patrick, an eyebrow raised in question.

''I'm Patrick Gallagher,'' he said. ''I have an appointment with Mr. Raleigh.''

She gave him a slow, once-over glance, then opened the door wide and stepped aside. Another time, he might have returned the glance, but now he had other things on his mind. He followed her up a blue-carpeted, oak-banistered staircase to a hallway lined with Ron Jensen seascapes. She rapped twice on a door at the end of the hall, pushed it open, smiled at him and turned back the way they'd come.

A tall, slender man in tennis whites came across the paneled study, hand extended. He was fit, with thinning gray hair and wire-rimmed glasses. He moved like Sin did, Patrick noted, with a grace that spoke of breeding.

''Mr. Raleigh,'' Patrick said. ''I'm Patrick Gallagher.''

''Welcome to Los Angeles,'' Raleigh said, leading Patrick to a chair that faced his desk. ''Can I get you a drink?''

''A gin and tonic, please.''

Raleigh went to a small bar across the study and was back in a moment carrying two frosty glasses with twists of lime.

''Sinclair tells me this has something to do with a hotel that's been in your family for some time. Please. Sit down.''

''The Candle Bay Inn,'' Patrick replied, easing into

the soft cordovan leather. "Near the mouth of the Co-lumbia. My great-grandfather built it at the turn of the century."

Raleigh took his chair behind the desk and nodded with interest. "Queen Anne architecture. Eighty rooms. You're talking about adding charter boats, tours of his-toric Astoria and a new chef."

Good. He was dealing with a man who did his re-search. "If you know all that," Patrick said, "you must also know that I'm taking over for my grandfather, who just passed away. Because the bank doesn't know me…"

Raleigh nodded again. "Because you've spent the last ten years in the military. You've been a civilian only six months. Go on."

Patrick calmly continued. "Because the bank doesn't know me, they're calling in the loan my grandfather took out to remodel and expand. The job's only half-done. Without remodeling, we can no longer provide the com-fort people look for in a hotel, and without expanding we won't be able to compete with the bigger houses in Seaside or on the Washington peninsula."

"You've talked to the bank?" Raleigh asked. "You've explained to them you grew up in the busi-ness?" He smiled slowly. "Explained that if you can take care of a company of young marines, you can do anything in this world you set your mind to?"

Patrick grinned. "Did your stint in the corps?"

"In the Navy, actually, but we had the standard ma-rine contingent aboard ship. They were fearless on duty and reckless on leave. Tough bunch to command."

Patrick nodded. "The bank wants to see my experi-ence on a profit-and-loss statement." He shrugged. "I can't give them that. I hoped you'd be more open-minded.''

''I might be. Tell me your plans.''

For an hour Patrick explained what he wanted to do with the Candle Bay Inn. The bed-and-breakfast certainly fulfilled a need, but many people wanted more than the usual room, shared bath, and croissants and coffee that the standard B&B provided.

''The Candle Bay Inn doesn't provide day care for guests' children yet, but that's something I'm working on,'' Patrick said, downing the last of his drink. ''But I know I can fill every other need if I can finish the remodeling and the addition. Right now I've got a crew of carpenters standing around, eating up money. If I let them go until the money problem's ironed out, they'll go to work for somebody else. It's already late April. I'll lose the season.''

Raleigh nodded thoughtfully as he refilled Patrick's empty glass. ''I might be able to help you,'' he said.

Patrick drew the first even breath he'd taken since Sin had dropped him off.

''After looking into your background,'' Raleigh said, freshening his own drink, then walking back to his chair, ''I thought you seemed like a good bet.'' He moved his glass in a circular, stirring motion and smiled. ''That's all a loan is, you know—a sort of bet on an individual. I never lend on the basis of a company's figures, but on the track record of the man guiding it. Now that I've met you, I'm convinced you'll give it everything you have.''

He took a long drink, put his glass down on a notepad on his desk, then leaned back in his chair and laced his fingers over his stomach. He met Patrick's eyes. ''But we both know that however good you are, lending you the amount of money you've asked for is still a risk.''

Patrick nodded. "Yes, it is.''

There was a long pause. Patrick waited. Then Raleigh said suddenly, ''I'm willing to take it. But there is a condition.''

Patrick's mind ran through the conditions a man of Raleigh's reputation might attach to a business deal. He couldn't think of one he wouldn't be willing to meet.

"Name it,'' he said.

Raleigh picked up his drink, took another swallow, then put it down again. "I'd like you to take my daughter back to Oregon with you—as your wife.''

For a moment Patrick could only wonder if he'd heard correctly. When Raleigh nodded in silent reply to his unspoken question, Patrick felt as though he were holding a grenade in one hand and its pin in the other; he had to think fast or he was going to get his head blown off.

"Why?'' he asked. Not a brilliant tactic, but bound to produce important answers and buy him time.

Raleigh smiled again. "Not prone to panic. I like that. Because she's been in one scrape after the other ever since she graduated from college.''

"Scrape?''

"Oh, nothing serious until this last thing with Yale Gardner. But she likes her friends a little wild. She's often in the tabloid headlines. Dancing in the fountain at the music center, being the cause of a brawl at some yuppy watering hole, picketing city hall because they were bullied into taking down an art show that contained nudes.''

That all sounded pretty tame to Patrick. "Who's Yale Gardner?''

Raleigh sighed with paternal frustration. "Two years ago she insisted on opening a design firm with a friend of hers from art school. I tried to warn her, but she wouldn't listen. Sank every penny into it." He raised both hands in a philosophical gesture. "Lost it all a month ago when her partner—" he emphasized the word scornfully "—stole jewels, antiques and artwork from their clients, raided their savings account and took off for parts unknown. She had to liquidate to try to make restitution to her clients. Now she doesn't have a dime until she comes into her inheritance from her grandmother when she turns twenty-six next March."

Patrick couldn't help the instinctive glance at his opulent surroundings. "You couldn't help her?"

Raleigh shook his head adamantly. "I told her, when she insisted on ignoring my warnings, that I wasn't going to bail her out when she got into trouble again. A parent has to stand firm."

"But you can't blame her for her partner's—"

"I can blame her for trusting every freeloader who comes along," Raleigh interrupted. "I can blame her for refusing to listen to sound advice. What I *am* going to do for her is take an old-world father approach and find a husband for her."

"Mr. Raleigh," Patrick said calmly, "I'm up to my neck in problems and debt. I—"

"I can solve the debt problems," Raleigh interrupted.

Patrick could almost see a wheelbarrow filled with cash rolling away from him. "You can't bargain marriage with money," he said, although considering the desperation with which he wanted to save the Candle Bay Inn, he wasn't absolutely sure of that. "At least...you shouldn't."

"Oh, I'm not," Raleigh assured him with an innocent

smile. "I've been looking for the right man everywhere. You're the only one with all the qualifications."

"And those are?"

"Toughness, tenacity, ingenuity, honesty."

Patrick shook his head and grinned at the impressive list of attributes. "Mr. Raleigh, you may know my background, but you don't know me. I—"

"The corps had a pretty detailed psychological profile on you. I hate to contradict you, but I think I do know you."

Patrick unbuttoned his jacket and leaned back in his chair. He had a feeling the rest of this interview was going to require some quick moves on his part.

"Regina's mother died when she was a baby," Raleigh explained with sudden sobriety. "I was very busy and didn't make enough time for my daughter or her brothers. The boys eventually came to work for me, but Gina's a right-brained kind of person—all feeling and artistic emotion. Bad qualities in an investor."

Patrick nodded.

"The minute she came into her trust at twenty-one she left the house. She supported every underdog that happened by. Then she took up with all her strange friends and went into business with Gardner. I watched all the money I worked so hard to give her go down the drain."

Raleigh's voice had risen, and Patrick could see that the notorious Regina had almost managed to crease her father's calm. Then he drew a breath and straightened in his chair.

"I'm within a week of launching my campaign for Congress, and I won't get very far with her making the headlines twice a week."

So, that was it. Patrick was desperate for Raleigh's

money, but not hard-up enough to coerce a young woman into marriage to further her father's political career.

He stood and carried his glass to the bar. Then he turned and faced Raleigh across the desk. "Thank you for your time and your interest, but I'm having enough trouble serving my own ambitions. I can't serve yours, too. I'll see myself out."

"You misunderstand me, Gallagher," Raleigh said. "Regina is not unwilling."

That stopped Patrick halfway to the door. He couldn't help a surprised "She isn't?"

"No," Raleigh replied, picking up a Mont Blanc pen and turning it thoughtfully in his fingers. "And that should give us both pause. But, for reasons of her own, Regina is perfectly willing to consider you as a husband."

Patrick absorbed that information and continued to the door. He stopped and turned with his hand on the ornate brass pull. "Thank you again, but if she's comparison shopping, I'm sure I'm not her man. Or yours."

"Wouldn't you like to meet her first?"

"No, thank you." Patrick opened the door and found the little brunette maid on the other side, her hand raised and prepared to knock.

Large gray eyes pinned him in place.

She no longer wore the apron but black leggings and a long yellow sweater. She looked into his eyes, apparently trying to read his expression.

"Hi," she said tentatively. He began to entertain a nagging suspicion.

"Regina," he guessed.

"Yes, Patrick." She folded her arms and asked anxiously, "You're not leaving?"

Raleigh was on his feet behind the desk. "You two have met?"

Patrick shook his head, casting her a scolding glance. "Not precisely. She let me in, pretending to be the maid."

"I let you in wearing an apron," she corrected with a smile. "You *assumed* I was the maid."

They stared at each other. Patrick liked to pride himself on the ability to read people and situations and find the most expedient way to deal with both.

She had thick, dark hair that reached her shoulders, and bangs that were swept to the side in a fanlike swoosh. She was average in height, small but roundly built, with a challenging angle in her shoulders and chin.

Something in him responded. "I was leaving," he heard himself say. He'd have sworn *I am leaving* was the impulse his brain had sent to his tongue. He fought to regain ground. "I understand you're considering marriage to me, but so far your father's explained that you're troublesome, quarrelsome and an exhibitionist. Is there something you'd like to add to that to make the notion more appealing to me?"

"MISS RALEIGH!" The judge's urgent whisper made Gina look up at Patrick. Now he was waiting for *her* answer and she wasn't sure she knew what to say. Could this possibly work? Granted, it had to work for less than a year, but that could seem like an eternity.

She was aware of the pulsing silence in the room. She was also conscious of the strong arm around her waist still lending support. She drew a deep breath and said strongly, "I do."

IN HER FATHER'S STUDY Regina considered Patrick Gallagher. So his polished civility was just a veneer. Considering her situation, that could be a good thing. "Would you like to talk in the garden?" she asked.

"Come on, Gallagher," her father prodded Patrick hopefully. "Can't hurt."

Patrick glanced doubtfully at him then back at her. He finally swept a hand toward the door, indicating that she should lead the way.

He kept abreast of her down the stairs and through the French doors in the kitchen to the velvet stretch of lawn behind the house. A colorful border of flowers, birds of paradise pointing their orange heads inward, surrounded it. She drew in a sweet breath and felt herself relax a little.

She led him to a canopied redwood picnic table. She slid into one side and he straddled the other. She looked up at him, prepared to make a laughing remark about the unusual circumstances, and found his dark gaze measuring and faintly disapproving.

"All right, so I'm not a bargain," she said candidly. "I'm rich and spoiled and like things my own way. I'm not much good in the out-of-doors with Mother Nature. But I could adjust."

He appeared unmoved by her candor. "Why are you doing this?" he asked without preamble. "Why would a pretty, intelligent woman let her father manipulate her this way? You don't want to go to work, is that it? You can't make an honest buck?"

She couldn't blame him for assuming that. "Not at the moment," she answered quietly. "At least, not in what I'm trained to do. My reputation in business has been destroyed."

"So you'd rather marry a stranger?"

She suddenly found it difficult to meet his eyes. She

looked up at the underside of the yellow-and-white striped canopy. "Actually," she said, "I agreed to my father's suggestion because I have my own agenda...and my own thoughts on how a marriage between us could be conducted."

When he said nothing, she lowered her eyes to his. He was removing his jacket. "Please," he said with a dry, sideways glance at her. "Elaborate. I can hardly wait."

She watched big shoulders ripple under his white shirt as he yanked the tie off and tossed it onto the jacket on the bench. Then he leaned on an elbow and gave her his attention.

She felt her mouth go dry. She decided to tell him the easy part first. "In eleven months," she said, folding her arms on the table, "I'll be twenty-six and come into the money my grandmother left me. It'll be more than enough to pay back the rest of what I owe my clients and start over again."

He frowned. "Then why not just wait for your inheritance?"

She made a point of keeping her eyes down, her voice casual. "Because I don't have a dime until then. You'd only have to put up with me for eleven months, then I'd walk out of your life forever." She grinned at him, but his expression didn't change. "I have another reason," she added seriously.

He was quiet for a long moment. "What?" he asked.

She'd had every intention of telling him the truth, but she knew what he would say: call the police; hire a private investigator. He was studying her across the table with a look of moral superiority—as though he was a man of purpose and direction forced to waste time with a silly young woman.

She quickly changed tack and decided to tell him another truth that would shock him.

"I want a baby," she said calmly.

For a long moment he stared at her. A breeze rippled through the fan palm at the other end of the lawn, insects hummed, and somewhere in the distance birds chattered. Then Patrick gathered up his coat and tie and started back toward the house. She caught him in the middle of the deep expanse of lawn.

"Hear me out," she pleaded, looping her arm in his so that he was forced to stop or drag her.

He came to a halt impatiently, looking down at her with an expression that brought color to her cheeks. This was not the reaction she'd expected, but she doubted he would believe the truth. And wanting a baby wasn't a lie. The perfect father had just never presented himself before.

"Where I come from," he said firmly, "we still cherish the traditional values. Babies are born out of love, not as a condition of a loan."

"I just thought," she said, trying not to sound desperate, "that I could help you and you could help me."

"I don't need a spoiled, selfish wife. I already have enough problems. I came to your father hoping to relieve some of them, not acquire new ones."

"Did I mention," she went on intrepidly, "that I'm a pretty good cook, I give a great back rub, and I'm good at staying out of the way?"

"Why," he demanded, annoyed by the fact that there was something touching about her persistence, "would you want a baby when you just suggested we go our separate ways in eleven months?"

"Because I've lived my whole life," she replied without hesitation, "alone and lonely. My father was always busy. My brothers are just like him. I love them but I want someone who is mine.''

"People," he said in a gently admonishing tone, "don't belong to other people."

She nodded and sighed. "Apparently. Even those who brought you into their world."

Patrick ran a hand down his face. "I'm sorry," he said. "I've talked to your father and I think I understand what you're saying. But I've lived hard all over the world, and I've maintained a certain...standard for my own behavior, which includes not impregnating women with whom I do not plan to spend the rest of my life."

She put a hand on his arm and saw something in his eyes react. "Patrick..." she began.

He grasped her wrist in his free hand and removed it. "There have to be a dozen blue bloods around here who would be happy to oblige you."

She stood still in his grasp and met his eyes. "I have a standard of my own, and that is not to make a baby with a jerk. I've read your file, too. I know what you're made of."

He dropped his jacket on the ground and pushed her down beside it, sitting knee to knee with her, his grip still firm. "You have no idea what I'm made of. I work long hours and I have a short temper. Married to me, you'd find yourself alone sixteen hours of the day unless you can wield a hammer, run a front desk or create a day-care facility that..."

He stopped midsentence as her whole countenance brightened. "A day-care facility? At your hotel? I could do that! Patrick, I could do that. I took classes in early-childhood education. I know all about..."

He released her and got to his feet. She sprang up

beside him. They looked into each other's eyes, he un-decided, she hopeful.

Then he reached under her hair to shape her head in his hand. His dark eyes warned her he was up to some-thing. She felt her breath stop as he lowered his head.

"Don't you even want to know if you'll like it with me first?" he asked softly. He opened his mouth over hers and gave her a kiss that wasn't hesitant or explor-atory or polite. It was a kiss intended to frighten her off.

He held her immobile, his tongue probed deeply, and his free hand ran down her back, over her hip, then up again.

Everything in her responded and quickened: heartbeat, bloodstream, nervous system. She felt strength in him and the suggestion of a powerful passion.

When he tugged her head back to look into her eyes, his were dark with surprise.

She dragged in a gulp of air and smiled up at him. "Yes," she said, her voice breathless. "I think I will."

He stared at her for one interminable moment, and she braced herself for his refusal. Then he leaned over her, still gripping her hair, until they were nose to nose.

"The first time you whine about the bad weather," he warned, "my long hours, the disrepair of the house or the lack of entertainment, I'm sending you back to your father fourth-class mail. Is that clear?"

Elation filled her, but she had the sense to look meek. "Yes," she replied.

"And the baby issue is not resolved."

"I want—" she began huffily.

He cut her off with a quiet but final "No. I'll marry you to keep you out of trouble until you come into your inheritance. In exchange, you will set up child care at the inn. That's the deal."

Gina was tempted to argue. But she'd felt that flare of passion. Maybe she didn't have to.

"Fine," she submitted.

"Good," he said, releasing her as he straightened. Then he closed his eyes and shook his head, and added, "I hope."

Chapter Two

"By the power invested in me by the State of California, I now pronounce you man and wife."

Gina drew a breath and turned to Patrick as the judge smiled. *Past the point of no return,* she thought. *I can do this.*

Patrick leaned down to give her a chaste kiss. *You've done it, Gallagher,* he congratulated himself. *You have the money. 'Course, you also have a wife.*

As she kissed him back, sweetly but with that suggestion of need he'd felt in her four days ago on her lawn, he was a little confused to find himself more fascinated with her than with the check in his pocket.

"YOU ARE CERTIFIABLE!" Bobbi Perducci, Gina's maid-of-honor, said as they stood in front of a bank of makeup mirrors in the ladies' room of the Woodland Restaurant. "You should have a box at the funny farm, life membership in the bin! You—"

"I get the message, Bobbi," Gina said, smoothing the hem of a pink sweater over matching tights. The wedding party had changed clothes, packed Patrick's canopied blue-and-silver Chevy truck, then found a quiet place for lunch before going their separate ways—Pat-

rick and Gina north to Oregon, Sin back to his law practice and Bobbi back to her small furniture-restoration
shop.

Gina kneaded the area behind her ears, hoping to relieve the tension there.

Bobbi stopped her diatribe to ask solicitously, "You
want an aspirin?"

"Oh, please."

Bobbi delved into a small leather bag and produced a
piece of round, red plastic that telescoped into a cup with
aspirin secured in its lid. Gina shook her head over her
friend's preparedness.

"I don't know what I'd do without you, Bobbi," Gina
said as she palmed two aspirin and held the cup under
running water.

"I don't know what I'd do without you, either,"
Bobbi said, watching frowningly in the mirror while
Gina tossed the aspirin into her mouth and swallowed.
"So please be careful. What did Patrick say when you
told him about the...?"

"Nothing." Gina tore a hand towel from the dispenser
and avoided the mirror as she wiped the cup. "I haven't
told him."

"You haven't—" Bobbi gasped. "Regina Jane, what
is *wrong* with you?"

Gina handed the cup back and smiled. "Well, Barbara
Elizabeth, I'll tell you. The gentleman doesn't like to be
used, and he was feeling pretty put-upon already."

Bobbi rolled her eyes. "Well, big surprise. Didn't I
tell you this was crazy? What man would dare take on
a wife just to get a loan?"

Gina brushed her hair, feeling the tension begin to
loosen. It *was* crazy, but she'd done it. That was all that

counted. "A man from Oregon, apparently. He put up a little resistance, laid down a few rules, then agreed."

"Because you didn't tell him the truth."

"I did. Just not all of it. But I will."

"You'd better make it fast. I'm sure it's Yale Gardner, or something to do with him. He probably wants to frighten you into keeping quiet about what he's stolen from you."

"Well, he's too late," Gina said. "I've already told the police everything I know."

"Maybe he wants retribution."

A little frisson of fear tried to shake Gina's new calm, but she refused to let it. "I'll be somewhere on Highway 101 with a two-hundred-pound ex-marine who has a vested interest in my personal safety."

Bobbi shook her head helplessly. "Gina, it won't be that simple. You should—"

"Bobbi," Gina said firmly, dropping her brush into her purse and turning her friend toward the rest-room door. "This is my wedding day. Though it came about in an unorthodox way, I'd like to enjoy it. Don't spoil it for me, okay?"

Bobbi turned at the door with a dreamy sigh. "He does have wonderful shoulders. Maybe something will come…"

Gina reached around her to pull open the door and push her gently through. "Snagging him was miracle enough. Thinking he might want to keep me when this is over is too much to hope for."

Besides, she thought as she followed Bobbi back toward their table, she was already beginning to wonder who'd snagged whom.

IN A CHINTZ-COVERED booth in a dining room decorated like a French country house, Sin looked at Patrick over his menu. "Can I have a drink?" he asked. "Or do I have to be on my best behavior?"

Patrick folded his menu and put it down. "Your best behavior is acceptable only around campfires on the John Day River, or possibly in the Sing Sing cafeteria."

Sin slapped his menu on top of Patrick's. "That's the thanks I get for coming through for you. Do you have another friend who could find you half a million dollars and a beautiful woman on a few days' notice?"

"I appreciate your putting the loan together," Patrick said, signaling the waitress. "I don't recall asking for a wife. You can have one drink. You have to drive Bobbi home when we leave."

Sin ordered a bottle of champagne, then leaned back in the booth and studied his friend with a thoughtful expression. "I didn't know Raleigh was going to make his daughter a condition of the loan. I guess I did too good a job selling you to him. My mistake. Actually, I think this'll be good for you."

Patrick raised an inquiring eyebrow. "How so?"

"Because you're so...military." Sin laughed lightly and shook his head. "Of course, if it hadn't been for your early-rising, schedule-keeping, everything-planned-in-detail approach to things, I'd never have graduated. But it was hell being your roommate. Go easy on Gina, okay? I like her."

Patrick sent a dark glance in the direction in which the girls had disappeared. He could still smell magnolias beside him. "She agreed to marry a man she doesn't know, to serve her own purposes."

Sin nodded and studied him levelly. "Isn't that what you're doing?"

"I'm trying to save a beautiful old inn that four generations of my family have loved and dedicated their lives to.''

''Why's she doing it?''

Patrick hesitated. He'd trust Paul Sinclair with everything he had including his life, but he divulged only half Gina's reason. He wasn't sure if he did it out of deference to her privacy or his unwillingness to be part of her baby plan.

''I told you about the thing with her business partner.'' Sin nodded. ''Well, she's flat broke, and her father refuses to help. He pawned her off on me until an inheritance from her grandmother becomes hers on her twenty-sixth birthday.''

''When is that?''

''Next March. Her plan is that we…help each other out for eleven months. Then both of us will have what we want.''

''You haven't made any dumb marriage-of-convenience agreements, like separate beds or anything like that?''

''No.'' Patrick reached for his water glass and studied it earnestly. ''Quite the opposite, in fact.''

Sin leaned forward in grinning interest. ''Really? Want to elaborate?''

Patrick gave him a studied look and shook his head. ''No. It's all very complex, but it's less than a year. I can handle it.''

''Just another skirmish,'' Sin said knowingly. ''You think this is going to be like any other battle where all you have to do is go in armed and ready and determined to be tougher than the enemy.''

''Don't knock it,'' Patrick said. ''It works.''

Sin leaned toward him earnestly. ''It works on other men. It does not work on women. Dealing with a woman that way would be like…like sending a military band to deal with guerrillas. She'll clean your clock." He straightened and grinned. "Then again, I think that could be a good thing. You need loosening up."

"So I can be like you?" Patrick challenged. "Going from woman to woman, looking for what you can't find because your life-style is *too* loose?"

Something altered subtly in Sin's eyes, and Patrick immediately regretted the gibe. He knew better than anyone why Sin was the way he was.

"Look, I—" he began.

"What I meant was," Sin interrupted him, dismissing any suggestion of hurt feelings with a swipe of his hand, "you might get something out of this. Relax and let yourself feel something." He paused and added quietly, seriously, "She has feelings for you."

"You're crazy."

"I can see it in her eyes."

"If that were true, it would only be because I can give her what she wants for a year."

"Because she needs something you have," Sin corrected with uncharacteristic gravity. "I recognize the look. I'll wager she was raised just like I was—alone. She needs a friend—just like I did."

The subject was dropped as the waiter arrived with a champagne bucket. The women returned to the table as the waiter popped the cork.

Patrick watched Gina laughing with Bobbi and felt that strange disruption she consistently caused in him. For a man whose entire adult life had required a brain and a body that functioned sharply and in harmony, the reaction was upsetting.

Then she turned to him, still laughing as Sin leaned across Bobbi and said something that made even the waiter laugh. She raised her glass, her expression sobering as her eyes met his.

He saw the look Sin had talked about—had seen it four days ago when they'd met. He didn't understand it, wasn't even sure he wanted to be needed in the way the look suggested, but he'd promised, and he took his responsibilities seriously.

He raised his glass in response, smiling. Her eyes brightened. Four glasses clinked together over the middle of the table. "To Gina and Patrick," Sin said, "and much happiness."

"To the middle of the rainbow," Bobbi said.

Sin lowered his glass and frowned at her. "The middle? Isn't the traditional wish for what lies in the pot of gold at the *end* of the rainbow?"

"Gina doesn't think so," Bobbi explained. "Her family has the pot of gold, and it's not what it's...cracked up to...be." She faltered as Gina caught her eye with a faintly embarrassed glance. "Well, there's nothing wrong with that," Bobbi said defensively. "I think you've got the right idea." She looked from Sin to Patrick. "She always says that getting what you want is like sitting on top, right in the middle of the bow."

Sin smiled at Gina and raised his glass again. "As another resident of the 'pot,' I concur. To the middle of the rainbow."

Glasses clinked again and everyone drank a toast.

"Are you going to take time and honeymoon along the way?" Sin asked.

"No time," Patrick said, giving him a dirty look. "All my crews are back to work. I should be there to supervise."

"So you're driving up the middle? Interstate 5?"

Patrick shook his head. "No, 101. I have to pick up new oak doors for the main building."

Sin closed his eyes and shook his head. "You're going to travel the California and Oregon coasts, a thousand miles of the most beautiful scenery God ever made, and I'll bet you'll still keep to a schedule."

"We're both anxious to get to Candle Bay," Gina said quietly.

Patrick saw the quick glance Bobbi sent Gina that Gina returned with the bland arch of an eyebrow. When she glanced his way and found him watching her, something disturbed the careful neutrality in her eyes and he saw something secretive there. Then she smiled at him and turned her attention to the menu.

THE GIRLS HUGGED goodbye while Sin and Patrick leaned patiently on the truck's front fender.

"God, I hope they don't start crying," Sin said. "I don't know how to handle it when they cry. And I have to take Bobbi home."

"Well, here's your opportunity to offer sympathy and comfort and turn her mood into one you know you can deal with."

Sin gave him a wry glance. "Don't get condescending with me because you're taking a wife home and not a stranger."

Patrick elbowed him and grinned. "Come on, you've never met a stranger. I think she likes you already."

Sin turned to study Bobbi with a narrowed glance as she and Gina walked arm in arm toward the truck. "Interesting woman," he said thoughtfully.

Patrick thought he could agree, though Sin found all women interesting. He straightened away from the fender as the girls joined them. They both looked a little grim, he thought. He'd observed how close they were that morning and how much they meant to each other.

Instinctively he put an arm around Gina as she came to stand beside him.

"Sin's coming to visit for the inn's yearly Memorial Day Weekend celebration," he said, surprised by the need to make her smile. "He could bring Bobbi with him if she can take the time."

He was rewarded when the girls exchanged hopeful smiles, and Gina looked up at him with gratitude. "I'd love that," she said.

He opened the passenger-side door and put her into the truck. Then he turned to give Bobbi a quick hug.

"You take good care of Gina," she said gravely, sounding a little, he thought, as though he were taking her off to war.

"I will," he promised. "And in exchange, I want you to keep an eye on Sin for me. He tends to get into trouble."

Bobbi looked from one man to the other. "What kind of trouble?"

Sin unashamedly wrapped his arms around Patrick. "You should talk," he said under his breath. "Which one of us ended up married?" Then he stepped back and clapped Patrick on the shoulder. "Take care. Call if you need legal advice."

"Right." Patrick climbed into the cab of the truck, backed out of the parking lot, then waved with Gina as he moved slowly toward the street. A final glimpse into the rearview mirror as he pulled out into the traffic showed Bobbi turning tearfully into Sin's shoulder and his arms closing around her. He guessed that in a matter of minutes Sin would have Gina's friend smiling once again.

PATRICK CONCENTRATED on the traffic as he turned onto the freeway. He waited until he'd slipped into the stream of cars moving sixty-five miles an hour before he glanced at Gina. She was staring moodily out the side window.

"Regrets?" he asked.

She turned to him, an eyebrow raised. "No. You?"

He shook his head. "I'm the one with a check in my pocket."

"And a wife."

"I'm assuming there'll be advantages to that as well as responsibilities."

She shifted, turning to face him. He heard the smile in her voice as he concentrated on the traffic.

"I told you that I'm a good cook, but don't count on breakfast because I'm a sack rat. Nothing happens that I care about before 8:00 a.m."

He checked the mirror to pass a pickup losing a top layer of trash and slid her a grin as he maneuvered. "Breakfast is my favorite meal. Do we need a counselor already?"

"Of course not," she said amiably. "You can fix it for me, and I'll prepare the other two meals. What time are you up?"

"Five-thirty," he replied, relaxing as the traffic moved comfortably.

She made a little sound of distress and teased, "You can just leave me something I can microwave." She added as an afterthought, "Do we have a microwave?"

"We do. The house is equipped with all the conveniences, it's just that the structure itself was built in 1887 and needs a lot of work. The plumbing and wiring are in desperate need of updating, too. On a scale of one to ten, if your father's place is a ten, mine's about a two."

"I make a point of ignoring scales of all kinds," she said, then she daintily covered her mouth and gave a great yawn.

He glanced away from the road to let his eyes run the length of her trim body in amazement. "No wonder. That was quite a lunch you packed away. You didn't tell me you have an appetite like a longshoreman."

"There's a lot I haven't told you," she said, finding a weird kind of relief in the veiled honesty. She batted her eyelashes at him. "A woman has to maintain an air of mystery, you know. Otherwise, what's to keep you interested? Although I don't suppose a marine wants that kind of a woman, does he? I mean, as a former officer in the corps, you would probably look for a woman who can take orders and hop to."

He considered that a moment, then inclined his head in a casual gesture. "As a former officer in the corps," he replied, "I know how to make anyone, woman or marine, do what I want whether they're willing to or not. In fact, the challenge of going head to head—" there was a brief, suggestive pause "—or whatever is at issue...is more satisfying than an easy victory."

Something inside her was warned and excited at the same time. "Have you ever had a serious relationship?"

"No," he replied. "No time. Six months here, a year there. It doesn't make for lasting liaisons."

She yawned again.

"Why don't you doze for a couple of hours," he suggested. "We'll stop for the night near San Luis Obispo."

"You can go farther if you want to." She tried to sound casual, without motive. "I know you're in a hurry to get there."

"Another few hours won't make much difference."

"You need help navigating or anything?"

"No. We'll stay on 101 all the way."

"If you're sure." She leaned down in her seat, then turned to grin at him. "You promise to wake me when you stop for dinner?"

He had to grin back. "You're not thinking about dinner already?"

She tucked her feet up on the seat and took the jacket he'd discarded between them and put it over her. "I'm always wondering about my next meal. Must be some primal thing that harkens back to my great-great-grandfather Raleigh who lost everything in a drought. He and his family ate nothing but potatoes and root vegetables one whole winter." She shuddered dramatically, then yawned again. "I can tolerate anything as long as I have a bag of potato chips and shortbread cookies."

"Between meals."

"Right." She sounded as though she was already drifting.

He glanced her way. A wave of dark hair fell over her cheek; her eyelashes lay against its pallor, impossibly dark and long; and her lips, pink and full, pursed together as though some troublesome dream had already claimed her.

He reached out to draw the jacket up when it slipped off the slope of her shoulder. She snuggled into it, and her frown turned to a smile. Unable to stop himself, he rubbed a knuckle along her satin cheek. He was suddenly consumed with wondering if her skin would feel like that everywhere.

He had to drag his mind back to the traffic to avoid driving up the back of the trash-laden pickup that had somehow gotten ahead of him again. Regina Raleigh, he

thought, then corrected himself—Regina Gallagher—
could be dangerous to his health.

He had no idea how prophetic the thought was.

Chapter Three

It was twilight. San Luis Obispo stretched out along the purple hills, strung with neon signs and street- and traffic lights. The night was balmy, the air perfumed with orange blossoms from an orchard that dotted one of the hills in a perfectly symmetrical pattern. Gina, who had just awakened, smiled at the fragrance. Orange blossoms, the classic wedding flower. Nature was teasing her.

Gina looked at the man beside her. In a navy blue cotton sweater and jeans, his dark hair rakishly disturbed by his open window, he looked like an ad for every woman's preconceived notion of the Northwest man. Sometime while she'd been asleep, he'd rolled up the sleeves of the sweater, revealing sturdy forearms that reacted as he controlled the wheel.

She could envision those biceps under a plaid shirt, chopping wood or reeling in a net gorged with fish. A plain gold band on his left hand matched the wider band on hers. Married, she thought in renewed wonder. She was married to him.

On the heels of that realization, she suddenly thought of lying in arms that had never held her, under hands that had never touched her. She was simultaneously eager to know what it would be like to make love with Patrick Gallagher and appalled that she'd used such means to get what she needed.

"You *are* a sack rat," Patrick observed as he turned the car into the driveway of a large motel whose marquee boasted a maximum of comfort and a minimum of noise.

Unsettled by her thoughts, Gina looked at him blankly for a moment.

He pulled up in front of the office and turned off the motor, frowning at her vaguely alarmed expression.

"You all right?" he asked.

She nodded quickly. "Just disoriented. What time is it?"

"Ten of seven. You slept quite a while. This doesn't mean you'll be watching midnight movies and racking up cable charges on the hotel television, does it?"

He was testing the waters. She looked nervous suddenly, and he was surprised. She'd been so matter-of-fact about the baby thing, so unconcerned that lovemaking would be a part of their relationship.

She smiled, but even on such short acquaintance, he knew it wasn't genuine. "No," she answered. "I spent most of last night packing and taking care of last-minute business. That was catch-up sleep."

The lady was frightened, he decided. That didn't upset him. It almost made her seem more normal.

"Want to come inside with me?" he asked. "Or wait in the car?"

"I'll wait," she said.

As he disappeared inside the office, she leaned back in her seat with a ragged sigh. God. She should have stayed awake. She should have been watching. She looked around at the cars already parked for the night in the huge lot around which the motel was built. No black Mercedes. She twisted in her seat to look over her shoulder.

Traffic sped past on the town's main thoroughfare. Nothing seemed out of the ordinary.

Patrick slipped into the truck and she started guiltily, as though her thoughts were written on her forehead.

"Relax," he said with a grin, dropping their room key into her lap. "I promise to beat you only with a little stick."

She returned his grin, hoping he'd hold to that promise when and if he ever found out why she'd really married him.

The room was spacious and immaculate. Gina's discomfort swelled. Patrick had placed their bags on the foot of the king-size bed and was reading a visitor's guide on the counter beside the television. *I should tell him,* she thought. *It would be so easy to just say it now.*

"We have Mexican food, Chinese food, French cuisine, seafood, barbecue and any number of fast-food restaurants." He turned to her before she could speak. "What sounds good?"

He was very large she realized, studying him in the concentration of light from a wall lamp near his head, very thick in the shoulders, very lean in the hips. From the lamp his dark hair picked up bourbon-colored highlights. His cheekbones and jaw were sharply defined. He looked gorgeous and dangerous...and she felt guilt-ridden and very nervous.

Patrick could hear the hum stretching from her to him. Though she stood in the shadows and he couldn't see her eyes, he could feel them on him. Her nervousness was a tangible thing. That was something he decided to take care of immediately. She was his now, and the unorthodox circumstances that had brought them together no longer mattered. They were married, and he'd never been half-committed to anything in his life.

He reached into the shadows and pulled her to him. "Relax," he chided quietly, holding her loosely in the circle of his arms. "The hard part's over. We've done the deal. All we have to do now is pretend fate brought us together rather than convenience. As though our eyes met across a crowded room."

It would have to be her secret that that was precisely how she felt about their relationship.

"It's just..." she said softly, aware of his thigh against hers, her breasts a hairbreadth from his chest, "that...doing the deal...is scarier than planning it was."

"You've read my file," he said, brushing a wave of thick dark hair out of her face. "Sin assured you I'm a nice guy." He grinned and she smiled. Then he added lightly, "All you have to do is be completely obedient and we'll get along beautifully."

Her smile became a laugh. "Because I *have* read your file, I know you're not teasing." She looked up into his eyes. "I'm sure from what my father's told you about me, you know that's a futile hope."

He didn't seem concerned. "We'll see. I can be pretty persuasive."

"Marine charm backed by a missile launcher?"

He shook his head, saying softly, "I have my own arsenal." And then he opened his mouth over hers again as he'd done on the lawn. That kiss had been meant to alarm her. This one had a coaxing, taunting purpose, and he used it with the skill of a master.

Her whole body tensed, though all he touched was the tip of his tongue to the inside of her mouth. He explored lightly, playfully, and she found herself leaning into him until her mouth was exploring his.

Then she felt his hand flatten against her back and draw her closer. She gasped and he swallowed the sound as he wrapped her tightly against him and took the kiss higher, deeper, farther than she'd thought a kiss could go. She lost awareness of everything but his roving hand and the beat of her body, rising and quickening.

Then he drew away and gave her a quick, punctuating kiss. She took a step back, annoyed, as she interpreted the point of the lesson.

"You want me to see what I'll be missing if I don't cooperate?"

He held the point of her chin between his thumb and forefinger and studied her face slowly, lingeringly, as though something there read very clearly.

"No," he said, pinching her chin, "I want you to know what you'll gain if you do. Ready to get something to eat?"

HE MADE HER PICK the restaurant, ordered everything she asked for down to the green-tea ice cream with almond cookies, and talked honestly about the hotel and what he intended to do with it. She had difficulty sustaining her annoyance. In fact, he was being so agreeable she began to have renewed confidence in her cleverness in selecting him.

"Tell me about Sin," she said when the waitress took their plates away and they sat over a fresh pot of tea. "How did you meet?"

"In school," he replied, the tips of his large fingers turning the tiny handleless Chinese cup. "We were roommates in the dorm at the University of Puget Sound." He laughed, still staring into the tea. "Hated each other on sight. I took him for a society snob and he thought I was a country rube. Then I explained the theory of relativity—or what we know of it—to him, and he backed me up in a brawl in the cafeteria. We've been friends ever since.''

"A brawl over what?'' she asked.

"What else? A woman, or in this case a nineteen-year-old cheerleader I had just dated that some jerk tried to tell me was...'' He hesitated, choosing his words.

Gina smiled, charmed that he edited his language because of her presence. Men seldom did that anymore.

"I understand,'' Gina said. "Was she?''

"Yes.''

"But not with you?''

"I hadn't asked her.'' He sipped his tea and grinned. "I *was* a rube. Anyway, getting back to Sin, he always had money and I always had a place to go to on holidays.''

"Is Sin orphaned?''

Patrick shook his head. "Abandoned, but not orphaned. His father runs a powerful international law firm, and his mother's from an old family in Philadelphia. He globe hops and she raises money for all the important causes.''

Gina nodded sympathetically. "I can relate to that. It's hard to be the last thing on your parents' mind.''

"I think your father cares for you,'' Patrick said. "He's gone to a lot of trouble to find you a husband.''

"Mostly he didn't want an indiscreet daughter to turn him into another press powder keg.'' She toasted Patrick with her cup. "So he called in the marines.''

Some subtle change was taking place in her. He didn't know what had precipitated it or where it was leading, but she was getting edgy.

"I'm a civilian now," he reminded quietly.

She sighed. "And I'm a bride. Isn't life interesting?"

He saw the flash of concern in her eyes and decided to approach it head-on. "Is that what's bothering you? Are you afraid of going to bed with me?"

She held his gaze as she sipped more tea. Then she put the cup down and reminded him quietly, "I'm the one who asked *you* for a baby, remember?"

"You're also the one who said doing the deed is scarier than planning the action."

Also harder on the conscience, she thought. If she told him about the possible danger from the black Mercedes, he could have her back home in a few hours.

If she remained in Los Angeles, the press would continue to haunt her, embarrassing her father as he began his campaign and making her own efforts to reestablish her reputation more difficult.

No. She needed this passport to Oregon and anonymity. But she wasn't going to bed with Patrick until she could explain everything. And she couldn't do it tonight.

"I...ah..." She rubbed a stiffening spot between her eyebrows. "I'm not scared, I'm..." She looked at him candidly. "I'm just not ready yet."

He held her gaze, his own dark and questioning but calm. She was beginning to like that about him.

"My stake in this," he said, "was the money, and I have it. Your risk was to come with me to Oregon. Whether you spend the nights in my bed or not is your call."

Perversely Gina found his tolerance a relief and a disappointment.

"Thank you," she said in a tone that didn't sound grateful.

PATRICK TURNED the truck into the motel parking lot, braking to a stop in front of the office and turning off the motor. "I'll get a second room," he said. "I'll just be a minute."

When he disappeared inside, Gina leapt out of the truck feeling quarrelsome and edgy. She headed for the room they already had, unwilling to examine the reason for her mood.

She found the third door from the end, then groped in her purse for the key Patrick had given her. It didn't fit. She looked at it in consternation, then at the room number. The brass numbers on the door said 200. The painted number on the tab on the key chain was clearly marked with a two and a zero, but the third digit was just a curve at top and bottom; the middle was worn away. Is it 203, she wondered? Or 208?

She walked along the gallery, her irritation temporarily supplanted by concern about finding their room. Gingerly, she tried her key in room 203.

The door flew open. Two men wearing black fezzes with a dagger symbol and silver tassels on them looked back at her. One was short and stout with a cigar in his mouth, the other tall and spare in a T-shirt and dress pants. Both were obviously inebriated.

"Well, aren't you a looker!" The stout man said with a broad wink. "Worth waiting for, after all. Come on in." He grabbed her wrist and tried to tug her into the room.

For an instant she thought they had something to do with Yale or whoever owned the black Mercedes. They'd found her!

"No!" she shouted, pulling frantically against him.

"Honey, this is the right room," the taller man said

urgently. "Gus and Billy from Eureka. We sent for you. Armstrong from the Fresno chapter set it up."

Gina glared at him.

"Got your money right here." He held up a spray of twenty-dollar bills.

A corner of Gina's mind was thinking this would make a hilarious story to tell Bobbi. The two inebriated gentlemen had nothing to do with Yale. It was a simple case of mistaken identity. But they were instilling panic in her, anyway.

She was tired and cranky, and her usually clear mind wasn't up at that moment to being mistaken for a hooker by two camel dealers from Eureka.

PATRICK TOPPED the stairs and rounded the corner just in time to catch a glimpse of a slim figure at the other end of the gallery pulling against a meaty hand inside a room.

"No!" he heard her say, her voice high and shaded with fear. "I'm not who you—"

"Now look, little lady," the stout man said around his cigar as he yanked Gina into the room. "We been waiting for you for more than an hour. First you're late and now you're teasing?"

She was now beyond finding anything amusing in the situation. "If you don't let me go," she said slowly, "I'm going to scream for my husband."

The taller man looked pleased. "The 'my husband is just outside the door' game. I like that one!"

But the stout man was looking at her narrowly, trying to push the door closed. "Your husband?"

The door shot back on him with a crash, knocking him onto the foot of a twin bed. "Her husband," Patrick said.

"Patrick!" Gina went to him in blind relief, her annoyance forgotten. He drew her into one arm, his eyes going over the two occupants of the room.

"What's going on?" he asked with ominous quiet.

"It's all right," she said quickly. "It was all a mistake. I misread my key and tried to get into the wrong room. They thought I was…oh, here." She stuffed the roll of twenties into Gus's hand. Or was he Billy? More than anything else she wanted to get out of that room.

He shook his head in disappointment. "You really aren't…?"

"She isn't," Patrick said quietly, looking from one man to the other. "I could call the police to find her for you." It was a threat rather than a suggestion.

The men looked at each other. The taller one smiled uncomfortably. "We'll wait. Sorry, little lady."

Patrick pushed Gina onto the gallery and closed the door with a slam. He unlocked room 208 and pointed her inside.

She stopped in the middle of the room, torn between laughter and a good cry. All in all, this wasn't the wedding night most girls dreamed about.

He frowned at her, hands on his hips. "You might think twice," he said, "about running off in a strange place among people you don't know."

She sighed. "I wanted to take a shower. I didn't expect to get the wrong room."

"I gave you a key."

She handed it to him. "The number's rubbed off. That's why I tried it on the wrong room."

She expected more condemnation. When he simply tossed the key with his jacket onto the bed and went to the coffeepot in the dressing room, she felt herself relax.

"No Vacancy sign went up while we were at dinner,"

he said over his shoulder. "You can't have your own room, after all."

Having to share this room was both good and bad news. She wasn't wild about being alone in a room if the Mercedes had followed her. But she also wasn't anxious to have to find a solution to sharing *this* room.

"Want some coffee?" he asked. "You can have first go at the shower while I fix it."

"Please." While she rooted through her bag for her nightgown and robe she tried frantically to think of a sophisticated way to bring up the problem of sleeping arrangements.

"We'll have to share the bed," he said, rather absently she thought, as he filled the carafe with water, then plugged in the cord. "But it's a king. Room for a lot of caution between us." He grinned. "I can be trusted if you can."

His easy dismissal of what had seemed to her an insurmountable problem set her further off balance. She was now sure of what she'd suspected when she'd first seen Patrick Gallagher—she'd never met another man like him.

WELL, he'd thought he could be trusted. Patrick poured coffee into a cup at the dressing-room counter, unable to keep his eyes from the sight reflected in the mirror of Gina walking to the bed. She wore a white silk thing that fell to her ankles and clung like a second, sinuous skin to the swell of her bottom. She bent to fluff her pillow. Coffee spilled onto his hand.

He swore silently and mopped up the mess with paper towels stacked on the corner of the counter. He carried the cup to her and placed it on the bedside table. His eyes fell to the soft ivory flesh disappearing into the white silk, then filling the fabric with a shimmering full-ness that threatened to steal his sanity.

"Thank you," she said, warily tugging the blankets up and holding them to her breastbone. "Shower's all yours."

"Right." He handed her the remote control for the television. "I've had my coffee. You can refill with what's left in the pot if you want it."

Then he went into the bathroom, leaned into the shower and turned on the cold water, not bothering with the hot.

FEIGNING SLEEP, Gina saw Patrick through the fringe of her eyelashes as he came out of the bathroom. He wore his underwear rather than pajamas, simple cotton briefs and a V-neck T-shirt. As he flipped off the bathroom light and came toward the bed in the glow from the television, she saw the thin fabric of the shirt strained across a broad expanse of shoulder and chest.

When he picked up the remote and turned to click off the television, she saw the taut muscles of his buttocks move under the briefs, before the room fell to darkness.

She closed her eyes tightly and tried to clear her mind. He was so casual about this. Surely she could be the same. But her heart was thudding.

She felt the mattress take his weight, felt him shift once to get comfortable, then there was silence.

ANOTHER SMOOTH MOVE, Gallagher, Patrick said to him-self several hours later when the lights were out and he'd been lying beside his bride for ninety-seven minutes. He knew exactly how long it had been because he was counting. It had kept his mind occupied. No, he consid-ered on second thought—it hadn't.

They'd begun this ordeal on their respective sides of the large bed. Gina had politely said good-night, turned her back on him and turned out the light. Ten minutes later he'd heard her even breathing.

In the last hour, he'd been acutely aware of every inch of progress she'd unconsciously made toward him. Restless, she'd tossed and turned, coming ever closer until seven minutes ago—when she'd burrowed into his side and finally stopped moving.

He hadn't budged, either. He'd been afraid to breathe, afraid the cannoning beat of his heart would wake her.

If it did, he couldn't be held responsible for what might happen. He'd married her, after all. She'd asked him to give her a baby! That implied a willingness, even an eagerness to be made love to.

He closed his eyes tightly and tried to clear his mind, but his body remained a raging frame of awakened testosterone.

Chapter Four

Patrick opened his eyes, stared at the pleated floral drapes and wondered where he was. Before his brain could give him an answer, his body became aware of another cause for confusion.

There was a warm, soft pressure against his back. A small, sleepy sound came from it, then a sinuous stirring against his hip and along his leg. There was a burrowing action against his shoulder blade, then stillness.

He remembered.

He resisted the urge to leap out of bed by reminding himself of all the conditions that attended this union. It was only for a year, she'd promised to stay out of his way, but she wanted him to make a baby with her. What more could a man ask for? Lack of permanence, freedom from restraint and sexual privileges. He was in clover.

However, he'd been a soldier long enough not to trust the obvious. The fact that they hadn't made love last night was proof that all the advantages weren't on his side.

There was a sudden, startled movement behind him and Gina sat up taking the blanket with her. He turned onto his back and looked up at her. Her dark hair was a silky tumble around her shoulders, bare except for the thin straps of a nightgown and the blanket clutched at her breast. Her gray eyes, barely darker than opal, blinked twice then settled on him with wary uncertainty.

He felt a sharp pang of lust coupled with a strange disorientation. Those eyes had talked him into this deal. They drew him, snared him and confused him while curiously keeping him at a distance. He should never have done this. He would live to regret it, he was sure.

But the deal was done, and he had to find a way to live with it. He suppressed a chuckle. Ironic choice of words.

He crossed his hands behind his head on the pillow and smiled. "Good morning, Mrs. Gallagher."

SOMETIME DURING the night he'd tossed aside the shirt. Gina knew he'd look like that without it—muscled, broadly proportioned, nothing lean or wiry about him.

He still had a trace of tan, probably from the months in the Middle East, and a wedge of dark, curling hair swept down his chest, over the jut of ribs to his flat stomach, then disappeared under the blanket.

Clutching the covers with one hand, she raised the other to brush the hair out of her eyes.

"Good morning," she replied, making herself smile. She was taut and nervous despite a good night's sleep.

Somehow, in the light of day, that tough, solid body suggested danger rather than comfort. Still clutching the blanket, she reached to the foot of the bed for the white silk robe that matched her peignoir.

"I like to have first dibs on the bathroom in the morning," she said lightly, hoping to assert herself. She pulled the robe on, then yanked the blanket out from under it when it was tied. She tossed the covers aside and stood, feeling amazing relief at putting the width of the bed between them. ''Although I imagine your house has two bathrooms?''

He propped up on an elbow, his lazy dark eyes roving her warm cheeks and knowing, she was sure, what was going on in her mind. ''Sorry, just one. It's an old house. But I'll get to that when I can. How long are you going to be?''

''Fifteen minutes,'' she replied, backing toward the bathroom. ''Twenty if my hair doesn't cooperate.''

He glanced at his watch, then his eyes lifted to her hair. She knew it probably looked like a broom in a state of apoplexy.

He smiled. ''Fifteen. Tie it up in a ponytail or something. I'd like to be on the road by nine.''

GINA CHECKED the light on her curling iron. She wouldn't wear her hair in a ponytail for anyone, and she was sure she could curl her hair out here in the bedroom before he was finished in the shower.

Feeling domestic, she straightened the covers on the bed and opened the drapes—and screamed.

Her heart pounded hard enough to choke her. A man was staring at her. He was tall and big, wearing a tweed sport coat a size too small. His eyes were large and blue and bulging, and his wide mouth drooped. He stood about six foot five.

Beside him was a much smaller, thinner man, whose beady dark eyes bored into Gina's, and whose lipless mouth curved into a leering smile. She knew without being told how they'd gotten there—the black Mercedes.

She screamed again and ran to the door to replace the chain lock. But before she could reach it, the door burst inward with a crash and the large man was upon her in an instant. He manacled her throat with one beefy hand

and bent her backward over the table. The other man snapped the drapes closed and leaned over the big one's shoulder.

"Where is it?" he asked.

Rapidly losing air and composure, Gina went slack under his hand. Beyond the bathroom door, the shower still drummed loudly. Patrick probably didn't even know she was in trouble.

She wrapped both hands around the meaty wrist at her throat and gasped, "Where's…what?"

"Don't get cute. You know what I mean."

She wished she did. "I don't," she gasped again. "Tell me." Little sparkly things were beginning to float before her eyes.

"Can I choke her, Larry?" the big man asked eagerly, his slack mouth taking on an anticipatory smile. "Can I?"

"Easy, Shrimp," Larry replied, leaning menacingly closer to her near-unconscious form on the table. "It's better when you give these things time."

Then everything erupted. Larry's body flew and Shrimp freed her, straightening up in surprise. Shrimp took a blow full in the face from Patrick's booming fist and wasn't even rocked.

Patrick, barefoot and barechested, hesitated in surprise. Before Shrimp could react, Patrick hit him again.

This time Shrimp blinked and shook his head. He looked at Larry crumpled on the floor, then at Patrick with childlike bad temper. Gina heard Patrick's round oath as he backed away and squared off.

"You hurt Larry," Shrimp accused. "I'm going to hurt you!"

Shrimp advanced on Patrick like Goliath after David,

and Gina tried desperately to drag in air and clear her brain. Then she remembered the curling iron.

When Gina reached them, Shrimp had big hands around Patrick's throat, completely oblivious to the blows being delivered to his midsection.

She put the hot curling iron to the back of Shrimp's hand and heard a satisfying sizzle followed immediately by an indignant yelp. Shrimp dropped that hand from Patrick.

As Shrimp shook the offended appendage, Gina applied the curling iron to the other hand with the same result. Now free, Patrick continued to batter at Shrimp. Gina ran around behind them to open the door.

Shrimp's long reach caught Patrick's throat again. This time Gina applied the hot barrel of the curling iron to the side of Shrimp's neck. He roared in pain and backed away, looking like a child surprised by another's unkindness. She advanced on him again. This time Patrick grabbed her wrist and slung her out of the way.

Larry appeared suddenly from behind them, running through the door and shouting for Shrimp to follow him. The big man lumbered after his cohort, seeming more than anxious to leave.

Patrick went to the phone while Gina locked the door. "God," he said, quickly reviewing the instructions taped to the table for a call to the desk. "Beirut wasn't this bad! Hookers and johns one minute, thieves and muggers the next. You okay?"

Gina put a hand down on the phone to break the connection. "I'm fine. Let's just go before Shrimp and Larry come back with reinforcements."

"Who?"

"Shrimp's the big guy." She was wrestling Patrick for the receiver as they spoke. "Larry's the other one.

Come on. It's quarter of nine and you wanted to be on the road by nine.''

Patrick yanked the receiver from her and held her away with his forearm across her chest from shoulder to shoulder. ''Gina, two thugs tried to rob us. We should report it to the management and the police.''

''No!'' she shouted. ''Please, Patrick, let's just go. My bag's already in the truck.'' When he tried to redial, she added anxiously, ''They're not thieves. At least, not the way you think.''

He frowned, his complete attention suddenly focused on her. He put the receiver down. ''What do you mean? You know those guys?''

''Not exactly.''

He replaced the receiver, his frown deepening. He folded his arms over his bare chest. ''How exactly?''

She sighed frustratedly and caught one of his arms in both hands. ''If I promise to explain in the truck, will you come now? Please?''

HE KNEW IT. A deal too good to be true always was. He flew around the room with her for two or three minutes getting all the rest of their possessions back into their bags and their bags into the truck.

''Can I take a minute to put shoes and socks on?'' he asked, sitting on the edge of the bed, prepared to do just that.

''You can do that in the truck,'' she said, snatching up his striped tube socks and Nike running shoes and leading the way to the door. ''I'll drive.''

''I'M A VERY competent driver,'' Gina said cheerfully, going much too fast along a truck route that led to the intersection of Highways 1 and 101. That little fracas had completely relieved her feelings of tension and nervousness, and though she should have been frightened that whoever Shrimp and Larry were working for had trailed her to the motel, she felt exhilarated instead that she and Patrick, together, had escaped them. "And you're very good with your fists," she said, feeling magnanimous. "Larry's probably still wondering what happened."

"Pull over," Patrick said.

"What?" Gina glanced at him as she braked for a truck carrying the famous Salinas Valley artichokes. He had a foot propped against the dashboard while he tied his shoe. His return glance was quiet and scary. Temper simmered under his cool control. "Patrick, we have to put some distance between us and them. We have to..."

He didn't bother to argue. He simply glanced into his side mirror at the traffic behind them, then put a hand on the wheel and turned them off the road and onto a long driveway that led to a group of warehouses.

"Stop," he said.

She braked and turned off the ignition. She turned to him with a judicious expression. "That was a dangerous thing to do. You should never take the wheel from another person."

"When a person lies to you," he said, "you don't usually want to follow where she leads. Now, who the hell were those guys and how do you know them?"

"I don't know them," she corrected, then rested her wrists on the steering wheel and stared through the windshield at the poplars that stood tall and green beyond the warehouses. She admitted reluctantly, "I just know they're after me."

"After you," he repeated, obviously waiting for her to explain.

When she couldn't, she just nodded and confirmed with a clear gray gaze on him, "After me."

He was silent a moment, then asked pithily, "Why?"

She shook her head. "That I don't know."

"Then how do you know they're after you, if you don't know *why* they're after you?"

"Because someone's been calling me and not saying anything. Because a black Mercedes has been following me for about a month. I had no idea who was in it until this morning."

He made a sound of impatience. "Did you call the police?"

She turned to him, her expression telling him she knew a little more about this than he did. "Yes. You know how everyone responds to nuisance phone calls? As though the one complaining is the problem. No one can do anything about it. You should hear what they have to say about my being followed by a black car that shows up in the damnedest places at the oddest times. Then they tell me they read all about me in the paper. That I'm the one who stole the Ming, the Renoir and the diamond necklace. They suggest that I'm delusional."

Patrick saw genuine distress in her eyes. He didn't want it to complicate his anger. "Surely your father has some connections that would help you out."

She studied her hands. "I haven't told him." When he responded impatiently, she said loudly, "Well, he wouldn't want to hear it. Trust me on that. He's about to launch a campaign, remember? The last thing he'd want is trouble from the daughter who's always embarrassing him."

Patrick remembered his conversation with Wyatt Raleigh. She was probably right.

She sighed. "No, this is something I have to do my-self. I just want to get away from them until they realize they have the wrong person. Or that I don't have what they think I have."

He stared at her for a moment without reaction, then he said, as though he finally understood the bottom line on this unconventional deal, "And I was your way out!"

He pushed his door open and stepped out of the truck. Sure he meant to abandon her, Gina followed, running to catch up with him as his long stride ate up the asphalt drive.

"Where are you going?" She reached a hand out, intending to pull him to a stop, but the look he gave her forced her to reconsider.

"For a walk," he replied.

"Now?"

"Either I walk off energy..." he said, a muscle ticking in his jaw, "or tomorrow morning they find your body in a Dumpster."

She continued to run along with him. "Look, Patrick, I know I didn't handle this the right way, but I..."

He had stopped so quickly, she was three steps ahead of him and still talking before she realized he was no longer beside her. She backtracked warily. His expression could have carved stone.

When she stood in front of him, he said gravely, "You lied to me. You and your father intended to use me."

"No," she denied. "I told you my father didn't know. He genuinely wanted to find me a husband he knew would take care of me, at least until my inheritance comes through. He trusted you. He didn't use you. And, anyway..." Guilt weighed heavily on her, but she folded her arms and looked back at him intrepidly. "You got half a million dollars."

"Like money and honesty are comparable." His expression made her lower her eyes, but only for a moment.

She put the shame she felt behind her, because she had to make him understand. She had to get to somewhere safe until her grandmother's money allowed her to start over. "It's a lot of money, Patrick. My father's a bold investor, but he's not stupid. Had I told you I needed a bodyguard to get me out of town and keep me safe, you'd have refused to marry me. When you did, my father probably would have turned you down. Where would honesty have gotten your precious Candle Bay Inn then?"

She had a point, and much as he hated to, he was forced to examine it. If it hadn't been for the check from Wyatt Raleigh, almost a century of Gallagher sweat and tears would have disintegrated into chapter eleven.

"All I did," she said, pressing her point with a cautious smile, "was save you from yourself. Now that you've got your money, you can keep the renovations going on the hotel and secure the season, and I'll help you start the best child-care facility any hotel ever had. All you have to do in return is keep the goons away from me."

He put his hands in his pockets and leaned his weight on his right foot. "I have the money," he said evenly. "I don't lose a thing if I let them have you."

She felt herself pale but answered quietly, "You'd lose peace with yourself, and for a man like you, that's a lot. You wouldn't do that."

He laughed ironically. "You overestimate my nobility, Gina."

She shook her head. "I don't think so. I read your

file, remember? Winner of the Bronze Star, for conspicuous courage.''

He started to walk again.

''You took a vow,'' Gina reminded him as she ran beside him, pressing her advantage. ''We're married. You can't just leave me. It wouldn't be right.''

''Right?'' He stopped again and caught her arm, his dark eyes boring into her cloudy gray gaze. ''As though you would know anything about what's right. You set me up, lied to me and played the role of lost little waif like a Hollywood veteran.''

She raised an eyebrow. ''Lost little waif?'' That wasn't the way she'd seen her performance.

He studied her a moment, as though perplexed. ''It was in your eyes,'' he said absently. ''This kind of... need.''

His gaze was so deep and dark that for a moment she lost herself in it. She lost connection with their surroundings, with the situation, with everything else but the gold flecks in the brown irises of his eyes.

Then he blinked once, straightened and squared his shoulders. She was forced to readjust to the here and now.

''You're telling me,'' he asked with cool distance, ''that you have no idea why those guys are after you?''

''I have a theory,'' she said, almost reluctant to share it. ''But it doesn't make sense.''

''What about you does? Let's have it.''

''Well, they may have been hired by Yale Gardner, my former partner.''

''Why?''

''I don't know.''

He shifted his weight again, studied the distance a moment, then looked back at her. ''You call that a theory? Theory is usually supported by reason. And, anyway, your father told me Gardner cleaned out your inventory and your bank account and took off for parts unknown.''

She nodded grimly. "He did. But I don't know how else to explain it. I have no other enemies.''

He laughed mirthlessly, turning back toward the truck at a reasonable pace. "Somehow I find that hard to believe.''

She turned with him. "You'll see for yourself. I'm really a very nice person.'' When he slanted her a doubtful glance, she returned a smile. "I'll make all this worth your while. I may have tricked you into this deal, but I'll keep my part of the bargain. When I'm not being chased by hoods, I'm an honest human being. I'm even fun to be with.''

"Apparently the conventioneers last night thought so, too.''

"That was a simple misunderstanding.''

"That was an indicator of things to come. You're trouble, Gina Raleigh, and I already have all the trouble I need.''

She stopped beside the truck and turned to face him. "I *am* trouble,'' she said. "My father's always said so. I attract it, even when I'm minding my own business. It's a fact I can't help. But you'd only have to put up with it for eleven months.'' She paused and lifted her chin. "And my name is Gina *Gallagher*.''

Patrick looked down at her, hands on his hips, waiting for his usually dependable brain to come up with a solution to the dilemma. But all he saw was a very pretty girl who now bore his name and still had that lost look in her eyes. Could it really be that the need in her was honest even if the woman wasn't?

If that were true, he couldn't in all conscience let himself off the hook. But he wasn't letting her off, either.

With a swift movement Gina hadn't seen coming, he grabbed her arm and backed her up against the truck door, planting a hand on the steel on either side of her head. Though her instinct was to flinch, she made herself look him in the eye as he leaned over her.

"There's implied honesty in all contracts, you know," he said with quiet intensity. "By rights, even a noble man can walk away from a contract in which he's been deceived."

That would be the end of everything. Gina swallowed. "In this case," she said, thinking fast and dangerously, "the noble man would be a foolish one. If you walk away now..." She hesitated, dropped her eyelashes significantly, then looked up at him with wide gray eyes and went on in an undertone, "You'll never know what you missed."

Long years of conditioned control prevented him from reacting to her suggestion. Everything he'd felt that morning when he'd awakened with her curled against his back came back to haunt him. He was beginning to wonder if half a million dollars would ever be worth the frustration.

"Please," he said dryly. "You needed more time, remember?"

She heaved a little sigh that he felt against his chin and said softly, "Tonight could be a new beginning. But not if you walk away."

His mind was made up.

"Oh, I don't intend to walk away." His eyes darkened when he saw hers flare with victory. She noted that subtle reaction and subsided when he moved even closer. "I'm going to get every last point of the contract that's coming to me, but if you lie to me again, we're history and you're on your own. Is that clear?''

She nodded, lowering her lashes this time so that the glow of success didn't show. ''You just have to put up with me for eleven months,'' she said, finally looking up at him again, her expression serene, ''and I'll walk out of your life. Hopefully, pregnant.''

He frowned. ''I said no baby.''

''I heard you.''

Patrick studied her calmly innocent expression and knew handling this woman was going to require every tactical skill he had. He straightened and lowered his arms. ''Get in the truck,'' he said.

She turned to open the driver's door, but he caught her arm and turned her to the passenger's side. ''From now on,'' he said, ''I'm in the driver's seat.''

Chapter Five

"You're taking Highway 1?" Gina asked in disapproval as Patrick took the marked turn that led them away from the pastoral stretch of Highway 101 through the Salinas Valley. "Have you ever driven 1?" Gina looked back over her shoulder at the traffic turning onto 101. "It's hours longer. It twists and turns and dips and climbs the Santa Lucia Range to its highest point. They make jokes about it. It's like driving the Alps!"

Patrick nodded, relaxing as the traffic thinned and the sun, now high in the sky, dappled the blue Pacific Ocean. "Sin and I drove it during spring break our senior year in college. The conditions will also make it difficult for whoever's after you to try anything on the highway. We'll have the cliff side. For them to mess with us, they'd have to take the water side and they're probably not that stupid." Then remembering Shrimp, he qualified that by saying, "Well, maybe the skinny guy isn't."

Resigned to her fate, Gina settled in her seat and relaxed. "His name's Larry."

"Right. I forgot you're on a first-name basis."

A sudden, vivid memory of the few moments Shrimp and Larry had had her bent backward over the motel table reminded her that she hadn't thanked Patrick for coming to her aid. "Thanks, by the way."

He set the cruise control and with the road ahead and behind them clear, gazed at the sparkling expanse of water. "For what?"

"A few more seconds with Shrimp's hand around my throat," she replied, "and you'd be a widower."

He glanced her way and smiled. It was the first smile he'd given her that expressed genuine amusement. She felt it warm her like the sun on the water. Until she realized it was probably thoughts of her death that had amused him. "Interesting prospect," he said, turning back to the road. "Have you had time to sign your life insurance over to me?"

She grinned grudgingly. "Sorry. But being a widower would still have its advantages. It would give you a great deal of appeal to young, single women. You could start fresh with some willowy blond thing bent on comforting you and who doesn't attract trouble or want a baby."

"I can do that in a year, anyway," he said. "I guess we'll just do our best to keep you alive."

"WE MISSED BREAKFAST," Patrick said, glancing at his watch. "Want to stop for an early lunch?" He turned briefly to give her a questioning look.

He was being remarkably civil, given the circumstances. She was anxious to cooperate.

"Please," she said with genuine enthusiasm. "I've usually had a full breakfast by now."

"We'll get a sandwich and walk along the beach. Stretch our legs."

He turned off the highway just beyond Cambria.

"Sounds good." She was already feeling stiff and confined.

"The only condition," he said, heading for the road that ran along the water, "is that you stay glued to me. No wandering off."

That condition had an appeal she chose not to consider at the moment. It was easy to agree to.

The small town faced the ocean and was set in a half-moon bay in the shelter of tall, steep bluffs. She gazed longingly at the inviting little shops as Patrick led the way to a fast-food restaurant near the water. When she paused to look into a bookstore window, he caught her hand and tugged her along with him. "No time for that," he said. "We need food, a little exercise, then we've got to get back on the road."

"Right." Her hand was enfolded in his much larger one, her shoulder bumping companionably against his upper arm. *This is nice,* she thought, recognizing candidly that it was far more than she deserved.

THEY ORDERED hamburgers, seasoned fries and colas and carried them to the water's edge where they found a low wall of boulders that stretched out into the ocean. Carrying the white bag that contained lunch, Patrick climbed up nimbly, then pulled her up after him and out onto the finger of rock.

A few feet short of the tip, he found a flat section, eased Gina onto it and folded up beside her. He distributed the contents of the bag while Gina inhaled the wonderful freshness of the breezy waterfront. Her gaze caught the flight of a bird, curiously prehistoric looking with its considerable size and angles. Long bill pointed downward, it made a kamikaze dive toward the water.

Gina pinched Patrick's sleeve between thumb and forefinger and shook it. "Look, a pelican!" She pointed with her other hand, then shaded her eyes with it as the big bird hit water with an awkward splash.

Patrick studied her speculatively as he handed her a straw. He wanted to throttle her after the way she'd tricked him, but some surprising ingenuousness in her kept surfacing and confusing him. "Never seen one?" he asked.

"Of course," she replied, absently tearing the end of the wrapper. "But I just don't get to the beach that often since I sold my place in Santa Monica."

He placed a paper napkin on her bent knee. "I didn't know rich girls got excited about things like pelicans."

"Are you going to pull some reverse snobbery thing on me?" Apparently unconcerned with his answer, she worked on sliding the straw from its wrapper.

He popped a fry into his mouth and shook his head while he chewed. "No. It's just nice to know you appreciate the simple things. For the next year that's all that will be available to you."

She raised a haughty eyebrow. "Maybe you could let me look through a Tiffany's catalog once in a while to keep me focused on what you think I consider important."

"Don't be snide," he admonished.

"Then don't assume you know me when you don't," she returned. "Did you get ketchup?"

He peered into the bag. "Nope. They're seasoned fries. They don't need ketchup."

"I always need ketchup."

"Try to manage without. Practice austerity for the year ahead."

He was surprised an instant later when a soft, harmless missile hit him in the face. He disentangled Gina's straw wrapper from his burger and balled it in his fingers, giving her a threatening look.

She contemplated a french fry. "I thought a soldier would have been better prepared for attack. Goes to show you. People aren't always what they seem."

He tossed the wrapper into the empty bag, thinking she was more trouble than he'd imagined she would be, but more interesting also. "You," he said, "appear to be trouble, and you are. It's been my experience—" he put the paper bowl of fries he held aside and dusted off his hands "—that those who initiate a conflict are seldom prepared for the counterattack."

In a move she never saw coming, he pushed her backward on the rock, cushioning her head in his hand. He leaned over her, grinning into her wide gray eyes. "They leave themselves vulnerable to the enemy."

She felt small and helpless as the vastness of the sky seemed to recede even farther beyond his head. He was always trying to frighten her, she thought. Always trying to keep her intimidated and at a distance.

She met his gaze intrepidly, though her voice was breathless. "I don't think of you as the enemy."

He studied her a moment with a mild frown, then straightened and pulled her back to a sitting position. "Maybe you should."

"You didn't leave me alone in this. You stayed with me. An enemy wouldn't do that. Thank you."

The need in her eyes was overlaid by a sweet, genuine gratitude. He had difficulty holding out against it, but he wasn't about to be fooled a second time. "Assuming you mean that, you're welcome. Whether you do or whether you don't, you're going to have to be the ideal wife to guarantee my continued support."

Her face fell, hurt feelings sharp in her gray eyes. She

got to her feet, her slim body in stirrup pants and a long white sweater silhouetted against the cloudless blue sky and the sparkling ocean. She opened her mouth to speak, then changed her mind and moved as far away from him on the rock as she could get and sat down and ate her lunch.

When she'd finished, she stood to leave, pretending he wasn't there.

Her progress was arrested immediately by the long leap required from their flat dining rock to the next one with enough surface to land on.

Patrick got to his feet, balled their bag of trash into the palm of one hand and made the leap. Then he turned to offer her a hand. She leapt, colliding with his chest on the scant surface of the rock. For a minute he held her there, her breasts against his chest, the lower part of her body pressed against him by the hand that anchored her in place. Everything inside her fluttered and beat.

Patrick felt the impression of her breasts against his ribs and her thigh between his. It incapacitated him for a moment. That gave him time to become aware of the floral scent of her hair, of the fragility of the frame he held to him with one hand, of the nervous flutter of thick, dark eyelashes. He had the sensation of having been caught by one of the sirens of legend whose cries lured men onto the rocks to their death.

Without taking time to consider the wisdom of the move, he lowered his mouth to hers. It was soft, cool and salty from the coastal breeze, and open in surprise. He took swift advantage.

He coaxed her lips into compliance, then teased her with his tongue, losing some of the frustration he'd felt during their long night without touching in the king-size bed. She responded with an eagerness that surprised him.

He took a fistful of the back of her hair and delved deeper with his tongue, needing to show her that he would be tolerant, but he would be possessive and demanding also.

Gina was surprised and delighted with his ardent kiss. She felt all the complications between them fade into the background until only holding him and being held mattered. She gave herself over to the comfort and excitement, feeling a kind of blessed rightness in his claiming touch.

"I WONDER," Gina said quietly, reverently, "if anyone would grow accustomed to the beauty of Big Sur? I mean, if you lived here and saw it every day?"

She had unbuckled her seat belt and was straining sideways to see beyond Patrick to the surf thundering against the cliffs. He glanced down to see the eerie mist created that made everything look like a page from prehistory.

Flanking the right side of the highway was a primordial mountain forest that was home to the southernmost stands of coast redwoods.

"The type of person who'd want to live here," Patrick replied, "is probably not the type of person who'd ever fail to notice his surroundings, no matter how familiar they became."

"Look," she exclaimed. "Mailboxes."

His eyes followed her pointing finger to a wooden benchlike affair that held more than a score of rural mailboxes.

She looked around, ducking down to look higher up, turning to look over her shoulder. "I wonder where the homes are. I don't see anything resembling a structure."

"I don't imagine someone would choose to live here

and then build right on the highway.'' Patrick guided the humming truck steadily along the curving road. "They're probably back in the folds of the mountains somewhere.''

Gina settled back in her seat. "You think you have these people all figured out, don't you?" she asked. "Just like you think you understand me.''

"You asked about where they live,'' he replied easily. "It's my job to know what people want in the way of shelter.''

She allowed him that. It made sense.

She put on her seat belt and leaned back, now watching the rich green on her side of the road.

"I wonder if there's a Bigfoot in there?" she asked. She rolled her head along the headrest to look at his profile. It was gorgeous, she noted. "Do you believe in creatures trapped in time, in things that can't be explained?''

He tossed her an indulgent glance and turned back to the road. "I believe in everything that I don't know for certain to be false. Do you believe in ever being quiet?''

She laughed softly. "I feel dozy, so I won't be talking for a while. Wake me if you lose your way or need a tire changed or something.''

Patrick glanced at her, then smiled to himself as she curled up in her seat as much as the seat belt would allow and closed her eyes.

GINA WOKE to busy, tree-shaded city streets. Old Spanish architecture rubbed shoulders with modern glass and stone amid a landscape lush with greenery.

"Monterey,'' she said, rolling her window down to get a closer look as Patrick stopped at a light. "Isn't it wonderful? If things go well with us,'' she teased, "I think we should have a summer home here.'' She turned to grin at him. "What do you think?"

His grim expression surprised her. What had she done now?

"I think," he said, glancing into the rearview mirror, "that you should close your window and get down in your seat. Now."

She didn't have to ask why. "The black Mercedes."

"Well, *a* black Mercedes. About four cars back. I don't know if it's *the* Mercedes, but we'll find out. I'm going to look for a turn sheltered by trees or bushes. If it's your friends, they'll be watching for me to do it, and they'll be right on us. If it isn't, we'll just find a gas station and catch our breath."

"I vote for the second choice," she said.

"Yeah." He pushed her head down a little farther as the light turned green. "Me, too."

Gina stared at the floor mats as Patrick proceeded with the traffic.

"Turn coming up," he warned quietly. "Hold on."

He flipped the signal on, took the left turn at normal speed, then took another sharp left, nosing the truck into a high hedge that marked the border of a park. He braked, put a hand on Gina's head to keep her down, then leaned over the steering wheel to wait.

A spiffy blue Dodge Shadow crossed the intersection and kept going, followed by a battered yellow Toyota truck, a bronze Cadillac convertible, and a black Mercedes. From this vantage point, Patrick could see that the driver was a woman and that there was a child's seat on the passenger's side.

He straightened with a sigh and let Gina up. "False alarm. Sorry."

Gina sat up and smoothed her hair, sending him a wry

smile as her pulse relaxed. "That's the kind of disappointment I can live with." She pointed across the street. "There's a gas station. Chevron okay?"

He turned the key in the ignition. "Fine."

She sounded relieved. "Good. I can see the candy machine from here."

AFTER PAYING the attendant and washing his hands, Patrick found Gina standing on the cement base of the chain-link fence that ran around the station. She was staring at the ocean about half a block away and at a row of gnarled cypresses that stood on a bluff overlooking it. As he watched, she took a bite of a chunky candy bar.

A little annoyed that she hadn't stayed by the truck as he'd asked her, he came up quietly behind her, waited until he saw her swallow, then snaked his arm around her waist, sweeping her from her perch. She uttered a little cry of surprise and kicked furiously. The candy bar went straight up in the air.

He held her against his side for a moment, squeezing her slender waist punitively. "If I were Shrimp or Larry," he said, "you'd be in the trunk of a black Mercedes right now."

"If you were Shrimp or Larry," she said, pink cheeked and breathless, "I'd have screamed for Patrick."

"You might not have had time to scream."

"Then I'd have bitten or scratched." Still dangling from his grip, she looked slightly backward at him and said gravely, "But I knew it was you."

He looked doubtful. "How?"

"I don't know," she admitted. "I just did."

"You struggled."

"I was surprised when you grabbed me, but I knew it was you."

He put her on her feet, apparently unwilling to argue further. "Next time do as you're told. Let's get moving."

Gina refused to look repentant as he put her into the truck. She *had* known he was behind her. It was as though a light had gone on inside her, as though some so-far-unrecognized radar connected them. The notion was unsettling.

"It's about an hour to Santa Cruz," he said, turning into the traffic. "We'll stay overnight there."

"Sounds good. I'm getting hungry."

He shook his head at her. "You just ate a candy bar."

"Two bites of a candy bar," she corrected. "Thanks to you I lost the rest of it. You owe me a large and wonderful dinner."

He cast her a glance as the traffic began to trace the crescent of Monterey Bay. It held challenge and warning and the suggestion of something else she couldn't quite define.

"I'll see that you get everything you deserve," he said wickedly. "I promise."

"I WAS HOPING for something with a sauna and a pool," Gina said as Patrick pulled into the driveway of a very small motel just outside of Santa Cruz.

"This is better," Patrick said, stopping in front of the office door. "You can't see the parking lot from the road, so they won't spot our truck unless they check every motel lot along the highway."

"Maybe they didn't follow us. Wouldn't we have seen them by now?"

"I don't know. Better safe than sorry. Come on in with me."

Moments later Patrick drove the car around the back of the simple structure that housed twenty units, ten on each of two levels. "Another advantage to this place," he said, parking in front of room 107, "is that there's only one wing. Impossible for you to get lost."

"Very funny."

"The restaurant looks good," he said, indicating the neon sign depicting a squatty little chef wielding a fry pan. Plaid curtains were visible from the windows, and a cozy glow of light promised atmosphere. He took her chin between his thumb and forefinger and gave it a playful pinch. "Maybe they'll have a big steak for you, a rack of ribs, a plump chicken and an all-you-can-eat salad bar. Will that keep you till breakfast?"

"If I don't have to work too hard," she said.

She got out of the truck and reached into the back for her makeup case and his tote bag. She handed him his bag with a grin. "Better carry your own so I can save myself." He took their large bags from the truck and unlocked the door to the room.

It was less Spartan than the outside suggested. The shower boasted a hand-held spray that went a little way toward making up for the lack of a sauna. They showered, changed clothes and headed for the restaurant.

"TELL ME ABOUT Gardner," Patrick said before they'd eaten dinner.

Gina looked first surprised, then grateful for a new focus of attention.

She sipped at her coffee and frowned, wondering how she'd come to this point when she and Yale had shared friendship and professional dedication only months before.

It wasn't hard to remember the curious chain of events, though she'd tried to make a point of putting it out of her mind. The press hadn't let her.

"Your father told me you'd met in school," Patrick said, thanking the waitress with a nod as she placed a coffee nudge in front of him.

Gina was momentarily distracted by the generous dollop of whipped cream on top of it.

"I gathered he wasn't in favor of your partnership."

She had to smile. "That's true. But I couldn't look upon Dad's disapproval as any kind of sign that I was making a mistake. He disapproves of me on principle because I don't revere money and position as he does. I think I'm a throwback to my maternal grandmother who turned her back on the family fortune and ran off with a trumpet player."

"What about Gardner?"

Gina shrugged, still surprised that what had looked so perfect had blown up in her face. "He'd been in my art history class. We met again after school at a party. We'd both been thinking about getting into the decorating business, but he didn't have enough capital and I wasn't sure I had the business sense to make it work." She smiled, reminiscing. "We talked about it after the party over a drink and decided we were the perfect business partnership." She had difficulty keeping her eyes off the whipped cream slowly dissolving in its pool of boozy coffee.

"No romance involved?" he asked. Then he noticed her greedy gaze. "You want a nudge of your own?"

She shook her head in answer to his first question. "Just friendship and business." To his second, she smiled winningly. "I don't like alcohol in my coffee, but I do have a thing for whipped cream." She looked at it anxiously. It was already seeping into the brew, marbling and lightening the coffee color.

Patrick dipped his spoon into it, captured a fat, curly blob and reached across the table to put the spoon to Gina's mouth.

She took the cream, feeling its coolness on the heat of the spoon as he drew it slowly back. The cream dissolved instantly on her tongue, but the look he gave her lasted into her dreams.

"What went wrong between you?" Patrick asked quietly.

"Simple thievery, I think." Gina tossed her head, having to take another sip of coffee to stabilize her pulse. "We worked together beautifully for almost two years. Our clients were more than pleased with our work, they told their friends, and our base was growing at a rate that surprised even me." She sighed, put her spoon down and took another sip of water.

"Then about three months ago a client called to tell me that a Ming vase was missing from the bookshelf in her husband's home office. Because we'd just redone the room for her and had a fireplace put in, I assumed she suspected the mason. I told her we knew him to be more than honest and completely reliable, that we'd used him countless times before. She considered us responsible because our firm had been in possession of her house key for the six weeks it took to finish the job."

"So you had to make good?"

"We're bonded. It was a relatively simple matter, but the same thing happened again three weeks later. This time it was a Renoir missing from the bedroom of a friend of my father's. Daddy almost had a stroke."

"You'd just finished a job there, too?"

"Two months earlier. Immediately after that it was a diamond necklace. I didn't want to believe the scenario that was beginning to form in my mind. Someone was copying the keys clients gave us and using them to steal antiques and valuable artifacts. And I knew it wasn't me."

"You confronted Gardner."

"I tried. He was supposed to be working on the soap star Susie Burns's winter home in Palm Springs. I called to talk to him and was told by the maid that he'd never arrived. She just assumed Burns had called us to change plans." She sighed, her mood grimly accepting as she recalled what happened next.

"I went to his place and found it locked up tight. But there was enough of a chink in the draperies to tell me he'd moved out. Everything was gone. I went immediately to a warehouse we kept near the shop and found that he'd cleaned it out. And that included pieces of furniture we were refinishing or reupholstering for clients. The next morning I discovered he'd cleaned out our business account, also. By that point I wasn't even surprised."

"What'd you do?"

"The only thing I could do. I called the police and began to liquidate. My place at Malibu had to go, along with my Carrera, and a few pieces of good jewelry I had. But I won't be completely out of debt until I come into my inheritance from Grandmother." She held her cup up as the waitress came by with the coffeepot. "The worst part is that I can't believe I could've been so wrong about someone."

Patrick raised his half-empty nudge and had it refilled. "Maybe it wasn't something he'd planned. Maybe he was the good friend you thought he was, then got into drugs or gambling or something that made him lose his head and turn to the first available source of salvation. It doesn't excuse him, of course, but it doesn't make you responsible.''

She put her cup aside and leaned an elbow on the table, propping her chin on her hand. ''You know, for a man who makes no bones about liking things his way, you can be very understanding and compassionate. Why is that?''

Momentarily surprised and disarmed by the compliment, he had to think a minute. ''I baby-sat teenage recruits for a lot of years. I guess it's a lot like being big brother or father in a very large family.''

''You know,'' she said thoughtfully, ''I'll bet you'd make a good one.''

''A good what?''

''Father,'' she replied. Then she smiled tauntingly. ''You're sure you don't want to have a baby with me? I mean, you have to consider it sometime. Who'll take over the Candle Bay Inn when you go to your reward?''

Patrick frowned at Gina as the waitress put their main courses before them. When she took the soup and salad things away, Patrick leaned forward and said quietly, ''If it's all the same with you, I'd rather not consider my death at this moment. I figure I still have another fifty years to make the next generation of Gallaghers.''

''All right,'' she said lightly, contemplating an aromatic chicken breast marinara with obvious anticipation. ''If you want to take that chance. What with global warming, El Niño, the imminent cataclysmic earthquake, not to mention the ever-present threat of nuclear...''

''Regina.'' He said her name softly, but with an edge of firmness that silenced her. He was forcing the sternness in his eyes, she knew, because a light of amusement flickered under it.

"Yes?" she asked innocently.

"Enough," he replied. "One more word out of you during dinner and you forgo dessert."

She looked injured. "But they had custard with hard sauce."

He was unmoved. "The decision's yours."

"Militarist."

"Motor mouth."

"COME ON," Patrick said, catching her hand as they left the restaurant. "Fresh air'll do us both some good." There was a break in the light traffic on the highway that bordered the beach, and he pulled her with him as he ran across.

The air was cool and salty. Gina shivered as she drew in a deep breath. In the distance a bright pattern of lights danced into the water.

"I wonder what that is?" she asked, shivering again.

Patrick stopped, pulled off his leather jacket and dropped it onto her shoulders. "According to the brochure I read in the room while you were showering, it's an old-fashioned boardwalk."

The silk lining was warm from his body, the leather pleasantly heavy. When Patrick put an arm around her to hold the jacket in place, Gina leaned into him as though it was the most natural thing in the world.

"I'll bet they have Skee Ball and a Ferris wheel and snow cones," she said dreamily.

"Don't tell me," he teased. "You once wanted to run away with the carnival."

She laughed. "No. I was just wondering what it would be like to take this trip in a relaxed way, without having to look over our shoulders to check the rearview mirror for a black Mercedes.''

As a strong gust of wind blew, Patrick stopped her to help her put her arms in the sleeves of the jacket and snap it closed. The jacket fell to mid-thigh, and her hands were lost halfway up the sleeves.

"Maybe you'll have that opportunity one day. Are you good at Skee Ball?''

"No, but I'm pretty good at the shooting gallery.''

"No kidding. Me, too.''

They walked on, arm in arm, the ruffly fingers of the surf milky white in the darkness. "Well, of course,'' she teased. "You have an unfair advantage. You've had training. I'm self-taught.''

"Then we'll have to shoot it out one day,'' he challenged. "See which approach is better.''

They continued on in silence for a moment, then she said quietly, "I'm sorry your return home has been delayed by all this. The coast route will take an extra day and a half.''

He dismissed the inconvenience with an inclination of his head. "It's all right. I like to be on hand, but I'm sure my staff's doing just fine without me.''

All kinds of things she'd had difficulty saying were suddenly easy to admit in the silky darkness. "I'm also sorry I lied to you.''

He stopped and turned to her. The sincerity in her tone dissolved whatever anger remained over their situation. "You've already apologized for that.''

She shrugged a shoulder hidden somewhere in the jacket. "I know. I'm just not sure one apology covers it. I…I'll do everything I promised. I'll set up a great child-care center for you. And I'll—you know…I'll try to be helpful and supportive and…I'll…'' She stopped on a sigh.

"Make love to me?" he asked, the quiet question still crystal clear despite the busy sounds of the surf. She felt her lungs dispel a gasp of air.

"Yes," she whispered with what little breath she had left.

He looked at her ivory face uplifted to him in the darkness and forgot how this had all begun, forgot that she'd lied to him, and knew only that at that moment he wanted her very much.

But he'd never in his life taken a woman who hadn't wanted him.

A fragrant breeze stirred her hair, and he put a gentle hand to the cold, silky strands to hold them in place. "We'll wait," he said, "until you *want* to make love to me. Not as a condition of a deal, but because you just can't do otherwise."

She caught his arm as he would have led them back the way they'd come. She didn't try to explain it. She didn't understand it herself. But the attraction she'd felt the first day she'd met him had grown steadily since, fueled by his tolerant if not patient handling of the difficult situation.

"I want to," she said.

He heard emphasis on the second word that gave the statement a flattering validity he had to accept.

He swept her up in his arms and started across the sand to the highway.

Her heart pounding, her face burrowed in his throat, Gina felt his warm, strong arms and knew without a doubt how right this was, however it had all begun. She wanted to make love with Patrick even more than she wanted the black Mercedes out of her life.

She heard Patrick's steady footfalls cross the highway, heard the sound of his tread stop as he crossed the grass that bordered the sidewalk, then held fast to his neck as he stopped abruptly, muttering a quick, emphatic expletive.

Then he suddenly dropped her onto her feet and pushed her into the darkened doorway of the office, jarring her languid mood.

She was so momentarily disoriented that she asked without considering the obvious, "What's the matter?"

Wordlessly Patrick pointed to the thin stream of traffic coming off the freeway. The black Mercedes swept past, gleaming like a breathing, threatening entity under the streetlights. It was not driven by a suburban matron with a child seat on the passenger's side. Larry was at the wheel with Shrimp beside him.

Chapter Six

Patrick grabbed her hand and ran toward the truck. He fumbled once with the key, then turned it in the lock and pushed Gina inside. She unlocked the driver's door as he ran around behind. He was backing out of the parking space before his door was closed, turning sharply toward the narrow alley of space between the office and a redwood fence that surrounded the motel.

"We're going to leave our things?" Gina asked as Patrick braked so sharply that only his arm, quickly thrown out to brace her, prevented her from hitting the dash.

"Depends," he said, easing the door open and slipping out. She scooted along the seat to follow him but he gestured her to remain in the truck with a sharp "Stay there!"

Frustrated, she watched him flatten himself against the wall of the office and peer around the edge.

If Larry and Shrimp made a casual tour of the parking lot, Patrick thought, straining to see in the dark, it might be safe at the motel when they left. If they started checking rooms, he was hitting the road.

He watched as the powerful halogens of the Mercedes

lit a large swath of asphalt as the car pulled up and purred in the motel driveway. He heard the bell jingle over the office door.

So, it was not to be a casual perusal of the parking lot. They were asking questions, probably giving a description of his truck.

In a moment the Mercedes pulled into a parking spot, and the hotel manger appeared with a ring of keys, looking concerned.

As Larry and Shrimp got out of the car, the manager led the way to room 107, saying, "I'd have never taken them for hardened criminals." Then he noticed the vacant spot where the truck had been. "They're gone!"

"Professional thieves," Larry said, "don't usually stick around to pay their bills. Let us into the room. Maybe it'll give us a clue to where they're headed."

That did it. A search of their room, however quick, would give him time to get miles ahead of them. Patrick turned to hurry back to the truck. He collided sharply with Gina, who had crept up behind him. She cried out as he stepped on her foot and knocked her backward.

"Shh!" he cautioned, steadying her. But it was too late. Loud voices from the parking lot told him someone had heard them. He pushed Gina toward the truck, stuffed her in through the driver's side, then followed, pulling the door closed and doing zero to sixty out of the alley faster then the five-year-old Chevy should have allowed.

"We *are* going to leave our things," Gina groaned as Patrick roared toward the freeway. Through the rearview mirror he glimpsed the great good fortune of a semi pulling up in front of the motel, blocking the exit from the alley as the driver, probably weary and anxious to put his head down onto a soft pillow, tried to maneuver his big rig into the three spots in front of the office.

In the time it would take Larry to wait it out or turn the Mercedes around and go out the way he'd come in, Patrick knew he could gain precious miles.

"Here's your chance to really come to terms with the simple life, Mrs. Gallagher," he said, taking over the fast lane and burning up the road. The rest of the light traffic ignored him. "You'll be living in jeans and a sweater for the next year. This is a good time to get used to it."

"I wasn't worried about my expensive things," she clarified, putting the visor down and checking the makeup mirror for signs of the black Mercedes. "Why do you always assume my concerns are material? I was thinking about my comfortable shoes and my makeup bag. I left it on the counter in the bathroom."

He cast her a quick glance as he swung back into the right lane and took a concealed position in front of a truck hauling feed. "I apologize for misjudging you," he said, "but we might have let them get ahead of us, which would have given us an advantage if you'd listened to me and stayed in the truck."

That was true. She didn't want to consider it. She folded her arms and stared out the windshield. The soft, seductive mood of only moments ago was left behind as they sped away. "I'm the one they're after. I have a right to know what's going on."

"You turned my life inside out to get me to protect you from Larry or Gardner or whoever. The prudent thing would be to let me *do* it."

"Just don't try to do it by pushing me around."

The temptation to pull over, back her into the corner

of the front seat and set her straight once and for all was almost overwhelming. But there wasn't time.

It was difficult to equate the testy woman beside him with the woman who'd only moments ago admitted she wanted him. Frustration frayed his patience and tautened his nerves. Instead of the romantic end to the evening that had looked so hopeful, he was behind the wheel again, racing through the darkness, pursued by more than one black demon.

As Gina fidgeted beside him, anxious and tired and probably as frustrated as he was, he shook off the discontent and made himself concentrate on what he had to do.

"I don't see them," Gina said, still studying the grill of the truck behind reflected in her mirror. "Can you see the other lanes of traffic?"

He glanced up. No sign of the Mercedes. "Why don't you close your eyes and get some rest. I'll wake you if he catches up."

"Want me to drive for a while?" she asked.

He shook his head. "Thanks. I'm fine."

"How far do you intend to go?"

"Past San Francisco," he replied.

"We could lose ourselves *in* San Francisco," she suggested, pushing her mirror up and turning toward him in her seat.

"I'm counting on them thinking that's what we'll do," he said. "While they're looking for us, we can get most of the way to the Oregon border. We'll find somewhere to hide for a few hours on the other side of town, then get an early start and be long gone while they're still combing Chinatown."

"You're sure that'll work?" she asked doubtfully.

"No," he said quietly, "but at the moment it's all the strategy I can put together. Be quiet and let me think."

She rested her head back and closed her eyes, tired and more than willing to leave him in charge. Particularly since nothing seemed to be going the way she'd hoped.

WHEN GINA AWOKE, there were pinpricks of light in the dark distance, and the freeway traffic had thinned even further. Everything they passed along the road was closed. The windows of gas stations and restaurants yawned hollowly, their security lights illuminating emptiness.

Gina suspected it was very, very late. She sat up, cramped and still tired, and looked at the clock on the dash. One thirty-seven.

Patrick glanced at her and gave her a quick smile. "Sleep well? You missed San Francisco completely."

Gina stretched her arms toward the dash and returned his smile. "I trust you stopped for a loaf of sourdough bread?"

"You're not hungry again?"

"Must be the excitement. Any sign of our 'friends'?"

"No. Ah, there's what I've been looking for."

Gina strained her eyes in the darkness for some sign of a motel. She saw nothing but night and the suggestion of the gentle shadowy roll of a hillside. As Patrick turned onto an unpaved road she hadn't even seen until they were on it, she noticed a tall, irregular shape against the faint, cloudy glow of sky.

"How did you see that?" she asked in disbelief.

"My platoon claimed I had nightscope vision."

Gina studied the ancient barn illuminated in the truck's headlights. Time and weather had dried the wood and left gaps between the boards. It had a cupola with a crooked weather vane, a gaping hayloft door and an open front door that hung drunkenly by one hinge.

"What if somebody lives here?" Gina whispered as Patrick nosed the truck into the barn. "What if there's a farmhouse right over the hill?" In the glow of the headlights he looked around the obviously long-abandoned structure with its piles of boards and hay littering the floor. She saw shadowy corners and asked doubtfully, "What if some*thing* lives here?"

He reached into the glove compartment for a flashlight, then killed the motor and the headlights. "You'd probably like me to roast it over an open fire so you can make a sandwich."

He opened his door and Gina caught his arm, her eyes wide in the periphery of the light he held away from her face. "I'm serious, Patrick. I don't like rodenty things. I'm not even crazy about chickens and stuff like that."

"Then stay in the truck and let me look around first."

"But you'll be out there and I'll be in here." She sighed and decided, "I'm coming. But if you let anything bite me, I'll see that my father cancels the check."

"Why don't you stay in the truck?" he suggested wearily. "Right now you're in more danger of being bitten by me than you are anything else."

She considered him a moment, then rolled her eyes and made a scornful little sound. He realized with resignation that he hadn't frightened her.

She followed him, holding on to his left hand as the right wielded the flashlight into all four corners and revealed nothing.

Gina sidled closer to him. "There *are* things in there, aren't there?"

"Probably," he said as a little pile in the shadows

changed shape. "But if they're smart enough to stay hidden, I'm willing to respect their privacy. How about you?"

"Yes, definitely." She watched as he flashed the light overhead into the loft. "Think we can get up there?" she asked. A ladder leaned against it, but it looked dry and rickety.

"We'll give it a shot." He handed her the flashlight. "Hold this. I've got a blanket in the truck."

He secured the blanket, handed that to her, also, then leaned a hand on the second rung of the ladder and pushed. It snapped in two. He tried a higher rung with the same result.

Gina looked longingly at the quiet security of the loft. "Guess it's the ground-floor suite for us."

Patrick went to the canopy doors. "Not necessarily," he said. He got in, turned the truck and backed it under the loft until the roof provided a step up to it. Then he parked again, climbed lightly onto the hood, then onto the roof. He was easily within reach of the platform.

He beckoned Gina to follow him. Reaching down to relieve her of the light and blanket, he gave her a hand up to the hood, then onto the roof beside him. He tossed up the blanket and handed her the light.

"Hold it," he said, "until I get up there."

She complied, waiting until he'd swung himself onto the platform. Then she handed up the light and waited while he trained it over the loft. Satisfied, he set the light down beside him, then lay down on his stomach and reached for her.

He pulled her full weight up with one arm so that she could get a handhold on the loft. But she was a few inches short. He steadied her and reached for the seat of her pants.

She squealed when he found nothing to grab of the tight leggings but what they contained. With time of the essence in their precarious position, he unceremoniously hooked a hand high up on her thigh and hauled her up.

As his body reacted strongly to that intimate contact, he wondered how in the hell he was going to survive life with Gina with his libido intact.

Gina wondered if she would ever forget the strength of the biceps she'd gripped for dear life. She didn't have to wonder if she would ever forget the hand wrapped around her thigh. She knew she wouldn't. It made her tingle...and want him.

She knew she would never forget any of this. It was like being trapped in a fable, lost in a dream. It had all seemed so easy when her father decided to marry her off at a time when she truly needed a man's protection. But like the princess in the tale, she'd brought the brave suitor danger, and for that she was truly sorry.

As they knelt facing each other in several inches of prickly hay, the light pointing away from them, illuminating the floor of the barn and the strange anomaly of a truck in it, she recaptured, as though uninterrupted, the passion she'd felt on the beach at Santa Cruz.

Patrick felt an unsettling sense of destiny as desire, hot and sharp, washed over him again. God, how he wanted this quirky heiress on the run. This wasn't a Frank Capra movie, he tried to tell himself, this was real life.

But there it was. He'd never been one to deny what he felt. And he felt lust. He also believed in calling a spade a spade. It was a lot more than lust. Every time he looked at her now, he felt an ever-growing weakness—not in his knees, but in his heart. He knew he was going to keep her safe no matter what it cost him. And it was going to cost him his sanity—he just knew it.

"You're exhausted," he said, looking into the opalescent eyes devouring his face. His body was clamoring for her, but this wasn't the right time.

"Actually," she said softly, running her hands over his shoulders, the peaked ceiling making her voice echo. "I'm wide-awake." She felt his strong heartbeat, felt it react to her touch.

He stroked her disheveled hair and warned gently, "The Mercedes could be right behind us."

"For now," she said, leaning into him, putting her teeth to the lobe of his ear, "could we just think about what's ahead of us?"

He had to make himself catch her hands and pull them from him. He kissed her knuckles. "Not until I'm sure you're safe."

"But you're with me."

He smiled wryly. "That's the problem. When I'm with you, I tend to lose awareness of everything else. I almost missed the Mercedes in Santa Cruz. I don't want to forget to listen for it until I'm sure we lost them in the dark."

He took her shoulders and pushed her gently back into the hay, then dragged his hands from her. He turned off the flashlight and lay beside her, pulling her into his arms and opening the blanket over them.

She snuggled into him, feeling remarkably comfortable considering the circumstances.

Patrick felt every inch of her in contact with every inch of him and wondered just how much a man could be expected to endure without snapping. He closed his eyes and tried to rest, knowing he wouldn't sleep. He was bone tired but would make himself listen for another thirty minutes. If Larry hadn't tracked them by then, Patrick would be fairly sure he'd eluded him. Then maybe he could do what he really wanted to do with this night.

GINA AWOKE with a start in the darkness.

"Easy," Patrick's voice said gently. "What's the matter?"

"I...don't know," she said, feeling the tension all around her as she leaned up on an elbow. Shafts of moonlight streamed through the roof of the barn, making silver stripes in the air. Motes of dust moved in them, giving them life. She was in the fairy tale again.

"I think I heard something," she whispered covertly.

"You did," Patrick replied, the palm of one cool hand finding her cheek unerringly in the darkness. His thumb strummed her cheekbone.

She felt herself go boneless.

"I said your name," he went on, the hand at her face slipping to cup the back of her neck and pull her gently down to him. "Regina," he said again, the low rumble of his voice now at her ear as he tucked her into his arm and leaned over her. "Regina Gallagher. Mine."

She raised both arms to circle his neck, coming sharply, tremblingly to awareness. The danger posed by the Mercedes was gone for the moment. But she wanted him to be aware that he faced a new and different danger.

"This will make you mine, as well," she said, sensation racing along her throat as his index finger traced a line to the V-neck of her sweater.

Patrick's brain told him that a dangerous pit yawned at his feet, but his body was attempting to tune out, listening only to the touch of fingers on the back of his hand. A part of him that was still soldier—that never relinquished control—fought to hold on.

He combed his other hand into her hair and tugged her head back so that he could look into her eyes. They were already lazy and languid.

"One unromantic question," he said, planting a kiss where his finger had stopped. Then he looked into her eyes. "Are you protected?"

She ran a teasing thumb over his bottom lip. "I don't want to be," she whispered.

"Gina…"

"Yes, I am," she said.

"You wouldn't fib to me? Again?"

She accepted the suggestion of censure in his question. "No," she replied. "That's no way to start a marriage."

Satisfied, he lay back, bringing her with him, shifting to lie beside her in the pleasantly spiky hay.

Gina felt confidence in his arms, in the artful mouth that teased her lips apart and in the tongue that delved inside. No man had ever made her feel like this before, as though he knew precisely what she wanted and didn't doubt for a moment his ability to give it to her. Body and soul, she gravitated to the security he offered.

Patrick felt her breasts spread against his chest. He drank thirstily from the mouth she opened to him, realizing how long it had been since he'd had the time to indulge his physical self. Something tugged at his consciousness, something suggesting that even now, before it had really begun, there was more than the simply physical here. But he tuned it out. The situation required simplification, not further complication.

He propped himself on an elbow and gathered up the hem of her long sweater. She raised her arms to allow him to pull it over her head. He placed it under her to cushion her against the hay, then turned his attention to the full breasts blooming from smoky gray lace cups. He unhooked the front closure of her bra and stared a moment at her rosy-tipped ivory perfection.

"You're beautiful," he said.

Then he leaned down to kiss her breast, to take one tight pearl into his mouth, then the other.

Gina shifted restlessly, feeling everything inside her tighten and wait. She tugged his sweater up and pulled it off.

Her eyes roamed the formidable proportions of his pecs and shoulders, glowing warmly in the dark. She planted kisses in the mat of dark hair, encountering warmth and washboard muscle.

He slipped her shoes off, peeled the stirrup pants from her, then hooked a finger in the elastic of her gray lace panties and pulled them down, tossing everything aside.

She unbuckled his belt and unfastened the button of his jeans. She raised her head for his kiss, momentarily hesitant.

Her head still cradled in his arm, he kissed her long and lingeringly, his free hand teasing her breasts, bringing sensation to such bright instant life that all thought of hesitation fled.

Drugged by his ministrations, she reached for the zipper of his jeans and pulled it down. Their snug fit required his help for removal, and she finally dropped them and his briefs beside her things.

He pulled her astride his waist, then wrapped his arms around her to pull her down to him. He stroked every inch of her with a touch at once reverent and possessive.

Fire raced under her skin where his fingers moved— over her back, following the curve of her hip, down her thigh to her knee, then up again, tracing slowly up the back of her leg. Then he reached inside her and her growing tension rose to a high, strained pitch.

She was mindless in a minute, unable to move, unable to think, afraid to breathe. Then he was inside her, his hands on her hips guiding her into the velvet rhythm of a perfect universe.

Even as climax broke over her, she shuddered under its impact, Patrick driving her higher and farther, and she thought she'd never known anything like it existed this side of heaven.

It went on and on, ripples of pleasure that broke one after another, assaulting her with sensation so exquisite she held on to Patrick's hands with desperation, afraid of slipping over into insanity.

Patrick held back until she began to breathe more normally, until that delicious, almost ethereal look left her face, then he pulled her down to him and rolled her over. He plunged deeper inside her and let the pleasure take him. Gina wrapped around him, tightening him into their sexual embrace, and he had a clear instant's awareness of having control wrested from him.

He felt her fingernails stroke from his hipbone up to his shoulder, over his buttocks and up his spine, vertebra by vertebra until his nervous system was a tangle of pleasurable impulses and faulty messages. He shuddered with the power of release, temporarily lost in the net of her sweetness, of the scent of her body and the silk of her hair.

When he could form a coherent thought again, he turned so that she was uppermost once again and yanked the blanket back over them. She lay limp atop him, still breathing hard.

After a moment she pushed herself up and crossed her

arms on his chest, her eyes still stunned. "That...I don't...we...God!"

"Yes," he agreed with a deep laugh. "That about says it. If your cooking is half as delicious as you are, I just might keep you forever."

She hid her smug smile in his throat, afraid he'd read in her eyes how much she already wanted that.

"If you prove to be as caring and exciting a husband as you are a lover," she said softly, "maybe I'll want to stay."

His chest moved under her as he laughed again. "Looks like we both have our work cut out for us."

As they lay cozily entwined, Gina snuggled even closer. "Do you think we've lost Shrimp and Larry for good?" she asked.

"No." He ran a thumb gently along her arm. "I think they want you, or something you have, very badly."

"But I don't have anything. Yale took everything we had of value as a company when he left." She sighed heavily. "He left some bolts of fabric, a few chairs that had to be repaired, a plant stand, a base, and a lamp. I sold everything except the lamp when I liquidated."

He looked down at her. "Why didn't you sell the lamp?"

"Because it wasn't worth anything. It's just a painted plaster piece—a sort of Renaissance thing of a couple with a picnic basket running together under the shelter of his cloak. Obviously a rainstorm has ruined an afternoon tryst." She smiled and kissed his chin. "Anyway, I've always rather liked it. I found it at a flea market and bought it on impulse, thinking I'd find the right place to use it one day."

He leaned up on an elbow. "Where is it now?"

"In the back of the truck," she said, scrambling up

with him as he got to his feet and started the cautious process to roof to hood to barn floor. "But, Patrick, it can't be the lamp. It's plaster. Believe me, I know a little about this stuff. It's not a valuable antique or anything."

He unlocked the canopy and she pulled open the carton in which she'd wrapped the lamp. He raised an eyebrow as she unwrapped the garishly colored base. The cloak was gold, the young woman's skirt and blouse a gypsy red and yellow, and the man wore purple pants and white shirt with billowed sleeves.

Gina ran a hand lovingly over the cloak. "Don't they look happy? As though they've found the middle of their rainbow." She held it to her and told him firmly, "I'm going to repaint it and find a place of prominence in which to put it, so you may as well resign yourself to it. Does your house have a mantel?"

He gave her a look that told her they would argue that later and removed another wrapped piece from the box. It was the tulip-shaped globe that held a flame bulb and fit into one of the hands with which the young man held the cloak.

Patrick turned it in his hand, frowning. "And this is it?"

She held up an old cellophane bag that held the crystal droplets that hung from the globe. "Except for these."

He winced. "Gina, maybe you should have left this at the flea market."

Indignant, she wrapped the base lovingly and replaced it in the box. "It spoke to me. I had to have it."

"What did it say?" he teased. "'Here I am, Gina. Waste five dollars'?"

She snatched the globe from him, her lips pursed in disapproval. "It said, 'One day you'll find the right man and you'll both be as happy as we are. Until then, you can look at *us*.'" She nestled the globe into the foot of the box, wove the flaps and replaced it in the back of the truck. She dusted her hands off and looked at him with a haughty tilt of her chin. "And I paid fifty. So go ahead and laugh."

But he couldn't. He closed the canopy, then leapt up onto the hood, drawing her after him. When they were back in the loft, he pulled her sweater off, kicked off his jeans and told her in no uncertain terms that for as long as they were together, he would do his damnedest to put the same look in her eyes as the girl in the lamp had.

Chapter Seven

"Come on. Gina, come on. Look alive." Patrick tugged at the arm Gina refused to put through the sleeve of her sweater. She was slumped sleepily against him, her eyes closed again.

"No," she grumbled as he reached into the cuff of her sweater, caught her fingertips and pulled them through. "It's still dark."

"That's because your eyes are closed," he said, now struggling with the other arm. "Open them. It's dawn. We've got to get on the road."

She smiled, her eyes still tightly closed. "Can't we stay here? Make love again?" As he tugged the sweater down she went on. "Why don't we just move here? I could redecorate. You could sell insurance or something."

"Gina, wake up," he said, sitting her up and patting her cheek until she finally looked at him. "There's nothing to eat within miles of here," he added gravely. "And you haven't had a bite since seven last night."

Gina's eyes widened and she came to sudden awareness. "Oh, my God."

"I thought that'd bring you around."

She stretched her cramped muscles. "I don't want to wear the same things again," she grumbled moodily.

"Lady Godiva had a horse, honey," he said as he swung her off the hood of the truck. "Not a Chevy. When we have time and opportunity, we'll get you a change of clothes."

"And makeup. I need makeup."

He looked at her pink-cheeked, sleepy-eyed face and couldn't imagine paint improving it. But she needed to be humored this morning. "Sure. Whatever."

In a moment she was opening the barn door and Patrick was driving out into the gray early morning.

The road climbed and wound and seemed to go on forever, reaching for the slow-rising misty sun. Like a ribbon the road undulated along a coastline of chiseled rock capped by a carpet of green.

On the land side of the road were tidy little farms where holstein cows grazed lazily.

A little farther, on the water side, they passed long, railed piers with small, brightly painted structures at the end of them.

"I love the privacy," Gina said, pointing to them, "but the places are a little small."

Patrick laughed. "I think they're boathouses. We have one at the inn, but it's a little bigger than those."

"Your guests go boating?"

"Fishing. Best salmon in the world at the mouth of the Columbia River. Have you ever fished?" He grinned and added before she could answer, "Or can you be quiet that long?"

She made a face at him. "No, I've never fished. Have you ever been antique hunting?"

"Can't say I have."

"I'll be happy to introduce you to the experience."

When he looked doubtful, she added brightly, "You'd enjoy it. I'm usually very serious and very quiet when I'm antique shopping."

"Then by all means, we'll try it."

"Patrick, I'm starving," she said plaintively. "One more minute without breakfast and I'm going to faint dead away."

"I was hoping we'd have found a restaurant by now." He reached across her to open the glove compartment. A bag of cheddar-and-onion potato chips fell out onto her lap.

"Oh!" she exclaimed as though it were pâté on crackers. "You've been holding out on me."

"I bought them last night when I stopped for gas while you were asleep." He gave her a teasing but indulgent glance. "I had a feeling an emergency would arise."

She tore the top off, dipped a hand in for a chip and chewed, her eyes closed in ecstasy. Then she removed a chip and held it to his lips. He snapped it with a nod of thanks.

"There's also a box of juice in there," he said.

"You're kidding!" She investigated the glove compartment and pulled out an apple juice with a small straw attached to the side. "Patrick, this is ambrosial. You're turning out to be prime husband material. Competent, resourceful, thoughtful."

Then she remembered last night and decided neither of those words described the tender power of his lovemaking. She glanced at him and found him looking at her, a smoky expression in his eyes telling her he was remembering also. It was the first thought they'd really shared, the first momentous experience on which they could look back together from the same perspective.

For the first time since she'd repeated her vows, Gina felt like a wife.

Patrick watched color fill her cheeks, watched her meet his eyes without apology or excuse or regret and felt fiercely and protectively like a husband.

"Competent?" he asked with a dry grin, stretching a hand out to take hers.

She brought his knuckles to her lips. "Last night was magical. You know it was." She sighed, then freed his hand as they came to a series of curves. She had to contend with a completely new impression of him—a passion beyond anything she'd imagined and a tenderness she could still feel in the light of day.

He concentrated on the road, but a corner of his mind that insisted on reliving those delicious hours in the hayloft told him in no uncertain terms that something had changed last night. He'd discovered a generosity in her that surprised him, and a sweetness that left him feeling drugged. He didn't like the uneven feeling, but the memories were too delicious to dismiss.

They found a small roadside restaurant in a little town just north of Fort Ross, a remnant of Russian presence and seal hunting in the nineteenth century.

"Two hamburgers," Patrick said in wonder as he headed north yet again. "I've never seen a woman eat two hamburgers."

She'd brought the rest of her fries with her and shook her head without remorse as she chewed. "One of them was a chickenburger," she said. "They're lighter. Want a french fry?"

"I should be entitled to one," he said. "They were mine after all, but, hey, who would dare stand in the way of..." He lowered his voice and intoned dramatically, "The Woman Who Ate the World."

"I'm trying to keep my strength up," she said, her side-glance righteous. "If we have to run for it or something, I wouldn't want to fall behind."

He gave her a half laughing, half serious glance. "I'd never leave you," he said.

Silence pulsed for one instant, then she asked softly, "Because I'm your wife?"

He stared at the road. "Because you're wearing the only jacket we have between us."

She battled with hurt feelings and disappointment for as long as it took him to lose the straight face. Then she hit him viciously in the upper arm.

He fended her off, reminding her laughingly that this was not a road that would forgive divided attention. Then he patted the middle seat.

"Move over here," he said, reaching behind himself to hand her one end of the belt.

As she buckled the seat belt and settled in next to him, hip to hip and thigh to thigh, she felt a shudder of excitement and a glow of warmth that made her forget this wasn't a real honeymoon.

Patrick rested his arm across her and cupped her knee in his hand. She rubbed her cheek on his upper arm and heaved a ragged little sigh.

Patrick felt her lean into him and tried not to notice how far he was falling.

"Where do you think the Mercedes is?" Gina asked, comfortably lazy, the thought of their pursuers like some fuzzy notion in the back of her mind.

"Ahead, somewhere," he replied evenly. "I think that by now they realize they got ahead of us last night and are waiting somewhere for us to catch up."

"What'll we do then?"

''Elude them again until I can find the right place to take them on.''

''You make it sound easy.''

''It's a military trick,'' he said, rubbing her knee. ''Reduce a complicated issue or mission to its simple components and you find that anything can be dealt with if you don't get caught up in the complications.''

She leaned her temple against his shoulder. ''That sounds like one of those things that isn't as easy in action as it is in theory.''

''It all depends on your attitude.''

Right now her attitude was too mushy to consider military strategy. She simply leaned against him and watched little clapboard houses go by, boxed-in water towers, split-rail fences from another time, steepled white churches and ruffled, scalloped coves.

''It looks like New England, doesn't it?'' she asked. ''Maybe we could have our summer home here. What do you think?''

''I think summer's our busiest time in the hotel business,'' he replied, ''and we're not going anywhere. February's a good time to travel, but you'd probably want to go somewhere tropical. I don't think this is a hospitable landscape at that time of year.''

She sighed. ''Hawaii's so pedestrian. Tahiti's so far.''

''What about Mexico?''

She sat up, interested. ''I've only been to Mexico City, but I loved it.''

''Good,'' he said, smiling at her enthusiasm. ''That settles it. But we should vacation somewhere you haven't been. Acapulco or Cancun.''

A strange thought occurred to her and she leaned back against him. ''By then we'll only have a month left.''

''A month of what?''

"Our marriage. I turn twenty-six in March."

He drove silently for several seconds, then he said philosophically, "Well, you know what they say about the best-laid plans."

She did of course. But was he blithely saying there was little point in planning? Or did the words suggest that the plan on which they'd embarked could easily change and follow another direction entirely?

By THE TIME he pulled into Rockport, about two-thirds of the way up the California coast, Patrick was beginning to feel as though he'd been born behind the wheel. The two-and-a-half-day drive down to Los Angeles on Interstate 5 had been quick but dull. The last two and a half days had been tediously slow and hair-raising.

He was beginning to feel as though he were dead from the waist down—a sad state of affairs for a groom of three days.

He couldn't wait to find a comfortable motel, eat something that wasn't between two pieces of bread, take a long walk, then take Gina to bed and share with her all the things there hadn't been time for in the hayloft. He smiled as he thought he would also like to repeat a few things there *had* been time for.

"What're you grinning about?" Gina asked. And as she watched, waiting for an answer, his grin froze then died. He made a last-minute turn onto a side street that earned him an emphatic honk and a rude gesture from the driver behind him.

"The Mercedes?" Gina asked, sitting up in her seat, suddenly alert, every vestige of the day's lazy coziness disintegrating.

"I didn't see it," he replied, turning up the street that

ran parallel to the main road through town. "But I saw Larry standing on a street corner, smoking a cigar."

"Did he see us?"

"Yeah."

"What now?"

"We do a trade-in."

"A what?"

"Just be ready to move in a hurry."

As they passed the town's main intersection from a parallel street a block away, Gina shouted and pointed, "There they are!"

The black Mercedes was parked in front of a gas station, and Shrimp and Larry were running toward it.

Patrick slowed at the next intersection, then proceeded, racing to the next one, where he made a small sound of satisfaction. "There it is. I saw it from the highway."

"A used-car lot?" Gina asked in surprise, seeing the rows and rows of vehicles that took up most of the block. Then she remembered his remark about a trade-in and frowned at him. "Patrick, the paperwork alone could take…"

"Trust me," he said, and pulled into the truck-and-van section at the back of the lot. A salesman at the other end could be seen pointing out the advantages of a late-model Cadillac to a pair of hot prospects. Patrick and Gina went unnoticed.

"If he's working alone," Patrick said, pulling into a vacant spot between a Ford long-bed and a Cherokee, "we've got it made. Get out and look for something with the keys in it."

"Patrick!" Gina gasped, "Then we'll have the police after us as well as the Mercedes."

He shrugged as though that was a negligible detail.

"We're not having much luck getting their help the honest way. Go!"

Patrick took one side of the lot and Gina the other. He kept an eye on the salesman and was relieved by his continued attention on the shopping couple. He blessed the tight economy that probably had him working alone.

But the vehicles on his side of the lot were locked up tight. He was about to race across to help Gina when he spotted the Mercedes doing a slow cruise down the street. He ducked behind a camper shell, trying to spot Gina and warn her. She was nowhere in sight. Now concerned, he crouched toward the back of the camper just in time to have the life scared out of him by a shrill set of brakes and the flat-faced front of an early-seventies Volkswagen bus stopping inches from his nose.

After a breath restored his composure, he saw Gina behind the wheel, grinning broadly and gesturing him to get in.

She was wearing a baseball cap for a feed company that advertised Udder Satisfaction. As the Mercedes rounded the corner out of sight, he climbed into the bus.

"Gina…" he began.

But she wasn't listening. She backed up to the truck with a screech of tires and said urgently. "Get my lamp from the truck."

"Gina…"

"Please!"

The screech had drawn the salesman's attention and there was no time to argue. Cursing the Fates that had gotten him into this, Patrick leapt down from the bus, ran to the truck, fumbled the canopy open, grabbed Gina's precious carton and the blanket and ran back to the bus. She raced forward, blithely ignoring the salesman who stood in the middle of the lot waving both arms.

"Gina…" Patrick warned.

"So what's a little hit-and-run after auto theft and an unpaid motel bill?" she asked calmly as the distance closed between the bus and the salesman.

Patrick was about to reach out for the wheel when she made a sudden turn to the left and exited the lot from a driveway he hadn't noticed. She glanced at him as she made an abrupt turn that slid him toward her. "Just kidding," she said.

"Gina, for God's…!" He began to scold her heatedly when she put a hand to the back of his head and pushed him so that he was doubled over in his seat—and possibly herniated in several places.

"The Mercedes!" she whispered harshly as she pulled up to the stop sign. "Right across from us. Stay down. They're not looking for a woman alone."

"Particularly not one with a hat promising Udder Satisfaction."

"You're just jealous 'cause you don't have a disguise."

"Quit playing around. What's happening?"

"They're staring at me."

"Oh, God."

"Relax. I've always had that effect on men." Gina proceeded toward the main intersection and the Mercedes raced past her, both men looking frantically around, obviously wondering what had become of their prey.

"You can get up now," she said smugly to Patrick. "They fell for it. We're home free."

"Not exactly." Patrick straightened and turned to her with a frown that was both judicious and resigned.

"Why not?" She glanced at him, the brim of the cap darkening her eyes. He swept it off her head.

"Because," he said frustratedly, "now that you've attracted the salesman's attention, he's definitely going to remember us when Larry and Shrimp spot my truck there and go in pretending to be policemen and wanting to know what happened to the felonious driver and his moll."

"Oh." Gina settled back, her shoulders sagging as she followed the highway out of town, picking up speed outside the city limit.

"And," Patrick went on, "we're traveling in a twenty-year-old red Volkswagen that sounds like it's in the last stages of emphysema. It'll be so easy to hide in."

She cast him a dark glance. "You said to look for something with keys in it. All the big-bore V8s with dual carbs were locked up tight. Don't be an ingrate. Uh-oh." The last was delivered in a tone of concern as the bus began to shimmy. She held tight to the wheel to keep it in a straight line. "What's the matter with it?"

"Feels like a bad case of the DTs."

"Patrick!"

Patrick unbuckled his belt. "I think the wheels are out of alignment. Speed up and see if it smooths out."

It didn't. It got worse. She gritted her teeth as the bus shook as though a giant hand were throttling it.

"Try slowing down!" he ordered over the loud racket of rattling seats, dashboard and inside furnishings.

She did, but nothing happened. Patrick slid into the driver's seat behind her and eased her aside, controlling the bucking vehicle while decreasing his foot's pressure on the pedal. At fifty the bus eased back into a comfortable ride. Patrick looked reluctantly into the rearview mirror.

The road behind him was clear. He stared in confused surprise. The black Mercedes should have caught up easily.

"Where the hell are they?" he asked.

When Gina didn't offer a smart reply, he glanced at her to see her staring glumly at him.

The focus of his concern changed abruptly. "What?"

"That means we can't go over fifty," she said worriedly, guiltily.

"It means..." He considered a philosophical way of putting it. "We'll have to be more cunning if we're moving more slowly. That's all."

She raised an eyebrow. "That's all?"

"Trust me. We can do this."

She was hungry and tired, but she didn't want to mention it—this was all her fault, anyway. And the fact that they were now traveling in something that couldn't even do the speed limit was also because of her.

The exhilaration of escape had been quickly eclipsed by the cranky behavior of the bus.

She looked moodily into the glove compartment, found an owner's manual, a flare and a mileage log. She closed it.

"No potato chips?" Patrick teased.

She sighed. "Just dull car stuff."

"Getting hungry?"

"No, I'm fine."

"Liar. You're always hungry." Disturbed by her suddenly quiet mood, he poked a finger at her ribs and was rewarded with an instant giggle. She slapped his hand away and leaned far back in her corner with a look of indignant but amused surprise.

"What are you doing?" she demanded.

"Ticklish, huh?" he said with a speculative grin. "That's something I'll have to take advantage of later."

"What are you so cheerful about?" she asked. "You've been driving for twelve hours on a hamburger and half a bag of potato chips, and we're about to be overtaken by two thugs."

"We're about a hundred and fifty miles from the Oregon border," he said, reaching out companionably to pinch her cheek. "My turf. Then the whole complexion of this will change. Relax. We're almost home."

Home, she thought. Home in his arms—at least for a while. Her mood began to lighten.

As the road turned slightly inland to skirt the King Mountain Range, they passed through a series of small towns just beginning to settle down for the night. The heavy canopy of redwoods brought an early dusk, and as the bus chugged along, lights went on, lining the highway and winking from the shelter of the woods.

"A restaurant!" Gina exclaimed, pointing off the road into a cozy little well of a meadow. "And cabins!" A dozen rustic little cottages were backed up against the trees. Beside them, a little restaurant named Mountain Mama's boasted the best stew around and homemade pie.

Gina's spirits soared. Patrick smiled at the obvious lightening of her mood as he made the turn. He passed the restaurant, following a road that probably led to one of the lights winking in the distance. Halfway up, he nosed the van into the trees and parked.

Gina didn't have to ask why. It was part of his plan to be more cunning now that they were moving more slowly.

They had their pick of cabins, and Patrick chose the

corner one nestled into the trees. The stew was hearty and delicious and accompanied by thick corn bread and the best coffee Patrick had had since he'd left home. The pie was apple and as aromatic as a grandmother's kitchen. And the restaurant was open for breakfast at six.

"I've died and gone to heaven," Gina said lazily as she and Patrick walked arm in arm to the cabin, satiated and relaxed. "Now, if we just had a hayloft to sleep in... Patrick!"

She exclaimed in surprise as he unlocked the cabin door, then swept her up in his arms.

"I haven't carried you over the threshold yet," he said, turning sideways to ease her into the room.

"Shall I get the light?" she asked.

"No," he said softly, kicking the door closed behind him. But instead of taking her to the bed as she expected, he took her to the tiny bathroom and set her down in front of the shower. Then he walked back to the door and threw the bolt, securing them from interference from the outside world.

Despite its rustic appearance, the cabin was warm and the shower stall modern, though very small. Patrick started the water, adjusted the temperature, then peeled Gina's clothes from her and put her inside. Dropping his in a pile beside hers, he joined her, closing the stall door and enclosing them in a steamy cocoon. He washed her hair and she washed his, she scrubbed his back and he scrubbed hers, she moved around to the front of him, soaping his pecs, down the center of his chest, along the jut of his ribs—and then he crushed her to him, the soap went flying and her feet were suddenly clear of the shower floor.

As she wrapped her arms tightly around his neck, he

braced her thighs around his hips and gently probed inside her with a deftness that made her gasp.

Patrick backed out from under the spray, never ceasing his taunting exploration. In a moment she was quivering like the lights that sparkled in the trees, like the stars in the sky, like the early-morning mountain air.

She opened her mouth over his, hungry for him. That delicious release only made her greedy for more of him, desperate to share what she felt, wild with the need to try to return the pleasure he'd given her—and everything else that had so changed her life in the small space of the last sixty hours.

She felt bound to him, part of him, more connected to his life than she'd ever felt to her own in the past twenty-five years.

He entered her without moving either of them, and she felt herself enfold and embrace him—and felt the same transformation she'd known last night in a hayloft.

Patrick couldn't believe the waves and waves of pleasure that wound through him as the water beat at her back, beat her against him as she swayed and squirmed to be closer, to hold him tighter and take him higher.

Her little cries of distress made him crush her closer and smile to himself. She was fearless and clever and unashamedly hedonistic—and putty in his hands.

A sudden blast of cold water earned a yelp from both of them. Patrick quickly elbowed the door open and set her outside, then fearlessly stepped into the water to turn the taps off.

He stepped out of the shower to be enfolded by Gina in a thick towel. Wrapped in her own, sarong-style, she rubbed warmth into his arms and shoulders and back.

When she came around in front of him, she remembered too late what had happened the last time—or remembered just in time, she thought with a smile as he swept her up and strode with her to the bed.

Chapter Eight

"I'm really tired of this sweater." Gina pulled on the bulky white V-neck she'd worn the past two days and stared disconsolately into the pocked mirror over the cabin's rickety luggage stand. Her image looked back droopily. She put a hand under her hair and held it atop her head, hoping to lift her appearance.

Patrick, walking out of the bathroom, seized the opportunity to kiss the back of her neck. The kiss became a nibble that worked to her shoulder then back up to her ear before he turned her in his arms and kissed her in earnest. "I think you look wonderful," he said.

She leaned back against his laced hands. "You're a liar, but thanks."

He freed one hand to run it over his chin, now dark with two days' growth of beard. "I'm the one looking shaggy."

"Oh, no," she said, running a hand over the wiry stubble, remembering how it had made her body tingle in its most sensitive places. She grinned affectionately. "I like it."

He chuckled. "Ready for breakfast?"

"I'm ready for new clothes," she said disconsolately. "I hate to sound like a whining wife already, but if I

don't have something different to put on, and something
with which to curl my hair..." She held out a strand of
glossy-clean but straight chestnut-colored hair. "I'm going to be very difficult to live with. Worse than I am
now."

His eyes widened dramatically. "I'm not sure I could
take that. We'll be in Eureka by mid-morning. If there
are no surprises on the road, we'll have a brief shopping
spree."

She hugged him close. "You're wonderful. Now let
me show you my appreciation."

THE MORNING was sunny and cool as Patrick pointed the
bus northward. The radio didn't work, but he'd cranked
the heat up, refusing Gina's offer to let him wear the
jacket for a while. For an hour they were alone on the
road.

"It's making me nervous that we haven't spotted
them," Gina observed as they drove through miles and
miles of sun-dappled woods. "Where do you think they
are?"

"Regrouping," he said. "Maybe getting reinforcements. They probably didn't expect you to be as much
trouble as you've become." He cast her a grin. "But
then, they don't know you like I do."

She huffed, then laughed. "Very funny. Maybe
they've just finally decided whatever they were after is
too much trouble and they've given up. I still can't imagine what it could be. Who did you call after breakfast
this morning?"

"Sin. He has a friend at the Department of Motor
Vehicles who's going to try to get us the registry on the
Mercedes. Maybe what Shrimp and Larry are after is
something you sold off when you cleared out the ware-

house. What was there again? That weird lamp, bolts of
fabric, a broken chair and…what else?''

''A plant stand and a vase. But none of them was
anything valuable. And if he'd wanted them, he'd have
taken them with him, wouldn't he?''

''Unless he was afraid he might get caught with it.
Didn't you say you were putting the pieces together by
then and brought the police to the warehouse?''

She thought that through. ''Yeah. You mean he was
planning to come back for it later?''

Patrick nodded. ''And when he did and it was gone,
he knew you would know where it was.''

''Why didn't he just call me and *speak* to me and get
it over with? Why annoy me with phone calls and follow
me around?''

''He must think you *know* you have it, whatever it is.
The calls were probably just to unsettle you. He followed
you, thinking he'd find you trying to sell or hock whatever it is and he could handle it from there himself when
you'd gone. He *kept* following you because you didn't
do anything with it, and he kept waiting for you to.''

Gina leaned back and closed her eyes, thinking
through the items she'd found in a heap in the middle
of the warehouse floor, discarded, she'd thought, as too
inexpensive to claim Yale's attention.

Unless there'd been something about one of them she
simply hadn't seen or been aware of.

''You're sure there's nothing valuable about your
lamp?'' Patrick asked.

She didn't have to consider. ''Positive. It's nothing
but plaster and glass beads. I love it for its significance
to me alone, not its value.''

He snaked an arm across her lap and tucked his hand
under her knee. ''The middle of the rainbow, huh?''

She leaned into him. "Right." And I think I've found it, she thought in wonder.

They passed a road sign that read Eureka—eighteen miles.

"Almost shopping-spree time," Patrick said. "Do me a favor?"

"What?"

"Buy more of that smoky gray underwear."

She laughed softly against his upper arm. "You took it off me so fast I thought you didn't like it."

"It matches your eyes," he said, glancing away from the road for an instant, his eyes alight with a vivid memory, "and when it's all you're wearing, it's like being lost in a cloudy heaven."

She dissolved against him. "I'll buy everything gray, how's that?"

"Unwise," he replied. "When we get home, I'll be expected to function in my usually efficient and competent manner. I won't be able to unless the gray you're wearing is covered up and waiting for me to discover it in the privacy of our home."

She sighed as the scenery rolled by. "You're making it hard for me to remember there's a time limit on this relationship."

"I've always ignored limits," he said lightly. "Or constraints of any kind."

She raised her head to look at his profile in surprise. "Surely the Marine Corps didn't let you do that?"

"Every man accepts a certain authority over his life," he said, guiding the bus easily as the road rose and curved. "But within those parameters, you set your own rules. And anyway, the corps doesn't own me anymore. No one does."

A subtle reminder, she wondered. She didn't want to

think about it. At that moment she wanted nothing in the world but to sit beside him in a loud and slow but cozy VW bus winding through a beautiful mountain road on the way to a shopping trip. Except for the black Mercedes, she thought, life was about as close to perfect as it could get.

EUREKA WAS a lively little town with absolutely everything they needed. When Gina fingered the contents of a new rack of summery shirts and pants, Patrick pushed her to what remained of the winter wear. "Turtlenecks, jeans, sweats, woolly socks," he said. "Candle Bay isn't sunny Southern California. You'll need warm clothes until late June, early July."

She found a blow dryer and curling iron and new makeup.

"I kind of like you without that stuff," Patrick said when he met her at the cosmetics counter and she asked for his credit card.

The clerk gave Gina a jealous look as she handed the card over.

There was some discussion over who should buy the new jacket.

Patrick pointed to the leather one he'd lent her. "It's way too big," he said. "You have to push the sleeves up and you could wrap it around you twice."

They stood in the men's department, and she turned to the three-way mirror. With her hair caught up in a new banana clip, and with no makeup, she looked about thirteen but, she thought, very chic.

"I like it. It's very fashionable. The big look is in and sleeves are always pushed up." She turned away from the mirror and perused the racks. She finally stopped at a rack of tweed stadium jackets, pulled down a black-and-gray one and held it for Patrick to slip into.

After they paid, they went to have coffee and bought a bag of donuts and muffins to take with them. "Just in case," Patrick said as they climbed into the bus. "You peering into an empty glove compartment is not a pretty sight."

Gina laughed and thought she might die of happiness.

"Oh, my new curling iron!" she exclaimed, looking over her packages again to make sure she hadn't put it in a bigger bag. Then she remembered. "I set everything down in the bakery to look at the display case."

In the act of snapping his seat belt in place, Patrick stopped and slipped out of it. "I remember," he said with a wry glance her way as he leapt out of the bus. "It was embarrassing when you pushed those little children out of the way. Wait here. I'll be right back."

"I didn't push them out of the way. I just asked them to move so I could get a better look at the Danish."

"Yeah, right. The little boy ended up sprawled on the day-old bread rack and the little girl's probably still flying."

She grinned and rolled her eyes at his exaggeration. "Will you go get my stuff before someone else picks it up?"

He turned back to add, "If you spot our 'friends,' honk the horn."

"Right."

Patrick was becoming concerned because he was having a good time. He shouldn't be. He should be taut and vigilant and aware of the possibility of danger at every turn.

Instead his mind was filled with Gina and the sensory

memory of the last two nights in her arms. He'd been anticipating nightfall since he'd awakened that morning.

He knew he had it bad because all her little quirks didn't annoy him.

Love, he wondered? A scary proposition, but he always faced the truth. He'd spent a lifetime being stronger and tougher than everything else that came his way.

He shouldered his way into the bakery and decided to think about that later. The clerk behind the counter remembered him instantly and pointed to the corner near an umbrella stand where the package still stood. He scooped it up with a wave of thanks and pushed his way out the door.

Fear lodged in his throat the moment he stepped onto the sidewalk. Parked two spots up the street was an empty black Mercedes. It hadn't been there when he'd walked into the bakery. And Gina hadn't hit the horn.

As he pressed back into the bakery doorway, his eyes flew to the bus, parked halfway down the street. He felt a sharp clutch of fear as he saw that it, too, was empty.

He started to sidle toward it through the spare midmorning foot traffic when he saw Shrimp and Larry approach the bus from the street side. He ducked into the front of a sporting-goods shop and watched as Larry tried the door and Shrimp walked the length of the bus, peering in through the windows.

At any moment he expected a shout of victory from the big man when he spotted Gina. But it didn't come. He began to wonder if they'd already taken her, maybe put her in the trunk of the Mercedes.

Panic fought with common sense and he had to assert his experience and training to keep his emotions in check. If they had her, they wouldn't be hanging around.

And he doubted they would bother looking for him. Still, he wouldn't be able to draw another breath until he knew.

Gina saw them coming, he told himself, and left the bus to hide. But why hadn't she honked the horn?

Shrimp and Larry looked around, exchanged a few words, then separated, one on each side of the street, apparently to begin a methodical, store-by-store search.

Shrimp took the bakery side of the street. Patrick hid behind an inflated rubber raft while Shrimp started into a drugstore. The big man was driven back by a group of young girls in very short skirts, arms loaded down with packages, hair teased into pointed spikes.

Shrimp gave them a wide berth and headed back into the shop. About to try to make it to the van and begin his own search for Gina, Patrick noticed a certain familiarity to one of the pair of legs.

As he watched, the owner of the legs handed a tall bag to one of the other girls and separated herself from the group. She slipped the sunglasses down her nose and looked anxiously up and down the street. Gina!

God! She'd bumped elbows with Shrimp! He wanted to hug her because she was safe, then he wanted to kill her. Patrick pulled the collar of his jacket up and made his way quickly but calmly toward her. She had started to move toward the bus. Then she spotted him and ran to him.

"Patrick," she said, grabbing his arm, "they're—"

"I know." He turned her swiftly to the bus, snapped, "Get in and get down!" then ran across the street to the Mercedes. He lifted the hood, removed the distributor cap and tossed it aside, then ran back to the bus and leapt into the driver's seat. He knew the moment he turned the key in the ignition he would have Larry's attention. Nothing else in the world could be mistaken for a VW engine.

He turned the key, the engine percolated loudly and he pulled out into the street. Through the rearview mirror he saw Larry come running out of a florist shop and race to the middle of the street. His features were growing too distant to be distinguishable, but the fist shaken at their exhaust wasn't. He grinned as he realized how the gesture would change when Larry realized the car wouldn't start.

Patrick did his best to eat up the road—or, in the case of the Volkswagen, at least nibble at it—while he could. It kept him from killing Gina.

GINA, brushing her hair back into order and tissuing makeup off her face, knew something was wrong apart from the fact that the black Mercedes had almost caught them. Patrick looked positively severe as he stared at the road, sparing only an occasional glance in the rearview mirror. And never one in her direction.

Not yet recovered from the fright she felt when she saw the Mercedes approaching through the makeup mirror, she was in no mood to baby *his* mood.

"What?" she demanded when they'd driven fifteen miles without speaking. "Tell me. How did this get to be my fault?"

He still didn't look at her. "We'll talk about it," he said in an ominously quiet voice, "when I can forget the image of you bumping elbows with Shrimp. You just have to push everything to the edge, don't you? You had to bump into him to show yourself just how close you could get with your clever little disguise."

"Oh, it's the disguise thing again, is it?" she asked angrily, forgetting to explain how the scenario had come about. "Well, next time we'll be sure and get *you* one. You get so testy when I have one and you don't."

"Gina…" There was warning in his tone, but she was too upset to hear it.

"We'll get you one," she went on, "the next time that I have three minutes to save my hide and you're nowhere to be found!"

"I went for the package *you* carelessly left in the bakery," he retorted, his voice beginning to rise. "Remember?"

"Well, pardon me! You're the one who made the decision to leave all our stuff in a Santa Cruz motel room. If I hadn't had to carry all the things we bought, maybe I wouldn't have forgotten some of it."

He shouted an oath. "I asked you to hold them while I paid for the half-dozen donuts that would keep *you* quiet until lunch!"

"So I have a healthy appetite!" she shouted back. "Five hundred thousand dollars will pay for a *lot* of donuts! Maybe I could expect a little tolerance."

"Why? It's your father's money. You blew yours through mistaken friendship and bad judgment!"

"Well, apparently that wasn't the only time I've exercised bad judgment!"

There was a moment's pulsing silence. "Hey," he said easily, "you've got a clear way out anytime you want it."

"Fine!" She was cut to the quick. Only moments ago she'd been thinking about how happy she was and how, for the first time in her life, her future looked promising. It had taken a very short time to change all that. "Fine. Just stop and let me out. Anywhere along here will be fine."

Patrick ignored her and continued to drive, always

checking the rearview mirror for any sign of the Mercedes. He would settle with her the moment he felt sure they were in the clear.

"Maybe you're deaf as well as irascible," she said quietly. "I asked you to let me out."

He shook his head at the absurdity of her request. "You may take my silence as refusal to comply."

"Fine." She put a hand out to reach for her door handle. He had her other one in a steel grip so fast he stopped her action.

"Put that hand down," he ordered, "or you'll wish I'd let you out, so help me."

Her hand remained suspended, but she glared at him despite the pain in the hand he held. "So you turn out to have a brutal side," she said.

He glanced at the road then back at her. "You want to see it?" he asked tightly.

She was more than happy to push him. She tugged on the handle and the door opened.

She'd never intended to leap from the bus. She'd been sure he would pull over the moment she opened her door. But the wind caught it and the door swung wide, pulling her with it. Pavement flew by at a startling speed.

She heard Patrick's shout, but for an instant she could do nothing but watch in fascination as the fog line streaked past. Then a yank she was sure had dislocated her shoulder pulled her back into the bus.

Patrick lost the fragile hold he'd kept on his control. Still holding Gina's arm, he pulled off the road and cut the motor.

He turned to her, fury in his eyes and in his grip. "You insufferable brat!" he shouted. "You don't need a contemporary husband, you need a nineteenth-century man who would take you over his knee and show you what your attention-getting games will earn you.''

She knew she was courting danger, but that seemed to be what life with him was all about. And he hadn't once bothered to ask her what had happened—he had simply accused.

She raised a haughty eyebrow. ''I guess the classic line here is, 'You wouldn't dare!' But you might remember where the money comes from in this relationship before you make up your mind.''

She should have remembered he was a decisive man. One moment they were face-to-face, and the next he sat where she'd been and she was suspended over his knee, her legs trapped under the dash.

''Patrick!'' she cried in mortified surprise.

''If you'll remember...'' His voice drifted down to her as she stared at the bus's old blue carpet and her clutch purse lying on its side. She struggled but a hard hand on her hipbone held her in place. ''You don't have a dime until next March, and my check's already cashed and being distributed. I would dare, Gina.''

He tightened his grip on her. She gasped and tensed, waiting for the first blow to fall.

Patrick heard the little sound, felt her fist clench on the thigh of his jeans and decided he'd made his point. He yanked her up and sat her down firmly in the driver's seat.

Her cheeks were flushed, her eyes overbright with anger and embarrassment. But he had her full attention.

''I *would* dare,'' he said again. ''In fact, for your own safety, the next time, I probably should. But I apparently have more respect for you than you have for me.''

Tears pooled in her eyes, but she willed them not to fall.

"I'd never deliberately hurt you," he went on, his voice calmer, "but *you* scared the hell out of me twice in the space of twenty minutes."

A tear fell, anyway. Furious at him, mad at herself, she swiped it away and folded her arms. "The horn didn't work," she said quickly because her voice was unsteady.

"What?" He frowned, forgetting for a moment what the horn had to do with it.

"You said if I saw them, to honk the horn." She remembered sharply how frightened she'd been for him. "I tried. It didn't work." She angled him a judicious glare and looked away from him.

He reached out to slap the palm of his hand against the horn. It didn't work. It was one of the vehicle's features he hadn't tried since they'd "liberated" it.

He fought feelings of guilt by remembering her pushing the bus door open and nearly falling out.

"Don't look so righteous," he scolded. "You opened the door of a moving vehicle."

She turned to him, fire under the tears in her eyes. "You *accused* me of playing games! When I couldn't warn you by honking the horn, I was going to come for you, only they got out of the car before I could reach the bakery. So I ducked into the drugstore."

He frowned, trying to unravel her meaning. "Why didn't you just stay where you were safe?"

She looked at him as though he was dim. "Because I was worried about *you* bumping into them."

"I told you to honk the horn," he said, "so I could come to protect *you*. You were not expected to come and protect *me*."

"Well, if it's any comfort," she said, looking away

from him again, "I'm sorry I did. I should have let you get shot or hauled away or whatever they have in mind."

She really had left the bus to save him. His anger was beginning to dissipate. But it wasn't gone.

"What," he asked, "does that have to do with opening the door of a moving vehicle?"

She sighed heavily and shook her head. "I was angry. I'm not always rational when I'm mad."

He reached across the space that separated them and pulled her into his lap. "All right. We've made each other angry and learned it isn't wise. We still have a ways to go. We have to do it in harmony, or we're not going to make it. Agreed?"

She gave him a warning gray glance. "If you're going to ask me to kiss you, forget it."

"I wasn't going to ask," he said, then took a kiss that gave her everything she needed at that moment. It was filled with passion, strength and tenderness.

It was easy to kiss him back, to wrap her arms around him and lose herself in his embrace.

She felt herself relax as his strong hand rubbed gently up and down her spine.

"I'm sorry I made the crack about the money," she said, planting a kiss under his ear.

He rubbed a hand gently along her bare thigh. "It's all right. I'm sorry I made the crack about the donuts. Incidentally…" He fingered the little scrap of delicate black fabric that barely covered the tops of her thighs. "Where'd you get the skirt? You were wearing sweats when I left you and all the stuff we bought was in the bus."

"It's not a skirt," she said, tugging on it to show him it was attached to the brief panties under it. "It's the skirt of my teddy. I bought it today, too, but I liked it so much I left it on.''

''Where are the sweats?''

''I had them tucked in my jacket. I tossed them in the back while you were busy messing under the hood of the Mercedes.''

He sighed and rubbed a hand gently along the silky skin from knee to torso. ''Well, you'd better put them on again if we're ever going to make the Oregon border.''

She slipped off his lap and he resumed his place behind the wheel. When she bent to reach her sweats, he took advantage of the opportunity to swat her backside.

She turned to him with a frown.

''Just a reminder,'' he said as he turned the key and the motor coughed to life, ''never to reach for the door handle in a moving vehicle.''

Chapter Nine

Gina felt as though she'd passed into a parallel universe when they crossed the Oregon border. She wondered if it was the suggestion that they'd almost reached Patrick's "turf" and some kind of safety that made the trees greener, the sky bluer, even the fat pewter clouds seem friendly.

"I'm glad you talked me into turtlenecks instead of halter tops," she said as they parked the van two blocks off the highway in Brookings and walked back to a little restaurant off the water.

A cold wind whipped around them, salty and fragrant. Gina tried to walk around the restaurant for a clearer view of the driftwood strewn on the beach, but Patrick pulled her back.

"No time for that," he said. "My guess is that when the Mercedes didn't start, they found another car. The next time they close in on us, we won't have the advantage of knowing they're coming." He'd decided to have the oak doors shipped, after all. The weight would slow the bus down considerably.

Gina placed their order while Patrick made a phone call. He came back to the table with a frown.

"The Mercedes is registered to R. P. Danforth," he said. "That name mean anything to you?"

She repeated it to herself, waiting for memory to kick in. It didn't. "No." She sipped at her coffee and shook her head. "That's weird. Why would someone I don't even know be after me for something I don't have?"

"Or don't know you have."

"I know," she insisted, "I don't have it. Apparently whatever they wanted wasn't in all the luggage we left behind in Santa Cruz. If it's someone Yale is connected with, the lamp and all the other stuff in the warehouse was obviously worthless to him because he left it. What else is there? Just…me."

Patrick's dark eyes locked on her, moody, faintly self-deprecating and curiously resigned. "Well, now you're mine. I'll just have to make that clearer to him once we cross paths again."

She patted his hand teasingly. "You should have fallen for some leggy Oregon girl who knows all about fishing and doesn't have people chasing her all over the country."

He shook his head. "Sounds dull. After the military, I have a thirst for adventure. Eat your lunch. We can make it to Newport tonight."

GINA STRAINED at her seat belt for a better view of the wild coast as they headed for Newport. Towering mountains pitched steeply into the ocean; surf battered against craggy bluffs spewing foam in dramatic displays. Long stretches of smooth sand and beautiful little harbors went on and on.

Then there were miles of sand dunes. "Look at the dune buggies!" Gina pointed to the spots of color crawling up and down the shifting landscape like bugs in a garden.

Patrick glanced away from the road, studied the dune buggies with disapproval and nodded. "If I were king," he said with a facetious smile, "I wouldn't allow anything with a motor on the sand."

"Erosion?"

He nodded again. "And mental erosion. Water washing on the sand, sand drifting, sea gulls calling, sandpipers running, are for enjoying without the interference of blaring noise. The beach should be for thinking and dreaming and restoring yourself."

She studied his grave profile in pleased surprise. "That's a poetic thought for a former soldier turned businessman."

He shrugged a shoulder. "Life and death make you philosophical. I suppose you grew up on water skis on the back of a motorboat."

She shook her head. "No. I grew up on a tennis court. Do you play?"

He nodded. "We have two on the hotel grounds. We'll have to settle all our arguments there."

"How do you know we'll have any?"

He smiled at the road. "We've had three already and we've only been married three days."

"This is our fourth day," she corrected.

"I apologize. Four days. That's not a hopeful average, do you think?"

She turned toward him and leaned her elbow on the back of her seat. "When you're being chased by hoodlums, it's probably not a bad average. I'm generally in a good mood. And you seem to be," she added, teasing carefully, "as long as no one does anything to frighten you."

He took the gentle criticism with a smile that had an edge of warning in it. "Remember that. You given any thought to what you'll need to help me with the child-care facility?"

She delved into the little clutch that went everywhere with her. "I've made some notes."

"You have?" he asked in surprise. "When?"

"Various times. Before we got married. Day before yesterday while you made the phone call to Sin. Yesterday morning, before you got up."

That surprised him into silence for a moment.

"So what did you conclude while I was asleep?" he asked.

She consulted a small leather-bound book. "We'll need the obvious. Bright paint, indoor-outdoor carpet, a carpenter who won't mind doing some 'fun' stuff."

"Fun stuff?"

"Small furniture, cubbyholes, hidey-holes, lockers for the children's things."

"Ah."

"Books," she went on. "Toys, craft stuff, pillows and blankets, and if the budget'll stretch that far, a VCR and movies."

He nodded slowly, marveling that she'd obviously given the project enough thought to have a pretty thorough idea of what she planned to do. Any notion he might have had that she'd do a halfhearted job was put to rest.

"Sounds good," he said. "We'll go over it when we get there. I've got two rooms that might serve. You can decide which one."

Gina tucked her notebook back into her purse and put it aside. "And when I'd finished making my notes," she said softly, "I watched you sleep."

That statement hung in the air in the confinement of the bus, gently suggestive, further unsettling. "Really," he said.

"Yes." She propped her head on her hand and studied him. She liked the little lines on his forehead. "You were frowning…" She reached a hand out and touched his forehead just above the bridge of his nose. "Just like you are now."

"Must have been wondering what to do with you," he said, sparing her a quick, unreadable glance. "Just like I am now."

"Mmm. Did you dream a solution?"

"You wouldn't want to hear about it," he said with a straight face. "It involved a gag and handcuffs."

PULLING INTO a rest stop a little while later, Patrick perused the map on the kiosk that listed tourist attractions on the coast, while Gina went to the rest room. Then he walked back to lean against the wall in front of the ladies' room and wait.

He frowned, thinking that for a woman who usually didn't dawdle in the bathroom, Gina was taking an awfully long time. He straightened, suddenly concerned.

"Gina?" he called.

She answered instantly. "Yeah?"

Relief relaxed him. "You 'bout ready?"

"A few more minutes," she shouted back. "I'm curling my hair."

"What?" He couldn't believe what he'd heard.

"I'm curling my hair," she repeated. "This Oregon dampness is making my ends frizzy."

He closed his eyes and counted to five. He didn't have time to make it to ten. "Gina!" he barked. "You're being chased by hoods and you're curling your hair? I'm going to frizz your other end if you don't move it!''

"Honestly," she said after a moment, her tone slightly injured. "I refuse to look a frump, even when I'm running for my life. I thought you were an understanding husband. I'll just be another minute."

He paused to count again, and that was when he heard the low purr of a powerful motor. It was cruising, not racing, and it was coming from the picnic shelter where he'd concealed the bus.

He hid himself behind the ladies'-room wall and watched as a buglike red Corvette cruised up the road from the camper side of the rest stop. A man of small stature drove, and the passenger's seat was empty. Patrick wasn't fooled. He'd used the trick of hiding his passenger enough times himself in the past few days.

He ran into the ladies' room, past Gina who still stood in front of the mirror, and into the stall directly below the air vent.

"Gina! Get over here!" he ordered as he clambered onto the seat, braced a foot on the paper dispenser and propelled himself onto the wall that separated the cubicles. Supporting himself with a grip on a light fixture, he slapped the flat of his hand against the vent. It didn't give. He heard the hum of the Corvette grow louder.

He hit it again and again and it finally flew upward with a loud clatter. The hum was now right outside the rest-room door.

Gina scrambled up after him, stood on the toilet seat, reached up to grab the top of the wall and hoist herself to plant a foot on the paper dispenser as he'd done.

One hand braced in the open hole, Patrick reached the other down to her and hauled her up beside him to stand on the narrow ledge of the wall. She wobbled precariously and he held her steady until she was balanced. Then he pulled himself up through the hole.

With pounding heart, Gina heard the slam of car doors, the sound of voices. Patrick reached down for her and she clutched his biceps for dear life. For an instant, she was just plain tired of the struggle. Then the awkward position reminded her of being hauled up into the hayloft. It gave her a suddenly different perspective on her situation. She walked her feet up the wall as he pulled and suddenly found herself on the slanted cedar roof of the rest room. Soundlessly Patrick replaced the air vent.

Knees braced against the pitch of the roof, Gina and Patrick lay back, listening to the conversation as Larry and Shrimp checked out the men's room, then the ladies'.

"Well, where the hell are they?" Larry's sharp voice.

"Maybe they stole another car," Shrimp said.

"Stupid. They'd have taken their stuff with them. It's still in the bus."

"They left their stuff before."

"No, they're here. I know it. I'm sure. All we gotta do is find 'em."

"Why don't we call the bo—"

"I'm not calling the boss again until I have her neck in my hand. Remember what he said last time."

There was an audible swallow. "We find 'em, or... nobody'll ever find us."

"Right. Start looking. Check everything everywhere. Start with the woods behind the rest room. I'm going across to the beach."

"Okay, Larry."

Clearly visible against the roof of the rest room, Patrick and Gina watched Shrimp lumber off into the thick trees, a gun clearly visible in his hand. He never once looked back over his shoulder. Gina breathed a sigh of relief when he disappeared.

"I hope," she whispered, "you've called for a helicopter to pluck us off the roof."

"Sorry." Patrick inched his way to the edge and looked down. "Piece o' cake," he said, turning to wave her to follow him. "Come on." He disappeared in a nimble leap.

Gina crab-walked to the edge and discovered that Patrick's piece o' cake was a considerable drop to asphalt. He waited, arms raised to receive her.

"Jump!" he whispered harshly, beckoning to her.

"Oh, God!" she grumbled under her breath, rolling onto her stomach and easing her legs and backside over the edge. She gripped with her fingers as she hung the length of her arms.

Patrick's hands clamped on to her calves. "I've got you. Let go!"

According to all reasonable laws of physics, she was sure the upper part of her body would pitch forward, she would tumble out of Patrick's precarious hold and land headfirst in the daffodils that bordered the rest room.

She was surprised to find trust more reliable than physics. She let go and Patrick's arms immediately snaked around her as she fell, one around her hips, the other just under her breasts. He eased her to the asphalt, caught her hand, and they headed off at a run toward the bus.

She heard Shrimp's shout behind them before they were halfway across the clearing toward the shelter of trees and the bus. They kept running.

The bus looked as though it had fallen into a hole. As Patrick jerked her to a stop, Gina stared at the vehicle that appeared to be sitting a foot lower than it had when they'd left it. She noticed the slashed tires just as Patrick whispered a pithy one-word assessment of their situation.

He yanked her around the bus and toward the woods. Breath was already burning in her lungs.

"Is this where I tell you bravely to leave me behind and save yourself?" she asked as she pumped after him for all she was worth.

"No, this is where you shut up," he retorted, slapping an overhanging branch aside as they ran into the shelter of Oregon firs, "and save your breath for running."

They continued to run. She ducked and dodged, fully expecting to get a faceful of bark at any moment.

She heard shouting and footsteps pounding behind them. Patrick took a left down a slimy slope. She followed, losing her footing. He caught her at the waist as she fell and pinned her there with his body, a leg slung over her to prevent her from sliding. He put a finger to his lips for silence. She nodded, but couldn't help gasping for breath.

They were just below the lip of the slope, she noted with a backward glance over her head. Footsteps pounded past.

When they'd gone, she stirred under Patrick, expecting him to leap up and lead the way back to the rest area. He shook his head at her and clamped a hand over her mouth.

Then she realized what was wrong. It had been only one pair of footsteps. Another came along more slowly and with considerably less sound. Larry.

Still pinned under Patrick with his hand over her mouth, Gina looked up at him, praying that he wasn't going to do what he appeared to have in mind. She watched his alert eyes track the sound just above their heads, saw the anger and the time-to-get-even look in them as the footsteps paused before going on.

She shook her head at him frantically, hoping to discourage him from his plan.

Patrick saw the fear for him in Gina's eyes and looked away from it, unwilling to consider it. He'd had it. The showdown was here and now. What had been for a while an interesting little adventure was becoming a pain in the butt. He wanted to get on with his life. He wanted to get on with Gina.

He waited until Larry was several feet past him, then he leapt silently up the slope. He was on him before he knew what happened. With any luck, he'd own Larry's gun before Shrimp even heard the fracas.

He hadn't been out of the military long enough to forget that luck was seldom on your side, but he was reminded sharply, anyway, when he had Larry pinned to the ground and heard Gina's scream.

Distracted, he took a knee to the gut and was suddenly looking down the barrel of a Colt .45.

A moment later Gina struggled up over the rim of the slope, her clothes muddy, dead leaves in her hair.

"I fell down the…slope," she said, hesitating as she looked at the obvious result of her distracting scream. Still breathing hard, she dropped her head onto her arms and groaned.

Larry encouraging him with an upward motion of the barrel of the gun, Patrick got to his feet and pulled her up beside him. This was going to require a few dangerous moves. He wished Gina were still at the bottom of the slope.

"Okay, so where is it?" Larry said testily, obviously as tired of the long northward trek as they were. He put the gun to Patrick's temple. "I want it in my hand now or I'm going to pollute this beautiful wayside with your brains."

Patrick pushed Gina to the side and backed away, hoping to draw Larry with him. "We don't have it," he said.

"Yes, you do," Larry cocked a bullet into the chamber. "The boss says you do."

"We left it on the road."

Larry considered that possibility with a frown, then shook his head, an angry tick beginning in his jaw. "You wouldn't do that. That would be stupid, and if there's anything you ain't, it's *stupid!* Now where is it?"

Patrick would have preferred to be a little farther from Gina. The gun could discharge when he hit him, but Larry was getting too itchy to dawdle with him any longer.

Patrick was just psyching himself to put everything he had into his right fist when Gina ran to him, interposing herself between him and Larry. She flattened her back against his chest and put both arms out protectively.

"Don't you threaten him," she said angrily. "He has nothing to do with this! He doesn't even know where I put it." That sounded believable, she thought frantically. Of course, *she* didn't know where she'd put it, either, because she didn't know what "it" was. She spared Larry that detail.

"Gina!" Patrick took one of her extended arms and spun her away from him with it while Larry looked on in confusion. Patrick pointed a finger at her. "You stay out of it!" he said, trying to convey with a look that he had a plan if she would just let him get to it.

He was not surprised when his silent communication conveyed nothing.

She flew back at him again, this time standing on tiptoe to wrap her arms around his neck and resist his efforts to dislodge her.

"You'll have to shoot me to get to him," she said to Larry, though she was looking at Patrick. "And then how will you find it?"

While Larry wondered about that, Patrick yanked Gina to the left and landed his right fist in Larry's face. The gun went flying and so did Larry. He landed with a thud and didn't move.

"What did you do to Larry?" Shrimp demanded, stepping into the clearing, his shaking gun pointed at Patrick. He walked to his partner's inert frame and nudged it with his toe. "I got lost, Larry. Are you okay?"

"I killed him," Patrick said, wishing he hadn't been worried about Gina and had watched which way Larry's gun had flown. He had one course of action left. When you didn't have a weapon, you had to have presence.

He strode toward Shrimp as though four men armed with M16s followed him. "Just like I'm going to kill you," he said, never taking his eyes off the quaking hand holding the gun. "Unless you give that to me. Now."

Shrimp handed the Smith and Wesson automatic over without a second thought. Patrick turned to Gina. "Run back to the rest rooms and see if there's a trucker there who can call the state police for us."

"BOTH MEN deny knowledge of Gardner or Danforth," the state trooper said. Patrick and Gina sat in chairs facing his desk in the office at Newport. "They said they just targeted you as a wealthy couple and thought they'd share your traveler's checks.''

Patrick closed his eyes and summoned patience. He was just beginning to understand Gina's frustration in getting law enforcement to help her. "We've traveled the last six hundred miles in a twenty-year-old Volkswagen bus. Would that make us sound like good pickings to you? And if they wanted to steal from us, why didn't they break into the van?''

"They slashed the tires," the trooper reminded.

"To disable it so we couldn't get away," Gina said. "We're telling you this isn't about theft. They've followed us from Los Angeles. And they'd been following me long before that. They want me!''

"Why?''

"I don't know. They're after something I'm supposed to have.''

"What?''

Gina looked helplessly at Patrick and subsided in her chair. "I don't know," she replied, defeated.

"And you have no witnesses to these previous attempts to kidnap you?''

"The hotel manager in Santa Cruz," Patrick said.

"Did you call him?''

The trooper nodded. "He never heard of you. Says you're not on his register.''

"We left owing him seventy-two dollars," Gina cried. "He *has* to remember us.''

At the trooper's raised eyebrow, Patrick stood and pulled Gina to her feet. "They bought him off. Big surprise.''

"Well, I've got both of them on violation of parole because of their weapons. Both have petty theft and assault records. I'm afraid that's the best I can do for you right now." He smiled genially. "Have a pleasant trip."

A pleasant trip. Patrick looked at Gina, saw the utter frustration of the past two hours registered in her eyes, and was surprised to find himself needing to laugh. When he smiled, her mood changed quickly, as though she'd just been looking for an excuse. They left the office arm in arm, laughing hysterically.

"IT DOESN'T FEEL like it's over, does it?" Gina asked wearily. She lay back against Patrick's chest in an old ball-and-claw bathtub in a Victorian bed-and-breakfast outside of Newport. The tub was filled with herby-smelling bubbles, and Gina soaped the arm with which Patrick held her to him.

"No," he said, raising his other arm to hold her so that she could sponge off the soapy one. "Because, technically, it isn't. Though Shrimp and Larry will probably do time, I'm sure whoever is after whatever it is will be back. But I have security people at the hotel, and until this is resolved, you're not going anywhere without me or one of my people."

That should rankle, Gina thought, but the past four days had taught her to respect and value his protection.

She soaped his other arm. "I suppose after what I've put you through you're already thinking about divorce," she said.

The hand that held her to him gently stroked her breast. She felt the little shudder of thrill deep inside. "Do I look as though I've hired a lawyer?" he asked.

She soaped the second arm. "You certainly have grounds. And your contract with my father was verbal, not written."

"I promised." He took the sponge from her and

tossed it to the foot of the tub. It landed with a plop and a spray of suds. He brought her back even closer to assure himself of her attention. ''I don't have to sign my name to feel committed to the deal—in business or in marriage.''

She leaned her head into his shoulder, feeling warm and safe, but suffering a nagging pang of guilt. ''I hate to think of you planning a big party in your remodeled hotel while worrying if your wife is going to be snatched from under your nose at any moment, ruining everything and probably getting you a lot of bad press.''

''Nothing gets snatched from me,'' he said, turning her so that she knelt astride him. ''If Gardner or Danforth or whoever the hell is behind this shows up, we'll be ready for him and you'll be safe.''

''But what if—?''

''Your job,'' he interrupted, ''is to concentrate on getting the day care ready, and try to make the adjustment from California girl to Oregon woman.''

She leaned forward on him, smiling when she saw the ready passion smolder in his eyes. ''You think there's really a difference?'

He combed the damp tendrils of her hair back with his fingers, his eyes consuming her face, feature by feature. ''There has to be. We raise no hothouse flowers here. Those of us born in Oregon have that strain of stubborn, sturdy pioneer who came thousands of miles in search of something that couldn't be found in the neat, quiet streets east of St. Louis.''

''You run an elegant hotel,'' she reminded him. ''Would your sturdy pioneer ancestry approve of that?''

''Of course.'' Unable to stop himself, he kissed her eyelashes. ''Those who visit Oregon come for the same things as those who live here are after—gracious living on the edge of the wilderness. Oregon is settled but it isn't tame.'' His lips moved to her mouth and opened over it. He kissed her deeply and hard, then withdrew, the smolder in his eyes igniting. ''And that's the way we like our women.''

Chapter Ten

"Oh!" Gina breathed, once again feeling as though she were trapped in a fairy tale. Patrick had stopped on a knoll overlooking Candle Bay and the inn his family had operated since the turn of the century.

The inn was a red-roofed masterpiece of Queen Anne architecture with a main, central building two stories high in classic Victorian style.

"Downstairs are the administration offices, the front desk, a dining room, the lounge and bar. Upstairs are rooms." He pointed to two long, low buildings, obviously later additions, that snaked down to the water from either side. A network of scaffolding was mounted against them, and Gina noticed molded fretwork trim being installed to match that of the main building. "Those are also rooms and that round building on the water with the cupola is a ballroom for special parties. A lot of local people use it."

A completely new two-story building was under construction, tucked against the hillside. "More rooms," he said, "and a cappuccino bar."

Beyond the ballroom was a dock and a small marina with three good-size fishing boats.

The whole was laid out against a rare sunny April day,

white clouds scudding across a bright blue sky over an even bluer bay.

Gina noticed a fussy little building near the marina, reroofed like all the others.

"Boathouse," Patrick explained. "We don't use it much. Our newer boats with the flying bridges are too tall for it. But it's so charming, I hate to take it down."

As they watched the riverbank, a heron rose and made its strangely graceful, awkward way across the bay.

Its flight led Gina's eyes to the hilly, fir-covered terrain across the water. Commercial buildings and an old power-plant stack rimmed the bank, and colorful houses dotted the hillside. Sunlight glinted off moving traffic and windows of homes nestled in the trees.

"What's that?" she asked, pointing.

"Astoria," he replied. "Oldest settlement west of the Rockies."

"It's beautiful from here."

"You should see it at night. It looks like a pirate's treasure trove, a mound of jewels in the dark." He put an arm around her and squeezed her shoulder. "Come on, I'll show you the house."

Gina couldn't quite believe it. The house, on a terrace between the hotel and the top of the knoll, was built in the same Queen Anne style, one round turretlike gable on one end of the house, surrounded by a screened-in crescent-shaped porch. There were rounded columns where the porch straightened across the front, and big, double oak doors with leaded-glass windows.

"It's in desperate need of repair," Patrick said, unlocking the door. "My grandfather had been alone for the last thirty years of his life and preferred to live at the hotel. So far I've had my hands full keeping things going there and have paid little attention to the house.

One of the hotel maids tidies it for me a couple of times a week, but that's all the care it's gotten. The plumbing's iffy, the wiring's reliable but a little spare, and it needs paint desperately.''

Gina only half heard him. She wandered from one wonderful room to the other, marveling at rich, carved woodwork, high ceilings, deep window seats, fireplaces everywhere and dilapidated though heart-warming charm her father's elegant home in Beverly Hills would never have.

"I love it!" she said sincerely, imagining the fun she could have restoring it. She turned to him under the dusty chandelier in the small library that looked out onto the crescent porch. "I'll do it over for you in my spare time. I can get everything at a good price, and Bobbi could handle all the reupholstering. That is, if you want it done over.''

"Well, of course." He looked pleasantly surprised. "I expected you to hate it.''

Her eyes widened. "Whatever for?''

He glanced around the room with its ancient, well-worn furnishings. "Well, it's hardly what you're used to.''

She frowned and folded her arms. "I thought we'd already decided to abandon all preconceived notions about each other. I'm spoiled, but I can appreciate beauty. And you're a strong and tough man, but you have the heart of a teddy bear. Could we not forget that?''

He winced. "Teddy bear. I *will* forget that, if you don't mind. It doesn't suit my image of myself at all. And if any of my old corps buddies heard you say that, they'd laugh you off the planet.''

She patted his cheek and said with playful drama,

"I'm your wife, remember? I know things about you others will never see." She glanced at her watch. "It's after one. I suppose you're anxious to get to the hotel and back to work. Should I fix us some lunch first?" She wandered toward the kitchen, asking over her shoulder, "Is there anything in the refrigerator?"

He grabbed his jacket off the back of the sofa where he'd left it when they'd come inside. "I'll get something in the coffee shop on my way in. Call room service and they'll bring you whatever you want."

"I'll pick up groceries this afternoon then. Where shall I…?"

He shook his head. "You don't leave the grounds without me, remember? Meet me in my office for dinner, I'll show you around the hotel, then tomorrow I'll have someone from security take you shopping."

She made a grim little face. "I keep forgetting. We've reached our destination, but the chase isn't over."

He cupped her chin in his hand and asked gently, "Is it starting to get to you?"

She sighed, catching his wrist and turning her lips into his palm. "No. At least I'm not in it alone anymore."

He pulled her to him and kissed her temple. "As long as you're on hotel grounds, you can pretend it doesn't exist, because there'll be someone to handle it for you." He pulled her away and smiled. "Try to relax this afternoon. It's been a rough week for you. Take a bath, read a book, order a giant lunch. After all…" He grinned. "You haven't eaten since we stopped for coffee in Cannon Beach and that was forty-five minutes ago."

Gina walked him to the door. "Keep it up, Gallagher, and you'll find out how difficult I can be."

He feigned a regretful look. "Then I'd have to show you how difficult *I* can be, and where would that get us?

I think we should continue the team spirit we developed on the road.''

She couldn't help the wicked grin that curved her lips. ''Disagree most of the day and settle all arguments in the shower or the bathtub?''

''Or the hayloft,'' he added, leaning down to give her a parting kiss. ''Unfortunately we don't have one here. Come on down about six.''

She took a few steps out with him onto the porch. ''You know, I don't have a dress to wear to dinner.''

''This is the Oregon coast,'' he said. ''Nothing takes second place to comfort. In our dining room you'll see casual and fancy dress.'' His gaze went to her hair, and the expression on his face accelerated her pulse. ''Wear your hair up. It always makes you look like a queen, especially when you're naked.''

AFTER PATRICK LEFT, Gina decided to take another tour and followed the overgrown stone path that led her through a corridor of mountain ash to the garden behind the hotel's central building. Sunny forsythia was in bloom, and white spirea, sweet-smelling lilac and hardy rhododendron. She walked slowly through it, inhaling the fragrances as they mingled with the wonderful but very cold river-fresh air. Tempting aromas also wafted out from the kitchen. She could hear the mild commotion of shouted orders, banging pots and pans and laughter.

She found herself hurrying as she walked around the building to go in through the front door and stopped just inside the hotel's lobby, gasping at its Victorian elegance. A dark oriental carpet brought out the warmth of the oak desk that took up one end of the enormous area. There were rose velvet draperies over delicate sheers and round oak tables and captain's chairs where people sat over drinks and conversation and watched the comings and goings in the lobby.

A subtle pink-and-green striped wallpaper rose up to the second level where she could see a gallery with more tables and books and magazines. Thriving fan palms stood near columns and in corners, and quiet music came from a trio near the lounge area.

Gina half expected to see the company of some Victorian drama, laughing and waving fans as they trooped out to a waiting carriage.

Instead a pretty young woman in a Victorian lace blouse and skirt came from behind the desk to greet her. "Mrs. Gallagher?"

"Yes." She couldn't help the little thrill she felt admitting it.

"I'm Katey. Mr. Gallagher asked me to watch for you." Petite and very blond, she leaned toward her conspiratorially. "We're all *so* happy for both of you."

Gina smiled as the young woman led her down a carpeted hallway toward an oak door at the end.

"When Mr. Gallagher came back to take over the hotel and moved into the old house," Katey whispered, "we could see him from Polly Dutton's window, looking out at the river. We were hoping he didn't end up like her, alone and lonely in that big old place."

"Who's Polly Dutton?" Gina asked.

"The Duttons founded Candle Bay," Katey explained. "Only it wasn't called Candle Bay then, it was just called Dutton. Anyway, Polly was supposed to marry a fisherman her father didn't approve of, only he was lost on the river. They never recovered his body. Polly kept a candle lit on her bedroom window every night for the rest of her life, on the chance that he was out there somewhere and needed a light to help him find his way home.'' She put both hands to her heart. ''Isn't that romantic? That's how this became Candle Bay.''

''So the house was here before the hotel?''

Katey nodded as she rapped on the door. ''The first Mr. Gallagher added the Queen Anne porch to match his hotel. But Polly Dutton's father built the house.''

A voice beyond the door shouted, ''In!''

Katey opened the door for Gina. Patrick sat behind a large desk, his feet propped on a corner of it as he spoke on the phone. He'd apparently showered and changed when he got to work because he now wore a three-piece suit and wing tips. Behind him was a breathtaking view of the bay and the rest of the hotel complex. He waved Katey a thank-you and pointed Gina to the chair near him.

''Right,'' he was saying. ''You'll pick up Bobbi, then?'' There was a moment's pause. ''Great. Gina's anxious to talk to her about helping decorate the house. It won't be ready for guests yet, but I'll put you two up in the hotel.'' He listened a moment and shook his head, absently studying an open book in his lap. ''No, we're both fine. Just look into those few things for me, will you? Right. Thanks. No, I'll tell you more about that when you come up. No. Sorry. It's a long story, and I'm sure Gina will want to add a few things, and she'll want Bobbi to hear. Okay. Take care.''

Patrick hung up the phone, leaned back in his chair and studied Gina in her new blue turtleneck and jeans and his ever-present leather jacket. She'd caught her hair up in a simple knot as he'd suggested, long bangs and dark tendrils framing her face.

He'd missed her this afternoon, and he'd felt the change in himself when she walked into his office. He'd worked like a fiend all afternoon. He'd written a check to Sin, who'd promised to send a check from his account to the motel owner in Santa Cruz and to the automobile dealer in Rockport. That would cover the bus he'd decided to keep and have the truck stored until it could be picked up. He knew Danforth and Gardner could certainly find him with some investigating, but he wasn't leaving any easy clues.

Patrick gave a long stretch and rotated his taut shoulders.

"How's Sin?" she asked.

He nodded. "Good. He says hi."

Her smile of anticipation filled him with a warm glow. "I can't wait to show Bobbi the house. She's going to love it. I spent all afternoon making plans."

"Did you order a feast from room service?"

She looked vaguely sheepish. "I skipped lunch."

"What?" Patrick brought his feet to the floor and studied her with exaggerated surprise. "You haven't had anything since mid-morning?" He glanced at his watch. "Almost eight hours? Are you feeling faint?"

She rolled her eyes at his teasing. "I got involved with floor plans and color schemes. I've been known to go into a trance at work and miss a meal or two."

"Horrors." He picked up the phone and jabbed a button. "And work gets done anyway without emergency runs for potato chips? Hi, Brian. Mrs. Gallagher and I will be in the restaurant. Then we're taking a tour of the hotel. I'll call again before we go home."

He cradled the receiver, stood and held a hand out for Gina's. "Come on," he said. "Let's get some food in you before your system fails."

The dining room was another model of turn-of-the-century elegance. Oak woodwork and gilded mirrors shone like jewels, snowy tablecloths were adorned with small pots of fresh flowers, and waiters and waitresses were dressed appropriately for the period.

The hostess led them to a table in the corner with a view of the bay and brightly lit Astoria on the other side. Gina drank in the beautiful sight for a moment, then turned to Patrick with a smile.

"I haven't seen you in a suit since our wedding," she said.

"That was only five days ago."

A waitress immediately filled their goblets with icy water and someone else brought an elegant silver pot of coffee. It smelled freshly ground and brewed.

"Seems like an eternity, doesn't it?" she asked, when they were alone again.

He shook his head, his eyes roving her face, feature by feature. "No," he replied softly. "Just a comfortably long time."

She sighed, ensnared by his warm gaze, marveling at the generous Fates that had crossed Patrick's path with hers. "That's what I meant," she amended in a whisper.

He handed her one of the menus the hostess had placed in the middle of the table. He ordered champagne and salmon with new potatoes and fresh asparagus.

They ate while companionably discussing her plans for redecorating the house. When they'd finished, Patrick took her on a tour of the hotel complex.

Gina zipped her jacket as they surveyed the construction of the new building. The night was now cold and spitting rain as they followed the recently refurbished rows of rooms to the water and inspected the empty boathouse.

It was dark inside and water lapped comfortingly along its middle, open to the water, where small boats had once been sheltered. "It's a shame you can't use it anymore," Gina said, looking at its octagonal leaded-glass windows and the old table and chairs in a corner that had never been removed. "What a charming building."

"I think it does get used," Patrick said, a smile in his voice as he came up behind her in the dark. "They think I don't know it, but there's a few romantic pairs on staff who come here during breaks and…do what lovers do."

Gina turned in his arms and raised her hands to his face. "You mean this?" she asked, raising on tiptoe to kiss his lips. He leaned down slightly to accommodate her, his mouth warm and pliant.

"Mmm," he said, cupping the back of her neck in one hand. "Maybe we could arrange to use this place, too."

She nipped at his lip. "Maybe. But I'm not giving up my lunch break for it."

He tugged at a tendril of hair until she yelped. "You mean you only skip lunch for your work?"

"I do sometimes forget food when I'm really distracted."

He fell for the taunt, nibbling kisses along her parted lips, drawing away when she tried to share the kiss. Determined to provide her with a distraction she wouldn't soon forget, he nipped along her jaw to her ear, then flicked his tongue into it until she hunched her shoulder and gasped.

"Patrick…"

"Shh," he said, nibbling along her throat as he held her to him with one hand and unzipped and removed the leather jacket with the other.

"My…jacket…" she complained in breathless distraction, her head thrown back.

He pulled up the hem of the turtleneck she wore as he backed her into the dark shadows of the boathouse.

"Whose jacket?" he asked, closing a hand over her breast. He caressed it, rolling his thumb over the taut tip until she uttered a ragged little moan.

"What time do you have lunch tomorrow?" she asked.

"One," he replied.

"I'll be here."

"I can't hold out until tomorrow," he said, tracing her ear with the tip of his tongue. She hunched a shoulder as it tickled, gooseflesh rising on every inch of her body. He was driving her backward into the darkest corner of the boathouse.

"What...what if one of the other couples...comes?" She tried desperately to keep a grip on sanity as his mouth replaced the hand that had taunted her breast.

"It's the dinner shift," he replied after a moment. "No breaks for another hour."

"But, where...?"

There was a small cruiser moored deep inside that she hadn't been able to see in the darkness. He leapt aboard, reached out to catch her as she followed and led her inside where it was even darker.

"I can't see a thing," she whispered as he turned her, flattened a hand at her back and eased her backward onto a narrow bunk. He tossed her jacket and turtleneck onto the floor and laughed softly. "We don't have to see. This exercise merely requires touch."

Then she felt his mouth on hers and his fingers at the snap of her jeans. He straightened and reached both hands inside to tug her jeans and panties down. Her body stilled and she felt the heart of her go liquid as his fingertips slid over the swell of her bottom, down her thighs to the back of her knees. He threw her clothes aside, then cast his slacks and briefs with them. They came together immediately, explosively, without time or need to prepare.

Nothing existed for her but that moment on the narrow little cot, the weight of Patrick's body and the spicy scent of him, the delicious delight he brought her to in less time than it took her to breath his name.

Then the mad spiral began, spinning her, moving her hips into its tightening pattern until that shimmering little dot of promised pleasure became the focus of her whole world. She cried his name as it flew apart.

Patrick marveled, as he had every time he made love to her, at the utter perfection of being drawn in and embraced by her. But tonight there was a special magic. Tonight they weren't running. Tonight they were home—and nothing had changed. It amazed him.

As she trembled in his arms, he drove her higher and higher, spurred by her desperate little whispers of his name. The gentle bobbing of the boat helped him take both of them beyond anything even he'd known. He abandoned all control at the same moment she did, and he clung to her, feeling her arms around him tighten as the sensation of a mutual climax rushed along both of them like a free-fall through the night.

Patrick was the first to hear the giggle. They lay lazily entangled, Gina sprawled over him on the narrow bunk. "Uh-oh," he whispered.

Her head snapped up, her hair tumbled in her face. "What?"

He put a hand over her mouth. "Company," he said in an undertone. "Just be still."

"Be still?" she pulled his hand down, her body tense. "We're naked!"

"Not completely," he replied calmly. "Shh!"

"Not completely, but where it counts! If we…"

He pulled her head down until her mouth was pressed to his rocklike pectoral muscle. Snatches of conversation drifted into the boat.

"No, I was foolish to get serious about a medical student." It was Katey's voice. "You'll have years of school before you say we can get married. Then there's residency, and if you don't want children until you establish a practice, I'll be too old to have them!"

An earnest male voice said, "We'll have them, but when we can afford them. When it's more convenient."

"Convenient." Katey snickered. "Nothing's ever convenient. Life is never perfect. Except maybe for Mr. and Mrs. Gallagher." There was a dreamy sigh. "Have you seen them together?"

"I thought we came here to talk about us."

"She's beautiful, and he looks at her like she just fell from heaven." Another sigh. "I'll bet *they* have babies right away."

Gina bit the sturdy muscle under her lips. Patrick pinched her hip in retaliation, then covered her yelp with his other hand.

"Katey, come on," the young man pleaded. "If I owned all this, I'd be able to afford babies, too. We've wasted five minutes already. Do you want me to show you how I feel or not?"

"How you feel as a man who needs a woman? Or how you feel about you and me?"

Gina nodded, as though she approved of Katey's tactics. Patrick looked heavenward.

"It's all the same."

"No, it's not."

"You want to kiss me and hold me because it gives you pleasure, not because I'm important to you."

The male voice became skeptical. "Like it doesn't give you any pleasure. Like you just don't care when I…" His voice trailed away as he apparently chose deed over words. There was a satisfied sigh then a dreamy one.

"All right, I do like it when you love me. But I don't want five or six years before this goes any further."

There was a long, thick silence. Gina and Patrick frowned, both waiting.

"Well, I can't marry you right now, Katey," the male voice said. "It wouldn't be fair of me."

Another silence, then Katey's voice, high and a little shaky said, "Then it wouldn't be…fair of me to go on seeing you."

"Katey!"

There was the sound of tears and running footsteps, then an abrupt silence.

Patrick and Gina lay together for a long moment, staring at each other. Then Gina propped herself up on her forearms and looked sadly in the direction the footsteps had taken.

"Couldn't you give him a raise?" she asked. "So he could support a family while he's going to school, too?"

He smiled and brushed her hair back. "The inn already pays better than other hotels. The kids have to find a way to work it out."

Gina's gray eyes coaxed him. "Come on. There must be something you could do. Katey thinks you're a demigod."

He grinned. "Only demi? And what do *you* think?"

Gina leaned her chin on her folded hands. *I think I*

love you was on the tip of her tongue, but she wasn't sure he was ready to hear it.

"I think we should restore this boat and sail it to Mexico when we go in February." Then she kissed his clavicle and began a slow, breathy path down his chest.

Patrick's breath caught in his throat as she reached her objective.

"Olé," he groaned.

Chapter Eleven

There were teddy bears suspended from heart-shaped balloons, dinosaurs riding bicycles, whimsical animals of all kinds having tea parties. Patrick studied the brightly colored wallpaper Gina held up and had to smile at it.

They stood in the middle of the room he'd first shown her three weeks before—the basement of the main building. It had once stored extra tables and chairs for the meeting rooms, but was now painted in the primary colors that predominated in the wallpaper.

Gina, dressed in dull gray sweats, swept a hand along one of the walls. "We'll have cribs and playpens here, and mats and pillows for sitting. Over there..." She pointed across the room, grabbed him by the wrist with one small, paint-spattered hand and tugged him with her. "We'll have stuff for the bigger kids, a comfy old sofa and a few decrepit chairs I found in your storage...." She added in an aside, "Bobbi can help me reupholster those when she comes. On that wall..." She pointed behind them. "We'll have all the cubbyholes where the kids can put their things, and that wall..." She walked to the front, still pulling him along. "I'll put half wipe-off boards and half bulletin boards. What do you think?"

He thought she was wonderful. In the paint-smeared sweats, with her hair pulled up and covered with his camouflage fatigue hat, she still made his heart beat like a jackhammer.

He couldn't believe how his perception of Gina had changed in the brief month they'd been married. He couldn't believe how his perception of *himself* had changed. The solitude he'd once valued had ceased to be a priority. He was now consumed with thoughts of their togetherness—memories they shared, plans for their future.

"I think it's great," he said, putting an arm around her and squeezing her to him. "Even better than I'd imagined. I appreciate how wholeheartedly you've attacked this project."

Her arms around his waist, she looked up at him, the brim of his hat shading her eyes against the fluorescent light. "You think you're the only one who feels tied to promises without a signature?"

They'd been so happy together that by some unspoken mutual agreement, they never mentioned that it wasn't forever. He was in so deep now, he even tended to forget.

They walked up the dark path home, arm in arm, Gina leaning against him, the light left on in their bedroom beckoning them home.

PATRICK TURNED his key in the lock and pushed the front door open. A spicy aroma wafted out to greet them.

He took an appreciative whiff as he closed and locked the door. "What is that?" he asked as he followed Gina toward the kitchen. "Gingerbread," she replied over her shoulder, tugging off the old sweater he had lent her to put over the sweats. "I ran home this afternoon to bake it so we could have it with our coffee when we came home. Brandied whipped cream or ice-cream topping?''

He put both arms around her when she stopped at the counter and nibbled at her neck. "You are *such* a domestic bargain. You wield a deadly curling iron, and you can bake, too. Sometimes I can't believe my good fortune. I'm going to be a very curly, very fat husband.''

She giggled, taking a fistful of his hair to stop his nibbling and to allow herself to plant a kiss on his cheek. "I'll still love you, don't worry.''

His eyes were an inch from hers, suddenly dark and intense. "You promise?''

Her eyes softened to gray velvet and her laughter gentled into a loving smile. "I promise,'' she whispered back.

He leaned an inch forward and kissed her with passion and tenderness and all the emotions growing between them he didn't completely understand yet. And with a promise for later.

He finally freed her and straightened. "Whipped cream,'' he replied to her previous question, his voice rusty and quiet. He turned to leave the kitchen. "I'll build a fire in the bedroom while you're fixing coffee. We can have it up there.'' He paused at the door to grin at her. "Okay?''

"Okay,'' she agreed.

Though the enormous old bedroom on the river end of the house was still desperately in need of fresh paint and new wallpaper, Gina had bought a new bedspread and curtains in burgundy and green, and they'd picked up an old love seat at a second-hand store in Astoria. She'd placed a matching green throw over it that she'd found in the attic. He'd come to love this room.

He built the fire and placed the kindling, then stood

to reach to the broad mantel for a match. His eyes fell on Gina's Renaissance lovers lamp that had urged them home, and he found himself smiling again. The tulip light glowed brightly and had become Gina's tribute to Polly Dutton.

Patrick took a moment to lean his elbows on either side of the lamp and study it. He remembered how he'd seen it for the first time in the beam of a flashlight in a deserted barn. He'd thought it gaudy then, even foolish.

Now he saw it in a different light.

"No pun intended," he told himself, batting with a fingertip one of the sparkling crystals that hung from the tulip cup. It dangled and shone crazily, as bright as the lovers' smiles.

"I thought you were building a fire?" Gina asked, shouldering her way into the room with a tray bearing their late snack. "Do I have to do everything?" she teased, placing the tray on the small table in front of the love seat and coming around it to the fireplace.

She thought much later that she should have been suspicious of his grin. He stood directly in front of the fireplace, hands loosely on his hips, his eyes blazing with a passion that had grown even since the momentous decision made in the kitchen.

"*You* build the fire," he challenged. "I dare you."

His suggestive double entendre wasn't lost on her. Eager to accept the challenge, she unbuttoned the top button of his shirt and put her lips to the warm, muscular flesh there. "Your whipped cream will melt," she warned, unfastening the second and third buttons and kissing her way down the open vee.

He inched up her sweatshirt and coaxed her backward toward the bed. He dipped his index finger into the cream as they passed the coffee table.

Gina sank into the mattress, Patrick kneeling over her, and she felt his finger touch the cool cream just beneath her bra and trace a line down to the waistband of her panties.

Everything inside her shuddered as he nibbled up the cream.

"The gingerbread can't be this delicious," he said, reaching under her to unhook her bra, then toss it aside. "But I'll have to have another taste to be sure."

"WE'D PROMISED a garden-view suite to the Websters," Brian Scott, the Candle Bay Inn's night manager said anxiously to Patrick as he walked into the office with the morning paper. "But they're due in an hour and there isn't one free. The plumber's still working on the stopped-up sink in the south suite, the couple in the middle suite extended their stay by two days because they just *love* the north coast..." A roll of his eyes said he wasn't particularly crazy about it himself at the moment. Patrick's hardworking employee was the young man who'd been with Katey in the boathouse the night he and Gina had almost been discovered. "And the north suite is occupied as scheduled."

Patrick nodded from behind his desk. "Do we have a river-view suite free?"

Brian frowned. "Yeah, but it's forty dollars a night more."

"Let them have it for the same price. Explain that the guests in the room they were supposed to have are enjoying their stay with us so much, they've extended, and that we hope the same happens with them."

Brian visibly relaxed. "Right," he said and turned away.

Patrick opened the paper, his attention immediately

arrested by the headline. Coastal Hotel Burns. He frowned over the three-column photo of a fire licking at the familiar pointed roof of a hotel just down the coast. He began to read the story.

"Mr. Gallagher!" A breathless Katey stood in his doorway.

Patrick looked up, bracing himself for yet another crisis, grateful, at least, that he wasn't in the Indian Beach Hotel owner's shoes.

"I have the president of the Northcoast Antique Dealers on the phone." She gulped a breath and shook her head. "He wants to know if we can host their annual meeting Memorial Day weekend. They'd booked the Indian Beach..." She indicated the newspaper open on his desk. "I could have buzzed you, but I wanted to make sure you'd read what happened."

He nodded. "Just reading it. How's the register look?"

"All the meeting rooms are free," Katey told him. "And he understands that their rooms would be scattered because it's so last-minute."

While grateful for her efficiency, he was torn between the bonus of having the hotel filled to capacity and the absolute havoc a last-minute booking that size would cause for him and his staff—particularly on the party weekend. But he already understood that the principle in commerce was "never turn down business or money."

He picked up the receiver, punched the blinking light, and made the frantic president of the Northcoast Antique Dealers a very happy man.

RAIN DROVE at the kitchen windows as Gina packed a picnic basket. The idea was crazy, but then, it hadn't been sanity that had put this marriage together.

She had promised to stay out of Patrick's way, but it was harder than she'd imagined.

Since he'd booked the antique dealers' convention, he'd worked long hours checking details and fielding the scores of crises that came up daily with so much construction and remodeling going on while the hotel remained open to guests.

She hadn't had a meal with him in days. They'd had little time to talk. She was determined to change that.

She picked up the wall phone and pushed the button that dialed his office.

"Gallagher," he said. He sounded preoccupied and she could hear the shuffle of papers.

"Hi," she said brightly. "I'm calling to announce that the center's ready for children. I put the last piece of furniture in place myself this morning."

"Terrific!" he praised, sounding enthused but still distracted. "I'll run by on my way home."

"I packed a lunch," she said. "I thought I could take you on a tour on your break, then we could drive to the lookout and eat."

"Sorry, Gina." He did sound apologetic, but still distracted. The tone reminded her of her father. "I've got a plumber here for a problem, and a shipment of red napkins is lost."

She hesitated a moment. "The dining room is oak and green and white."

"Exactly."

She sighed. "You can't spare twenty minutes to eat?"

"Not this afternoon. Why don't you come down to the coffee shop for lunch? Katey's there."

She huffed impatiently, determined to get through to him. "I don't miss Katey, I miss *you*."

DOWN THE SLOPE, in the proprietor's office in the main building of the Candle Bay Inn, Patrick heard Gina's words and for a moment was lost for a reply.

He'd been afraid this would happen. Sometimes, down in the depths of his soul, he admitted there'd been times when he'd been afraid it *wouldn't* happen. But that was confusing, and he liked things plain and simple.

"I told you the day you proposed this marriage," he said reasonably, "that I work long hours."

"I know," she countered blandly. "And the first time I complained you would send me back to my father by fourth-class mail."

There was a long pause. She waited for him to say he hadn't meant it. He didn't.

He waited for her to say she'd never want to leave— ever. She didn't.

So Patrick did what years of military training had taught him. He attacked while the opportunity was his.

"Do I have to buy stamps or what?" he asked.

Gina was hurt for just a moment. She let herself compare him to her father and remembered all the times Wyatt Raleigh's work had taken precedence over her needs.

Then she remembered that as a child, she'd been powerless to change that. She was a woman now—a smart one.

She drew a breath and said evenly, "Forget the stamps. Save your money and buy a hard hat. You're going to need it before I'm finished with you."

Patrick stared at the receiver for a moment after the line went dead. Then he cradled it, not sure whether to laugh or worry.

PATRICK LOOKED UP at a complex arrangement of dripping pipes in the basement of the main building while the plumber explained that a large part of it had to be replaced.

"It was quality work," the man said, "but it's very old. I'd suggest—"

"Mr. Gallagher!" A bellman wound his way between the drips and handed him a cordless phone. "A problem at the desk."

He'd done something to offend the Fates today, Patrick thought as he pressed the Phone button.

"Mr. Gallagher," Katey said anxiously. "There's a problem in 209 and the guest wants to see the manager. Brian isn't here yet."

He frowned. "What kind of problem?"

"I don't know. The implication was that I'm too much of an underling to discuss it with."

Oh, good. An unhappy guest with a Caesar complex. Just what he needed to round out his day. "On my way," he said.

He handed the phone back to the bellman, told the plumber to do what had to be done and took the elevator to the second floor. He tried to adjust his attitude on the brief ride up.

He'd been thinking about Gina since she'd hung up on him two hours before. His brain told him he had no reason to feel guilty, but his heart longed to chuck aside the rest of the day's responsibilities and go to her. He'd find a way to make it up to her after the big weekend.

The elevator doors parted and he stepped out onto the soft blue carpet. He rapped on the door of 209.

"Come in," a faint feminine voice shouted.

Patrick stepped into what seemed to be an empty room. It appeared in perfect order, the softly shaded nautical decor spotless and fresh.

"Hello?" he called.

"Yes?" a slightly louder voice replied.

"It's the manager," he called back. "I understand there's a problem."

"It's in here!" the voice called back.

It came from somewhere inside the dressing-room arch. He studied the shadows there in mild concern, reluctant to venture farther.

He stopped to lean against the molding. "Something wrong with the shower?" he asked.

"No, the bed," the voice replied silkily.

He turned to look at it. Then something yanked his tie and turned him back. He found himself face-to-face with Gina—naked.

A flare of annoyance warred with an eruption of hormones.

"And what precisely," he asked, "is wrong with it?"

She pressed herself against him and bit his chin. "You aren't *in* it."

"Gina..." he said in laughing protest, trying to disengage her hands as she unknotted his tie. "I told you I can't..."

The words died on his lips as her bent knee rubbed along the inside of his thigh. His resistance went down and his blood pressure went up—and it wasn't alone.

His tie was off and she was working on the buttons of his shirt.

"I know," she said, planting a kiss on the jut of his ribs. "You don't have time. But I knew you'd make time for a guest. I've booked the room."

He took a handful of her hair, prepared to pull her away and explain the complete attention to detail required to keep the inn running smoothly, to tell her that she was being childish and demanding.

Then she lifted her eyes to him. They were large and soft and filled with love, and he knew she hadn't been motivated by selfishness.

Every other thought fled in his mind. There would be a time to deal with them. He nobly decided to let her have her way.

She tugged the shirt and jacket off. As she hung them on the hanger just inside the dressing room, he stepped out of his slacks and briefs and tossed them over the luggage rack.

She crooked a finger at him. "Follow me," she said, turning to the bed.

He reached out and pulled her back, lifting her into his arms and tucking her legs around his waist.

"I don't follow," he said softly, covering her mouth with a deep, drugging kiss. "I was taught to lead. But I'll take you there."

His arms were crossed to support her, a hand cupping each hip. She wriggled closer, wondering if anything in the world ever felt as right as the warm, naked flesh of the one you loved against your own.

"Then do," she whispered, kissing him back.

He leaned over the bed to drop her in the middle, but she kept a grip on him and tugged so that he fell with her, then she rolled him over and knelt astride him. She braced her hands on his shoulders and looked down into his dark eyes, heavy lidded with anticipation, yet soft with amusement.

"I was never an officer," she said, tracing a line from between his pecs to his navel with the tip of her fingernail. "But, I've always been my own boss. *I* invited *you* here. We do this my way."

"I think *tricked me here* is the term," he said, his

fingertips roaming up her sides and circling her breasts. "But do go on. I'm more than happy to cooperate."

"Good." She began to kiss a trail across his chest, then down his torso. She scooted backward to kiss and nibble over his hipbone and down his thighs, ignoring that part of him straining for her touch.

He groaned. "Little witch!"

She started back up again, making him mindless with taunting forays that led everywhere but where he wanted her most.

"Gina," he finally pleaded huskily, "have a heart!"

She poised over him. He took hold of her waist and assumed control, entering her with one smooth but desperate thrust. "I do," she whispered as they began to move together, swaying in opposing directions to make the ultimate circle, the quintessential yin and yang of life. "And it beats for you."

Pleasure erupted with a power that awed him. And he knew it wasn't merely because of Gina's ardent ministrations, but because of the love he felt for her.

She whispered a high-pitched little cry and collapsed on top of him.

"See," she said after a moment. "Don't I beat the traditional lunch at your desk? I've got a picnic basket in the closet and—" She tried to push herself up to go and get them.

But Patrick wrapped his arms around her and rolled them over. She blinked up at him in surprise, then raised her wrist to look at her watch.

He began to do to her what she'd done to him.

"Patrick, we've already used half your lunch—" She broke off to gasp feelingly, "Oh, my! Oh, Patrick, I don't think I could take another. Ooooooh!"

"You weren't very merciful with me a few minutes ago."

"I thought you needed to slow down, to…"

She arched up in his arms and he felt her body shudder with the pleasure he'd given her. He entered her again and took her possessively, completely, deliciously.

NAKED, Gina peered into the picnic basket she'd earlier brought to the chair beside the bed. Leaning against the propped-up pillow, the blankets drawn up to his waist, Patrick smiled and enjoyed the view.

"An orange?" she asked, glancing at him over her shoulder. "Or an oatmeal cookie?"

He raised an eyebrow. "Since when does the kitchen have oatmeal cookies?"

Taking that for assent, she grabbed the baggy of cookies and crawled back into bed. Patrick lifted the blanket for her and pulled her into his arm.

"I baked them last night while you were working," she said, putting one between his lips.

His strong even teeth snapped off a bite. He made a sound of approval as he chewed. "I'm glad to see," he said finally, "that you were usefully occupied. The chicken and salad were also wonderful. This lunch was an inspired idea."

She nibbled delicately at the rest of the cookie. "I just didn't want you to think I'd put up with that forever."

He reached past her to the bedside table for the glass of wine they were sharing. "Put up with what?"

"Being last on your list of priorities because you're afraid to face the fact that you need me."

He looked at her in surprise. "Of course I need you," he said. "I thought I'd made that more than clear."

He offered her the glass. She took a sip and handed

it back. "I mean in ways that aren't physical." Their faces were so close that she could see the gold flecks in the depths of his brown eyes. She looked deeply into them, desperate to read there what he truly felt. "I came to this room because I knew I could get your attention this way." She sighed in self-deprecation. "And because I feel as though my life starts all over every time you love me. But I want you to know I won't settle for just this."

She took her courage in both hands and admitted candidly, "I don't think I'll be able to leave you in March, Patrick."

He put the wine aside and enfolded her in his arms. "That's good," he said, "I'd hate to have to chase you down."

He wasn't quite getting the point. "*Why* don't you want me to leave, Patrick? Because we're so good in bed, because there's someone in the house when you come home? Don't you want to share more with me?"

He wanted to tell her it was because he loved her and wasn't sure he could live without her, but he'd been a soldier too long. The most important lesson he'd learned was that vulnerability meant defeat.

"Because you're mine," he said, holding her to him. "And it still isn't safe for you out there. The fact that whoever's after you hasn't appeared, doesn't mean he isn't out there waiting."

"Patrick..."

The phone rang shrilly. Patrick reached for it. "Yes?" He listened a moment. "Yes, Katey." He cast a scolding glance at Gina. "No, that's all right. I'll be there in fifteen minutes. And you and I have to have a talk, young lady, on where your loyalties lie."

Gina heard but couldn't decipher Katey's reply.

Patrick looked at the receiver, then replaced it in the cradle.

"She said her loyalty lies with Polly Dutton." He frowned at Gina. "What in the hell does that mean?"

Gina laughed softly, settling for half a victory. He hadn't said he loved her, but he did say he wouldn't let her leave.

"I imagine," she said, pushing the blankets back, "I remind her of Polly. She, too, was always trying to lure her lover home with a light in the window."

He caught her arm and pulled her back against him when she would have gotten to her feet.

"You're going weird on me, my love," he said, kissing her temple. "Maybe you've been confined too long. I was going to send the hotel limo to the airport for Sin and Bobbi, but maybe we'd better pick them up."

The idea delighted her. It would be wonderful to have him to herself for the few hours it would take to drive to Portland and back.

"But can you leave the hotel with the big weekend starting tomorrow?"

"Wasn't that the point of this lesson?"

She grinned up at him. "You mean, you've learned it?"

He laughed softly. "I don't know. But I've sure as hell enjoyed it."

Chapter Twelve

"Oh, Bobbi!" Gina hugged her friend to her then held her away, drinking in the warm and robust look of her. She hadn't realized how much she needed a friend until that moment. "You look great! Just the same!"

Bobbi made a face. "It's only been five weeks. Did you expect me to have aged?"

Gina swatted her arm, then tucked hers into it. "Of course not. Come on. I can't wait to get you home and take you through our wonderful house."

Bobbi hesitated as Gina tried to lead the way. "The bags..."

"Oh, don't worry," Gina said, smiling over her shoulder at Patrick. "I brought the Candle Bay Inn's chief bellman with me."

As the women headed toward the parking lot arm in arm, Sin picked up Bobbi's large piece of soft-sided luggage and handed it to Patrick. "Well," he said, "I see marriage has really improved your status. From owner of the hotel to bellboy."

Patrick laughed and started to follow the women, then waited to give Sin a minute to catch up. "It's improved a lot of other things about my life."

Patrick took two steps back to his friend as Sin, holding his own large bag, tangled with a small, masculine-looking tote, a larger brocade one and a camera he was trying to loop on his shoulder. "What is your problem?" Patrick asked.

"You'd think she could carry her own camera," Sin said, casting a disgruntled look in Bobbi's direction.

Patrick took it from him. "That better?" he teased. "What's the matter? She hasn't fallen for you yet?"

Sin straightened and glowered, the expression half playful, half serious. "If you've invited me here to torment me, tell me right now and I'll turn right around...."

Patrick frowned at him worriedly. "Sin, you're losing your sense of humor. You want to talk about it?"

"No."

Patrick watched Sin march off after Gina and Bobbi, and grinned. Sin didn't have to explain what was bothering him. Patrick thought he knew.

"I'll use CORDOVAN leather," Bobbi said, running a hand over the torn upholstery of the library chairs. "Or maybe brocade? And I think Patrick should have a throne chair for that spot by the window." She pointed to the leaded-glass window that looked out onto the hotel. Now a threadbare upholstered chair sat there, a book on its arm.

Bobbi straightened, her arms wrapped around herself. "Gina, this place is a masterpiece! I'll make a list of everything before I go and I'll send you fabric swatches. I'll come back in August and spend my vacation doing the living room for you, then I'll ship whatever you decide on for the other stuff and you can have someone local do it. By this time next year, it'll be like something people pay money to tour."

Gina hugged her. "It's so good to see you. I wish the

bedrooms were in better shape so you could stay here instead of the hotel.''

"Oh, I'll be fine." Bobbi put an arm around Gina's shoulders and wandered with her back into the dining room. "So…" Her voice took on a careful quality as she dropped her arm and walked slowly around the round oak table, fingertips rubbing lightly over the smooth, burnished surface. "Things haven't worked out precisely the way you planned, have they?"

Gina's eyes widened with surprise. How could she know?

Bobbi smiled and slipped into a ladder-backed chair. She propped her elbow on the table and a chin on her hand. "You fell in love, didn't you?"

Gina sat two chairs away and nodded. "Deeply. Desperately. Unreservedly." She sighed and added, "Unfortunately."

Bobbi crossed one arm over the other and frowned. "Why? Patrick's wearing precisely the same look you're wearing. I'd say he fell in love, too."

Gina grimaced. "The point is, *he* won't say it."

"You know men." Bobbi sighed. "They're not always quick about these things. They haven't the vaguest idea what to do with a woman. Except the obvious, of course."

Gina stood, restlessly pacing around the table. "You think I should settle for being wanted instead of loved?"

Bobbi shook her head, obviously not requiring time to consider the question. "No. Don't ever settle. But bide your time. You have ten more months to this bargain, haven't you?"

Gina sighed and sank into a chair opposite her friend. "Yes. I guess I feel this way because his attitude is a lot like my father's was. He's always so busy.…"

"Hey." Bobbi reached across to place her hand over Gina's. "Have a little faith. He stayed with you after he learned you'd tricked him, he kept you safe during that awful trip. I think you're so used to your father's remoteness that you don't recognize genuine busyness when you see it."

Gina had told Bobbi about their chase up the coast while they'd unpacked her things. She thought now that her memories of it weren't awful at all. Was she being paranoid and selfish?

"And he seems very attentive," Bobbi went on. "He'll come around. I'll bet you fifty bucks."

Gina laughed. "Fifty bucks? On my future?"

Bobbi shrugged. "Love's a dangerous game. The stakes don't matter as much as your courage to play."

"I APOLOGIZE if suggesting you bring Bobbi ruined your long weekend," Patrick said to Sin. They were testing a new forty-foot boat just purchased for the inn. Patrick handled the helm, while Sin leaned against the safety rail and stared quietly over the water.

Sin shook his head. "Nothing could ruin this place. She's just kind of...I don't know...cold. Remote. I hate that in a woman."

Patrick remembered their easy amity the day of his and Gina's wedding. "You two got along so well the day Gina and I got married. What happened?"

"Who knows?" Sin turned his face into the wind, then zipped his jacket up the last three inches. "I called her for a date and she turned me down. Coldly. So I guess I misread her." He turned back to Patrick as the wind tossed his short blond hair. "Isn't it ever going to warm up? It's Memorial Day weekend, for God's sake.

Spring. Maybe you should have bought a ski lift for the inn instead of a boat for charter trips.''

"Come on. You love your boat."

"It's a sailboat in sunny Southern California. Sailing in balmy waters isn't the same as sitting on deck in a survival suit waiting for something to nibble on your line."

Patrick turned the boat in a wide circle and headed back for the inn's dock. "You Southern Californians," he teased with a grin as Sin braced himself against the spray shield. "Bunch of wimps. Any dude can wear shorts, lie in the sun and hold a sail line. It takes more guts and brains to go fishing here than it does to compete in the America's Cup down South."

Sin groaned. "And I suppose you have as many preposterous stories about the fish that get away, don't you?"

"Of course not." Patrick grinned. "Nothing I go after gets away." He turned suddenly serious. "You have a detective on staff with your firm, don't you?"

"Yeah. Jason Watters. You want him to look into the two guys who attacked you and Gina on the road?"

"No. I'd like to fax him our list of guests for the convention. Make sure everyone on it is who he says he is."

"You have suspicions?"

"I don't know." Patrick hunched a shoulder. "I have a house full of antique dealers. Could be coincidence, but I'd like to be sure."

"Right. We'll do it the minute we get back."

"YIKES," Bobbi said under her breath. "It's like Times Square in here."

Sin kept a hand on each woman's arm as they wound

their way through the crowded lobby toward the main dining room. The antique dealers were registering, along with the regularly scheduled guests. The elegant lobby was thick with irregularly formed lines of people talking and laughing, checking touring brochures and getting acquainted.

Gina noted quite a few children in the group and thought the new day-care center might be full tomorrow.

"This looks good for Patrick," Sin said into Gina's ear as they cleared the worst of the crowd. "You two will be able to retire young, live and travel in the lap of luxury."

His casual remark made Gina turn instinctively to Bobbi with a questioning if not accusing look. Bobbi's expression told her she'd pay later for even thinking she'd shared her confidence.

The headwaiter seated them and gave Gina the message that Patrick was held up and would join them as quickly as he could.

Sin groaned dramatically. "Two women all to myself. Whatever shall I do?"

Bobbi smiled blandly at him and batted her lashes. "Take comfort in the fact that one of them has a jealous husband, who's just a little bigger than you, and the other has no interest in you whatsoever."

Sin returned Bobbi's bland look. "Thank you, Miss Perducci. I'm so glad I drove all the way from Malibu to Burbank to pick you up, made all your flight arrangements and carried your two-ton bag of makeup the three miles from the terminal to the car. Your gratitude, not to mention your good manners, are overwhelming."

"Guys…" Gina began placatingly.

Bobbi took Sin's bait. "Travel arrangements. You must have been on the phone for hours to arrange to

have me seated next to a little boy who got Slimer String
all over me, and to have had me served a vegetarian
dinner that was specially planned for the person who was
supposed to have my seat.''

''Didn't I get you another lunch?''

''Who can eat,'' she demanded, ''after one mouthful
of lasagna made with eggplant instead of meat!''

''Bobbi—'' Gina tried.

''You could have restrained yourself,'' Sin interrupted
stiffly, ''from pouring your cola on the stewardess.''

''The little boy,'' Bobbi said, low in her throat, enunciating every word, ''threw his drink at the stewardess
when she gave him ginger ale instead of cola. Had you
stuck around to see that my problem was taken care of,
you'd have known that!''

''Bobbi? Sin, really...''

''You had just told me,'' Sin retorted, his color deepening, ''that I was free to leave the plane. That you could
handle it. Considering we were still at thirty thousand
feet, I chose simply to return to my seat.''

''Which was seven rows back from mine,'' Bobbi
said, pointing a finger in the air. ''If that doesn't prove
that you wanted nothing to do with...''

People were beginning to turn their way.

''I'll just go see what's keeping Patrick,'' Gina said.

Sin and Bobbi, still battling, failed to notice that she
was standing. She found the headwaiter, asking him to
bring champagne to their table and to keep pouring, hoping to add a little effervescence to her friends' disposi-
tions, and headed for Patrick's office.

She stopped halfway across the lobby when Katey
beckoned her to the desk. The clerk held out her left
hand with a giggle of delight. It sported a beautiful pearl
flanked by diamond chips. Gina exclaimed at its beauty,

but looked into Katey's eyes, unsure that it indicated what she suspected.

"We're engaged!" she bubbled. No champagne necessary there, Gina thought with a pleased smile. "We couldn't afford a diamond, but I think this pearl is the most beautiful ring I ever saw."

Gina leaned over the desk to hug her. "That's wonderful, Katey. Congratulations! What happened to change Brian's mind?"

Katey glanced surreptitiously left and right. "Mr. Gallagher."

Gina stared at her a moment. "What?"

"I'm not sure what happened exactly," Katey said, "but all I know is he went into Mr. Gallagher's office to talk about a problem at the desk, stayed quite a while, and that night he invited me to dinner and proposed. It was the same afternoon you booked the room." Katey beamed, apparently pleased to have been a conspirator in the little ruse that had gotten Patrick there.

Gina gave her another hug, surprised that Patrick had taken Katey's side. She thought cautiously that it could be a good sign. Maybe Bobbi was right. "That's terrific. Just goes to show you a good boss can fix anything."

Gina turned from the desk to go in search of Patrick and collided with an elegantly mustached gentleman in an overcoat and an Irish bog hat.

"Oh, my gosh!" She juggled the small square box she'd knocked from his grasp. She lost it once, caught it with less style than luck with her fingertips, watched it do a complete turn just above her head, then caught it against her with a gasp of surprise.

"Well done!" the man praised.

Gina held the box out, but he hesitated before taking it. She thought she saw recognition in his eyes for a moment, then he smiled, doffed his hat, took the box and said in a deep, rusty voice, "If you don't play for the Trailblazers, you should."

She shrugged a shoulder, liking the *Field and Stream* magazine-cover look of him. "I tried out," she said. "Too short. Have we met?"

He shook his head regretfully, extending his hand. "I wish I could take that line and run with it, unfortunately I'm due to host a welcome meeting in ten minutes and, as you can see..." He indicated the luggage at his feet and the fact that he hadn't checked in. "I'm hardly prepared. Ah, Miss...?"

Gina placed her hand in his. "Mrs.," she corrected. "Gallagher. You're with the antique dealers?"

"I am."

"Well, let me get a..." She turned to call for a bellman and found one standing right behind her, along with Patrick, who'd apparently been watching her encounter.

He gave her one brief indeterminate glance, then extended his hand to their guest. "Welcome to Candle Bay. I'm your host, Patrick Gallagher. This is my wife, Gina."

The man grinned broadly and shook his hand. "Dan Porter. I own Newport Niceties. It was good of you to take our group at the last moment like this."

"It's our pleasure, of course." Patrick gestured to a second clerk just coming out of the office. "Would you register this gentleman, please?" He turned to the bellman. "After you've taken him to his room, please escort him to the Cormorant meeting room."

"Yes, sir."

Patrick smiled affably. "Enjoy your stay."

"I will, thank you." The man nodded politely to Gina. "Mrs. Gallagher."

She smiled over her shoulder as Patrick led her toward the dining room. "He was ni—" she began, smiling up at Patrick only to find he was frowning down at her.

"'Have we met?'" he quoted her question with a suggestion of mockery. "You didn't ask him what astrological sign he was, did you?"

She looked at him in surprise. Jealousy? Another good sign. She grinned. "Oh, we cut through all that. I'm meeting him later at the boathouse."

He stopped several yards from the dining room to look down into her eyes. His held a hint of ill temper.

She put conciliatory hands to his chest. "Really, Patrick. I bumped into him—literally—while I was on my way to look for you. Sin and Bobbi have done nothing but quarrel, and I was looking for a more amenable dinner companion." She raised an eyebrow. "You are going to be, aren't you?"

He ran a hand down his face and sighed wearily. "Maybe if I have a lobotomy. It's been a hell of a day."

"Come with me." She took his hand and pulled him with her to the back of the lobby, down a utility corridor and to a door marked Supplies. It was locked.

She smiled at him. "You have the key, haven't you?"

He was looking at her warily. "Yes, but..."

She leaned against the doorjamb, her pose indolent and suggestive. "My surgery tools are in there."

The ill temper slid away instantly to be replaced by lazy amusement. "Really." He handed her the key. "Show me."

She opened the door, flipped on the light and led the way inside. The space was narrow, crowded on both sides with front-desk and office supplies.

He reached to a pencil cup that held half a dozen stainless steel, no-frills letter openers. He tested the dull tip of one with his index finger. "You're not going to operate with this, I hope."

She took the opener from him, plopped it back in the cup and put her arms around his neck. "No cutting. I prescribe an oral medication."

His eyes ignited. She loved it when that happened. "Then dose me, Doc," he whispered, lowering his mouth to meet hers.

Every tedious, unmanageable detail of his day dissolved as she ministered to him. She toyed with his tongue, nibbled at his bottom lip, drank from him with a thirst that made him feel humble. Could she really need him that much? As much as he needed her?

"That better?" she asked, moving her lips along his jaw to his ear.

He groaned, wishing desperately that they were home.

"Almost," he said, injecting a pathetic quality into his tone.

"All right," she said, working little kisses back toward his lips. "One more application. We don't want you overdosing when Sin and Bobbi are still waiting for us."

"Just go back to the dining room and tell them I broke something—I swear I'm about to."

"They're your friends."

"I want my doctor."

"I'll be going home with you, remember?" She kissed him again, more deeply, more thirstily than before, then pulled away and drew a deep breath to restore herself.

Patrick took a handful of her hair and looked with mock severity into her eyes. "All right, but don't you dare order dessert."

Love and passion blazed in his eyes. They were hot, sincere, honest.

The sound of a key in the lock made them move apart and turn to opposite sides of the narrow little room. Katey walked in and stopped short with a little cry of surprise.

The airless room was now warm from their bodies and smelled of her perfume, his cologne, and the suggestion that they'd mingled.

"Looks okay to me," Gina said in a tone of cool efficiency. She held an open box out to Patrick. "What do you think?"

He gave the long forms the box held a deliberate scrutiny. "I think we should reorder. Three copies of this form aren't enough. I know they come in quadruplicate. Make a note of that." He turned to Katey with a calm smile. "Hi, Kate. Everything all right?"

She looked from her boss to his wife, apparently unsure which of the three of them should feel guilty. "Fine," she answered absently. "I needed another box of pens. You know how they're…always disappearing."

"Right." Patrick turned Gina to the door and pushed her through. "We'll leave you to it. We'll be in the dining room if you need me."

As the supply-room door stood open behind them, they heard Katey's voice say in obvious confusion, "Laundry tally forms in quadruplicate?"

Chapter Thirteen

"Now, when Hilton calls and tries to lure you away to handle his hotels in Europe," Gina teased, walking Patrick from the coffee shop, where they'd met Sin and Bobbi for breakfast, to his office, "don't act eager. Everything here is going so well, I'm sure you'll be able to name your price."

As they walked across the lobby, conventioneers with matching notebooks in hand hurried past in laughter and eager conversation. The man from Newport Niceties, in conversation with two other men, spotted Patrick and Gina and smiled and waved as he and his companions stepped onto an elevator.

Patrick put an arm around Gina's shoulders as they turned down the administrative corridor. "You want to see Europe?"

She stared a moment, surprised by his question. "No. I was teasing."

"Good. Because nothing's going to budge me from Candle Bay. I got to see the world in the corps, but I've known I'd settle down here since I left to go to college." His gaze probed hers. "You're happy here."

His statement had a vaguely tentative quality—an unusual tone for him. He was always so sure of what he knew.

She parted her lips to assure him that she was happy, but she was concerned enough about how she would live without him if he couldn't come to love her that the words stalled in her throat.

Patrick saw her hesitation. Instantly the glow of success this weekend had built in him was snuffed as though someone had pulled a shade. He knew what she wanted to hear and was angry with himself for being unable to say it, and with her for making him feel that way.

Gina saw frustration and confusion in his expression, and the beginnings of temper.

"Patrick, we—"

"Mr. Gallagher, can you come to the Cormorant meeting room?" A bellman out of breath skidded to a stop beside them. "A guest fainted. We called 911, but we thought you should..."

Patrick hesitated only long enough to give Gina a stiff, quietly spoken, "We'll talk later," and headed off for the meeting room at a run, the bellman chasing after him.

PATRICK STOOD under the hot shower in the bathroom off his office and decided there were advantages to a foul mood he hadn't anticipated. People left you alone. He hadn't had a whole day of peace since he'd first taken over for his grandfather.

He dried off briskly, pulled on briefs and a T-shirt, then the tux he kept in his office.

He ran over the evening's details in his head, knowing all the various department heads would carry out their responsibilities with their customary style and efficiency. All he had to do was appear, looking successful and in control of everything to assure everyone that the young Gallagher ran the same fine house his grandfather had.

The news media would be there in force, and as far as he knew, every travel agent they'd invited had accepted.

The antique dealers' convention was going exceptionally well. Even the woman who'd fainted yesterday awoke laughing, refusing to be taken away in an ambulance. She'd insisted she'd fainted from too much good food and too much partying—she blamed the Candle Bay Inn for its great chef and hospitable atmosphere.

Patrick was startled to a stop when he walked out of the small bathroom into his office, yanking at the bow tie already strangling him, and found Gina staring out his window. The ballroom visible beyond the glass glittered like a crown in the darkness. Against the backdrop of brightly lit Astoria, it looked like a tiara that had slipped from some hidden treasure trove.

Gina also looked like part of the booty, in an electric blue dress woven with silver threads and beads. The back was cut almost to her waist, and her hair was piled in a complicated twist. He studied her creamy skin and the enticing line of her neck with a familiar quickening in his gut.

Sensing his presence, she looked over her shoulder to give him a tentative smile. "Hi," she said softly, then turned back to the view. "It looks like something out of *Ali Baba,* doesn't it?"

He came to stand behind her, leaving a hairbreadth between them. Her fragrance wafted around him, making him feel as though he just might lose his head.

GINA HAD DRESSED for the festivities, determined to pretend to herself that she was loved.

"It does," he replied, unable to stop himself from putting a hand on her arm and stroking her silky skin. "Do you feel like Scheherazade?" He turned her to him, looking deeply into the same expression he'd seen that morning that had troubled him all day. She tried to hide it with a smile, but failed. He asked gently, "Or are you Aladdin with your unconventional lamp?"

She laughed and the sound ran over him like a balm. She took his hand in her two and began to lead him away.

"I have a thousand-and-one tales to tell you, O Sultan," she said.

At the door he flipped the office lights off and they stood together in the semidarkness of the empty administrative corridor. "There's only one story I'm interested in hearing," he warned softly. "I want you to tell me you're happy."

"I love you," she said softly, "but that's not quite the same thing, is it?" She tugged him toward the sounds of revelry already beginning in the dining room. "But now we feast and dance."

"HOWARD WANTED to go to Mexico, but I said, 'Howard, sunshine is so ordinary! I want to visit the Northwest. I want the power and passion of nature…'"

Patrick was absolutely sure that whatever Belinda Suffolk wanted she got. As he led her around the ballroom's dance floor, he wondered if he would have permanent handles where her stubby, bejeweled fingers had gripped him.

He looked longingly across the room to where Gina danced with Belinda's husband. She'd been claimed by one laughing male guest after another all evening, and he had yet to dance with her.

As he watched, Sin cut in on Howard and whisked Gina away. Patrick sighed, resigned to having to listen to more of Belinda's dramatic oratory.

"Where men are men and women still know how to respect them and get the most of their marital investment."

Patrick glanced down at Belinda. "Pardon me?"

"Well, marriage isn't all 'separate but equal,' you know," she said, giving him a slap on his shoulder that he was sure dented it. She smiled broadly. "I suppose being a newlywed, you don't know that, but you can't treat marriage like an integration of neighborhoods. It's more complicated than that. It's down and dirty. It's love. If you think you're going to get back exactly what you give, then you need to invest in safe stock, not another human being." She jabbed an index finger at him, making a hole in the dent she'd left previously. "Marriage takes both of you giving one hundred percent and taking up the slack when the other just doesn't have it to give. Next time it'll be your turn. That's what makes marriage work. Not being perfect, but knowing how to give."

Patrick felt a jab on his back. For a moment he thought Belinda had developed some form of rear attack, but he turned his head to discover Sin behind him, Gina in his arms.

"Change partners?" Sin suggested. To Belinda he said, "Howard told me you have a sailing story about snapping a mast off at Newport, Rhode Island, that'll curl my hair."

Preening at the invitation, arms still raised in dancing mode, Belinda sailed toward Sin like a racing sloop with its spinnaker set.

Patrick drew Gina into his arms. Happy laughter and

the cheerful strains of a contemporary ballad filled the room as he fond a quiet corner and moved slowly with the music.

"It's after eleven," he said, "and I've yet to hear one of your stories. I'm afraid I'll have to take my scimitar to you at midnight."

Gina wrapped both arms around his neck and felt his arms tighten around her waist as he drew her closer. They touched from nose to knees, and a little anticipatory shudder ran through her.

Patrick felt her tremble and knew without a doubt it was futile to struggle any longer. She belonged to him, but in making that happen, he'd given himself to her. Independence be damned. He was in love.

He kissed her cheek and whispered into her ear, "Come on. We're going to disappear for a while."

Gina heard the urgency in the softly spoken statement and drew back to look into his eyes. They were dark and steady but turbulent.

Her heart gave an uncomfortable thud. Maybe she shouldn't have told him she loved him. It wasn't part of the deal. Was he about to declare it null and void?

"Where did you want to go?" she asked.

"The boathouse," he replied.

She suspected he wasn't taking her there to set sail for pleasure on the little cruiser.

He caught her wrist and led her through the crowded ballroom. The level of fun and excitement was rising, and the music grew louder to combat it.

They stepped outside and the door closed behind them, muting the sound but not silencing it. The music followed them as they headed up the walk toward the low row of rooms. They took a right turn in the direction of the boathouse. The night was cloudy and blustery and Gina had forgotten her wrap in the dining room.

Patrick pulled off his tux jacket and put in on her shoulders. "I'm surprised you didn't wear the leather jacket tonight," he teased.

She smiled up at him, that bittersweet quality still there. "I was thinking of sewing pearls onto it so I can wear it on formal occasions. But you do still grab it once in a while. You'd probably have difficulty explaining the pearls to the guys you go fishing with."

He put an arm around her shoulders as they headed for the boathouse. "Tell you what. Consider it a gift. I formally turn over ownership of the disputed leather jacket to you."

Gina stopped, frozen on the slab-stone walk. "Why?" she asked. Was it a parting gift?

He squeezed her closer as he urged her on. "Why not? I thought you liked it."

She stopped him again and pulled him under one of the old ornate lights that lit the path to the water. Beyond, in the darkness, water lapped and a freighter blasted its horn to call for a bar pilot. She looked up into his eyes, straining to see what he felt.

"What are you saying?" she demanded.

He frowned at her. "That you can have the jacket. Why? Am I speaking in code?"

"To go *where* in it?"

He rolled his eyes, wondering why this always happened. She often made him feel as though he needed an interpreter. "It doesn't come with restrictions," he replied. "You may go where you like in it."

"With or without you?"

He was beginning to understand. That bittersweet look in her eyes had become desperation, and suddenly what

he'd brought her out to tell her had finally, unequivo-
cally lost its power to threaten him. It was hard to be
afraid of your own love when it glowed from your
woman's eyes.

He folded his arms and grinned down at her. "Well,
how do you prefer to travel?"

Tears stung her throat. "In an old VW bus with you
behind the wheel and me feeding you potato chips."

He laughed and wrapped his arms around her, locking
her against him. "Then that's how we'll spend every
anniversary," he said tenderly, lowering his head to kiss
her lips. "We'll pack up the old red bus and take off
down the coast."

"*Every* anniversary?" she asked. "Like there'll be
more than an eleven-month one?"

He framed her face in his hands and let her see how
much he loved her before he spoke the words. "God, I
hope there'll be sixty or seventy. I hope we set a record.
I love you, Gina. I hope you're prepared for this marriage to last a lifetime."

"Oh, Patrick." She melted against him with a softness
that turned his spine to mush. "I love you, too." She
squeezed him again. "You don't feel obligated...?"

He silenced her with an emphatic kiss. "Look, let's
make another deal, all right? You won't try to second-
guess what I'm saying if I make a point of trying to put
what I'm feeling into words. I love you. Plain and simple." He thought about that a minute, then corrected
himself. "Actually, it's not plain at all. It feels kind of
baroque and even a little convoluted."

She laughed softly, happy enough to burst. "Sounds
like the real thing, all right. I—"

She was interrupted by a tall, slender man in kitchen
whites running toward them in the darkness.

He stopped before them, his face sooty, his eyes wide with distress. "The kitchen, Mr. Gallagher!" he shouted. "It's on fire!"

Gina turned to the main building, half expecting to see fire bursting through the windows, but it looked just as it always did, like a beautiful old lady, bejeweled with lights for nighttime.

Patrick turned her in the direction of the ballroom. "Go back to Sin. Tell him what's happened, and don't let any of the guests come back to the main building until I know how bad it is."

"But I want—" She made a move to go with him as he started for the building at a run.

"Go!" He pointed her back to the ballroom, then ran with the sous-chef in pursuit.

Gina hurried to go back to the party, still startled by his admission of love.

"Mrs. Gallagher." The sound of her name jarred Gina. She turned to find the man from Newport Niceties ambling down the walk from the long arm of the refurbished addition. He was dressed in evening clothes, hands in his pockets.

She smiled. "Good evening. How are you?"

"I'm fine." He pointed in the direction of the small commotion in the doorway of the main building. "Something apparently isn't fine up the way."

"There's a small fire in the kitchen," she said, smiling like a stewardess trying to reassure her concerned passengers. "Nothing to worry about, I'm sure, but I'm going to the ballroom to keep everyone at this end of the complex until we know for sure what's happening."

He caught her arm and corrected her with a faintly disturbing smile. "Actually, there is something to worry about."

There was also something disturbing in his tone.

"I set the fire," he said with a rumbling little laugh. Then he started toward the boathouse, dragging her with him. "Come along, Regina. We have to talk about what you've done with my diamonds."

PATRICK BURST into the kitchen, expecting to find it empty of staff, thick with smoke, a wall burning. But Emil, the chef, was calmly setting up a fan to divert the smoke to the back door, and everyone else was grilling steaks, pulling things out of the oven, slicing *gâteau,* while absently waving a light fog of smoke from their faces.

"No, we did not overdo ze flambé," Emil said with a roll of his eyes as he noticed Patrick. He directed the sous-chef to see that the fan was properly placed and all the windows opened and took Patrick's arm to lead him to the small room off the kitchen where dishes were done and trash disposed of.

There the walls were blackened, and a heavy pall of smoke still hung in the air. Here, too, a fan had been set up. Two waiters wearing napkins over their mouths were cleaning up. Emil led Patrick to an area in the back, walled with cinder blocks, where the trash was kept. One of the large trash containers usually kept in the clean-up area was soggy from having been doused with a pot of pasta water.

"What happened?" Patrick demanded.

"Ze trash went 'poof!'" Emil said, making an exploding gesture with his hands. "Ze flames were very high. Must be somezing smoldered in ze bottom of ze can, but we are very careful with ze paper trash."

"One of the staff got careless with a cigarette?"

"*Mais, non!* No one smokes in my kitchen. Zey know I would guillotine them."

"Then what happened?"

Sin burst out of the kitchen's back door, breathless. "Patrick. Got to talk to you."

Patrick looked up at Sin in mild annoyance. "Sin, we've had a fire here—"

"So did the hotel down the coast, remember?" Sin pointed out. "Little too coincidental, don't you think?"

Emil said something emphatic in French. Patrick frowned. He'd been so concerned about the safety of his staff and guests, he hadn't made the connection. "My call from Watters just came through," Sin went on. "Guess who's here as part of the Northcoast Antique Dealers?"

An icy ripple of foreboding ran down Patrick's back. "Gardner," he asked, "or Danforth?"

"Danforth, registered as Dan Porter. Owns a shop called—" he raised an eyebrow significantly "—Newport Niceties. It's him. Watters faxed me a photo."

Patrick had a clear picture in his mind of the affable man whom Gina always seemed to run into in the strangest places.

"Did you leave Gina at the ballroom?" Patrick asked.

Sin looked confused. "She left with you."

The chill now went up Patrick's spine. "I sent her back when James came to tell me about the fire."

Sin's confusion turned to distress. "I wasn't there. The desk sent someone to tell me Watters's call had come through."

Patrick grabbed Sin's arm and started pulling him with him as he backed away. "Emil, I want everyone in security looking for Mrs. Gallagher," he said.

"But what—"

"Just have them find her and hold her! I don't want them to let her out of their sight. Come on, Sin."

They raced for the ballroom where news of the kitchen fire hadn't reached, or if it had, hadn't dampened the party spirit. The music and the laughter were still loud and fast.

Patrick looked over the room, praying that his eyes would fall on Gina, safe and sound in some guest's arms. But she wasn't there. He did another quick scan of the room, his heart fisting into cold resolve when he still didn't find her.

Patrick spotted Bobbi, dancing with a guest. He had spun her away from him in a daring twirl, and she flew out, colliding with Sin with a gasp of alarm and a swirl of red taffeta skirt.

They stared at each other for a moment, unmoving. Impatiently Patrick grabbed Bobbi's arm and pulled her toward him.

"Where's Gina?" he demanded.

She looked at him blankly. "Well…she left with you."

"Oh, God," he muttered. It was suddenly all too clear.

Patrick left the ballroom at a run, Sin and Bobbi close behind him.

THE BOATHOUSE was dark and cold, the lap of the water in the slip a curiously languid sound in an atmosphere tight with anger and quiet panic. Gina's arm was twisted up behind her, her strained shoulder a hot throb of pain. She'd lost Patrick's jacket somewhere in Danforth's headlong rush to get out of sight.

"Now." Danforth shoved her against the wall. She landed with a jarring thud, trying desperately to make her mind work despite the fear. She turned to face her captor, rotating her painful shoulder and making every effort to appear calm.

"What have you done with the diamonds?" Danforth demanded, keeping the distance of a few feet between them. His voice, deep and quiet, closed the small space and crawled over her like something alive.

She tossed her head to shake the feeling. "Why would I," she asked reasonably, "have diamonds that belong to you?"

He heaved a deep sigh. "Regina, don't do this," he said quietly. "You have to have them. Gardner insists that he left the lamp in the warehouse. But when I went to pick it up, it was gone. You have it."

"The lamp?" Gina said in surprise. "You don't mean the lovers'—"

"I do."

"But it's just plaster and—" Suddenly she had a clear mental picture of the crystal drops that sparkled like stars in the firelight.

Danforth came to within a foot of her, the elegant planes of his face a blotch of ugly shadow in the darkness. "So, you *didn't* know," he said in mocking amazement. "Yale took the piece apart and replaced the crystals in the plastic bag you had them packed in, in the warehouse. Didn't you wonder that such an ugly lamp should have such finely cut crystals?"

She hadn't, she thought with a fatal sense of her own naïveté. Until she'd brought it along with her on the trip, she hadn't had much time to look at it. She'd stored it, waiting to refinish it.

She shook her head. "I've never worn diamonds. I like simple gold, myself. You worked for Yale?" she asked.

Danforth snickered. "Yale worked for me. He piled up some gambling debts. I leant him the money to get out from under, and when he couldn't pay me back, I suggested we might...move some merchandise together. I've done this successfully for years. I have many collectors who'll pay a high price for special pieces whose market route they never question."

"The Ming," she whispered. "The Renoir and—"

"And a diamond necklace." In a move made more shocking because of his indolent voice, Danforth grabbed a fistful of her hair and yanked her to the water's edge. "What have you done with the stones?"

"How do you know," she asked, having to swallow to get the words out against her strained throat, "that Yale *doesn't* have it? I...certainly wouldn't take his word."

He shook his head and smiled. "I found him at the airport, about to make his getaway. After what I did to him, I'm sure he told me the truth. He was smart enough to leave me my share before trying to disappear. Now, come on," he said almost amiably, "do I have to do the same to you?"

He yanked her violently to her knees. Pain exploded in her legs at the impact, and her scalp stung from the pressure of his fist in her hair. "Now, where are they?"

She couldn't tell him. She didn't want that animal setting one foot inside Patrick's house.

"I...sold it at a little second-hand shop in Burbank," she said in what she prayed was a convincing tone. "Where I sold the rest of the things Yale left in the warehouse."

"You sold it," he repeated in that soft, menacing voice. Then he gave her a vicious shove that landed her in the slip.

Gina drew cold, brackish water into her mouth and her nostrils. Real panic closed in on her as she tried to surface and Danforth's strong hand held her head under. For an interminable moment all attempts to think clearly were swept away as her lungs threatened to burst.

Then the hand that had held her down yanked her up by her hair. Gasping for breath, she clung to the deck of the slip.

"You didn't sell it," he said as she choked and gasped for air. "Yale assured me you had a sentimental attachment to it. It wasn't on the invoice of things you sold that little shop. I checked." His voice lowered as he crouched down to get nose to nose with her. "And security's too tight around here for me to try to check your house. Is that where it is? Somewhere in your cozy little Victorian love nest? If I don't get the right answer this time," he said in an infuriated whisper as he straightened, "your body's going to wash up somewhere in Cannon Beach! Now where is—?"

There was a hollow thud, then Danforth sailed over her head with a high, shrill cry, arcing into the water with a loud splash. Wiping water from her face, Gina found herself being hauled up by two rescuers she didn't recognize in the dark.

One gave the other a quick shove. "Go find Mr. Gallagher!" a young man's voice said urgently. She recognized it as Brian's. "Hurry!"

"But…" Katey's voice.

"Hurry!"

Katey ran off as Brian hauled Gina onto the deck. Then he pushed her to follow Katey. "Go!" he said. "I'll take care of him."

But Danforth rose out of the water swearing and spitting and promising Brian an ugly death. Gina knew what

Danforth was capable of. She couldn't leave Brian. She searched around frantically for a weapon, but there was nothing. So she stood beside Brian, waiting for Danforth, who'd wisely leapt out of the water on the other side of the boathouse.

"Mrs. Gallagher!" Brian said impatiently, trying to push her toward the door. But Danforth was too close and Brian quickly changed tactics. He pushed Gina behind him and began to back away.

"All right!" Danforth roared, advancing on them as water streamed off him. "I've *had* it!" The dip in the water seemed to have shaken his calm. "Do you have any idea what you've put me through? Do you?" he demanded. "I've wasted weeks of valuable time, had a forty-five thousand dollar car disabled, two men thrown in jail—"

"Car disabled?" Gina leaned around Brian to scoff. "It was only a distributor cap! You're not much of a mechanic, are you? And your henchmen are pathetic."

"Mrs. Gallagher!" Brian pleaded desperately, trying to push her back behind him.

"I'm very good," Danforth said, picking up his pace toward them, "at getting rid of what gets in my way. Now getting you out of my hair has come to mean almost more to me than the diamonds!" And he lunged at them.

Chapter Fourteen

Gina could only hear the tussle. She'd landed at the bottom of the pile like a running back who'd been dumped at the Super Bowl.

It occurred to her that it seemed inordinately loud for a two-man scuffle, then she heard Patrick's voice, then Sin's and Bobbi's and Katey's.

When Patrick hauled her to her feet, Danforth lay on the deck, mouth open, eyes closed.

Patrick wrapped her in Sin's jacket, tucking it high around her neck. "Gina, are you all right?" he demanded.

She felt his cold hand against her face, felt her body trembling wildly under the warm jacket. She was aware of being very cold and vaguely disoriented. Patrick was holding her close and rubbing her arm and back. Bobbi was studying her worriedly.

"I'm fine," she said in a voice that surprised her with its strength. She certainly didn't feel strong.

Then the men from security appeared with flashlights and weapons and Danforth was taken away. Brian gave the assembled group a blow-by-blow description of everything he and Katey had heard and seen from inside the cruiser.

''What were you doing in the cruiser?'' Bobbi asked, obviously puzzled.

Sin rolled his eyes.

''We were, ah, making wedding plans,'' Brian said, clearing his throat.

Patrick gave him a hearty hug with his free hand. ''Thank God for wedding plans. You two go back to the hotel. I'm sure the police will want to talk to you. Sin will go to my place to turn over the stones.''

Sin nodded.

Patrick held Gina closer. ''I'm taking Gina to the emergency room.''

''I think that's an excellent idea,'' Bobbi said.

Gina struggled feebly, trying to rouse herself out of her woolly state. She felt fine. The only problem seemed to be with her brain. She could almost hear it slowing down, clouding over.

Gina said firmly to her friend, ''I'm fine.''

Bobbi folded her arms. ''It wouldn't hurt to have a doctor make sure, would it?''

The faces around Gina began to recede, and the beam of the flashlight the security team had left with them began to undulate. She summoned her waning energy to say emphatically, ''I do *not* want to go to the doctor.'' Then counteracted all that effort by fainting dead away.

GINA AWOKE in the emergency room as a middle-aged woman, glasses perched halfway down her nose, took her blood pressure. A badge on the pocket of the woman's lab coat said she was Dr. Davidson.

She pulled the stethoscope from her ears and dropped it around her neck, smiling at Gina as she did so. ''Good. You're both fine. I understand you've had quite an evening.''

"*Both* fine?" Gina asked, trying to surface to full brain capacity. "Patrick!" she said in sudden alarm. "Was my husband hurt?" She couldn't quite bring back the details that had brought her here. She remembered being frightened, being in the water, fainting. But Patrick had seemed fine.

Then he came from behind her to stand beside the doctor. He appeared in perfect health.

"Oh!" Gina put a hand to her heart in relief. His declaration of love came back to her, those few wonderful moments on the walk before James came from the kitchen to report the fire. She smiled at him, love bright in her eyes.

His expression remained carefully neutral, something remote and vaguely angry in his eyes. Gina stared at him, confused.

"By *both of you*," the doctor said, reclaiming her attention, "I meant you and the baby."

"What baby?"

Dr. Davidson turned to Patrick, then back to Gina with a concerned, maternal smile. "*Your* baby, Gina. Didn't you know?"

Gina felt her mouth gape. She slowly shook her head. Then she smiled as she dealt with a flash of ebullience. A baby!

Her eyes flew to Patrick's, and the smile died on her face as she finally interpreted his curiously remote expression. He'd obviously learned the news before she'd come to. He probably thought she'd done it deliberately, that allowing herself to get pregnant had been a ploy to keep him in the marriage once she'd reached her birthday.

She must have gotten pregnant one of the first few times they'd made love—long before he'd declared his love and while he was still adamant about not wanting to father her child. He must think she'd tricked him—again.

Dr. Davidson looked from one to the other. "I know this hasn't been the ideal way to find out such happy news," she said gently. "Maybe you should go home and start this evening all over again in the light of what you know now."

She swung Gina's legs over the side of the gurney. "You had a very normal reaction to the circumstances." She looked up at Patrick. "She should lie low for a few days—maybe just rest through the holiday. By Tuesday, she should be good as new."

Patrick nodded, gave Gina a quick, cursory glance and handed her a pile of clothes.

She recognized a pink sweat suit from her closet and looked at him in confusion.

"Sin and Bobbi brought them," he said stiffly, "so you could change out of the wet dress. I'll be in the waiting room while you get dressed."

GINA PRETENDED interest in downtown Astoria as Patrick drove through it toward the bridge that would take them back to Candle Bay. At just after one in the morning all the shops and businesses were closed. Her mind made a quick parallel between this drive and the part of the trip where she'd awakened just outside of San Francisco at about the same hour of the morning. It was shortly after that that they'd found the barn and the hayloft—then found each other. Now she was about to lose him.

She didn't know what to say. He hadn't spoken a word to her since he'd put her in the Firebird he drove when he wasn't hauling building materials.

God, she thought unhappily. Was everything she'd gained a few hours ago about to fall apart because of a misunderstanding?

Patrick knew precisely what he wanted to say, but he needed time to calm down. Had her surprise at the news been an act? Had she not even suspected she was pregnant? Or had she known and kept it to herself so that if it all did fall apart between them she'd have what she wanted without interference from him?

Part of him found that hard to believe of her, but another part remembered that she'd lied to him before.

As he drove onto the bridge, the only car on the road, he glanced her way. She looked pale and small wrapped in the blanket he'd given her, and very miserable.

He'd forgotten until that moment what she'd been through tonight. From the time she'd fainted in his arms, he'd handled more fear than he'd ever felt in combat.

He kept his eyes on the lights of his hotel in the distance, trying to find an answer to his questions. All he could see in his mind's eye was her laughing beside him in the passenger seat of the truck, then the old bus, talking chattily, nibbling constantly on chips or cookies. Then he remembered her putting herself between him and Larry's gun. Held against his suspicions, nothing computed.

He pulled into a lay-by off the road where tourists stopped during the day to look at the sights of Astoria, and where lovers stopped at night to look into each other's eyes.

He turned the motor off, and silence boomed in the small space of the car. He stared through the windshield for a slow count of ten, then turned to her.

"Explain to me," he said quietly, "what's happened here."

Gina felt like she might burst from the joy and the fear warring within her for supremacy. She was ecstatic that she was pregnant, but she knew that the reason for her delight could also cause her to lose Patrick.

She turned to him with a smile because she was simply unable to dredge up any guilt. "It's called life," she said. "It's the result of love."

He couldn't dispute that. "What I want to know," he said, "is how did it happen? I thought you were protected."

"So did I." She pulled the blanket tighter around her.

"How could you have no idea you were pregnant? The doctor guessed you to be about six weeks along. There are signs—"

"I've just been moving too fast, I guess," she said, shrugging so that the blanket rose and fell. "I haven't counted days because I wasn't worried about it. I thought I was safe. I had a little mild nausea, but I put it down to nerves."

Her face was alive with excitement, happiness, trepidation and concern. But she was absolutely sincere; he was sure of it.

Gina found him difficult to read. Impatient because she didn't know what to think, she said moodily, "Undoubtedly this will be a baby that makes a lot of noise, eats you out of house and home, and draws trouble like a magnet. Not a convenient distraction for a busy innkeeper."

He made a small sound of amusement. "Noise, food and trouble sort of define our relationship. It's probably been the most inconvenient marriage of convenience on record."

"And I guess that's *my* fault?"

He shrugged a shoulder. "You're the one who tricked

me into this, was responsible for the fact that we were chased a thousand miles, and placed a half-million-dollar lamp on our mantel that put us both in danger.'' With a trace of a smile, he continued. ''I don't see how you can blame anyone else.''

Anger rose in her like fire up a draft. ''Oh, really! Well, let me tell you a thing or two!''

She rounded on him. He braced himself. He'd hear her out, and then he'd tell how it was going to be.

''Everything is your fault, Patrick,'' she said emphatically, dropping the blanket to allow herself free use of restless hands. She stabbed one in his direction. ''Had we done it my way in the beginning, we'd have gotten along just fine, made a baby and gone our separate ways. But no!''

The same hand swiped in his direction to reinforce the negative. ''You had to be all tough and noble and responsible!''

He thought that through. Toughness could be debatable as a virtue, but weren't nobility and responsibility sought after in a man by most women?

Her eyes filled. ''You had to be brave and concerned and fun. You had to make love to me in a damned hayloft!''

He smiled and put a hand to her face. ''Now, I wasn't solely responsible for that. You sat there on a moonbeam looking like an angel. What was I supposed to do?''

''It's just possible…'' she began heatedly, then hesitated when his words played over in her mind. Like an angel? Refusing to be distracted, she gave her hair a toss and began again. ''It's just possible you could come to love this baby, but if you don't want to give yourself the chance, it's fine with me.''

''I'm thrilled about the baby,'' he said, his tone annoyed because he was mad at *her*. She was second-guessing him again. "I love it already."

She stared at him, afraid to believe him. "I don't want you to love it because you feel obligated," she said.

Patrick closed his eyes, shook his head and turned the key in the ignition. That did it.

"I've been there," she said. "And my baby will not grow up having just half of her father's attention."

He backed onto the road and roared toward the inn. "It isn't *your* baby, it's our baby, and you're second-guessing me again. Have you ever had only half of my attention, except when you were being a pill? Like now?"

When she didn't answer, he cast her a quick, dark glance. "Then just shut up about it until we get to the office."

She subsided in her blanket. "Why are we going to the office?"

"We're going to do what the doctor suggested," he said. "We're going to start this evening over in the light of what we know now." He pulled into the spot marked with his name and turned to her and warned quietly, "And you'd better get it right, Mrs. Gallagher. Come on."

He pulled her out of the car, blanket and all, and strode to the side entrance of the main building with her in his arms.

The grounds were quiet now, though the ballroom was still brightly lit.

He stopped at the door to his office, propped one knee against the wall, balanced her on it and unlocked his door. He put her on her feet in front of his desk, turning on the low light on the credenza in the corner. The soft light did not interfere with the glittering view of the ballroom and Astoria beyond the bay.

He took the blanket from her, tossed it in a corner and positioned her before the window where she'd been earlier that evening when he'd walked out of the bathroom.

He stepped back a few steps, reaching out to turn her back to the window when she tried to follow him.

"We're going to recreate this evening," he said. "Only this time we're going to do it better. Do you remember how it went?"

"I remember every minute of how it's gone," she said without turning away from the window, "from the day you opened the door in my father's study and found me standing there."

"Good," he said. "Then you're on. I've just closed the bathroom door."

Gina drew a deep breath, then turned to look at him over her shoulder. "Hi," she said, her voice barely there. She cleared her throat and said it again. "It looks like something out of *Ali Baba,* doesn't it?"

Patrick moved to stand behind her, thinking how beautiful she looked in the sweats, with her hair a mess. He ached with love.

"It does," he replied, putting a hand on her arm as he'd done earlier, fighting the urge to crush her to him. "Do you feel like Scheherazade?" He turned her to him. "Or are you Aladdin with your unconventional lamp?"

"I have a thousand-and-one tales to tell you," she whispered, feeling choked with what she saw in his eyes. He did love her and their baby. All the doubt had been hers.

He put a hand to her face. "To tell you, *O Sultan,*" he prompted with a grin. "I really liked that part."

"To tell you, O Sultan," she laughed softly. But instead of leading him away as she had earlier, she pushed him gently into the deep chair behind his desk. They *were* going to do this right this time. "The first is a long and complicated one," she said.

He pulled her into his lap. "Then go slowly, wife."

She settled comfortably against the arm that held her and thought back to their almost fairy-tale beginning. "There was a mighty sultan," she began, "who took a vizier's daughter to wife."

Patrick nodded sagely. "A tale of woe."

Gina scolded him with a look. "A tale of love."

"Ah," he said. "Continue."

"The sultan and his wife began a perilous journey on a magic carpet. Thieves were in pursuit, for the sultan's wife had a magic lamp."

"Were they overtaken?"

"Very nearly. To escape they were forced to trade the magic carpet for a very slow camel."

Patrick kept a straight face with difficulty.

"But the sultan and his wife," Gina went on, putting a finger to his lips, "were as much in peril from each other as from the thieves."

He kissed her fingertip, then pulled her hand down. "Why was that?"

"The survival of his kingdom," she replied, "and her personal safety depended on their close alliance. But he was a leader of men and sheltered his person, like his people, in a fortress. His wife was taught by the vizier, her father, that love is painful if not returned."

He combed a wisp of her hair back with his fingertips. She stared out the window, her voice quiet and haunting as she continued.

"And so they mated during the starry desert nights, each thinking the heart could be held apart from the body. When they reached the sultan's palace, his soldiers captured the thieves and threw them into the bowels of the palace.''

''And the sultan and his wife lived together to a happy old age?''

Gina leaned her head on Patrick's shoulder and sighed. ''The sultan discovered that his wife was with child,'' she said. ''He thought it was a trick to make her more important to him than his other wives.''

''Other wives?'' Patrick asked.

''One wife in particular,'' she said, ''was very large and very powerful and demanded his attention.''

''Mmm. I hope he was wise enough to see the treasure he had in the vizier's daughter.''

Gina leaned her elbow on his shoulder and looked into his eyes. ''This is where the tale grows weak.''

''I know this story,'' Patrick said, sinking deeper into the chair and pushing her head gently back to his shoulder. ''Shall I conclude?''

Gina snuggled into him and closed her eyes and prayed.

''Despite the noise made by the large wife,'' he said, a smile in his voice, ''he remembered all the pleasures the vizier's daughter had given him. He remembered the balm of her laughter, the sustenance her gentle ways provided, the whiteness of her body in the moonlight and its generosity always.'' He was silent a moment, then went on quietly. ''Their child would be a part of them, and the sum total of their special singularity.''

Gina raised her head, tears streaming down her face and kissed him desperately, ardently.

''You want the baby?'' she whispered. ''Honestly?''

''Of course I do. The only thing that worried me was

that you knew and hadn't told me so that you could leave with it if anything went wrong.''

''I didn't know. And I'd have never done that to you.''

He tucked her knees up higher and crossed his feet on the windowsill. He turned the chair so that they could see the glittery reflection of Astoria in Candle Bay.

''The sultan—'' he picked up the threads of the story to tie them off ''—ordered feasting and dancing. He gave his wife a necklace of pearls and put the lamp in a place of honor in the palace because keeping it safe had brought them great love.''

''He placed it in their chamber window,'' Gina corrected, ''so that whenever he left the palace, it would shine for him like her love and call him home.''

Patrick laughed softly and kissed her forehead. ''You're getting your Scheherazade and your Polly Dutton stories all mixed up.''

''No.'' Gina pointed to the glimmer of light visible from their bedroom window in the uppermost corner of the office windowpane. ''It's *our* story, and the middle of my rainbow.'' She wrapped her arms around his neck and kissed him.

HARLEQUIN®
AMERICAN ROMANCE®

and **Muriel Jensen**
present

WHO'S THE
DADDY?

*A*t a festive costume ball, three identical
sisters meet three masked bachelors.

*E*ach couple has a taste of true love behind
the anonymity of their costumes—but
only one will become parents
in nine months!

Find out who it will be!

November 2000
FATHER FEVER #858

January 2001
FATHER FORMULA #855

March 2001
FATHER FOUND #866

HARLEQUIN®
Makes any time special ™